# THE MÉNAGE À TROIS

## A LORA WEAVER MYSTERY

## KATY LEEN

ISBN: print: 978-0-9936165-8-7

Cover: Team KL

# DEDICATION

This one is for my hubby. If in every life a little rain must fall, I'm glad we've shared an umbrella.

---

"*T*HIS IS IMPOSSIBLE," I whispered into my mobile. "How am I supposed to get pictures of the guy from inside this sweatbox?"

It was late at night and spring had just sprung in Montreal. Which meant rather than arctic winter temperatures outside, evening lows hovered closer to 0°C. But where I was, it felt more like August in New York.

Camille Caron, my best friend and co-boss, sighed at me through the phone. "*Regarde*, Lora. At the second level in the front. There's a hole in the frosting. Use that." And she clicked out.

I scoped the enclosure that surrounded me. It was circular. There was no front.

"I think she means there," the woman crouched beside me said and pointed a lace-gloved finger to her right. The woman's name was Marlene but she went by Silver Spoon. So far, I'd avoided calling her that. It was hard calling a grown woman Silver Spoon.

I squinted, trying to see better in the near dark, the only source of light in our sweatbox abode coming from a tiny battery-powered dome globe resting on the floor, its glow weak, like a night light with a dimming bulb. I clicked on the flashlight mode on my phone and directed the beam of light towards where Silver's finger pointed to a small, rectangular wedge cut into the side of our accommodations. A tiny knob stood out in the center of the wedge and hinges held it in place at the top.

I shut off the light beam and crept forward, careful not to ensnare Silver's frilly spaghetti strap draping from her shoulder. We were scrunched together tighter than raisins in a box. It was enough we were sharing limited space, we didn't need to be sharing clothes, too. Especially since she didn't have many to spare and my jeans and blouse were staying put.

I neared the wedge and reached up to grab hold of its tiny knob, but Silver got to it first. She lifted it to reveal a tiny opening to the outside.

"Oops," she said, looking out through the hole. "It's almost time."

She let the flap close and eased back, pausing to take a swig from her water bottle, place the bottle at her feet, plump her chest, and steady the mesh fabric flowing from a bejeweled crown on her head.

I waited until her elbows lowered, then I squeezed past her to the makeshift lookout and peered out. The lookout opening was maybe two inches long, an inch tall, and three inches deep, and it narrowed towards the exterior end so that my view focused on the round table I'd seen on my way in. Empty then, the table was kitted out with poker greens now, seven twentysomething men crammed around it, cards in hand, booze in reach. On the wall behind them, some action movie played, sound off, rock music playing in its place.

One man at the far side of the table had a lacy, red garter stretched around his forehead. Johnny, the guest of honor I figured, just a typical groom-to-be enjoying his last night as a bachelor. And my *objet d'intêret* of the evening.

Either that was one giant garter he wore or he had one puny head. It was hard to tell which from my funnel-lookout. But that wasn't my concern. My concern was how I was going to get a clear shot of Johnny in his wheelchair if the poker table was in the way. Not to mention the husky guy sitting with his back to me, crew-cut hair standing at attention, ears like coasters. His backside shifting sideways, back and forth, like a dog dragging his hindquarters to scratch.

"Is there any way to move this thing?" I asked Silver.

She stopped primping and looked at me. "You mean this hunk-a-junk fake cake we're in? Not from inside. It's got wheels to push it around but no motor or anything." She paused when the music in the room slipped into a thumping beat, then she started up the short ladder leading to the trap door in the narrow fifth tier up top. "Here we go," she said. "That's my cue." She nodded down at me and dropped her voice to a low whisper. "Ready?"

I nodded back at her, held my cell phone up to the lookout, and clicked on the camera function. The phone's display area mirrored back my own face—blue eyes blinking, wisps of auburn hair escaping my pony tail and clinging to my cheeks, spooky shadows shading my pale skin. I tapped the "reverse camera" icon and my reflection disappeared and the poker table came into view. I panned the phone over the men at the table, watching as Johnny's friends exchanged small grins.

The music got louder and the men stood, some tottering a bit, some faster, and whisked aside the poker table. Johnny looked up, his face growing angry, his mouth spewing expletives. Above me, Silver whipped open the top hatch on our fake hunk-a-junk cake and popped out, stopping Johnny's rant short when his glassy eyes locked onto her.

He whistled and let out a hoot. "Come on a little closer, sweet thing. Johnny don't bite," he said, intertwining his fingers into a stretch, his face relaxing into a smile.

The music thumped and a giant image of Silver replaced the movie on the wall screen. Then my phone camera picked her up "live and in person" gyrating over to Johnny in her skimpy fantasy bride get-up, peeling off her long gloves and flinging them away as she lowered herself onto his lap.

His arms opened and his hands disappeared from view.

Eww. I had to force myself not to turn away. This was the picture Camille wanted. Johnny caught in the, er, heat of the moment with Silver, hopefully moving his back. Even better, getting out of his wheelchair.

I, on the other hand, wanted a shot of Johnny exactly where he was.

*C'mon, Johnny, don't move, I silently begged him. Let's show that insurance company you're not cheating them out of your big fat disability check.*

I kept the camera focused while Silver did her thing. Nothing extra, nothing to trick Johnny into moving. I specifically asked her not to. That would be entrapment. I worked for C&C, a reputable PI agency. Camille and her ex-cop brother Laurent ran a clean shop. No setups or entrapment allowed. Just pure observation. And if that observation happened to get caught on camera in a club, all the better to show the client, *Assurance Lion*—the insurance company paying Johnny disability for the back injury he got some two months ago at his warehouse job where an accident left him so incapacitated he needed a wheelchair, only not so bad off that he needed surgery.

Johnny claimed to have done in three of his disks when a co-worker nearly ran into him with a forklift. Johnny'd had to dive out of the way and slipped in a puddle of grease he said had leaked from said forklift. The accident happened in a corner of the warehouse with limited security camera angles, making it hard to substantiate the details. And Johnny's x-rays came from one of those slipshod doctors popular with the insurance scamming crowd, so naturally *Assurance Lion* was suspicious of the validity of the injury. Or at least the extent of it. It was my job to prove they were right about it being a faulty claim and save them the big bucks of paying Johnny indefinitely.

Only I believed in giving people the benefit of the doubt. After all, maybe Johnny had no clue his doctor was fuzzy on ethics. This was Montreal. People had public health care and referrals to specialists came from primary physicians. Probably Johnny had nothing to do with choosing which doctor he saw. Probably Johnny was in legitimate pain, slipshod doctor or not.

I had better lighting now that the cake lid was open, and I snapped a few pictures, trying not to look too closely at the view screen on my phone. The music had morphed into a new song and Silver was dancing for Johnny now, maybe a foot away from him, allowing me a clear view of his glazed eyes and partly open mouth. His foot tapped to the music and his butt stayed in his chair as the other men rhythmically clapped off-camera.

Then the song ended and so did Silver's dance. And the clapping was replaced by grumbling. But not for long. Silver said something to the crowd that got them happy again and put a grin on Johnny's face. Probably Silver's résumé included wrangling drunken men as a skill.

She moved out of view and I heard a door open. A short man walked into my sight, lots of dark hair shellacked to a high gloss finish, lots of coat flapping. Behind him, two larger men trailed in, both reminding me of bookcases with feet—tall and wide but lacking in depth.

The short man barked something at Johnny and the two bookcase goons widened their foot stance and crossed their bulky arms over their bulky chests.

Johnny's face went pale, and I brought my phone down and peered out directly, my head pressed up as close as I could get to my peek-a-boo slot. With my wider scope, I could see more now, a few of the poker buddies unsteady on their feet, the others nearly rigid in place. Silence fell on the room, and I was getting the feeling the three new arrivals were attending the bachelor-party-poker-shindig sans invitation.

One of the bookcase goons broke the silence when he stepped forward and swept up the pile of poker money on the table. All of it, the pot in the middle and the small mounds the men had left by their cards.

Then the room started spinning.

No, wait. That was me. I was spinning, the hunk-a-junk cake suddenly whirling like a merry-go-round.

The cake lid slammed shut and I tipped over, my phone dropping from my hand and skidding away. I flailed and managed to grab onto the base of the ladder inside my cake sweatbox-cum-merry-go-round, hoping I wouldn't hurl. I heard thuds out in the room, a few high-pitched wails, some heavy breathing. The cake got knocked, alternating the spinning. Something crashed into the side and bashed it in, and I gripped the ladder harder and tucked my head between my arms.

I held tight until the spinning started to slow and come to a winding stop, the noise in the room coming to a stop along with it.

My hair had come loose from its ponytail and dipped onto my face as I let go of the ladder and crawled over to look out my peep-hole. The table was overturned, chairs were broken, booze bottles were smashed, Silver's veiled crown lay on the floor. And everybody was gone. Except Johnny, his head slumped to his chest, still sitting in his wheelchair.

*C*AMILLE ARRIVED JUST about the same time as the authorities. And after the paramedics took Johnny, unconscious but alive, to the hospital.

So far, I'd learned squat about what happened to Johnny. I'd sloshed through puddles of pooling alcohol from the broken bottles, sidestepping shards of glass, and rushed to his side when I got out of the cake. But all I got from Johnny when I reached him was a head roll, a groan, and a handsy pass at my derrière.

Once the paramedics arrived and took over, I was whooshed away and Johnny went quiet and still again, a bruise starting to show on his cheek and a trickle of blood tainted with the stench of Scotch seeping from the side of his mouth. More blood was splattered on his shirt and the tips of his bright white Nikes. I listened in as he was examined, but the paramedics spoke lots of French and I spoke little, making eavesdropping difficult.

Then Camille blew in and chatted up some young cop before making her way over to me. Her long, fitted, blue trench coat hugged her lithe body. Her pixie-cut blonde hair was smoothed back. And her tall, black boots were darker near the bottom and along the toes, dampened no doubt from the monsoon of rain that had soaked Montreal all day in a spring marathon of torrential baptisms.

Camille looked me up and down and shook her head. She didn't have to tell me what she was thinking. This turn of events would bode about as well for us as it did for Johnny.

But like best friends sometimes do, we were going to gloss over that bit for now. "*T'es correcte?*" she asked me. "You're okay?"

I nodded. I gave her a brief report on my photo shoot mission and told her about my ride in the spinning cake. Then I asked if her conversation with the cop had shed any light on exactly what happened to Johnny.

"*Probablement* too much drink or too little head protection," she said. "Maybe both. We'll know for sure after a head scan."

"I can't figure out how Johnny's friends could just leave him like that."

She shrugged. "Maybe not by choice." She ushered me to the corner of the room and held out her hand. "*Passe-moi ton cellulaire.*" She wiggled her fingers. "Your phone, Lora. Let me see the pictures. They will tell us more, no?"

When I hesitated, she leaned towards me and lowered her voice. "Don't tell me you gave the phone to the *police* already. *Mais voyons*, Lora. I told you before, always wait for me before giving anything to the *police.*"

"I did wait." I reached into my pocket, pulled out the phone, and held it out to her. A drip of water trickled onto my finger, easing out from the phone's edge where the seam sat loose. Another bit of water squeezed out from the glass top now etched with web-like cracks, cracks forming an intricate pattern that would make Charlotte the spider proud.

Camille looked down at my hand and back up at me, and she

shook her head again.

I wanted to shake my head, too. She wasn't nearly as upset as I was that the phone hadn't survived the spinning, bashed-in cake episode well. Not to mention the attempted drowning the phone endured, a drowning I could only guess came courtesy of Silver's abandoned water bottle spilling during the whirl and twirl. I'd had the phone barely two months, courtesy of my first undercover case. When the case ended, I'd been given the souped-up phone as a souvenir bonus of sorts. And now that it was bashed and water-logged in the line of duty, I'd have to go back to my old clunker phone.

I felt a tap at my shoulder and a plastic baggie appeared at my side.

"Drop it in here, *mon petit lapin*."

The *lapin* nickname was another souvenir from the undercover case. One my other boss, Camille's brother Laurent, gave me and still used now and then.

He looked me up and down like Camille had, only slower, his eyes resting briefly on the tear in the thigh of my jeans where they'd snagged on the ladder on my way out of the cake. Laurent had dark unruly hair, perpetual three-day scruff, nearly black eyes, and he was wearing a brown jacket and jeans and stood like he'd just come from the gym.

"Which one of you wants to tell me what Lora was doing in that cake?" he said, his tone low but slipping into cop voice. The voice that drove women nuts and made men spill their guts. The voice he'd honed during his days on the police force before he quit to open the PI agency.

Camille narrowed her eyes at him, and I focused on the now blank movie screen on the wall. Just once, it would be nice if Laurent weren't such a great PI. Or if he would at least save his skills to use on someone other than me.

9

I willed myself not to succumb to cop voice but truth be told I was seconds from cracking. Camille and I had committed a big no-no. I was still a lowly PI in training on assistant status. It was against the rules for me to do any field work solo without supervision by a licensed investigator. Not being a huge fan of rules, I may, on occasion interpret that rule a little broadly. As did Camille, who was known to bend a few rules when it suited her. But not Laurent. Laurent liked his rules nice and straight. Probably he wouldn't buy that Camille was supervising me by phone while I took pictures from inside a tiered slab of cake-shaped plastic dressed up in faux frosting and rounded curves. Nary a straight line in sight.

"*Mais voyons*," Camille said, saving me from cracking. She nodded her head in my direction. "*Regarde*. She fit better, no?"

I smiled. This was true. Petite, barely five foot two little old me had to crouch and contort myself to take up my vigil in the cake. Camille was at least half a foot taller. She never would have fit. Not along with Silver. The way we saw it, we weren't so much breaking rules in this case, we were just doing our best to serve the client.

Laurent shot us each dark looks before his eyes darted over to one of the cops walking the room, notebook in hand. "And the police? What did you tell them?"

My face grew warm. I knew full well the agency could be in a lot of trouble if anyone questioned my no-no.

"Relax, big brother," Camille said. "*Probablement* the police think I was with Lora."

This was news to me.

"Probably?" Laurent said.

"*Oui, oui.* I told officer Tessier that I did not see anything from my position, only Lora had a view. I did not tell him my position was nowhere near the cake."

All three of us looked over at the fake cake, smashed in on one side. Hard to imagine anyone would believe three grown women could fit into the cake. But then Tessier was a man. Maybe he liked to think three women crammed into a cake was sexy.

I glanced over at young officer Tessier, the cop Camille had chatted up earlier. He oozed newbie from the tip of his buzzed red hair to his regulation uniform to his polished boots. It was just possible he was rookie enough not to pick up on Camille's avoidance technique. And more importantly, not connected enough yet to be wise to her reputation for manipulating rules and men. And not necessarily in that order.

Laurent let out a slow breath and turned to me. "And what *did* you see?"

I told him everything. Just like I'd told Camille. And before her, the manager of the club that rented the meeting room to Johnny's friends for his bachelor/poker party.

"*Et puis?*" Laurent asked when I was done. "Where did everyone go?"

"I don't know. Everyone but Johnny was gone when I stopped spinning."

Camille and Laurent exchanged one of their quasi telepathic sibling looks then gazed back at me.

"How long before someone from the club came in?" Camille said.

"By the time I pried the cake lid open, two staff guys were in the room. Louis and Manuel. At least those were the names on their nametags. Manuel was the one who helped me climb down from the cake."

Laurent's eyes rose from mine and scanned the room.

"He's there," I said trying to gesture without pointing. "That ripped guy in the corner with the Buddy Holly glasses." I motioned again, over near the doorway this time. "And that's Louis. The older guy with the earring."

Camille turned to get a good look. *"Ah, oui.* I'll take Manuel," she said, already walking off in his direction leaving Laurent and me alone.

"Aren't you going to talk to Louis?" I asked Laurent.

He stood quiet a minute. "Later." He tugged at my sleeve, gently navigating both of us out of the room and a ways down the hallway, stopping near a planter filled with a tall leafy tree. The hall had minimal pot lights, no windows, and smelled of carpet deodorizer and beer. I was guessing the tree was fake. The leaves looked too good for a real plant living in these conditions.

"Tell me more about when the men came in and took the poker money," Laurent said.

I told him again, trying not to leave out any detail. Laurent was big on making me recount things over and over until I remembered more details, so I tried to do my remembering quickly.

"What did the men look like?"

"Nothing special. Two big goons, boss with a Napoléon complex, face like the Penguin from Batman." The guy sounded like the Penguin, too, now that I thought about it. If the Penguin had a French accent.

Laurent's mouth showed a brief hint of a smile. "Movie Penguin or TV Penguin?"

"TV."

"Anything special about him? Tattoos? Scars?"

I shrugged. "Nope. I couldn't see much detail from inside the cake."

"And after you got out, anything else you remember?"

"I don't think so. After Manuel lifted me down, my focus was on Johnny."

Laurent's eyes went dark then glinted. "Lifted you down?" he said, looking back to the rip in my jeans. "Were you hurt?"

I straightened my posture. Camille and Laurent were big on the protective thing and I was big on the independent thing. "I'm fine," I said, working to keep an edge out of my voice. "Probably Manuel was confused and concerned to find the room such a mess and he was just trying to be helpful."

Laurent's eyes lingered on my face then trailed away above my head and went dark again.

I turned to see a cop coming towards us—dark curly hair cut short, body like a battery, clothes ironed stiff. Samuel Brassard, a fellow trainee Laurent met back in his days at the police academy. And an even bigger stickler for rules. They weren't friends exactly, more boot camp bondees who occasionally ran into each other when our investigations and police matters intermingled. Mostly, Brassard worked homicides, though, not brawls.

He gave Laurent a chin nod. "*Heille*, Caron. Don't keep our only witness to yourself." Brassard shifted his look to me with that last bit, his French accent stretching out the two syllables of "only" like they were two words: "own-lee" and hitting them softer than the rest of his sentence. Probably he wasn't buying the three-ladies-in-a-cake idea. I wasn't surprised. Mister big-time stickler didn't have far to go to become mister big-time suspicious.

Laurent placed his hand on my shoulder and I felt my stomach flip. Somehow I had to convince Brassard I wasn't the only witness, just the only one inside the cake with a view. And I had to do a good job or mister suspicious stickler could become mister tattler, and Johnny wouldn't be the only one of the evening who played the odds and lost big.

"NICE SHIRT, BRASSARD," Camille said as she strolled down the hall towards us, talking as she moved, carrying her cell phone in her hand. "Your *maman* dress you or you filling your lonely hours ironing again?"

Brassard pivoted to get a look at Camille. "Why? You offering to keep me company, *belle* Camille?" He paused to pout his lips at her and add a note of pity to his voice. "You and Luc on the outs again?"

Luc was a cop and Camille's on-again off-again beau, currently set to off. Her on switch was set to Paul Bell, aka Puddles, a man about ten years her senior we'd met on an earlier case who had a key to her flat and was working on securing one to her heart.

Camille kept her face blank. "I've seen what you have on offer, Brassard. Not interested. Luc or no Luc. There's a minimum size requirement to go on this ride."

Brassard's jaw clenched and his cheeks notched up from pink to red.

I moved closer to Laurent. What was Camille doing getting Brassard riled up? I'd never convince him I wasn't alone in the cake now. He'd be gunning to trip me up just to get back at Camille.

Brassard turned to me and narrowed his big bushy eyebrows into slanted lines, like two caterpillars forming a slightly disjointed V. "Maybe we should go over your statement at the PDQ, mademoiselle Lora."

I stiffened. The PDQ was Montreal talk for police station. PDQs were scattered around the city and numbered like precincts back in my old stomping grounds in New York. I hadn't been interrogated at a PDQ before, but an image popped into my head of being whisked off to a tiny, stuffy room with a two-way mirror, hard chairs, and even harder questions.

"I wouldn't want to waste your time," I said, big smile coming to my lips. "I didn't see much." Then before Brassard could stop me I blurted out everything I'd seen and heard.

Camille's mobile buzzed in her hand when I was done and all eyes shifted to her. She clicked on her phone, listened, then spewed out a bunch of French words I wasn't fast enough to catch and clicked the phone off again.

"*Je m'excuse*," she said. "All night with the phone." She turned to Brassard and shimmied up to him, bringing her hand to his shoulder then slipping her fingers into his shirt collar and smoothing it down. "*Je m'excuse aussi pour tantôt, Samuel.* You hit a nerve, *là*. I've been fighting with my *chum* all night. Thank goodness for Lora. She held down the fort while I was busy on the phone."

She smiled over at me and I smiled back. My smile more one of shock. If I heard right, Camille just apologized. Even when she was manipulating someone, it was rare to hear Camille apologize. A beat passed before I found my voice to play along. "That's what partners do, right?" I said.

Brassard brought his hand up to remove Camille's hand from his collar, gripping her fingers a few seconds before letting go. "All right, ladies. Have it your way. For tonight." He went on to ask me for more specifics about the goons I'd seen break in on Johnny's poker party, then Brassard walked away. "*À bientôt tout le monde,*" he said as he rounded the corner, his boot steps fading.

I glared at Camille as soon as I thought Brassard was out of earshot. "What was that? You poked the bear. Everyone knows you don't poke the bear."

"Brassard?" she said. "Brassard is no bear. And I was not poking. I was tenderizing. Men are like meat, Lora. It helps to beat their tough skins a little to soften them up. Throw a few contradictions at them and they're thrown off their game. And it worked, *n'est-ce-pas?*"

"Worked how exactly?" I held my thumb and index finger up at Camille. "I was this close to being marched down to the PDQ."

She waved her arm in the air in my general direction. "Pfft.

Close doesn't count." She turned and took the same path as Brassard.

I glanced at Laurent. "Is she right? Do you think Brassard bought that she was with me?"

"*Non*. But he has no proof. And he has bigger things on his mind. Your mister Penguin with the Napoléon complex for one. If I'm right, he's not just any fish in a tuxedo. He's THE fish. The one Brassard has been chasing for three years. The head of a construction family that gives the trade a bad name and plays fast and loose with regulations."

Immediately I thought mafia. The mafia was alive and well in Montreal and the TV news shows often prattled on about connections to the construction industry. But probably I was getting ahead of myself. I'd also heard a lot about less sinister corruption in the construction industry. Probably this Penguin guy was just one of those types. "You mean like crooked deals, kickbacks, contracts for fake work?"

"*Non*," Laurent said. "His contracts are written in cement. The sucker on the other end of the deal only reads the fine print when the cement is being poured onto his body and he's made into a pillar. Or when the Penguin's cheap building collapses. Whichever comes first."

Okay, that didn't sound good. Mafia or not, the Penguin sounded like he deserved the villainous nickname I'd dubbed him.

I let Laurent's words sink in as he led me out of the club into the dark night, through the biting late March rain, and into his car. As we drove away, I wondered what could possibly connect Johnny nobody to a guy like the Penguin. And if they were connected, how Johnny got lucky enough to be spending the night in a hospital bed instead of a bed of cement.

## 3

*I* STUMBLED OVER boots and paws when I got home to the house in NDG that I shared with my boyfriend Adam. The house had two-storeys, three-bedrooms, one bathroom, plenty of brick on the outside, plenty of century-old charm on the inside, and a lineage of being owned by Adam's mother before she passed away a couple years ago from cancer and left her only major asset to her only child.

Her illness and subsequent passing had prompted Adam's move from New York, where we'd met, to his hometown of Montreal. I'd joined him, leaving behind my old life and starting a new one—including trading in a lifetime of living in apartments for house life. At the beginning, the place had seemed huge to me, but now that I was used to it, it seemed just right. Except the anteroom which was barely bigger than an appliance box and not designed to accommodate two four-legged beings at once, let alone adding in any of us two-legged ones.

I navigated around my dog Pong and my cat Ping, squeezed through the vestibule, and made my way into the living room and onto the sofa. I stripped off my coat and boots en route and collapsed lengthwise, landing in cushy couch comfort and seriously contemplated staying put for what was left of the night. A much better idea than going upstairs to bed at nearly one A.M., likely waking Adam and having to explain that I'd spent part of the night in a bachelor party cake playing photographer, and the other part standing in booze-soaked boots in a club corridor playing witness to a crime involving the Penguin and his goons.

My dachshund sniffed at my legs and my cat jumped onto my stomach and sat looking down at me, her nose in the air, her tiny nostrils inhaling in small, audible puffs. Like my boots, probably my pant cuffs still smelled of the booze puddles I'd stepped in getting to Johnny. Not my usual scent. Usually when I got home from work I smelled of coffee and chocolate.

The hall light blinked on and my eyes closed in retaliation. Heavy footsteps shuffled down the stairs, and I tried to think of a good explanation to give Adam for the distillery odor around me that seemed to be upping by the minute. Then I caught a blast of fake floral chemicals mixing into the scent and realization hit. With every shuffled footstep, the floral brew was getting stronger. And it didn't belong to Adam.

Realization seemed to hit Ping as well because she leapt from my stomach, and I opened my eyes to see her disappear into the dining room just as Adam's old friend Tina appeared in the hall doorway.

Tina's blonde hair hung loose halfway down her back, over two inches of dark roots showing, and she wore a pair of Adam's pajamas under *my* fluffy blue robe.

I called on the tongue-holding superpower my British ancestors had bestowed on me and willed myself to remain calm. Tina was wearing *my* boyfriend's pajamas. And *my* best robe—warm and soft and comfy. And now it had Tina cooties on it.

"I heard you come in," Tina said, dropping herself into an armchair across from me. "Have you ever tried to sleep in that hide-a-bed you guys have, Lora? It's awful. It's killing my back." She rubbed her stomach. "And these two aren't helping. They're starving. Could you make me some warm milk and a sandwich? Tuna maybe?"

I looked at her large belly and allowed myself an internal sigh. For someone who didn't like sleeping in the sofa bed in Adam's home office upstairs, Tina was doing an awful lot of it lately. This had to be the eighth time this month. And every time she complained about something. One time, it was noise from the neighbor kids playing in their yard in the morning when Tina wanted to sleep in. And last time, it was the dog barking at the doorbell when Tina was talking on the phone. Now it was back pain and hunger. The last thing I wanted to do at one o'clock in the morning after a rough night at work was make our unhappy houseguest a snack. But, I reminded myself, Tina was over seven months pregnant with twin boys. And them I was happy to feed.

I got up, passed through the dining room into the large kitchen at the back of the house, and flicked on the light. The kitchen was original to the house except for a few upgrades Adam and I had made since moving in—granite counters, energy-efficient appliances, fresh coat of powder blue paint on the cabinets, French country café curtains on the windows that lined the back wall overlooking the backyard. At the moment, the room also had piles of dirty dishes sitting on the counters and dirty pots stacked in the oversized white apron-front sink, the stainless steel pots gleaming under the light above.

Pong danced right by the pile of dirty dishes and over to the sun porch door off the back of the kitchen—her all-access pass to the backyard. I let the dog out, waited while she scurried into the rain to answer her call of nature and scurried back, fur damp, feet slipping slightly on the tile floor as I toweled her dry. When I returned to the kitchen, Tina was sitting at the round table in the corner, her legs propped up on a chair beside her.

"If you haven't got tuna, I'll go with bologna," she said. "With pickled beets. These days I'm just crazy for pickled beets."

I went to the pantry and searched the shelves for pickled beets. "Beets I can do," I told Tina, spotting a jar tucked in behind a tin of tomato paste. "But no tuna or bologna. Unless you want soy bologna."

Tina heaved a long breath. "That's right. I keep forgetting you and Adam are vegetarians."

That was true. She often did forget. Tina couldn't be bothered remembering details about other people. She had herself to think about.

"I'll take an omelet then. You do have eggs, right?" She held her hand out. "I'll just have the beets while I wait."

I passed her the jar of beets, a plate, a bowl, and a fork and spoon, just to cover all my bases, and I got to work on her eggs.

"What's all this?" a groggy male voiced asked a couple minutes later.

The voice came from behind me and belonged to Adam. I turned from the stove to find him standing in the doorway, nearly six feet of lean man, hands working to belt the striped robe he wore, T-shirt visible below. His short, brown hair pressed in on one side of his head and his long, bare legs ended in gym socks. His five-o'clock shadow had passed from shady to prickly and his mouth was still relaxed from sleep.

"Tina was hungry," I said.

He shot me a sheepish look that turned anxious when he spotted my hand still gripping the big knife I'd used to dice vegetables for the omelet. He closed the distance to me in quick steps and eased the knife from my grip. "Why don't you go up to bed. I'll take over here."

A few months ago, I may have argued with him and insisted on finishing the eggs myself. A few months ago, Tina had been like a bad cold, only cropping up a few times a year. But ever since she and her third husband Jeffrey had had a misunderstanding and she'd temporarily bunked at our house, she'd become more of a recurring rash—turning up at odd times and causing low-grade irritation. She and Adam had been friends since college when she started playing the role of dingy girl-in-trouble and he started playing the role of her mister fix-it. Their roles hadn't changed much over the years, only gone through hiatus now and then. Until Tina got pregnant, named Adam as godfather to her forthcoming twins, and added needy-mom-to-be to her act.

There was a scratch at my legs, pulling my attention to the floor where Pong sat expectantly, the smell of eggs firing up her appetite, too. I dropped a pinch of egg into the dog's bowl while Adam plated the rest onto Tina's dish. Then I said my goodnights and headed for the hallway.

As I started up the stairs, Adam caught up with me, spun me around, and planted a kiss on my lips. The extra height I'd gained standing on the first step easing his incline down to my mouth and bringing our bodies into close contact.

"Last time. I promise, hon," he whispered when we broke the kiss.

My eyes were too tired to work up a good show of disbelief. Which probably wouldn't have gone over well anyway, so I tried a small smile. Even if his words were more wishful thinking than true, his heart was in the right place.

"Really," he assured me. "Jeffrey comes home tomorrow from that law conference. Tina won't need me anymore."

Probably Adam was deluding himself if he thought Jeffrey's

return would reduce Tina's neediness, but I wasn't going to be the one to pierce the illusion.

I hugged Adam goodnight, and he nuzzled my neck and planted a squeeze south of my back before completely letting me go and I darted up the stairs.

When I was sure I'd cleared Adam's sight line, I reached around to my rear pocket, to the exact spot Adam had just squeezed. The spot now sore from the feel of something solid being forced into my flesh.

I pulled the something from my pocket and looked it over. A tiny doll. Felt. Female. The shape of a skinny nesting doll but the look of '60s hippie. Blue floral dress, added layer of tiny pink felt circles on the cheeks, stitches for eyes, yarn for hair, painted on love bead necklace. Homemade looking. Like something I would have seen at my grandmother's house. I turned it over for a look at the back and something dropped out of the bottom. A metal flash drive with strips of blue plastic running along the sides like racing stripes.

I stared at it, flipping it in my palm, then held it up to the doll in my other hand. Neither the doll nor the flash drive were in my pocket when I'd left the house.

And neither belonged to me.

## 4

ATURDAY MORNINGS ARE great days for sleeping in. Except when I have to contend with a roughed-up, potential scammer in the hospital. Not to mention a narcissistic pest in my guest room and a mysterious doll and flash drive in my possession. The latter also ramping my curiosity up to high alert when I'd discovered before going to bed that the drive stored password-protected files I couldn't open.

I was washed up, dressed, and on the phone to Camille before Adam and Tina were awake. Camille loved delving into other people's gadgets and I knew she'd be thrilled to get her hands on the flash drive. We made plans to meet at the office, and I cleared the front door with a note to Adam left on the fridge and the pets walked, fed, and kissed goodbye.

A half hour later, I stood on the stoop to the C&C office in the Plateau, dodging yet more rain, and waiting for Camille to show with the key. I'd made the dash from my car to the stoop sans umbrella, sputtering rain from my lips as I ran, then I pressed myself as close to the building as possible in an attempt to keep my hair from getting completely soaked through.

Not two minutes in, the door opened behind me and Laurent poked his head out. "Catching rain drops with your tongue, *mon petit lapin?*" he said. "We both know there are better uses for your tongue than that."

I waved my arm at him in an attempt to imitate Camille's gesture for dismissal. On a previous case, Laurent and I had shared a kiss. One kiss. While we were undercover as an engaged couple. A kiss I did not initiate and tried never to speak of since. A kiss he spoke about as often as he could. Probably to see me blush. But I refused to let him bait me anymore. "Enough with the kiss already," I said. "You need to get some new material."

He widened the door opening and beckoned me in. "*Bon ben.* I'm game if you're game."

I stepped inside and slipped off my boots. There's nothing worse than an incurable flirt with attitude and a French accent. Unless it's one with charm and good looks. And a hot kiss I was not going to think about.

"It's Saturday," I said. "Shouldn't you be off somewhere chasing a puck with a hockey stick?"

"That's on Sundays. On Saturdays I chase bad guys with flash drives."

I slipped past him and into the nook that served as C&C reception, glancing into the first doorway to the right as I went to add my coat to the hooks on the far wall.

"So Camille told you about the flash drive?"

"Everything but where you found it," he said.

"My back pocket."

He glanced down at my jeans and smiled. "Any idea how it got there?"

I'd asked myself that question, too, and come up with two

possibilities. "I'm thinking either Silver or Johnny. Silver and I were pretty tight inside that cake, it wouldn't have been hard for her to slip the drive into my pocket without me knowing."

"*Et* Johnny?"

"Johnny had a moment of lucidity while he was passed out and chose to use the time to grope me."

"*Ben*, maybe he thought he was being friendly."

I rolled my eyes as I fished in my shoulder bag for the flash drive. "I think drunk had more to do with it. As soon as he sobers up, I'll pay him a visit, make up some story about why I was at his party, and ask him."

"*Non.* Not now you won't. He's in a coma."

I stopped fishing and looked up at Laurent. "Coma?"

"Medically induced. Something about brain swelling. May be a week before they take him out."

"A week? But he's supposed to get married today. His fiancée must be frantic." It wasn't enough she was marrying a guy suspected of insurance fraud and roughed up by goons. Now the guy was in a coma. I shook my head. "Nothing good ever comes from a bachelor party."

Laurent smiled. "You think this happened because Johnny had a party? The party wasn't the problem."

"Are you saying bachelor parties are good?" I said, edge creeping into my voice. "Seriously? Some arcane, patriarchal ritual that tells men they need to ogle women and maybe even sow a few wild oats before they marry. Like somehow they need to mourn what they're losing by getting married instead of celebrating the miracle that they found a life partner? Do you really—"

He put up both hands in the stop position. "Whoa. One man's problem at a time, no? Johnny's not hurt because he had a party. Johnny *est un con* who got himself into trouble and is paying for it."

"You don't know that. We didn't prove Johnny was faking his

back injury. And that Penguin and his Neanderthals may have busted in on the party at random. Maybe they rob parties all the time."

"And steal all the guests?" Laurent said. "None of Johnny's buddies have been seen since last night."

Hmm. That didn't sound good. "What about Silver?"

"Not her, either."

"You really think the Penguin took them?"

"*Non.* I think they got scared and are hiding until they think the Penguin won't go after them, too."

"Because they were witnesses to what happened to Johnny?"

Laurent moved closer to me. "Maybe, *mon petit lapin.* Or maybe because the Penguin wants something from Johnny. Something Johnny did not give. Something the Penguin now thinks Johnny gave to someone else at the party." Laurent was standing over me now, peering into my bag. "Something like that flash drive you found in your pocket."

**I HAD A** sudden rush of gratitude for the pop-up cake keeping me out of sight and off the Penguin's radar. Then I got another rush of curiosity about the contents of the flash drive, and I moved into the kitchen and dumped everything out of my bag and onto the table.

The C&C office was a flat reconfigured from an old, two-storey stone house of two attached semis. Each level had been reborn as an office suite, one up, one down on either side. C&C had a main level suite with the original living room at the front now Camille's office, the dining room in the middle now Laurent's office, and the kitchen at the back now shortened to allow for a bathroom beside it. The receptionist, Camille and Laurent's cousin Arielle, had a desk in the hallway nook, along with minimal

cabinet storage and a visitor chair. I had a voice mail box, no desk
no chair no cabinet. Mostly, I played assistant or part-time PI out
of the office and musical chairs when I was in. The café table in the
kitchen was as close to a work station as I had carved out for
myself.

I scavenged through the purse paraphernalia on my makeshift
desk, found the hippie doll, and passed it to Laurent.

He arched an eyebrow at me.

"Don't look at me like that," I said. "I'm not the one who stuffed
a flash drive into a doll. It came like that." I tugged the flash drive
out from the bottom. Without the hard metal filling it out, the doll
deflated like a retired finger puppet.

"You've touched both?" Laurent said.

"Well, yeah. Who puts on gloves to handle stuff in their own
pocket?"

He bagged the doll and used a cloth to shield his hand from the
drive as he took it from me. I hoped he'd have more luck opening
the files than I'd had when I tried the night before. Camille and
Laurent were both way more tech savvy than I was, so chances
were good one of them would at least be able to figure out who
owned the drive. Then I'd know for sure if it was Silver or Johnny
who'd chosen my pocket as a safety deposit box. Laurent was right,
the smart bet was on Johnny, but I was crossing my fingers for
Silver. I didn't like the mojo of possessing something that landed
its last owner in a coma.

Either way, my curiosity was aroused. As was my sense of
duty to protect whoever had entrusted me with the drive. At
least until I knew why I was chosen and what exactly I was
protecting.

"This is just staying between us for now, though, right?" I said
to Laurent.

He raised an eyebrow at me again. "*Ben*, let's wait and see what's on it before we make plans for its future. I'm not making any promises. It could be evidence if they arrest the Penguin."

"*If* they arrest him? Didn't they already do that? I figured they'd have picked him up overnight."

"They did. His lawyers got him released."

"Why?"

"He's got very good lawyers."

Sheesh. "If only my phone didn't break, I could show the police pictures. His lawyers would have a hard time explaining away those."

Laurent shook his head. "*Ben*, even if they were admissible evidence, you didn't get any pictures of the fight."

"How would you know?"

He pointed up. "The Cloud. I checked the iCloud account for your phone. It backed up everything. You've got Johnny, Silver, some poker game. No Penguin fight."

I thought back. He was right. When the Penguin came in, I'd moved the phone away from the peephole so I could see better. Another mistake. Oy.

"What about the club. Don't they have security cameras?" I asked.

Laurent grinned. "*Oui*. There was one in the room, but the lens got covered."

That got my attention. "Covered? You mean someone blocked the camera view in advance like they knew there was going to be a fight?"

"If they did, it was not the best choice of cover. White lace."

Lace? Oh right. "You must mean Silver's gloves," I said. "She tossed them in her act." I shook my head, recalling the lace flinging through the air. "If one landed on the camera, it was dumb luck. Her attention was on Johnny the whole time."

The front door banged opened, and Camille stomped in and

pushed the door closed with her booted foot. "*C'est vraiment trop-là cette pluie*. If it keeps raining like this, I'm buying a canoe."

"Car trouble?" I asked her.

She threw off her boots, flung her coat and purse onto Arielle's desk, and flew past me to the Nespresso machine on the counter beside the fridge. Cupboards slammed as she gathered her coffee supplies and geared up the Nespresso, pouring enough cream into the whipper sidekick machine to threaten an overflow. "No car," she said. "*Taxi*. Bell has my car. He took it this morning to Lachute to see his mother. His motorcycle is no good in this rain, and he won't change it for a car. It's him who needs the canoe."

The Nespresso geared down, and Camille added the cream to her coffee and dropped two squares of dark chocolate into her cup. Laurent took one look at the melting chocolate in Camille's cup and retreated into his office. Barely 10 A.M. and she was already augmenting dosage of her three CCs of "meds"—coffee, chocolate, and cream. He knew his sister well enough to know it was wise to steer clear of her until her "meds" took effect. Probably I would have steered clear, too, if I was a man, but we women understood about the three CCs.

Camille brought her mug over and sat across from me at the table, eyeing my purse contents still strewn across the table top.

"*Heille*. Where's your screamer?" she asked me.

My "screamer" as Camille called it was an alarm gizmo most people used to ward off assaulters. She'd given it to me a week earlier after her third attempt to teach me some self-defense moves ended in me cringing when she showed me how to crush someone's windpipe.

I held my bag at the edge of the table and swept its contents back in. "Isn't it in here? Maybe I left it in my other bag."

She stirred her three CCs into one harmonious brew. "Nice try. You don't have another bag. You drag that huge thing everywhere."

She was exaggerating about the bag. I did have other purses. I just didn't use them very often unless I was on a case that called for something small and subtle. I'd seen those old TV commercials that advised me not to leave home without IT, and I had a lot of "ITs" so I preferred to carry a bag big enough to hold them all. The screamer was new and hadn't quite qualified for IT status yet. And truth be told, still a social worker at heart from my previous career, I didn't much like the idea of the screamer. Social workers were big on inspiring trust and bonding with their clients. Carrying around a screamer was like signaling the world at large I didn't trust anyone. Not the vibe I wanted to give out. That's why the screamer was currently residing in my closet along with other gifts I couldn't bring myself to chuck but couldn't bring myself to use.

"Okay, fine," I confessed. "It's at home. I appreciate it, but I don't need it."

She stopped stirring and took a gulp of her coffee. "*Voyons*, Lora, you need something. You can't just talk your way out of everything."

I smiled. Camille didn't have much patience for the art of talk. She was no stranger to using talk as manipulation, but she much preferred the art of physical communication. She'd been holding her own and then some since she got her black belt when other girls were just getting their boobs. But talking was actually the best tool I had so far in my PI arsenal. That and some lingerie I had leftover from my first undercover case. Turns out, there are more uses for garters than holding up stockings. And in a country like Canada that frowns on citizens carrying guns, tasers, pepper spray, and the like, PI arsenals had to get creative. Which probably meant Camille was right and I should add the screamer to my toolbox for backup, distrustful vibes notwithstanding.

"Which reminds me," she went on, "where's that little memento you got in your pocket last night?"

"Laurent has it. He's checking it now."

She tapped her fingers on the side of her cup. Slowly, not fast like she did when she was annoyed. I'd learned a while back that the Carons had a slew of sign language all their own, and I was all too familiar with Camille's tapping. I'd expected fast tapping when Camille found out Laurent was getting first crack at the flash drive. But this slow tapping meant Camille had something bigger on her mind. And with Camille bigger was almost never better.

"*Okay*," she said. "Then you can come to *l'hôpital* with me to follow up on our fraudster, Johnny."

"Seriously? Now? Isn't it enough we have the flash drive to worry about? Shouldn't we let Johnny be for a while. After all, the guy's in a coma."

"*Oui, oui.* But his doctors are not. Surely they will know if his back is really hurt. He can't hide behind the shoddy diagnosis he got before. Not with examinations by ER doctors and staff specialists. Opportunity, Lora. *C'est ça qu'on a.* This could be the perfect time to get the information we need. Whatever happened to Johnny last night doesn't change our commitment to the client."

Ah yes. Opportunity. I'd learned, too, about taking advantage of opportunity on my first undercover case, and Camille was making some good points. But I had another good point. "What about privacy laws? Doctors don't just give out patient info to anyone. And we can't ask his fiancée. I doubt she'd rat on Johnny even if he is faking and she knows about it. Plus, talking about it with her would out our client, *Assurance Lion*, wouldn't it? Didn't they want a discrete investigation?"

Camille chugged the last of her coffee and stood. "No need to worry. *Probablement* the fiancée will go home for a break this morning. But Johnny has a sister in Toronto. The doctors will talk to family, no?"

I didn't like the look in her eye. Now we were coming to what her slow tapping was about. I could see where this was going. "You have a plan to get the sister to talk to you, right?"

She shook her head. "The sister's not here. But we don't need her. We've got you. You can be the sister."

"Me? No way. I am not impersonating a real person." On the undercover case, I'd pretended to be someone else, but she didn't actually exist. Representing myself as a real live, flesh and blood woman was completely different. "That has to be illegal or breaking some PI rule somewhere, doesn't it?"

"Not if we don't get caught. Then it's fine."

"If it's so fine, why don't you do it?"

"*Mais voyons*, the sister is Anglophone, like you. You think I pass for Anglophone that easy?"

Not likely. Camille's French accent was heavy. And getting heavier by the minute, I noticed.

She motioned for me to get up and continued, "*Vite*. We have to hurry."

I stood and walked out to reception to get my coat. "Why?"

"We have to get there before the real sister shows up."

"I thought you said she was in Toronto?"

"She was early this morning when I called posing as Johnny's nurse to pump her for information. She said nothing, but she was expecting to come for his wedding and still now to see him in *l'hôpital*. The drive is only five hours."

I hurried out to the foyer to put on my rain boots. "What time did you call her?"

Camille finished getting on her own outdoor wear and shrugged. "I don't know. It was dark and my eyes were not awake to see the little numbers on my phone."

That was a big fib and we both knew it. She knew exactly when she spoke to the sister, and I'd bet my weight in ice cream that time was ticking down fast. I grabbed my car keys from my bag, and she reached over and took them from me.

"I drive, *hein*," she said. "You drive like *ma grand-maman*."

I'd spent time with Camille's grandmother but had yet to see her drive, so I couldn't comment. But I did obey traffic laws. Camille not so much. Camille treated the roads like race tracks. I just hoped Johnny's sister didn't, too. Having two sisters show up at the same time could get messy.

## 5

*I* TOOK ONE look at the man in the hospital bed and felt my knees grow weak. My vision lost focus and my head felt as though cold air was being pumped in while warm air drained out.

Camille's murmured voice came at me through the gauzy sensation in my ears. *"Qu'est-ce qu'il y a, Lora?"*

I blinked my eyes closed. "Nothing. I'm fine."

"You're not fine. Your eyes are closed. And you're swaying. Another minute and you'll be in bed with Monsieur Lavoie."

I snapped my eyes open. Monsieur Lavoie was probably a very nice man. But at the moment, he was full of tubes and attached to more machines than my TV. His skin drooped away from his face like silly putty, and his head was covered in more dandruff than hair. Plus, he smelled faintly of urine.

I moved away from my vigil at bedside and closer to the curtain separating Monsieur Lavoie from the other bed in the room. Johnny's. "Let's switch places. You play visitor and I'll keep lookout."

Camille didn't budge and shot me a look, part petrified cat, part mother bear on attack. Camille didn't do well with doctors or anything medical. It ignited her flight or fight response faster than real threats like imminent violence or earthly disasters. The only thing on par with her aversion to doctors was her aversion to relationships.

Which was a problem because I was a tad on the squeamish side. How either of us thought we could pull off hospital duty on a case was beyond me.

I eased up alongside Camille and moved the edge of the curtain aside to look out at the bed on the other side where Johnny lay unconscious with his sister sitting in a chair at his side. His *real* sister who also turned out to be a *sister* sister—as in nun—complete with prayer beads and head covering, which she periodically adjusted giving me the impression she probably didn't wear it on a daily basis. Probably she was only donning it now to score brownie points with the big guy upstairs so he would help her brother heal.

Jane, or Sister Jane, the name we'd heard the nurse call her, had already been sitting pretty when we'd arrived at the hospital, effectively putting the kybosh on Camille's plan for me to play the sister role. Secretly, I was relieved.

Until I realized Camille had a Plan B that involved waiting around for Johnny's doctors to come in and give Sister Jane an update on Johnny's condition. An update we would conveniently overhear since anything above a whisper could be heard easily given we were only one bed away. Which is how we got to be Monsieur Lavoie's visitors for the morning, crammed into his side of the room. The stuffy side, with the window painted shut. Both of us now crowded together by the curtain, our backs to Monsieur Lavoie.

I nudged Camille and she nudged me back and said, *"Mais voyons!* We can't both stand here. It looks odd."

I scanned behind me, from the curtain to the dusty window frame on the outside wall, careful to avoid lingering my gaze on Monsieur Lavoie and his tubes. "Who's going to see us? Nobody can see that we're here let alone where we're standing. Unless someone's training binoculars on Monsieur Lavoie from the building across the way." And even then it was a stretch given the smudged panes in the window lowering the chances anyone could get a clear view.

"This isn't going to work," Camille whispered, moving to pace at the end of Monsieur Lavoie's bed, her footsteps muffled by the thick soles of her Doc Martens as she turned direction after barely three steps.

I resisted the urge to shoot back a sarcastic quip and instead moved to take up Camille's place by the slit in the curtain where I could see that Johnny's doctor had come in. I signaled Camille to cut the pacing thing as I kept one eye positioned ahead on the doctor—a man in his early fifties wearing a lab coat over suit pants. His hair prematurely silver, short, and combed. His skin tanned and leathery.

His French accent was apparent but not intense as he explained to Sister Jane in English about Johnny's injuries and the rationale for keeping him in a coma. There was a look of relief on Jane's face when she understood Johnny's prognosis was good so long as the brain swelling went down. He had no other internal problems of major concern aside from a somewhat weakened liver which the doctor attributed to heavy drinking. Sister Jane bowed her head at that news, possibly from upset, possibly from embarrassment. Hard to tell which.

Aside from Johnny's fiancée, who'd apparently left a bit ago, I heard no mention of Johnny having had other visitors. Not a surprise since all his buddies were still MIA. But at least it meant, too, that the Penguin and his goons hadn't stopped by, either.

When the doctor left, Camille nudged me and pointed to the curtain.

"*Voyons,*" she whispered. "The doctor said nothing about Johnny's back. Do your social worker thing and talk to Johnny's sister. See what she knows."

My social worker thing, as Camille put it, was my biggest asset as a PI and the best tool in my PI toolbox. Back in New York I'd gotten my degree in Social Work and worked in the field for almost ten years honing my skills. I knew how to foster trust and how to read people. Most of the time. When I wasn't distracted by hospital machines, IV tubes, and the overpowering smell of disinfectant tinged with various bodily fluids and fear.

"You said his sister didn't know anything when you spoke to her this morning," I whispered back. "Why bother talking to her?"

Camille shook her head. "*Non, non.* I said she didn't *tell* me anything, not that she didn't *know* anything. *Vas-y.*"

And with her last word Camille shoved me forward, outing me from the curtain and causing Sister Jane to nearly jump out of her chair when I suddenly stumbled in beside her.

"I'm sorry," I said to the Sister, putting the brakes on my feet and stretching my arms out, hoping to right myself before I belly-flopped onto Johnny's bed. The hospital room was small and crowded. More than two or three steps in any direction and a gal was almost guaranteed to bump into something or someone. Lucky for me I ended up at the bottom of Johnny's bed, otherwise instead of doing a palms down on his thin cotton blanket I could be waltzing with his IV pole.

Sister Jane resettled herself in her chair and offered me a polite smile. "Are you all right?"

I sprang back from the bed and stood. "Fine," I said. "I didn't mean to intrude." Instinctively, I wiped my hands on the side of my jeans, pausing when I saw her watching me, afraid she would think I was some sort of germaphobe. I may have a wee thing about hospital bed cooties, but I was no germaphobe. Just a gal with common sense who may have watched too many exposé shows about the spread of superbugs in hospitals.

My eyes slid over to the curtain still sheltering Monsieur Lavoie's side of the room. I could swear the curtain was moving and I imagined Camille laughing at me from the other side.

"Would you like to talk about it?" Sister Jane asked.

I shifted my attention back to her. "Excuse me?"

She folded her hands in her lap, a softness settling onto her face, the large crucifix around her neck hanging heavy like an anchor grounding her in calm. "You seem upset," she said. "Maybe I can help."

Hmm. That was a twist I hadn't expected. Maybe stumbling out wasn't so bad after all. Stumbling out may just have stumbled me in to an opener with Sister Jane. Okay, so maybe I'd have to pretend to be sad and upset. But I could do that. I didn't even have to fake the second part. One look at Johnny's tubes and machines and the bruising on his face, made greener by the fluorescent light on the wall above his head, and I could feel the woozies coming back to me.

I quickly looked away from him and back at her. Then did a double take. Minus the green shading, his face was remarkably similar to his sister's. Like boy and girl versions of the same person. Same acorn-shaped eyes, same wide nose, same pointed chin. Under her head covering, she probably had the same brittle brown hair, too.

"You're very kind to offer," I said. "It is hard when someone you care about is sick, isn't it?" A safe thing to say I figured even if I wasn't supposed to know Johnny was her brother. Even if he'd just been a parishioner or friend, he'd still fall under the heading of someone she cared about.

The softness in her face went from tranquil to tired. "Yes. Illness can be trying." She gestured to a plastic chair stuffed into the corner. "Would you like to sit?"

I thanked her, brought the chair closer, and sat.

"Is it your grandfather you're visiting?" she asked me.

Hmm. Given Monsieur Lavoie's age, grandfather wasn't a bad fib, but it seemed too personal. Tough to explain away if any of his real family showed up. "Not exactly. He's an old, um, neighbor. But he feels like family, if you know what I mean." I held my hands in my lap and resisted the urge to cross my fingers. Not that I was Catholic or super religious, but fibbing to a nun felt like all kinds of wrong.

She nodded.

"And you?" I said, happy to move on.

She looked at Johnny. "My twin brother," she said.

Twin? No wonder they looked so much alike. But I was guessing their resemblance pretty much ended there. After all, she was a devout nun with connections to God and his disciples. Johnny was a gambling drunk with connections to the Penguin and his goons.

Still, twins tended to share a special bond. This had to be tough for her.

"I'm sorry," I said. "You must be very close."

A sadness flitted through her eyes before reserve whooshed it away and she nodded again.

"Is he very ill?" I asked.

"I'm hoping not. And your friend?"

There was a muffled sound behind the curtain. A muffled sound with the unmistakable pattern of Camille taping her soft-soled boot. If she was sending me some kind of Caron Morse code about what to say, I couldn't make it out. Probably it had less to do with Monsieur Lavoie's condition and more to do with her wanting me to find out about Johnny's back injury already.

I smiled at Sister Jane. "I'm trying to be hopeful, too." I glanced at Johnny. "But my old neighbor isn't young and strong like your brother."

Johnny's skin didn't look all that young at the moment and his sunken cheeks and stringy body didn't exactly scream virile man, but a little flattery couldn't hurt. Everyone likes to think the best about family. Plus, it wasn't like I could just come right out and ask about Johnny's back. I had to try and steer the conversation around to it gradually and ease into the subject.

"The Lord makes each of us strong in our own ways," Sister Jane said. "A strong spirit is just as important as a strong body."

Hmm. This might be harder than I thought. She was fully in nun mode now. Totally deflecting her own emotions and offering up words meant to comfort me rather than sharing her own feelings. Nun mode and social work mode might just cancel each other out.

Unless maybe I donned my imaginary Wonder Woman bracelets, practiced a little deflection of my own, and matched my instinct to help others with hers.

I smiled. "Well, if your brother is anything like you, he must have both, and he'll be back to his old self in no time. Up and around, talking and walking and just itching to go home."

She glanced at his inert body in the bed, propped up slightly here and there by pillows probably meant to aid circulation and reduce bed sores. Her eyes didn't linger on his back or his legs or his bruised face. "God willing," she said. "He was supposed to be dancing at his wedding tonight."

Hmm. Dancing. Maybe Sister Jane and Johnny weren't as close

as she thought. She didn't even seem to know about his hurt back, let alone if it was a real injury or not.

She stood, catching me off guard, and I stood, too, automatically, prompted by the manners my mother instilled in me as a child.

Sister Jane bent, extended a hand to the floor, and straightened again, a strip of something white in her fingers. "*Investigations C&C,*" she said holding the something white out to me. "An investigator. That must be an exciting job."

I looked at the something white in her hand—a business card, *my* business card, and quickly accepted it. Must have fallen from my pocket when I sprang up. Whoops. Good thing I hadn't given her a fake name along with my fake reason for being at the hospital.

"It's an okay job," I told her, not bothering to detail my training status. "It has its moments, but it's not as exciting as it looks on TV."

Her face stayed blank a moment before she smiled, and it occurred to me she may not watch much TV. Did nuns watch TV?

"Well it was nice to meet you, Lora," she said. "I enjoyed our chat, but if you'll excuse me I've had a long drive and I must stretch my legs and get something to eat."

I nodded at her. "Of course." The thought skittered through my brain that I should keep her talking, probe a bit deeper, confirm that her comment about the dancing wasn't just an expression. But her mention of Johnny dancing at his wedding coupled with the fact she hadn't asked the doctor anything about Johnny's back or twigged to my earlier prompt about Johnny walking, had me thinking I already had my answer.

She faced Johnny's bedside, reached for his hand, and gave it a light squeeze. Then she adjusted his covers, picked up a sweater draped over the footboard of the bed, and walked the sweater over to the locker-like closet by his headboard, across from where she'd been sitting vigil.

Inside the locker, I could make out Johnny's bachelor party clothes, blood stains and all, along with his shoes and a small bag hanging on a hook. The bag and the sweater in Sister Jane's hand I didn't recognize, the shoes I did. Sister Jane lifted them up, moved the bag down to their place on the floor, placed the shoes on top, and set the sweater on the hook now free of the bag. She closed the locker door, turned a weak smile my way, and wished me well before she left.

When Sister Jane was gone, Camille whipped open Monsieur Lavoie's curtain and hurtled forward. "So much for that," she said as she crossed to the other side of Johnny's bed. "That got us nothing."

"Maybe not nothing," I said, making my way to the closet, checking the doorway was clear of onlookers as I passed by. Quickly, I eased the closet open, took out Johnny's shoes and held them up to Camille, whose eyes locked onto the soles as she smiled. Mud and fresh grass were caked onto the bottom of the shoes. Shoes still stiff and except for the bloodstains on the toes, pristine white, smelling of new leather and fresh laces. Brand spanking new shoes used only by a man who swore on his soul he was wheelchair bound, but whose soles were telling a different story.

CAMILLE PASSED LAURENT HER MOBILE, a picture of the underside of Johnny's shoes filling the phone's screen.

"*Voilà*," she said. "Shoes hardly worn, fresh mud caked into the treads. Caked in deep from walking. *La preuve que* Johnny is lying."

She moved away, heading out of Laurent's office at C&C and

into the hall. I shifted into her vacated space and peered over Laurent's arm where he sat in his desk chair, studying the photo.

Camille was right. Things didn't look good for Johnny. Which had me feeling bad, especially with him all banged up in the hospital. Not to mention how his sister the nun would feel when she heard in addition to a drinking problem weakening Johnny's liver that could land him a repeat stay in the hospital after he recovered from his beating, he also had a lying problem that could land him in jail for insurance fraud.

I kept my eyes on Camille's phone as Laurent flicked the shoe picture away and zipped through more pictures on her camera roll. I wasn't sure if his move was one of idle curiosity or disinterest in the shoes. Maybe both. But it unnerved me. Laurent had been working on the mysterious flash drive when Camille and I had come in, and if he'd learned anything he wasn't sharing. Which also unnerved me. He had an old cop habit of picking and choosing when to share and when to not. In this case, that could mean he knew something already or he didn't know anything yet. When he went into cop mode, the man was impossible to read. Threw me off balance every time. Plus, it annoyed me since I was trained to read people. And I was beginning to think he knew how cop mode affected me and sometimes did it just to push my buttons.

"The shoe mud's not much to go on really," I said, not wanting the off-balance thing to keep me from putting in a good word for Johnny. Even though I was the one to spot the shoe clue I didn't feel happy about it. "Probably circumstantial at best."

Camille strolled back into the room, cup of coffee in hand. "*Mais alors, Lion* didn't hire us to be judge and jury. They hired us to catch Johnny moving with no signs of injury. Or to find some *informations* that show he's lying and pass it over. It's them who

43

decide what to do with the informations. The shoes are just one piece. We'll get more."

I smiled at Camille's determination. If it wasn't for pesky laws getting in her way, she would have scoured Johnny's apartment or hid out on his fire escape waiting to snap a pic of him dancing in his underwear. Whatever it took to get the proof she wanted.

But, Johnny's lease ended a month earlier. He'd thrown all his stuff into storage and moved into his fiancée's place until after the wedding when they planned to get a bigger home. Which made staking Johnny out without being spotted even trickier. And now with him in the hospital, I wasn't even sure it was possible.

"How are we supposed to get more now?" I said. "The guy's in a coma. We're not exactly going to catch him jogging in the park."

"*T'inquiète pas*. There are ways."

She went on to say something about his fiancée and the hospital, but I was only half listening, distracted by the photo Laurent had stopped on. A picture of me on a recent visit to Camille and Laurent's tante Claudette's house. Snuggled to me was *Mignon*, tante Claudette's mini white poodle and a former roomie of mine when I looked after him temporarily while Claudette was *ailleurs*. Seeing the pup made my eyes want to tear. I missed the little guy. He'd only been with me a short time, but we'd been nearly inseparable for most of it. It had been hard to return him to his rightful home. Lucky for me, tante Claudette understood that and let me visit him as often as I wanted.

Laurent scrolled past the picture and stopped on another, his head tilting to the side. I bent to get a closer look, my head tilting, too, trying to make out the image. Dark hair maybe. And was that skin?

"*Heille. Ramène-le moi,*" Camille said, lunging to wrench her mobile from Laurent's hand.

I watched them wrestle over the phone and my mind flashed

back to Johnny. "You know what's strange?" I said. "There was no cell phone with Johnny's things at the hospital. Everyone has a phone these days, so where was his? Camille and I went through every inch of the little closet in Johnny's hospital room. His clothes were there, but no cell."

Camille gave one final yank on her phone just as Laurent released it, propelling Camille back a step, sloshing coffee out of her cup and onto his desk.

We all glanced at the coffee spill, neither sib making a move to wipe it up.

"*Probablement* the fiancée of Johnny took it," Camille said. "His wallet wasn't there, either. Maybe she was worried they would get stolen."

Sounded logical. If I was in the hospital, though, I can't imagine wanting anyone taking away my purse for safekeeping. I'd feel naked without my purse.

The doorbell went and both Camille and Laurent rushed out to answer the bell. Expecting someone maybe. Or maybe both avoiding picking up the coffee spill lest the other think it was an admission of responsibility for the wrangling that caused it. In their work, they were consummate professionals and they would defend each other to the death from outside threats, but neither admitted weakness in petty sibling squabbles. Being an only child, occasionally I envied them their sibling ways. The rest of the time I thought they were nuts.

I grabbed a wad of tissues from a nearby box and soaked up the coffee. The social worker side of me knew I was probably just enabling their craziness, the rest of me wanted to avoid coffee forming into a tiny river staining the table forever with some crazy Caron mini form of De Nile. En route to the kitchen to toss out the soppy mess, I stopped short in the reception area, finding myself nose-to-chest with a man. His chest firm and wet and smelling of rain.

I took a step back, got a look at his face, and felt my cheeks flush. The man wore black jeans, a colorful shirt, an open jacket, and a toothy grin made brighter by his dark skin. All of it much more than he'd been wearing the last time I'd seen him. Last time, he'd been buck naked, hands cuffed behind his back, sharing his tongue ring with Arielle, the C&C receptionist aka Camille and Laurent's twenty-one year old cousin, about ten years their junior. And mine, too.

The man's name was Jason and he was Arielle's live-in boyfriend. He hailed from Trinidad, had a degree in engineering, a tendency to sneeze around pets, and a twentysomething body that looked like the Gods themselves had chiseled it into smooth, hard perfection. Everywhere.

"Hey Lora," he said. "How's it going?" His words had a slight sing-song to them, mellow and happy, like he'd just finished meditating. "Long time no see."

Hmm. That was a matter of interpretation. "Good," I told him. "How's it going with you?"

"Very good. I'm meeting Arielle for shopping and a movie on this fine rainy day. But the little lady left her credit card here and I've come to fetch it for her."

Hmm. Shopping and a movie did sound like a good way to spend a rainy day.

Camille slammed a drawer shut in Arielle's desk and passed Jason a card holder, its backside aglow with a purple glittery cover.

Jason shoved the holder into his jacket pocket and sauntered towards the door. His body moved fluidly, like all his joints had just been oiled, as he called a thanks to Camille over his shoulder and a good day to us all.

On his way out, another visitor scooted in. This one wet and thin, long hair slicked down with clumps here and there, reminding me of a bedraggled puppy.

"I'm not here," the visitor said, voice low, eyes in constant motion.

The eyes were much bigger and rounder than I remembered, but the voice was familiar. Silver, my fellow hunk-a-junk-fake-cake dweller.

She shook her head from side to side, her hair whipping back and forth flinging water at us. Each of us stepped back as she went on to slip out of a droopy jacket, oversized for her medium frame, to reveal her outfit from the night before, legs bare and wet, strappy shoes glistening with dampness.

"A towel," she said, placing her coat on a nearby hook. "Does anyone have a towel?"

Laurent walked into his office, came back with the blanket he kept on his small sofa, and draped the throw over Silver's shoulders.

Good call, considering the only towels around were hand towels in the tiny bathroom and maybe a tea towel or two from the kitchen.

Camille disappeared into the kitchen and came back with a mug of steaming coffee just as Silver finished "toweling" off and squeezing excess moisture from her thin long hair, rubbing the ends until the augmented blonde bits showed color again. Resting the blanket across her back, cape style, Silver let the long blanket fold together across her torso and trail down to the floor as she reached for the coffee cup.

She took a test sip of the coffee then gulped back some more. "I've come to warn you," she said, focusing in on me. "That thug from last night is coming for you."

I felt my eyes stop mid blink. "Excuse me?"

"He's not happy. He heard the police questioned you as a witness to what happened at Johnny's party."

I glanced from Camille to Laurent, thinking Silver must be talking about the Penguin. "How would he know? He was long gone by the time the police got there."

Silver finished her coffee, passed the mug back to Camille, and shrugged out of the blanket. The skimpy fantasy bride outfit she wore looked more tacky in the light of day. And wilted somehow, lost without the hair piece and veil. "He knows everything. I'm telling you, Lora, you don't want to mess with that guy. When he tracks you down, give him whatever he wants." She reached for the wet coat she'd ditched earlier, and I noticed fresh bruises on her bare upper arms.

I saw Camille's eyes narrow as she took in the bruises, too. "*Attends.* Don't go. We can help you."

"Don't worry about me," Silver said. "He's done with me." She hurried to the door. "Worry about your friend. She's the one on his must-see list."

And with that she was gone before we could do more to stop her or ask her about the flash drive. Only a dirty mug, a damp blanket, and a wet floor left behind to show she'd ever come at all.

## 6

"**Y**OU REALLY DIDN'T have to come home with me," I said to Camille as I tossed my house keys onto the little table in my hall. "It's Saturday night. I'm sure you have better things to do than babysit me."

I glanced behind me to where Camille stood, sock footed, halfway between my vestibule door and the stairs leading up to the second floor of the house. Her head was turned, her gaze fixed on the living room, so she missed the look I was shooting her. The look that added the subtext to my comment, ie.: That I didn't *need or want* anyone to babysit me, that I could take care of myself even if I didn't know how to crush a man's windpipe with my bare hands.

"You and Adam redecorating?" she said.

"What?" I went over to stand beside her, my living room coming into view as I did. Or at least what used to be my living room—couch under the large front window, the far wall a bank of short built-in shelves flanking a wood-burning fireplace, worn armchair tucked in front of the shelves to the right, rocking chair on the left. The whole thing open to the dining room with a wide archway delineating the spaces.

Camille moved slowly into the room and smiled. "A bit crowded, no?"

Crowded was right. I couldn't even see my couch and chairs anymore. They were completely blocked by large boxes and a half-built crib standing where my coffee table used to be. Another crib in pieces sat leaning against the fireplace front. Above, various tools and nuts and bolts looking things were strewn along the fireplace mantel, a long rubber fish front and center like a fisherman's trophy catch. A fisherman who probably fished with a plastic rod in the bathtub.

I eased past Camille over to the fish and picked it up. It squeaked under my grasp, its squeak followed by a bark to my left. A bark reminding me that no pet feet had greeted me at the door. I tracked the bark and peered over a box to find my dog Pong penned in near the couch, her tiny dachshund mutt legs too short to raise her head above box level, even when standing on her back feet.

"What are you doing back there?" I asked her as I leaned down to pick her up and out.

She wagged her tail at me when I put her down. Her big brown eyes darting between me and Camille, my own eyes glancing away from her to scan the room in search of my cat Ping. The debris may have confined Pong, but Ping wouldn't let a few boxes limit her run of the house. She'd be in kitty heaven jumping about like she'd finally gotten the feline jungle gym she deserved, scratching her signature in every scrap of cardboard she could land her claws on.

I checked the living and dining rooms then went through to the kitchen. No sign of her. I left Camille fidgeting with a plastic hose on some gizmo she'd de-boxed and I headed upstairs. Three of the four doors were closed. Only the bathroom open. I knocked briefly on the first closed door I came to before I poked my head into Adam's office. The sofa bed was open, sheets askew, and the room was cluttered with Tina things and clouded in her perfume. But free of Ping or anyone else. Ditto my tiny home office at the front of the house.

Panic seized my chest as I hurried to the bedroom, hoping with every step that the cat hadn't gotten out of the house. Ping was a house cat. No telling what would become of her outdoors. She was a creature of comforts—fluffy pillows for napping, warm laps for snuggling, full bowls for nibbling, clean litter for piddling. She'd be lost in the outside world.

In the bedroom, her sleep spot was empty. Her lookout on the radiator by the window all clear. My last hope was the closet. I rushed over to see what was behind door number five, and as I passed the bed I felt a breeze brush past my legs. I looked down to see a blur of fur whiz by. A blur that could only have come from under the bed and had already made it to the hallway.

By the time I caught up enough to catch a proper glimpse, I could see the blur was unmistakably Ping, rounding the bottom of the stairs, dashing on towards the kitchen. Gone when I got downstairs, the little pet flap in the basement door slapping shut.

"*Que-est-ce qu'il y à?*" Camille asked me. She stood by the door from the dining room, moving to sit at the kitchen table as she spoke. "Why is your face all red like that?"

I touched my cheek. I used to be much better at hiding my emotions. Lately, it was all I could do to keep from shouting them from rooftops. My panic had gone, but watching Ping zip to the basement had riled up something else. The cat only went downstairs for one reason—to use her kitty facilities aka litter box. Her rush made me think she'd been denied access for far too long, and I wondered who had shut her in the bedroom and how long she'd been exiled there. It was one thing to turn my living room into a baby store outlet. But banishing my own baby to a marathon time-out was something else. When Adam got home he was definitely in for an earful from me. Either he or his houseguest was responsible, and as far as I was concerned nobody puts my "baby" in a corner. Make that "babies" since Pong had also been cornered in that makeshift box pen in the living room. I'd thought that was accidental, but now I wondered if that was true. Just exactly what happened around here when I wasn't home?

"*Tiens*," Camille said, up again and handing me an open carton of ice cream with a spoon sticking out on top. "*Mange*. Your face gets any redder and I'm slathering you with the stuff."

I accepted the carton. She was right. I needed to cool down. I had other things to think about. Like the reason Camille was in my kitchen instead of her own. Silver and her message about the Penguin and his goons.

"Thanks," I said, feeling calmer after just a few spoonfuls of ice cream and grateful to have a best friend who knew me so well. "I'm good now. Seriously, you can go. Nobody's going to bother with me here. I'm home, all safe and sound. Don't you have some big Saturday night plans with Puddles?"

She helped herself to a chocolate chip cookie from the cookie jar. "Not really."

"What does that mean exactly?"

"He's at my place I think."

Her place. Right. Unofficially Puddles had moved in with Camille a bit ago but officially she still refused to see it that way. "And?"

"*Et alors*. I see him when I see him."

I stopped shoveling in my ice cream and caught her eye. Camille may not have been big on relationships, but she cared about Puddles. I knew that much. I thought back to her talk about phone calls to her *chum* the night of Johnny's party. Maybe that hadn't been just a line to give Brassard after all. "You guys okay?" I asked her.

"*Oui, oui.* Of course. It's you with the problems. With your house in new decorations and your friend from the other night."

I sat at the table and watched her a beat. She hadn't really answered my question. She was deflecting. Plain and simple. Laurent may have perfected the art of cop mode, but Camille was brilliant at deflection. The difference was I knew Camille would eventually share when she was ready. Laurent not so much. Laurent seemed to like to keep me guessing.

Still, something was clearly going on with Camille and Puddles, and I was dying to know what. Probably if I pushed the topic, she'd spill. But she wouldn't feel good about it. Better to give her time to come to it in her own way and allow her to change the subject for the moment.

"By 'my friend' you talking about Silver or the Penguin?" I said.

"What penguin?"

Right. I'd taken to thinking of the badie from Johnny's party as the Penguin after my chat with Laurent, but I hadn't mentioned that to Camille. I quickly filled her in on the nickname and she grinned.

"I'm curious now," she said. "Maybe it's good if he shows up tonight. I'd like to see a man who looks like a penguin."

"You think he'd show up here? At my house?"

She shrugged. "Why not?"

I capped the ice cream and set it aside, afraid I was hitting bottom, unsure how full the container had been when I started. "But we don't even know what he wants from me. We still can't be sure he's after the flash drive. It could have come from Silver. We didn't get a chance to ask her."

Camille rolled her eyes.

Okay, so I didn't really think that. The part of me that had been holding out hope for that knew better. "What does it matter anyway? I don't even have his stupid flash drive anymore. I can't help him."

"He doesn't know that."

"And we don't even know what's on the flash drive. Laurent didn't say if *he* even knows yet."

I added in that last bit in case Laurent had told her something he hadn't told me. But if he had, the look on her face told me she wasn't going there. I may work for the agency and they may be training me, but I'd learned that didn't gain me access to all things. At least not as quickly as I'd like.

She grabbed my ice cream, got up, put it away, and plucked a handful more cookies from the jar. "*Regarde*, Lora. I'm not leaving you here alone. Did you see the dancer's arms? The Penguin man is no door-to-door salesman. If he shows up at your door, he'll do more than talk."

"I'm not afraid," I said, accepting the cookie she offered me.

Ping came whizzing back through the pet door, the door clacked closed, and I jumped.

Camille smiled. "You want me to show you the windpipe move again?"

I frowned and crunched a bite off my cookie.

**I GOT THROUGH** the next few hours unscathed and without any need for the windpipe move. In fact, probably not having it at my fingertips was a good thing. I may have been tempted to use it on Adam when he'd come in around ten-thirty, smelling like a mix of Chanel N° 5 and Pampers.

Turned out, Tina's husband Jeffrey had run into a last minute snafu at his conference and couldn't make it back in time to attend their birthing class. So Adam had graciously agreed to take Tina, who then decided she wanted to take the baby care prep class that followed and he'd gone to that, too. He came home with a new-found fear of childbirth and a new-found fascination with swaddling and diapering.

Normally, I'd applaud him for stepping up and being a good friend. But not when he'd gotten so caught up in Tina's forthcoming babies that he'd left our "babies" without a thought to their well-being.

Not to mention that it would have been nice if he'd called to let me know where he was, so I wouldn't have to worry that he could be sitting in his car on the side of the road somewhere with a chunk of overpass lodged into his windshield. On the news the other night, I'd seen that happen to someone. Scary. And the kind of image that sticks with a gal.

With Adam finally home, Camille took that as her cue to leave. The whole safety-in-numbers logic thing probably. Or maybe it was the whole self-preservation thing. Camille was no stranger to drama, but she much preferred her own to anyone else's and she'd have to have been asleep not to feel the tension rise in the air the minute Adam walked in. He wasn't home five minutes before she was gone, leaving me making vain attempts to pretend I was cool with his waltzing in so late and him making even more vain attempts to share what he learned at baby class.

"And you know babies can recognize their mother by smell?" he said.

I was standing at the kitchen counter facing the window, back to Adam as he filled a glass with something from the fridge, and I was thinking that if what he said was true Tina's poor babies would be mistaking any woman dripping in perfume for their mother. They'd have to be born with noses like bloodhounds to sniff out Tina's real smell.

"What about their sense of hearing?" I said, turning to face Adam.

"What?"

"Babies sense of hearing," I said again. "Is it better than yours? I must have called you three times in the last few hours."

He set his glass down on the table and pulled his phone from the pocket of his sweatshirt. "Oh, right. I forgot I turned my phone off. They don't allow phones in the classes." He eyed his phone display. "Yeah, sorry about that. I'll switch it back on."

"You could have at least let me know where you were."

"I did." He shoved his phone away and gestured at the fridge. "I left a note like always."

I glanced at the refrigerator. Our usual spot for posting messages to each other. All the magnets were bare except two that held photos of us. Selfies we'd taken and printed out, one of us outside the villa where we'd spent Valentine's day in Saint-Adèle and one from the summer before at the Old Port in Vieux Montréal.

"There's no note," I said, pointing out the obvious.

The tiny lines by his eyes formed a parenthesis and his chin jutted out, equal parts defiance and annoyance. "It was there, Lora. What do you want me to say."

"I want you to say you're sorry," I said. "I want you to tell me why you locked the cat in the bedroom and left the dog stuck behind all those boxes in the living room. I want you to tell me why we *have* all those boxes in our living room!" By that last sentence I was shouting and not proud of it.

Adam's face relaxed faster than a balloon losing air. His eyes went to Pong resting on the floor by the water dish and moved on to Ping asleep on a chair. "What are you talking about?"

"When I came home that's where I found them. If it wasn't you who put them there, it had to be Tina."

He shook his head. "Tina was in the car when I locked up. And Ping was asleep in the rocker. Pong was gulping down a Milk-Bone in the hall."

I was looking at the floor, avoiding Adam's face, trying to decide if he was telling the truth. He wasn't prone to lying, but he did sometimes cover for Tina. Especially if he thought she'd done something that might upset me. Cloistering my pets would definitely qualify, but this didn't feel like Adam fudging. I was trying to decide what it did feel like when out of the corner of my eye I spotted an edge of white paper between the fridge and the counter. I bent, tugged on the paper, and found the loose edge attached to a balled-up wad. Unraveled, the wad of paper had Adam's message to me scrawled on one side. The other blank. Proof Adam was telling the truth. And fodder for the feeling that was slowly creeping into my system. Something was off.

If Adam or Tina hadn't penned in Ping and Pong, who did? And who scrunched up Adam's note? If it had simply fallen, it would be flat. The scrunching was man-made. And I had a sinking suspicion that scrunching man was not Adam.

# 7

ONLY ONE NAME came to mind of course. The Penguin. Probably not him directly, but his goons. Probably on the hunt for the flash drive. The mere thought of it gave me the heebie jeebies.

Even worse, it meant Adam and Tina weren't responsible, either purposefully or accidentally, for Ping and Pong's sequestered afternoon. I was. Indirectly, but still I was. Which had me feeling a wave of guilt followed by one of relief that both pets were fine.

Adam crossed over to me and took my hand. "Earth to Lora. What's going on here?"

"Nothing." I forced a smile. "Let's forget it and go up to bed."

He kept a firm grasp on my hand when I moved to leave the room, and he used his other hand to reach for the note. "Not so fast."

I let him ease the note from me and waited for the inevitable. Adam tried to be supportive of my work, and we both worked from home now and then. He wouldn't have a problem with my work following me home. But he would have a problem with it surreptitiously following me home and breaking in all on its own.

He looked from the note to me. "Okay, so missing note explained. But if you didn't ball it up, who did?"

I took a deep breath, debating how much to tell him. I did have client confidentiality to think about, but Camille and I also had an agreement that sometimes I shared bits of information with Adam on a need-to-know basis. The Penguin goons breaking into his home may not count as need-to-know, but it might border on right-to-know. Unfortunately, telling him would also make me look bad for going on at him about the pets and Tina. I hated that.

Plus, was I really sure it was the Penguin goons? I mean, when goons break in and search a place, don't they leave a mess? Tossed cushions, bashed in TVs, underwear streaming out of drawers? If it was the goons, they'd taken pains to leave things neat, like they didn't want anyone to know they'd been here. And I wouldn't have known, either, if it weren't for Ping and Pong's odd confinement. Which now that I thought about more, may have come about by accident. Pong cornered when the goons shuffled boxes. Ping hiding under the bed when she heard strangers come in. Ping hid under the bed when the plumber came or when she sensed an impending trip to the vet. She'd be smart enough to hide from goons.

But she wouldn't close the door. Someone else had to do that. And the goons were the most likely candidates.

"Okay, now you're freaking me out, Lora. You look like you just found out they discontinued your favorite ice cream. What's wrong?"

Adam had moved his hands and now his whole arms held me. Blast. My face must be giving me away again. That was twice in one night. I had to work on that.

I made an effort to relax and explained to him that there was a possibility we may have had a break-in. That I was working on a case and someone may have come looking for something. That it was over now and they wouldn't be back. I crossed my fingers as I said that last bit, hoping it was true.

He released me and took a step back. "Geez. Have I told you lately that I'm starting to hate your job?"

"Uh huh."

"I mean it, Lora. You get on me for missing some phone calls. But I have to put up with your gallivanting around all day with miscreants and inviting them into our home."

Gallivanting? Miscreants? Inviting? Really? Most PI work was boring stuff. Cheating spouses, lost relatives, missing witnesses. And Johnny's case would probably be boring, too, if the Penguin hadn't gotten involved.

Still, embellishments aside, Adam may have a small point.

He walked over to where our portable phone sat in its charger on the counter and picked up the handset.

"What are you doing?" I asked him.

"What do you mean what am I doing? I'm calling the police to report the break-in."

I moved close enough in to hit the phone's 'end' button before his call connected. "You can't do that. We don't have anything to report. Nothing's missing. Nobody's hurt. There are no signs of forced entry." At least none that I knew about. But then I hadn't been looking for any.

He lowered the phone to his side and wandered out of the room. I heard the front door lock tumble back and forth, window locks click, swearing from the living room.

I rushed in. "What?"

Adam was leaning against the fireplace, one foot on the ground, the other in the air, fingers rubbing his airborne toes. "Nearly cut my foot on that darn crib leg," he said. "Darn things are supposed to be safe for a baby's room. How can they make them so sharp? First thing tomorrow that thing's going back."

I held back a smile. Camille and I had rearranged all the baby paraphernalia so we could get to the couch and watch a movie while we waited for the Penguin to show. The boxes were neat and orderly sitting mostly around the perimeter. And we'd shoved the half-built crib to the fireplace front, out of the way of foot traffic. Or so I thought.

"Let me take a look." I went to Adam, pulled his sock off, and found his big toe reddening but no cuts or blood. "I think you'll live, patient."

He sighed and shifted over to sit in the armchair crammed in beside the crib. "What are we doing? This is crazy. *You* make me crazy."

I started to respond, but he talked over me. "No. I don't mean you make me crazy. I mean all this makes me crazy. Your job. Your even knowing people who could break into our house." He paused for a breath. "I know it's not your fault. But it just makes me crazy."

I smiled. Crazy I could understand. For him it was my job, for me it was his ties with Tina. "Okay. So maybe we both need to do some adjusting. Couples do that. We can do that."

He reached for me and pulled me onto his lap. "Adjusting, eh."

I nodded. "You know, compromising and accommodating each other's careers." I glanced at my cluttered living room and held in a grimace. "Supporting things that are important to the other person. Understanding each other's positions."

"Hmm," Adam said, his voice softening. "That's quite a list. Let me finish checking the house, then I'll meet you upstairs and we can get started on that last thing, the position one. Sounds fascinating."

I rolled my eyes. "Will you take this seriously!"

He played with a curl at the end of my hair. "I assure you I take everything about our positions seriously, and I plan to give both of them a lot of thought. Deep thought. All night if that's what it takes to come to a mutually happy understanding."

**"WHY DIDN'T YOU** call last night?"

The voice that spoke to me through the phone was quiet, even, controlled. Very male, very French, and very heavy on the breathing. Laurent. I'd called to ask if he'd made any progress cracking the passwords on the flash drive, filling him in on my suspicions about my impromptu house call from the Penguin goons. Which I still felt creepy about in the light of day. I still had no other explanations for the pet quarantine or the moving of Adam's note. I'd even checked with Camille about the note on the off chance she knew how it ended up as a paper crumble, but she didn't.

"It was too late to call when I figured it out," I said to answer Laurent's question. "What was the point? Anyways, I'm calling you now. You find anything on the flash drive that links it to the Penguin?"

Silence from the other end and then, "I'll collect you in an hour." Click.

I held the phone away from me and stared at it a beat before hitting the disconnect. I was on the landline, my new cell phone gone, my old clunker phone languishing in a drawer somewhere, only coming out now and then for an occasional charging. Knowing I couldn't avoid the old thing forever, I put the landline down, rooted around, found the old mobile, checked to make sure it still had service, and tossed it into the shoulder bag hanging off the back of my chair. The chair where I sat, barely awake, clad in my robe, in my little home office. Second floor of the house, tiny window overlooking the street.

The room held the castoffs of my Soho apartment—loveseat

under the window, desk and chair on the wall bordering the bedroom, tall bookcases and a file cabinet on the opposite wall. Impossibly small closet crammed impossibly full with remnants of my New York life. The whole space my homeland oasis amid the foreign land of Adam's mother's house, now ours, but filled to the brim with decades of home game advantage.

My own parents had died years ago, leaving me with little family and no home to go back to. Just a few things now residing in my closet. And my mother's locket that I wore every day which held pictures of both my parents when they were young. My parents had never owned property to leave me. Instead they left me a legacy of peace rallies and granola recipes. All very nice, but not the sort of things that prepared me for break-ins or a shady Penguin with goons.

"Let me guess," Adam said to me from the doorway. "You were talking to work." His arms were folded across his chest, partially covering the vintage Rolling Stones tongue sticking out at me from his T-shirt. He still wore the sweats he'd dragged on to take Pong out for her walk, but he'd added a plaid shirt open down the front. The look was weekend casual, the stance not so much.

I shrugged. "What do you want me to do? Sit around and do nothing when someone broke into our house?"

"It's Sunday, Lora. Is it so much to ask that you don't work on Sundays? Any other job and you wouldn't be working."

"That's not fair. Plenty of people work Sundays. What about doctors? Cashiers? Realtors? Priests? Besides, you know I hardly ever work weekends. And, you're one to talk. You work weekends all the time when you're on deadline. *And* holidays. Did I complain when you left the country last Christmas?"

His forehead lines did that parenthesis thing again. "I made it back by Christmas Eve. And as I recall you were off with the Carons then, too."

I sighed. Our truce from the night before seemed to be showing an expiration date. Good thing we weren't handling peace talks for the Middle East.

"Look. Why don't you come to the office with me?" I suggested. "I'm sure it won't take long." How could it? Couldn't do much on the insurance case with Johnny in the hospital. That just left the little matter with the Penguin and how long could it take to look at files on a flash drive? "We can go out after. Maybe lunch or a walk?"

He shifted. "Can't. Have to return Tina's cribs this afternoon."

Oy. Busy with Tina again. We were some pair. I wasn't sure if I should laugh or cry and decided on the laugh.

I got up and went to Adam. "What we need is a date night," I said. "The works. Dinner out. Maybe a movie. Something fun just the two of us. What do you say? Seven o'clock tonight?"

He was quiet a minute then kissed the tip of my nose. "You got it." His eyes left my face and loitered behind me. "You know, sometimes I miss our days back in New York," he said. "Everything was so easy. Your dinky little apartment. Me working on my degree, you working regular hours for social services. And when we first came here and were helping my mom those last few months, we were together almost all the time. When did it get so hard to find time together? When did life get this complicated?"

He was right. Our early days together had been different. More focused on each other maybe. More simple. "I don't know," I said, letting the warmth of his hug seep through my bathrobe, both of us going quiet, lost in our own thoughts. I had no idea what he was thinking, but I was seriously rethinking the whole work on Sundays thing. At least I was until the sound of breaking glass hit my hears and I felt Adam's body shudder against mine.

We bolted apart and headed for the stairs, his arm out, urging me back. My arm navigating between his, moving us both forward.

The sound had come from the main floor. Ping and Pong were on the main floor. No way was I waiting upstairs. Not with the Penguin and his goons possibly staging an encore performance of their sneaky B&E the day before.

Two glowing eyes came into view when I came to a stop alongside Adam at the downstairs landing. The eyes peered out at us from behind the edge of a box in the living room, then the eyes disappeared. In front of the box, shards of colored glass decorated the floor.

"Oh, no," Adam said, advancing towards the glass. "The Superman lamp. That was the last one at the store."

The slight thumping that had started in my chest slowed and a hungry stomach growl gurgled up instead. A broken lamp. Was that all?

Ping scurried out from behind a box and made a beeline past me up the stairs, guilt in her eyes, speed in her gait. I hoped for her sake the speed outran the guilt. With the living room so cramped, it was hard *not* to knock over something.

"And it matched the action figure, too," Adam said. He glanced around. "Wait, what did you do with the Superman figurine, Lora?"

I tiptoed around the glass and over to him. "What figurine?"

Adam pointed at the mantel. "It was there. With The Flash and The Green Lantern."

I gave him a palms up, shoulder shrug.

He shot me a duh look. "You know, from the Justice League."

"Um..."

He shook his head at me. "Superhero action figures, Lora. I left them right there beside the fish."

Okay now we were getting somewhere. "I didn't put any Super-heroes anywhere," I said. "Didn't see any." I stopped myself from joking that maybe the grinning fish ate them. Adam's mood had shifted. Probably levity wouldn't go over very well.

He pivoted and began hunting through the mess of boxes, maneuvering his feet around the bits of broken lamp on the floor, waving me off when I started to help. "Go. Get ready for work. I'll find them."

I nodded and headed back upstairs to take a shower. Not at all sure he *would* find them. Camille and I had shuffled everything around when we tidied the space. If there'd been any little Superhero people, I would have seen them. My guess was they were long gone. Probably taken by whoever broke in. Probably that whoever looking for a doll with a flash drive tucked up its tush.

**I WAS NEARLY** DONE blow drying my hair when I heard the doorbell go. I shut off the dryer and got dressed. Jeans, long crochet sweater, locket. The outfit that had become my mainstay the last few weeks. Especially the locket. I'd come close to losing it recently and now had a hard time letting it out of my sight. I finished off my ensemble with some fluffy socks and rushed downstairs to find Laurent standing in my foyer. His dark hair damp, flatter on top, tousled on the sides. His coat, unzipped, hanging loose over a beige sweater, hand knit, and dark jeans. His boots off.

He passed by me through to the living room and stood stock still on a chunk of wood floor free of boxes or furniture. Without moving his body an inch, his eyes scanned all the windows in view with the methodical precision of a clockmaker checking faulty gears for a glitch.

"I'll need to see the back door," he said.

Adam stood by the couch, small paper bag in his hand that I was guessing held remnants of the broken lamp. "For what?" Adam said to Laurent. "If you're looking for signs of the break-in, I've already checked. There aren't any. We have no idea how anyone could have gotten in. But it looks like whoever it was might have taken something after all. I'm missing three mint-condition action figures."

Laurent glanced over at me. "Action figures?"

"Little plastic dolls of Spider-Man and stuff," I said.

Adam sighed. Loud. "They're not dolls. They're action figures. And there was no Spider-Man. It was Superman. And The Flash and The Green Lantern."

Laurent nodded at Adam, saying nothing. Probably Laurent didn't have a clue about guys like The Flash and The Green Lantern. Probably when Laurent was a kid he was more interested in being a Superhero than in playing with any.

He moved off to pick a path through to the dining room then went on to the kitchen, checking windows as he went.

I should have expected the impromptu inspection when Laurent said he was picking me up. I chalked up his carpool plan to more babysitting because of the Penguin situation. I hadn't factored in the break-in. But naturally Laurent would want to scope out the house, too. Gauge things for himself. He liked to be sure of his facts.

I took the hallway route to the kitchen and met up with Laurent as he got to the door to the sunroom. Adam trailed close behind me, his weight heavy on his heels.

Laurent yanked open the door that separated the kitchen from the sunroom, and Pong appeared from nowhere and barreled out, tail in a mad wag as she waited by the exit to the yard.

I moved to let her out, stopped by Laurent's hand on my shoulder, one of his sign language signals I'd come to know well. No words. No heavy pressing of the hand, just a gentle touch that meant I needed to hit my pause button. Which I did, watching as

Laurent inspected first the door and then the bank of windows, checking the large panels below and the slim panels above. The windows were original to the house. The lower ones Guillotine-style with warbled glass. The top, lever-style, same glass.

"*Ici*," Laurent said. "This one."

I pulled my cardigan tighter around me and went over for a closer look. The sunroom was the three-season variety. Unheated. Most houses in these parts needed heating until the end of April. On a clear day, the abundance of windows helped the room heat from the warmth of the sun. On cloudy days with rainy spells like we'd been having this week, not so much.

"See here," Laurent said, running a finger in the air following the window line. "It's damp on the inside edge. The dust unsettled below."

Adam's head popped in between us to take a look. "Well, yeah. I didn't check those little windows. Nobody could fit through them."

Laurent caught my eye and Adam dipped back, registering the exchange. "Well nobody except maybe Lora," he added. "Or some kid."

I was with Adam on that one. I couldn't picture either of the bookcase goons fitting through. Or the Penguin. He was short but too stocky. But Laurent was right. Someone had disturbed the window. Which got me wondering if I was wrong about who. Maybe some kid had broken in. Maybe it wasn't about me and the flash drive after all. Maybe it was about Adam and his figurines. He had said they were in mint condition. Maybe they were worth some ungodly sum or so rare collectors stole for them.

I turned to Adam. "Were the figurines expensive?"

His face reddened some. "Not worth stealing for."

I eyed him, waiting to see if he'd get specific about cost. Not surprised when he didn't. He'd been spending money on Tina and the babies like he was *The* Godfather not *a* godfather. Only he didn't like to admit it.

Almost as much as I didn't want to admit wanting to offload some of my guilt about the B&E on Adam and his figurines even when I knew better. I couldn't see anyone bothering to break in for collectibles and not nabbing a computer or something, too.

Pong barked and we all looked her way. She added a scratch to the back door in case we missed her cue. She'd been out less than an hour ago so her interest in outdoors was more want than need, but the girl was on the cusp of spring fever so to her the whole want/need line had blurred.

Since the window seemed to be the B&E entry point, I figured it was okay to use the back door now and stepped towards it to let the dog out. But again Laurent stopped me.

"*Attends*," he said. "Better to wait until the police come and have their own check of everything."

"The police?" I asked him. "For some missing action figures?"

Laurent ushered us all back into the kitchen, me grabbing Pong on my way, hugging her to me until the sunroom door was shut tight behind us before letting her down.

"It's always a good idea to report a break-in," Laurent said.

Maybe or maybe after his own look around he was agreeing with my first assessment. As an ex-cop, Laurent knew the police were overworked and had little to no chance of recovering major stolen property, let alone minor stuff. Probably he wouldn't bother them for that. Probably like I had, he suspected the B&E had nothing to do with good guy Superheroes and everything to do with the bad guy Penguin. And Laurent wanted this logged officially just in case.

Fifteen minutes later, two cops were at the door. Another fifteen minutes more, after a slew of questions and a walk-through of the house, they were gone.

"And now we go," Laurent said to me when the last cop was out the door.

I darted my eyes to Adam. He'd barely spoken while the police were around and showed no signs of breaking his silence. Mostly he'd kept swiping at his hair and did that annoyed thing with his chin twice. Not good.

He watched from the hall as Laurent and I traipsed into the vestibule and got on our coats and footwear.

"I won't be long," I assured Adam, voice all casual, as though having cops out to the house was a common way to spend Sundays. Like going to church or watching sports on TV. "I'll be back in plenty of time for seven."

"Yeah, me too," he said.

Right. I'd forgotten he was making the crib-return run. That would leave Ping and Pong alone. I turned to Laurent. "What do you think the chances are the burglar will return?"

"This afternoon? Probably none."

I nodded, hoping he was right, and I gave Adam a quick kiss, letting him know to call my old cell number if he needed me. Then I grabbed my umbrella in case the weather turned rainy again and I headed out.

When I got to the bottom step of the balcony, I paused and glanced back at the house. "Just how sure are you?" I said to Laurent.

He joined me on the step. "Very."

"Why?"

"Because what the Penguin wants now is standing right next to me."

8

"*I* THOUGHT WE were going to the office?" I said to Laurent from the passenger seat in his Beamer. We'd made it out of my NDG neighborhood and sat at a red light after taking an off ramp from the Twenty—the highway that ran west to east, south of the city, following a similar path to the Fleuve Saint-Laurent.

There were several possible routes between my house and the C&C office in The Plateau, but this didn't fit any of the usual ones.

He slid his eyes to me then back to the road. "*Non.* No office. We're going to my place."

I sat up straighter, seat belt strap digging into my shoulder. I'd never been to Laurent's house before. Curiosity mixed with guilt in the pit of my stomach. I so wanted to see where Laurent lived, but I knew Adam wouldn't be happy about me leaving our house for Laurent's. Plus, I wasn't sure what to make of the change in venue given Laurent's eerie remark about me and the Penguin.

"Is this about protecting me?" I asked, my arms instinctively folding across my chest like Barbara Eden in *I Dream of Jeannie*

71

getting ready to blink someone off to a desert island. "Because I *don't* need protecting."

His eyes strayed my way again and he smiled. "This isn't about protecting you. This is about showering me. Your call came this morning at my hockey game. I left fast. No time to clean up."

My arms relaxed back into my lap, this time my hands resisting the urge to whack myself in the side of the head. I'd totally forgotten about Laurent and his Sunday hockey games. He often played at some ungodly early hour and usually out in the boonies. Ice rental time was tight, and early was the only time his league could secure. No wonder he'd been breathing heavy when I called. He'd probably just come off the ice.

"Sorry," I said. "I totally forgot. I hope I didn't ruin your game. I didn't expect you to come running over."

"*Non*? What *did* you expect me to do?"

"I don't know. Nothing. Tell me about the flash drive, I guess. What's going on with that anyway? Did you crack it?"

He stopped the car at a driveway outside a short blocky building, red brick, old but nicely so. Rooftop carved like a crown, chiseled medallions adorning it like jewels. Laurent punched a code into a metal box sitting on a short pole, and a garage door opened at the end of the drive. The Beamer moved into the garage, the door sliding shut behind the car.

Inside, there were seven parking spaces, each bearing little placards with numbers on them. Four spots to the left, three spots to the right. Laurent pulled into the last slot of the three set and parked.

We got out of the car, he pulled a duffel bag from the trunk, and we headed for the only door in sight—thick metal, painted white, small glass window inset near the top, thin black vertical lines etched in the glass about a half-inch apart.

Laurent unlocked the door, and we walked through to a wide

cement staircase, went up three flights and through another door to a short hallway maybe five by six feet wide with tall, round-topped double-doors at each end. He turned a key in the set of doors to the right and gestured for me to pass through.

I got two steps in and stopped at the edge of a large square throw carpet.

Laurent dropped his duffel bag to the side of the carpet and punched more numbers into a box attached to the wall, disarming an alarm.

I stared ahead of me and shifted so he could close the door. My feet teetered a bit as my gaze swung up towards what had to be at least a fifteen-foot ceiling with exposed white fat pipes running here and there.

I felt a warm hand press into the small of my back. "Steady," Laurent said. "My insurance is high enough. All I need is someone falling and breaking a leg. My premiums will skyrocket."

I nodded, thinking that there was sure enough "sky" around to house a few rockets. To go with the high ceilings, plenty of light streamed in from nearly floor to ceiling windows marching across a back wall that ran the expanse of the place. White painted brick walls, muted wood floors, huge open kitchen, and a large wood and glass staircase to a second floor spilled out before me. All of it furnished with charcoal brown comfy seating, wood tables, iron lamps, and bookcases filled to the brim.

Laurent guided me nearby to sit, and I found myself settled on a short bench similar to a church pew but not. I ran my hand over the smooth surface, my finger lingering in a tiny notch. "What is this?" I asked him.

"A seat from an old *calèche*."

"*Calèche?*"

He took off his shoes and dropped his jacket onto a hook beside the bench. "I don't know the name in English," he said.

"Where the man sits to drive the wagon with horses. Like in Vieux Montréal for the tourists."

"Oh, you mean like a carriage. I took a ride in one of those once in Central Park when I was a kid. I didn't know you could buy the seat. It's beautiful."

I pulled off my boots, stood, and walked my boots over to where I'd seen Laurent drop his shoes.

"Take a café if you want," Laurent said. "Machine's on the counter. I'll be a few minutes only." He headed for the staircase, went up, and disappeared around a corner.

"Thanks. Think I will." The way my day had been going, I could use coffee. I barely slept, worrying about the Penguin and another break-in. And the day had gotten off to a rousing start what with Adam's superhero woes and playing host to cops. But even if none of that had been true, I'd have jumped at the chance to poke around Laurent's loft. I was feeling like Dorothy about to learn the magic behind the Wizard of Oz. And this magic would have nothing to do with a little man behind a curtain. In fact, there wasn't even a curtain in sight.

I wandered into the kitchen zone to start my poking around and found cement counters, natural wood cabinets, same charcoal brown color as the couches and chairs, and stainless steel appliances. A long counter spanned along the back wall, string of windows above. And a large island with stools on one side housed a stove top. Double oven, pantry, and fridge made up a short wall that met the back counter at ninety degrees. No overhead cabinets anywhere. Instead, open shelves tucked into the brick walls that gapped the windows. Stacks of dishes, glassware, mugs, mixing bowls, and the like sat in orderly sections on the shelves. The dishes and mugs all white, mixing bowls a soft blue.

Under a window, I spotted the gleaming steel coffee maker on the counter. Beside it, under a shelf, a row of dark glass jars just transparent enough to make out their contents. Beans. I lifted a lid and the scent hitting my nose confirmed my suspicion. Coffee beans. Five little jars of them. Uh oh. I barely had the hang of the Nespresso at the office and its pods. Laurent's machine was not Nespresso. Laurent's coffee machine was serious. Laurent's machine looked like it could make coffee with one lever behind its back while it mixed a cake and baked it up in a pan.

I explored a bit, found the machine's bean box, and eenie meenie minied my way to a bean selection, hoping my pick's strong aroma didn't mirror its potency. I was a coffee lightweight. Anything with too much caffeine and I was bouncing off walls faster than a two-year old stuffed full of cotton candy and cookies.

I used the handy scoop inside the jar to ladle the beans into the machine, pushed a button, and crossed my fingers. Nothing happened so I tried another button. Instantly, the machine began to hum. Success! I grabbed a mug from the shelf and shoved it in front of what looked like the spout. The machine hummed some more. Then some more, puffs of steam rising out, grinding noises bookending the puffs. Rattling coming from the back end. Foul smell seeping out in gusts.

Yikes.

I pressed at buttons, trying to shut the thing off. "Laurent," I yelled upstairs. "Laurent! Help! Your machine's gone crazy."

"*Qu'est-ce que tu dis?*" I heard him call from somewhere upstairs. Seconds later, he appeared beside me, pulling the coffee's electrical cord from the wall.

"What did you do?" he said.

"Nothing. I swear. I just pressed that button." I pointed. "Then that one."

He pulled the machine away from the wall. "*Ah. Okay.* We let it rest, it will be fine."

I let out a long breath. What a relief. I thought I'd killed it and would have to replace it. Probably cost me more than a year's worth of coffee at Starbucks. Maybe two.

"Sorry," I said, turning to face him. His wet hair dripped and soaked the shoulders of his T-shirt. His jeans were unfastened, hint of white underwear showing.

My eyes darted away when they spotted the underwear and I added, "Not just about the machine but about pulling you out of the shower."

He zipped and buttoned his jeans and dabbed his hair with a clean tea towel he pulled from a stack on a shelf. "No worries." He tossed the towel aside, felt the side of the coffee maker, and plugged it back in. He fiddled with the bean chamber and a couple other gizmos, poured water into another chamber, pressed a button and the maker started purring like a tomcat, deep and steady. No puffs of steam. No rattles.

Barely minutes later, the scent of fresh coffee hit the air and two short mugs were filled. As were two plates, with croissants Laurent pulled from a paper bag on the counter. Little pats of butter joining the croissants along with mini blunt-edged knives with blue handles.

"Fancy," I said to Laurent as I inspected my knife. "Gifts from a girlfriend?"

He grinned but said nothing, picked up our coffee mugs, walked off past the wall with the fridge, and disappeared around a bend.

I was beginning to realize the loft had quite a few bends as I followed with our plates and discovered that beyond this bend was another space. This area raised up by a step, same wood floors, more windows on the outside wall, built-in bookcases with glass fronts along another wall, and tall French doors at the far end. A round table with fours chairs was set up directly in front of me, a worn blue couch sat centered in the space under the windows, and a desk was tucked into the corner by the French doors.

I set the plates on the table and walked over to the doors, drawn by the view.

"You want to step out?" Laurent asked me. "Go, it's fine. All dry from the rain."

I unlocked a door and went outside onto the patio—a tall brick wall closed it in on one side and two short walls completed the square. Standing over by the corner of short walls, I could see church tops and buildings at least a couple hundred years old. Beyond them, a bit of the Fleuve Saint-Laurent. It surprised me how much I could see given that we were only three floors up. Somehow, Laurent had managed to snag a patio angle with very few buildings blocking its view. It was beautiful now and this was a gray day. I could barely imagine what it would look like with a bright blue sky and shining sun.

"I don't know how you get any work done," I said to Laurent. "If I lived here, I'd never want to leave this spot."

He joined me outside and passed me my coffee. "You like it?"

"Oh, yeah. Who wouldn't?" I turned to look back at the apartment. Two dark round spots stained the patio floor on either side of the French doors. Round spots that I suspected matched the ones on the base of two planters sitting in the far corners of the terrace. Planters I suspected Laurent pulled over in the summer to hold open the doors.

A café-sized white table and two chairs sat flush with the tall brick wall, nearly shielding what I realized now was a small door. "What's that?" I asked Laurent.

He turned to look. "Nothing. Small box in the wall for storage."

"Handy," I said, wondering if in older days the box had stored coal or wood. Even though it seemed to have gone through a fairly recent conversion, the bones of Laurent's building probably dated back over a hundred years or more. Maybe two. The brickwork and masonry detailing had to be done far before machines took over construction. His front doors looked like they belonged in an old European city, and his floors were worn in a way that only comes from decades of use.

"You're cold," he said.

"No, I'm not." A shiver went through me. Well maybe I was and hadn't noticed. "Okay, maybe a little."

He ushered us both inside and we went to sit at the table. I picked at my croissant and took a sip of my coffee. Maybe it wasn't just the cold that was slipping my mind. Maybe I was letting my magical mystery tour distract me from the task at hand. "So, about that flash drive…" I began.

"*Ah, oui,*" Laurent said. "Your pocket friend. Records of shipments for construction supplies."

"That's what was on it? Files of shipments."

"*Oui.*"

"Something fishy about them?"

"Can't tell. Need more specifics, more details about the shipments."

Made sense. The files had to be relevant somehow, though. Why else would Johnny have slipped me the drive and the Penguin want to get his fins on it?

I pondered that as I pulled a chunk off my croissant and slathered it in some butter.

Laurent said something more, but I didn't hear him. My taste buds drowned him out with their ooing and awing over the silky bread and salty butter melting on my tongue.

I nodded, hoping Laurent had said something worth nodding about, and smeared more butter on my croissant. Going in for another smear a couple seconds later, my knife coming up empty.

Still talking, Laurent took his own butter, covered my remaining croissant, and passed it back to me.

I took a bite and slowly tuned back in to him, catching the tail end of what he was saying. Something about the Old Port in Vieux Montréal.

He sat back and finished the last of his coffee. "You ready?" he asked me.

"Umm. Ready for what?"

He smiled and watched me lick the butter off my fingers. "How much did you hear?"

"Everything." I looked down at my plate. "Everything but that last bit."

"*Ah ma belle menteuse*," he said and laughed.

I didn't understand what he said, but I took the laugh as a sign that even if he knew I was fibbing, he was going with it. "So what am I ready for?" I asked him as I stood to clear the dishes.

His phone buzzed from his jeans and he held up his "wait" finger while he answered a call, which gave me time to finish clearing the plates and load the dishwasher. The dishwasher I discovered also had stainless steel on the inside and was nearly empty, the fresh smell of detergent lingering.

Laurent was still on the phone when I was done, and I wanted to pay a visit to the little girl's room before we ventured out again. My eyes trailed over to the staircase leading to the second floor then over to the two doors along the wall across from the kitchen island. The Dorothy in me really wanted to check out the bathroom upstairs, but probably I should try the doors first for a guest powder room.

I opened the first door and found a closet. The walk-in variety. Large and rectangular. The front used as a coat closet, the rest stocking various household items and multi-sized storage bins. I moved on to check the next door, found a small pristine washroom, and went in. New fixtures, vintage look. Mini white marble tiles on the floor, larger tiles halfway up the walls, pedestal sink, traditional toilet, standing tub, no shower. The same soft blue from the kitchen bowls was painted on the upper walls. Mirror over the sink, no medicine cabinet. All very nice, but nothing to shed any light on the magic of Oz. Probably Laurent kept that kind of thing upstairs. Out of the prying eyes of snoopers like me.

When I got out of the bathroom, Laurent was already waiting. He'd added a sweater over his T-shirt and a scarf loosely wound once around his neck. And he stood holding my coat out for me. We made it all the way downstairs and into the car before it hit me that I still didn't know where we were going, and I asked Laurent as we left the garage and pulled into traffic.

"Back to your place," he said.

I was about to ask him why when my phone buzzed in my purse, and I gave him the same "wait" finger he'd given me earlier, pulled my phone out, and checked the caller ID. Adam.

"Lora?" he said when I picked up. "What's going on? What are these men doing at our house?"

"What men?"

"I got home from the store and a van full of guys surrounded me before I got my keys in the door. I thought I was being swarmed. They say you sent them."

"Me? I didn't send anybody." I felt Laurent's eyes on me and slid mine over to meet his gaze. "Wait," I said to Adam. "Maybe I did. I'll be right there."

## 9

---

"**I** DON'T WANT an alarm in my house," Adam said.

Laurent, Adam, and I were standing in my incredibly-shrinking living room, single file, on the only bare strip of floor left, surrounded by even more boxes than the day before.

"If I wanted an alarm," Adam went on to say, "I would have put one in. I've lived in this house practically my whole life and it's never needed an alarm."

My feet shifted, and my eyes moved from Adam on my right to Laurent on my left.

"The office will pay for it," Laurent said.

"It's not about the cost," Adam said, my eyes pinging back to him. "It's the principle. I live in a safe neighborhood. I don't need an alarm."

"We," I said.

Both men looked at me. "*We* live in a safe neighborhood," I added to clarify.

"This isn't about neighborhood," Laurent said, putting his focus back to Adam. "This is about work."

Adams's jaw clenched and released. "I don't care what it's about. I'm not doing it."

The front door banged open and a burly man appeared in the hall. One of the guys from the van. He barked out something French directed at Laurent who turned to me and said, "He wants to know if it's okay to let in a big blonde woman with a teddy bear."

"That's Tina," Adam said, making his way out of the living room. "Of course it's okay. Geez are these guys bodyguards, too?"

He wasn't really asking, but I wouldn't be surprised if the troop of men did all sorts of "security" work. Laurent had connections to all kinds of people. All on the straight and narrow now, but how they got there may have involved a few crooked paths.

"I guess it's a no on the alarm," I said to Laurent when Adam followed the big guy outside, presumably to get Tina.

"You've had two break-ins in six months," Laurent said. "You're getting an alarm."

"Two?"

"*Ben oui*, two. You think I don't know about the one in the fall?"

Oh, right. On my first big case. I'd nearly forgotten about that. "You can't count that," I said. "That was nothing. Practically over before it even started. Anyway, you heard Adam. He's not taking an alarm, break-ins or not."

Some feet stomped into the hall and stopped in the doorway. The feet belonged to Tina. "You had a break-in?" she said, turning towards the vestibule. "You didn't tell me about a break-in, Adam." She turned back to the living room and ambled along the path, knocking boxes as she moved. "Did they take anything? They didn't get my breast pump did they? That's the best one on the market. We paid a fortune for that thing."

The breast pump was the gizmo Camille had unboxed. I knew

exactly where it was. Safe and sound tucked back in its box. I'd put it away myself. "The breast pump is fine," I assured Tina.

"Oh, thank God," she said, lowering herself onto the couch. "These puppies are going to need it." She hiked up both breasts and they nearly popped out of the V in her sweater. The sweater that looked tighter on her than when she'd worn it just a week before. Ditto the blue stretch pants she wore that formed to her legs like pantyhose, the fabric stretched to nearly the same transparency, too. I felt for her. It couldn't be easy carrying twins.

Her eyes travelled the room and finally landed on Laurent, beads of sweat appearing on her forehead, faint blush creeping up her cheeks. "Laurent, right?" she said. "The charming Frenchman."

He shot her a smile and I thought she'd fall off the couch. "Good to see you," he said. "You're looking well. To be pregnant agrees with you."

Her cheeks reddened some more and I had a sudden urge to get Laurent out of the room lest her blood pressure soar and cut off nutrient supply to the babies or something.

I tried to catch Laurent's eye and tapped his arm, hoping to lead him out and away.

He avoided my look and stood his ground. "It is bad news about the break-in, *hein?*" Laurent went on to say to Tina. "Adam said the thieves took some toys of your babies."

My eyes closed briefly. Just fab. Now we'd never get out of here. Bad enough he was ratting us out about the break-in, but he was doing it in his best French accent, dropping his "THs" for "Ts. Not in that fake French accent way, the real one that sounded quite posh. Tina was a sucker for that accent. She'd keep him talking forever if she could.

"Oh my God," Tina said. "Which toys did they take? How could that happen?" She started to fight her way up from the couch, leveraging her weight side-to-side to get some momentum. "This is awful," she huffed out. "This place isn't safe. I have to get my things out of here. This is why I live in the suburbs. I'm never bringing my kids here. This city isn't safe anymore."

Adam slipped past me and over to Tina. "Stay put. It's nothing to worry about. It's perfectly safe here." He sighed and glanced back at me. "We're getting an alarm. Your things will be fine, Tina."

I felt Laurent edge up against my body as he slid his way along the narrow path and out to the front door.

Minutes later the pack of burly guys were inside, spreading out like ants at a picnic, in orderly trails, each with his own set of orderly tools.

I left Adam rooting through boxes and holding up various baby doodads for Tina to check off a list she had pulled from her purse, and I made my way over to where Laurent stood at the bottom of the stairs, overseeing the burly men.

"You totally played Adam and Tina back there," I said. "You didn't need to do that. Adam was right. We don't need an alarm. You already know what's on the flash drive. All you had to do was let that be known and the Penguin wouldn't bother with me or my house."

"Maybe," he said. "But I don't like to take chances."

I looked at him sideways. "No. What you don't like is losing."

He nodded as one of the workman went by. "That, too."

"HOURS LATER, THE house was plus one fancy alarm and upgraded wiring and minus Laurent and the burly men. Tina and her boxes still sat, status quo, reigning over the living room. No sign of either giving up their governance any time soon.

I checked the time, close to dinner hour. So much for Adam's and my date night.

"I'm gonna make a quick run to the market," I called to Adam from the kitchen. I opened and closed the fridge, looking for something to be out of to substantiate the errand. "We need milk and bread." I clanged a cupboard and strolled out to the living room where Adam sat keeping Tina company while she waited for her husband Jeffrey to pick her up. She'd been waiting over two hours, and I was beginning to wonder if he would show up at all.

"Maybe you should get some takeout for dinner while you're out," Adam whispered to me, swinging his look to a snoring Tina flaked out on the couch, feet hung over the armrest. "For the three of us."

"Uh, sure. I could do that. Pizza?"

He nodded, got up from the chair he'd pulled into the middle of the room, and walked me out to the hall.

"Maybe get enough for four in case Jeffrey's here by then. He's supposed to be borrowing a minivan from his brother to haul some of this stuff out. No idea what's keeping him."

That was the most Adam had said to me since the cops' morning visit. Either he was softening or worn out from the day. Probably the latter. Too much edge in his voice for a softening. Probably he was still sore about the alarm. Couldn't blame him really. Especially since he'd insisted on footing the bill. Nobody liked paying for things they didn't want. Plus, he had to feel ambushed and even though I hadn't been the one to ambush him I felt responsible.

"I'm sorry about the men showing up out of the blue like that," I said. "And the alarm."

He sighed. "I hate it. But it makes sense. I just don't like that it makes sense."

Right. So not so much about an alarm as about my job again. "Me either," I said. "I'm thinking our date night isn't working out so great, either."

He ran a hand through his hair. "Darn. Forgot about that."

I nodded understanding. "It's been a long day."

Tina coughed and sputtered, and Adam leaned closer to me, this time his eyes softening along with his voice. "Look. I'll call Jeffrey again. See what I can do. Give me half an hour and I'll see if I can clear the place out."

I nodded again and felt his lips graze mine before he darted off back to Tina. I grabbed my jacket and car fob and left, thinking maybe just maybe, Tina and Jeffrey and their baby loot would be gone when I got back.

THE SIDEWALK WAS dry and the evening air fresh. Eager buds glistened on trees under the streetlight haze. In the driveway, my Mini sat beaming white, gleaming after its bout of spring showers. I took one look at the car, pocketed my fob, and turned on my heel. City living had many perks and one was having stores and restaurants in walking distance, and I was in the mood for a stroll. It would do me good to stretch my legs and clear my head.

At the end of the block, I slowed my gait and unzipped my jacket, letting it swing in the light breeze. Temperatures had warmed, all the rain driving the cold away, and the dusk skies had all the making of an early spring night. I made a right at the corner and three doors down placed my order at the pizza place. Pickup was in fifteen minutes, plenty of time to get the groceries. I headed for a little épicerie across the street that stayed open late on Sundays. Its wide, plate glass window showcased bin after bin of fruits and vegetables, and its aisles beyond exhibited end displays of boutique chocolate bars, fine wines, and wholesome cookies. All glowing under soft ambient lighting.

I went in, picked up a shopping basket, and walked to the fridges in the back. I snagged some yogurt and ice cream along with the milk, veered over to the bread section and grabbed a paper-wrapped baguette from a basket, then I loitered over one of the wine displays. Ordinarily, Adam and I weren't big wine drinkers, but it *was* date night. And we did need to unwind from a long day.

I put my basket on the floor and picked up a bottle of red. Then replaced it with a white only to replace it with the red again. I had no idea which wine went with pizza. Or which one would console me best if I got home to find Tina still on my couch.

"*Le Merlot*," a man said, coming up beside me.

"*Merci*." I started to smile as I turned to my new wine buddy. People around here were often quick to offer their thoughts or strike up a chat. I loved that, and my new wine buddy's advice was sweet. Not necessarily reliable since the guy had no idea what I was pairing with the wine, but sweet.

I felt the wine bottle being removed from my hands at the same moment my eyes landed on my new buddy's face and recognition hit. The Penguin. Ugh, maybe I was too quick on the sweet thing.

I kept my smile in place and willed the rest of my face to stay blank. It took a lot of will. My heart wanted to race ahead and take the rest of me with it. My head wanted to show no fear. Show the Penguin he meant nothing to me, just a man in a grocery store. A man who had relieved me of my wine.

I reached out and took the wine back, hoping the tremble in my hands didn't show. I picked up my basket, offered him another *merci* for his "help," and turned to go, a goon appearing at my other side, blocking my path. Another one coming into view by the exit, arms crossed over his chest, biceps bulging through his jacket. Seriously? Who was this Penguin guy? Lead singer in a goon rock band? Did he go anywhere without his backup group of goons?

I took a deep breath and turned back. "Is there something I can help you with?" I asked. This time, I didn't try to match his French with any of the limited French phrases I'd memorized. If he wanted to talk to me so bad, he could do it in English.

"I think you know there is," he said. His squinty eyes unblinking, his mouth less penguin and more shark.

My free hand reflexively reached to my chest for my locket. A while back, Laurent had fitted the locket with a tracking device I'd since removed. A decision I was starting to regret. The chill emanating off the Penguin had me thinking I was seconds away from a visit to his ice float. And not for wine coolers and cheese.

"I think you've got the wrong gal," I told him, with far more bravado than I felt. "And if you don't mind, I have somewhere to be." My gaze ventured up to the security camera in the corner.

The Penguin took a long look at me and snapped his fingers at the goon to my side. The goon moved enough for me to pass, but not so much that when I passed him I wouldn't feel the bulk of the gun tucked into the beltline below his coat.

When I got up to the cash, I took my time, pulling up my items one by one, bantering with the clerk, Louise. Easy to do. I came in a lot and she served me frequently. Plus, my body had to do something with the excess adrenaline revving it into overdrive.

Louise rang up my total and started to bag my purchases while I rooted through my wallet for the cash to pay. "I hope that wine is good," I said. "I had no idea which one to get until that guy recommended one." I passed Louise the cash and watched as she glanced behind me to the Penguin still standing in the aisle I'd just fled.

Satisfied she'd had a good look at him, I thanked her and hightailed it out of the store.

Glancing behind me, I dashed along the street. The Penguin and his goonie backup group stood on the sidewalk, watching me. I rounded the corner to my house, checking back every few steps. Nobody followed, but that didn't slow my pace. By the time I reached my door I was out of breath, my hand making several attempts before it managed to connect my key with the lock.

Once inside, I slammed the door closed behind me and clicked the bolt. I dumped my grocery bag on the hall table, moved to the new alarm box on the wall, and studied the buttons, blowing out a sigh when I realized they were all labeled in French.

I barreled upstairs, closed myself in the bathroom, pulled out my phone, and tapped through my contacts until I got to Laurent.

"How do you alarm this thing?" I asked when we connected.

"Lora? I can hardly hear you. Talk up."

"I can't talk up. I don't want Adam and Tina to hear. Just tell me how to set the alarm."

The doorbell went and I missed Laurent's answer, so I asked him again and clicked off. I eased open the bathroom door and peered downstairs, expecting to see Tina leaving with her husband. Instead Adam looked up at me.

"It was just the pizza delivery guy," Adam said.

I zipped down the stairs. Dang. Totally forgot about the pizza. "What pizza delivery guy?"

"I don't know. Some guy we never had before. Older. Kinda short." Adam laughed. "Looked more like the dad of a delivery guy. Maybe he was filling in for his kid."

Adam walked off to the kitchen, plunked the pizza on the counter, and took a piece from the box.

I caught up to him, grabbed the slice from his hand, and tossed it in the garbage.

"What'd ya do that for?"

I leaned back, ducking through the dining room doorway, checking the living room for Tina before I answered. No sign of her. Just her boxes. "Tina upstairs?" I asked Adam.

"No. Jeffrey took her home. He's coming back for the boxes

tomorrow. Couldn't get his brother's van. Now answer my question."

I walked over to the pizza box and lifted the lid. Heavenly scents of tomato and gooey cheese wafted out. I sighed, closed the lid, smushed the box in half, and dumped it in the garbage.

Adam stared at me, chin hanging down. "What is with you?"

"That wasn't our pizza," I said. I walked into the hall and over to the alarm, setting it as per Laurent's instructions. "I ordered the pizza for pickup not delivery."

A green light blinked at me from the alarm signaling it was armed, and I said a silent thank you to Laurent and his burly men. I turned, spied my grocery bag on the table, and bent to pick it up. An envelope with my name on it sat beside the bag. I ignored the groceries and picked up the envelope. "What's this?"

"The delivery guy left it for you. Figured you dropped it and left it behind when you made the pizza order. Figured he was returning it."

Adam came to stand beside me as I opened the envelope and pulled out a napkin. Scrawled on it in fat loopy letters it said, "You look just like her. Keep the doll."

"Just like who?" Adam asked me.

I frowned. If the note was referring to the flash drive doll, I looked nothing like her. "No idea," I said. But I did have an idea who the note was from and it was no pizza delivery guy.

## 10

"*I* **LOOK NOTHING** like that thing," I said.

It was the next morning, and Camille and I were sitting in a café near the office. The place had a brick wall along the back and scads of little square tables with mismatched chairs. It served strong coffee and delicate pastries, and Camille and I had each ordered both and were devouring them under the watchful stitch eyes of the flash drive doll.

I picked up the plastic baggie that held the doll. "She's dressed like an escapee from a hippie commune. I don't dress like that."

Camille raised an eyebrow. Okay, maybe sometimes I dressed like that.

"And her eyes are stitched on in slits for goodness sake," I said. "Mine are big and blue."

"The stitching is blue," Camille pointed out.

I squinted at the doll. Well, navy blue maybe. "And look at her hair. The yarn is practically orange. I do *not* have orange hair."

Camille glanced at the waves of hair drifting past my shoulders and she shot me two raised eyebrows.

I looked towards the ceiling. "It's those Edison lights. They're bringing out my ginger bits. But ginger is not orange." I sat back and let out a long breath. When I'd called Camille and told her about the doll message, I hadn't expected her to bring the doll to breakfast. Now that she had, I wished she hadn't. Comparing myself to a doll wasn't going to get me anywhere. "What do you think the Penguin's trying to pull with that note?"

She picked up the napkin note, also now in a baggie. Not that I thought it needed one since I and goodness knows who at the Pizzeria had already handled the napkin, but bagging anything connected with work was becoming a habit.

"*Aucune idée,*" Camille said, having no more ideas about it than me. She put the bag back on the table, took the doll from me and placed it alongside the note, leaning it against the sugar dispenser. "How did you explain the note to Adam?"

"I didn't. I told him with all the strange goings on with the house, I didn't trust a pizza that showed up on its own. I didn't tell him I thought the delivery came from a Penguin with a penchant for cement. I said the note was probably somebody's idea of a joke."

Camille sat back and eyed me.

"What?" I said. "Adam was upset enough over the break-in and Laurent putting in the burglar alarm. If he knew the Penguin had just been at our door and was sending me personal notes, he'd go berserk. Anyway, by today some guppy in the Penguin's eco system will probably tell him the flash drive is no longer in my possession, and since he doesn't seem to care about the doll, that'll end his interest in me. Then Adam will never have to know a thing."

I glanced at the doll. Propped up by the sugar jar, she was looking right at me. Her little red felt mouth all smiles, her stitch eyes rag-doll friendly. Tiny yellow flower drawn on near the top of her left cheek. That right there setting her apart from being a mini-me. I would never paint a yellow flower on my cheek.

"And if the Penguin doesn't lose interest?" Camille said.

"Why shouldn't he? Laurent said there was nothing but shipping logs on the flash drive. If there's anything off with them, that's got nothing to do with me. And I can't see a guy like the Penguin still worrying about me as a witness to what happened at Johnny's party. There were plenty of witnesses there who saw way more than I did."

Camille tapped her finger on the side of her cup.

Okay, so I may have been overselling things. I was totally creeped out that a simple case of possible insurance fraud had led to goons breaking into my house and a dodgy Penguin delivering pizza to my door. But I refused to let the creeps get the best of me.

I ignored Camille's tapping fingers and went on, "What say we forget the Penguin for now and get back to Johnny and his insurance claim. Here's what I don't get. I know things work a bit differently in Canada than in the U.S. because of your health care, but wouldn't his insurance company be privy to his hospital records now that he's in a coma? Wouldn't the doctors there have done tests for say, internal injuries, that would show the condition of Johnny's back?"

"*Peut-être*, but there are rules about protection of personal information. There has to be a reason to share the information. Johnny's care at *l'hôpital* is paid by the government. But if he applies for his personal insurance to cover extras like a private room or something that is not standard care, then the insurance company is brought into the loop."

"But Johnny doesn't have a private room."

"*Exactement*. Johnny has nothing extra so far. Not even a TV. And nobody has asked for insurance help yet on his behalf. Legally,

*Assurance Lion* has no role so no automatic access to his files. Any other type of access would take time if allowed at all." She paused to check the time on her phone. "Anyway, what *Lion* really needs is proof Johnny was lying before this. Now he could have injuries to his back from his assault. It could be hard to prove what damage is new and what is old. Back problems can be tricky."

"Right," I said. "And all we've got so far is the wet shoes and that's not much. So unless we can prove he or his back doctor were lying before, we're stuck."

Camille raised her coffee cup to her mouth and wrinkled her nose. She placed the cup back on the table and waved over a server. Not all cafés had table service anymore. Part of the draw of this place was that it did, and Camille could get as many coffee refills as she wanted without having to stand in line at the counter. Camille was not big on standing in lines.

The server appeared at Camille's side. Tall woman, late-fifties, cat-eye makeup, hair dyed in light streaks that covered gray, slice of roots showing when she bent to wipe a crumb from the table.

*"Oh, c'est vraiment cute,"* the woman said. *"Je peux le voir?"*

She'd been looking at the flash drive doll as she spoke, and I watched as Camille passed it to her, baggie and all. They went on to chat some more in French before the server returned the doll and went off to get Camille another dose of caffeine.

"What was that all about?" I asked.

*"La serveuse"* was a camp counselor up north somewhere when she was young. She tell me they made dolls like that in crafts time."

I was surprised. I never went to sleep-away camp as a kid. Just day camp. We never made anything more than bracelets and baskets. "Small world," I said. "But probably lots of people make dolls like that. Could have come from anywhere." And that was the truth. I thought at first the doll had come from Johnny. Just some-

THE MÉNAGE À TROIS

where to hide the flash drive. I could maybe buy Johnny as a camp kid. Or even his sister the nun. But since the Penguin had offered me the doll, that suggested some kind of ownership on his part. And I had a hard time imagining the Penguin sitting around a camp fire sewing a doll. Probably the Penguin snatched the doll from some old lady's needlework basket when she was looking the other way.

The question was, if the doll came from the Penguin, how did Johnny get it? And why did he give it to me?

I waited while the server plunked Camille's coffee on the table and whisked off to another table, then I leaned in to Camille and said, "Do you suppose if Johnny is guilty of insurance fraud that there's a connection to the Penguin?"

She shrugged. "*C'est possible.*"

I thought back to the party and the goons busting in and stealing the poker money. "Like maybe Johnny has gambling debts and owes the Penguin money. Maybe when he's not busy with his dodgy construction business, the Penguin's a bookie or a loan shark. Maybe Johnny was looking for an insurance windfall to pay off his debt. I'm not sure how the flash drive figures in, but it might explain their connection."

Camille swigged more coffee and shook her head. "*Non, non.* I don't think it's about a windfall. Johnny isn't suing for damages. He only filed for disability. *En plus*, no debts we could find. Just car payments."

Hmm. So much for the deadbeat debts theory. "What about the fiancée? What do we know about her? She have money problems?"

"Nothing came up in preliminaries," Camille told me, waving over the server again as she spoke. This time to get the bill and pay it. Then she stood, scooped up the doll and Penguin note, and tossed them into her purse.

"Maybe we should talk to her," I said, wriggling into my jacket as we left and walked up Saint-Laurent boulevard, sidestepping the Monday morning crowd and some tiny puddles left over from an overnight rain. "I don't think she's likely to rat Johnny out about any possible insurance scam, but she may know something about the Penguin. And since he just had her fiancé beaten and ruined her wedding day, she may be in the perfect mood to rat *him* out. Probably we can catch her at the hospital."

Camille pulled out her phone and made a quick call. "*Non, non.* She's not there." She made another call, this time stopping at a store window until she ended the call. "Found her," Camille said. "She's at her work."

Truthfully, that was a relief. Much better than going to the hospital. I barely just got my breakfast down. Hanging out with tubes of bodily fluids and watching Johnny's face change color like autumn leaves was not high on my wish list. Nor was reprising my role as his roommate, Monsieur Lavoie's, visitor, especially if said roommate was conscious and got to questioning how we knew each other. Or worse yet, had real visitors spitballing the same questions. Wherever the fiancée worked had to be better than facing that.

"Is it very far?" I asked Camille. We'd both left our cars at the office and walked the four blocks to the café. With the walk back that was eight blocks. Eight big blocks. I liked exercise as much as the next gal, but saving my parking space near the office was not worth hoofing it all the way to the fiancée's work place if it involved much more hoofing. I didn't eat enough pastries at the café to exceed my morning walking limit.

"*Le Port,*" Camille said.

"You mean the Port in Old Montreal?" That would be good. Much too far for hoofing.

"*Oui!!!*" Camille's gaze wandered back to the store window and fell on black boots, knee high, three inch heels. *"Attends-moi,"* she said, slipping into the store, asking me to wait for her.

I went in after her and walked the side wall of shoes and more boots. I picked up a pair of shiny silver pumps, red soles, fancy lining.

*"Jolies,"* Camille said. She sidled up beside me, bag tucked under her arm, black boots like the ones in the window on her feet. "You should get them."

I looked at the silver shoes some more. It had been a long time since I'd been anywhere that called for shoes like these. Adam was right, we didn't get out as much anymore. But maybe if I bought the shoes...

Camille nudged my arm and winked. "That little doll would never wear shoes like that."

I laughed. Camille was so bad for me. And she knew me so well. She knew just what to say to push me over the cliff of indecision.

I trotted the shoes up to the cash and asked for a pair in my size. Five minutes later, we were back on the street and I wasn't minding the walk back to the office quite so much.

**"THAT'S JOHNNY'S FIANCÉE?" I said.**

Camille held her phone screen up for me to see. On it was a photo that matched the woman standing twenty feet in front of us. Camille created files for every case and the picture came from the file on Johnny for *Assurance Lion.* Background info mostly. But the woman standing ahead was far from background anything. Everything about her screamed foreground from her platinum blonde hair to her purple Lycra pants to her sequined purse to the giant rock on her finger. And her bulbous belly that tested the strength of a long-sleeved white top that didn't quite cover her midriff.

The woman stood by a vending machine, smacking gum, laughing with a man beside her. The guy, a big bear of a man, laughing right along with her.

"She's gotta be six or seven months pregnant," I whispered to Camille. "I didn't know she was pregnant. And what's she even doing at work? She was supposed to be married two days ago. Shouldn't she be on holiday time for honeymoon days? Or maybe visiting her comatose honey in the hospital?"

Camille tucked her phone in her purse and flexed the toes on her new boots. "*Allons-y*. Let's go find out."

We walked straight for the woman, both of us coming to a stop when we reached hand-shaking distance from our target.

"Mademoiselle Malouf?" Camille said. "Chloé Malouf?"

The fiancée turned, gum stilling in her mouth. "*Oui?*"

Up close, Chloé looked all of twenty-four years old. Creamy brown skin, eyes alert, nose pert, nails long. Cracked orange polish wearing at the tips. Probably from working the machines in the building we were in that processed goods coming in and out of the country. A building very much like the warehouse Johnny worked in not far away. Only his was more about storing than shipping.

Camille lowered her voice, slipped closer to Chloé, and gave her some spiel in French about the club where Johnny'd had his party, dropping the name of the manager we'd spoken to that night. Either I lost something in the translation, or to hear Camille tell it we were somehow connected to a follow-up investigation on the assault and Johnny's condition.

Chloé's face lost the laugh, she exchanged a look with the man beside her, and he put a protective arm around her shoulder as she went on to say what we already knew. That Johnny was in a coma in the hospital.

"We're so sorry to hear that," I said. And I was, too. No matter

Johnny's possible connection to the Penguin, no one deserved to be beat up.

Chloé smacked her gum from one side of her mouth to the other, lodging the wad in her cheek, and glanced at her companion again, barely acknowledging my sympathies.

"Do you have any idea if Johnny knew his assailants?" I asked. "Or why he was attacked?"

Again Chloé looked at her friend. Making me wonder if she was looking for input, or if we were having a language barrier.

The man tightened his grip on Chloé's shoulder and said, "Those assholes got off scot free. They should be locked up. And that shit ass club should be shut down for letting those assholes in."

And with that the man steered Chloé away, griping something about the club having good insurance and hearing from her lawyer.

I watched as Chloé and her companion headed to a set of doors, presumably out of the break area and back to work.

"Well that wasn't much help," I said to Camille. "They didn't even answer my first question. But I gotta say, insurance sure is popular with this crowd."

Camille nodded, her eyes focused in the same direction as mine, on the testy twosome.

The guy dropped his arm from Chloé's shoulder and punched a code into a box on the wall. Then he grabbed for the door handle and shook his head, thin vertical folds of skin forming in his wide neck and running up into his buzzed hair as his head moved back and forth, ears tipping side to side. The wiggly move reminding me of something. The saucer ears even more so.

"Hey, I know that guy," I said. "That's one of the guys from Johnny's party." From the front, I couldn't place his face, but from the back, I recognized him as the guy who hampered my view of Johnny from the hunk-a-junk-fake-cake lookout.

The guy hunched closer to the box and tapped the numbers again. This time the door opened when he pulled the handle, and he and Chloé went through, the door easing closed behind them.

Camille and I turned and walked for the door we'd entered by on the other side of the room. *"T'es certaine?"* she asked me, wondering if I was sure about the man.

I nodded.

"He looks good for someone in a fight two days ago," she said.

"He does, doesn't he? And he's not MIA anymore. Wonder what that means."

We'd made our way out of the building and into Camille's car. She pulled out her phone and tapped the screen, sharing it between us so I could see that she'd pulled up info on the guy with Chloé. Thomas Duncan. Listed in our files as a poker party guest and an old high school friend of Johnny's. One year older, no Cegep or university. Moved here shortly after Johnny, going to work straight out of high school and still doing the same job, working for the same company as Chloé.

Camille ditched her phone and navigated the car out of the side lot and into traffic, bumping the car along cobblestones streets as it wound its way out of Old Montreal. *"Alors voilà,"* she said. "Maybe you got your answer. You wanted to know why Chloé was at work and not at *l'hôpital* with Johnny. Maybe because of monsieur Thomas Duncan."

"You mean like she's cheating on Johnny with this Duncan guy?"

*"C'est possible."*

I wasn't so sure. They had looked cozy and close, but cozy and close could be relative. Plus, there was the whole pregnant thing. If Adam was any indication, that could bring out the protective thing in men. This Duncan guy may just be stepping up with Johnny temporarily out of commission.

"I don't know," I said. "Maybe Chloé just stopped by work to pick something up, they chatted a bit, and she's on her way to the hospital as we speak. Or maybe on her way home. Probably Chloé met Duncan through Johnny."

Camille glanced at me. "Or the other way around."

Interesting idea. "Either way, even if Chloé is cozying up to Duncan, I can't see how that has anything to do with Johnny and his insurance claim. It's got nothing to do with us. That's their business."

"*Voyons*, Lora. Our whole business *is* poking into other people's business."

She had a point. One I contemplated as we left Old Montreal and met a main road. Camille flicked on the car's left signal, made a turn, and we soon found ourselves in a neighborhood of older houses densely situated on treed streets. I didn't recognize the area but that was no surprise. Montreal was a big city. It would take me years to know the place. Longer, since I rarely ventured out of my regular haunts and work kept me pretty localized.

"Where are we?" I asked Camille.

"Saint-Henri. Chloé's *quartier*."

"Chloé's neighborhood? Why? We just left her at work."

Camille smiled. "*Exactement*."

Oh right. While the cat was away, Camille could play. A computer and phone got you plenty of intel on people these days, but now and again Camille liked to supplement that intel with other forms of information gathering. Like peeping through windows and chatting up neighbors. I was good with the neighbor bit, but I got less excited about the window peeping. Especially in broad daylight.

We went a few more blocks, the car turned again and slowed as it neared a row house—car missing a tire in the adjoining driveway, awning over the front door hanging on for dear life, patch of dirt lawn. Two goons standing on the stoop.

Two goons in long black coats and short white scarves. Two goons I recognized all too well. And two goons whose beefy necks were turning in my direction.

## 11

*I* SUNK DOWN in my seat, waved at Camille, and whispered, "Don't stop! Keep going. Those are the Penguin goons."

I felt the car coast on, round a corner, and slow to a stop.

"*Vite*," Camille said, grabbing for the door handle.

She didn't have to tell me where she was going. Exactly where I wanted to go. Back to the row house. I knew firsthand about surprise visits from the goons. If Chloé was on her way home, better she find me and Camille on her doorstep than the goons.

I scrambled up and out of the car, nearly bumping into Camille who had come around to my side and had the rear door open and her body bent over the back seat.

She backed out and passed me her blue trench coat. "*Mets ça*," she said.

I glanced at the sky, overcast but no signs of rain. I smiled and slipped the coat on over my jacket. Bit tight in the shoulders, but I didn't want to lose any time ditching the jacket first. "Do I get dark glasses, too?" I said as we hurried along the street.

She smiled. "Wouldn't hurt. We don't want the goons to recognize you and get scared off before we see what they're up to." She rummaged in her bag. No glasses, but she did find a scarf and passed it to me.

I wrapped it around my head, kerchief-style, and slowed my pace as we neared the house.

"Too late," I said. "They're gone."

Camille let out a loud breath, her eyes focused on Chloé's empty stoop.

I walked on so I could get a better view of the driveway. No goons there, either. I glanced at the parked cars on the street. If I hadn't dipped down in my seat so fast I'd have a better chance of remembering if any cars were missing. It would help, too, if I knew the make of the goonmobile, but I didn't. I imagined it would be long and black, though, and didn't see anything like that on the street. Mostly I saw compacts or old sedans with rust stains and cracked paint.

Still, I couldn't rule out the possibility that the goons were lurking about or had broken in to Chloé's house and were simply inside, waiting or prowling, whichever option suited them.

Camille stepped past me, made her way to the door, and rang the bell. I stood back in case one of the goons answered and Camille wanted to play some role like "hapless neighbor borrowing a cup of sugar or locked out of her house." Which was usually my role. Camille didn't do hapless well. Camille's version more sly than shy.

No answer to the bell and Camille rang it again. Still no answer. I glanced at the front window. Too high to peep in and too far from the stoop to access.

I looked back to the door, movement catching my attention when the door swung open. No one in the doorway, Camille's hand on the doorknob.

She shrugged. "*C'est ouvert.* We have to check it's okay, no?"

She slipped inside before I could object and gestured at me to follow. I dashed in and stopped cold, bracing myself in case an alarm went off or a goon popped out.

"*Qu-est-ce qu'il y a?*" Camille said. "Why are you standing there like that?"

"We shouldn't be in here," I told her.

Camille waved her arm towards the living room to our right. "*Non,* it's your goons who shouldn't have been in."

I scanned the room. Furniture askew, papers on the floor, dirt spilled out of plants, doors open on the TV unit.

We did a quick walkthrough of the tiny house. Downstairs, the kitchen and dining room were in similar condition. Upstairs the three cramped bedrooms, too. All ransacked, valuables intact. Unfinished basement, pretty barren, harder to judge. On the upside, no bodies anywhere, warm or otherwise.

Back in the living room, Camille pulled vinyl gloves from her pocket and handed me one. "I have one set only. We'll have to share." She took her one glove, slipped it on, and headed for a desk tucked into the dining room. "*Mais voyons,* Lora," she said, looking back at where I still stood rooted to the spot she left me.

"I know, I know. Opportunity," I said. "We should look for anything about Johnny and *Assurance Lion.* But I'm just wondering what the goons were looking for. The Penguin knows I had the doll with the flash drive or at least thinks I did. What could they want from Chloé?"

Camille shrugged again and went back to rifling through mail at the desk, her gloved fingers doing the walking through stacks.

I lowered my kerchief and started my search at the hall closet. Jam packed with coats at either end. Long, puffy wedding gown hanging dead center. Thin, wrinkly plastic bag draped over the dress in a clingy uneven shield. Crooked shelf above piled with hats, a couple bicycle helmets, a grungy pair of mukluks. Inside closet door covered with a shoe organizer, two pointy heeled pristine white Mary Janes loosely set in the bottom row.

Beside the Mary Janes, stuffed into an adjacent shoe compartment, I spotted a wallet and pulled it out. Flimsy leather cracked at the seams. Johnny's driver's license, debit and credit card inside along with some loose change. Proving Camille had been right and Chloé did take it from the hospital. I tucked the wallet back and checked a wad of papers stuck in the next pouch. A few bank receipts, some work notes, and a parking ticket. I took a closer look at the bank info. Nothing but bill payments and a low balance.

I stuffed the wad back, closed the door, and waded through the debris of the living room, poking at papers, resisting the urge to fetch a broom and scoop the dirt off the floor and back into the plants. Aside from a skimpy collection of DVDs, a few pregnancy books, and a slew of wedding magazines, nothing stood out. No notes with insurance letterhead. No phony medical records. No to-do lists or how-to tips about insurance fraud. No computer laying around for perusing. I moved on to the kitchen, hearing Camille overhead, upstairs banging drawers, muttering to herself.

"Anything?" I asked her.

"*Rien*," she called back.

I thumbed through a wedding magazine I'd found on the kitchen counter. Thin blue stickies bookmarked page after page of do-it-yourself tips for wedding favors, bridesmaid gifts, even wedding cakes. But no little notes were tucked inside about Johnny's faux or real back injury.

I chucked the magazine and checked out a big pile of mesh-balled candies set in a basket on the table. Each ball was tied with purple ribbon and had a small white card attached with Johnny and Chloé's names and their wedding date printed in tiny cursive purple type. Home-made wedding favors nice and neat. I sank my hand in the basket and rooted through the candy bundles. Nothing hiding I could find. "It's a bust down here, too," I said.

We met back in the living room where Camille pulled a coin from her pocket and tossed the coin in the air. "Call it," she said.

I frowned. Coin tosses were a Camille and Laurent thing. Usually when they wanted to decide unpleasant tasks. "I'm not calling it," I said. "I don't even know what we're calling."

The coin landed on her right hand and she covered it with her left. "If you don't call it, then I will. Heads you call in the goon break-in to Laurent and I make the call to the police. Tails you call it in to the police and I tell Laurent." She started to raise her left hand.

"Wait!" I said. "No, make it the other way around." Odds were the coin was heads and no way did I want to be the one to tell Laurent. I already got us into trouble with the hunk-a-junk cake mishap. I didn't want to admit we entered Chloé's house uninvited and rifled through her previously rifled belongings, too. Goons or no goons disappearing from the stoop. Laurent's PI rules never took opportunity as far as Camille's.

"*Okay*," she said and looked at the coin, a smile coming to her lips. "Tails."

"No way." I moved nearer to see for myself. A cute deer shined up at me from the coin. Drat. "Let me see the other side," I said. Not that I didn't trust Camille would play fair with me, but for all I knew she had a fake coin on hand for when she didn't feel like playing so fair with her brother.

She tipped the coin over and the Queen's face smiled up at me. She dropped it in my hand for further inspection.

"Okay fine," I said. "I'll call Laurent."

We each pulled out our phones and made our respective calls, Camille talking on a mile a minute when she reached her party. Me stammering along when I reached mine.

"*Ah, mon lapin.* Just the person I wanted to talk to," Laurent said before I got much out.

I glanced at the coin in my hand and paced in front of the closet. "Yeah, um, me too."

"Your new client is here," he said.

I stopped pacing. "My new what?"

"*Ta nouvelle cliente. Soeur Jane.*"

Soeur Jane? Omigod. He meant Sister Jane. Johnny's sister.

I waved at Camille to get her attention from across the room, wagging my hand furiously like I was fanning myself on the worst day of a heat wave. In the desert.

If Sister Jane was at C&C, she had to have remembered my contact info from the business card I dropped at the hospital. The business card I failed to mention outing myself with when I was supposed to be incognito. This couldn't be good.

"She'd like to hire you," Laurent was saying as Camille shot me a look and stuffed her phone away, her call evidently done.

"Me?" I said to Laurent. "She wants to hire me?" Okay so that was a little good, right? A *real* client wanted to hire me to be a *real* investigator. The budding PI in me would have been doing a happy dance if it wasn't for the accidental outing thing that brought me to the notice of said real client. And the fact that Sister Jane found herself in need of an investigator. I hoped she wasn't in trouble. But then, how much trouble could a nun get into?

"Wait. Hire me for what?" I said, Camille beside me now, her foot tapping, her ear pressing close to my phone.

"How soon can you get here?" he asked without answering my question.

I figured we'd have to wait for the police first. Then there'd probably be questions. Then the drive back. I had no idea how long all that would take. "I'm not sure," I said.

"Get sure. Your new client has a pressing problem. Someone just tried to kill her brother."

ISTER JANE SAT in a hospital chair, one hand gripping prayer beads, the other gripping Johnny's hand. Much like the last time we'd met, only this time we were in a new room. This one private and on a different floor. A cop stationed outside the door.

Johnny, too, looked much the same as the last time I saw him. Tubes and wires attached to various places on his body, machines blinking near the top of his bed, bruises coloring his face like a relief map.

"If I hadn't come in right when I did, Johnny'd be gone," Sister Jane was saying. "Someone turned off his machine *and* unplugged it. Poor Johnny wouldn't have stood a chance." Her eyes moved to one of the blinking machines. I had no idea what it did, but apparently it held the power of life and death.

She looked back to me. "There's no way it was an accident," she said. "I want you to find out who did it. And I want security cameras in his room. I'm afraid to leave him."

I nodded and pulled up a chair beside her. "We can do that," I said, not entirely sure the camera bit was necessary given the guard cop at the door. Or doable. I'd have to check later with Laurent and Camille. Laurent was off getting more info from the police and Camille was with hospital security.

"Now I'll be honest with you," Sister Jane continued, "Johnny's got himself into some trouble before. But nothing big. Nothing to make someone want to kill him."

"What kind of trouble?"

She let go of his hand and let her beads sit freely in her lap. "He gambles some. And he drinks. He had the drinking under control until he lost a friend a few months ago. I'm afraid he's had a hard time getting over it." She cast her eyes downward. "And I think he's stressed about the wedding. He hasn't known his fiancée very long. I'm not sure he's ready to get married. He was kind of pushed into it."

Hmm. Pushed or thrust? If she was talking about Chloé being "with child" I'd say Johnny had a part to play in that. If there was any pushing going on it wasn't all Chloé's doing. But I couldn't very well point that out to a nun. Plus, how would I explain what I knew? Better to let that sit and see if I could learn other specifics.

"Aside from the drinking and stress, Johnny tell you anything else was troubling him?" I asked. "Money problems? Health issues? Work worries?" *Insurance scam woes?*

She looked up and shook her head.

"Anything he may have shared with other family members?"

She shook her head again. "Our parents died in an accident when we were teenagers. We didn't have anyone else. Johnny quit school, left Toronto, and ended up in Montreal." She gazed over at him. "He's a little rough around the edges, but he's a good man and he's trying to make something of himself now. I can't imagine anyone wanting to hurt him. I've only met his fiancée a few times, but I'm sure she would say the same."

If she were here, that is. And not dealing with the goon break-in at her house. Camille and I had hightailed it out of there before Chloé arrived, but we were there long enough to know she'd been notified. Probably around the same time someone told her about Johnny.

I glanced at Johnny, his body looking small and fragile under his thin blanket, and my heart went out to the kid he was when he lost his parents. I knew what it was like to feel orphaned. Like you didn't belong to anyone anymore. Maybe Johnny had felt that, too, and tried to find his belonging on the streets while his sister found hers in the nunnery.

My phone trilled in my purse and Sister Jane glanced at it, frown on her face prompting one on mine, too. A sign on the wall had a big red line through a picture of a cell phone, but I'd ignored it. Partly to keep up the whole "supervising" thing Camille and I had going and partly in case Adam tried to reach me. I couldn't complain about him not taking my calls when he was with Tina if I didn't take his.

I excused myself and went out to the hallway to answer my phone. Not one of Adam's numbers I knew on the call display, but I picked up anyway.

"Mademoiselle Lora, I thought that was you," a man said.

The phone went dead in my hand, the man's voice coming at me again from the guy coming to a stop in front of me. Dour face, trench coat open, big gun bulging under his side pocket. Samuel Brassard, super cop.

"Let me guess," he said, ushering both of us a few steps down the hall. "*La belle* Camille is supervising you from under the hospital bed?"

I glanced back at Johnny's room and smiled up at Brassard. "Good to see you're on the case, inspector Brassard. I'm sure Johnny's sister will be happy to know one of the city's finest is watching out for her brother."

"*C'est pas pire.* Laurent is wearing off on you."

"Excuse me?"

"Very deft sidestep of my question."

I smiled some more. "Did it work?"

He bunched his eyebrows at me and pulled a pen and small pad from his breast coat pocket. "Did you find out anything from your little tête-a-tête in there?"

"Not really. Sister Jane doesn't seem to know why anyone would want to hurt Johnny."

Brassard's chin did a set of small nods, taking it in, no doubt his own wheels turning with questions for Jane.

"And what about you? I hear you had a break-in at your house. Maybe a visit from Johnny's assailant?"

"Maybe," I said. "I can't say for sure."

He scratched a note in his pad. "What about the little gift you got from Johnny. You can say for sure about that?"

I gritted my teeth at his sarcasm and nodded. Not surprised he'd heard about the flash drive. Probably Laurent had already made a copy that made police rounds until it landed on Brassard's desk. If Brassard had a desk. I was starting to think he spent most of his workday hovering, like a drone, gliding about in hopes of capturing something nefarious.

Brassard clicked his pen, his eyes steady on mine. "Why do you suppose Johnny picked you? Of all the people at the party, why would he give the drive to you?"

I snatched a look down the hall, hoping to see Camille coming around the bend. Brassard's tone felt like it could use some tenderizing. His questioning was starting to feel more like a grilling. By a cop with his barbeque set on high.

I gave him a shoulder shrug. "I don't know."

"*Et je suppose* you don't know anything about the break-in at the fiancée's house, either?"

I felt a flash of heat rush to my face. Guilt rising like mercury in a thermometer. Or maybe guilt mixed with anger. Just who was in trouble here? Sure, maybe Camille and I had searched the place "unofficially" but it's not like we were the ones to toss the place.

"You know I do know something about the break-in," I said, my hands going to my hips, my voice more assured. "I saw the same men at Chloé's who attacked Johnny the other night. Two of the goons were on Chloé's porch minutes before Camille and I discovered the break-in and called the police."

Brassard scribbled some more in his pad with his clicky pen.

"I don't know why you ever let them go free after the attack," I added. "None of this would have happened if you'd kept them in jail in the first place."

Brassard looked up, head weighted to one side, gaze looking off before refocusing back on me with hard, unmoving eyes.

Uh, oh. Now *I'd* poked the bear. I took a step back and felt a hand on my spine, warm and firm, fingers moving slightly up and down, and Laurent came into view beside me.

"*Des problèmes, Brassard?*" *Laurent said.*

Brassard went back to his pen clicking, repeatedly exposing and recoiling the tip. "Just talking with your new recruit. *Et toi?*"

"I'm good."

Something in the air changed from hospital brew to locker room stew, and both men went quiet.

I tried to inch away, but Laurent's hand at my back grabbed hold of my coat. I crooked my arm up behind me, trying to undo his clasp, and his hand transferred its hold from my coat fabric to my fingers.

Brassard watched us a sec then walked on past the cop outside Johnny's door. He turned and nodded his chin at Laurent, his gaze travelling to me. "Careful, Caron, or this one will get you into trouble," he said and disappeared into Johnny's room.

Laurent's eyes met mine. "Don't I know it."

**"IF ALL COPS** are like him, I can see why you left the force," I said to Laurent once we were in the elevator.

"Brassard made detective in record time. He closes more cases than anyone else. The force is lucky to have him."

I turned my head so Laurent wouldn't see me roll my eyes. "Okay. I'll give him that. But the guy could use work on his people skills. And why are we leaving? I wasn't finished talking with Sister Jane. She did ask for our help. We should be in there with her and Brassard."

Laurent shuffled me closer to the elevator wall, bowing his head towards me. "Right now we can help *Soeur* Jane better by keeping you away from Brassard," he said, voice low, accent deepened. "We'll go back when he's not there."

"But she wants us to put security cameras in Johnny's room. She won't leave without the cameras and she can't stay there all day. She needs rest, food, a shower maybe."

Laurent smiled, jostling into me when the elevator jerked to a stop and several people got on and off before it started up again. "Once a social worker, always a social worker, *hein?*" he said. "Not to worry. *Un policier* is with Johnny. She can come and go as she wants."

This time I didn't try to hide my eye-roll. "What she *wants* is the cameras."

The elevator doors opened again and Camille strolled on, surprise in her eyes, a grin on her face.

I made room for her near me, distancing myself from a guy on crutches.

"We're in luck," she said. *"L'agent de sécurité* gave to me a copy of the camera footage for Johnny's floor."

"He gave it to you?" I said.

She turned her focus to above the elevator doors where the numbers blinked as we past floors. *"Mais oui,* close enough."

Beside me, Laurent grimaced.

Camille shifted her look and narrowed her eyes at him. "You want to see it or not?"

I looked over at Laurent. The grimace was gone, cop face in its place. Not hard cop face, more non-committal, like a Magic 8 Ball in the "answer fuzzy, try again later" mode.

While he may have been fuzzy on his answer, I wasn't fuzzy on mine. I totally wanted to see the video. I was almost certain it would show the Penguin goons going into Johnny's room, and I couldn't wait to tell Brassard and his clicky pen all about it.

"**THIS DOESN'T EVEN** SHOW Johnny's room," I said. "There's nothing but a view of the elevators and the stairwell door. Everybody passes by those. This is no help."

Camille shifted the chunk of dark chocolate in her mouth from one cheek to the other, letting the chocolate melt slowly and ease its way into her system. Beside her, Arielle crunched her own chocolate and got up from her end of the couch in Laurent's office where we were watching the hospital security tapes on the big computer monitor.

*"Oui,"* Arielle said. *"C'est vraiment* boring. The opening of the mail was more interesting. We got a coupon for that new salon on La Gauchetière. I think I leave early and go there." She raised a lock of her long red hair up to eye level. "Maybe I try something new."

I glanced at the nose ring she got last week. Just one of her many piercings, the others currently covered by her blouse, save for the four holes in her ears that held tiny gold hoops. Then I took in the rose tattoo near her shoulder and the chain of flowers etched into the skin around her wrist, and I wondered if decorating her body was more about Arielle's yen for self-expression or a form of shopping therapy.

Arielle left for the hall and Camille stretched out on the sofa, keeping her eyes on the monitor, her fingers working her laptop to control the screen. "*Ici,*" she said, pausing the footage. "This is backed up to when we see *Soeur* Jane arrive on the floor." She stood and marched out after Arielle. "Back it up some more and watch. See if anyone familiar leaves."

Camille's voice dimmed and picked up again somewhere outside Laurent's office. Arielle's voice chimed in, too, their words humming along in French, tones rising and falling, providing an out of sync audio for the video I watched. Arielle's voice rose just as an orderly crossed the screen scooting an IV in front of him, a stooped old man in patient garb trailing behind, straining to keep up. The orderly glanced back and with the sound of Arielle's voice hitting a spike, it made it seem as though he was shouting at the poor patient. It didn't fit at all but at least it added interest to my viewing. Arielle was right, the footage was super boring.

No wonder Laurent had begged off watching and disappeared on some mysterious errand. Laurent had experience watching security footage. Probably he knew it was boring and figured it was better left to me and Camille to wade through it and weed out any points of interest. Of course, with Camille begging off, too, that just left me wading through and feeling like the flunky left to do busywork. And this busywork was about as fun as sharpening pencils.

Worse yet, it was a major disappointment. My hopes of spotting the Penguin goons were dashed. No one I recognized passed anywhere, except Sister Jane.

I stopped the video and cued up the other one, the one that showed the view of the stairwell exit. Nothing caught my eye on that one, either, so I wound both back farther, about an hour, opened a second screen and started up both videos, side by side.

"Find anything?"

I paused the videos and looked to Camille crossing the room towards me.

"Not yet," I told her.

She handed me a round cardboard container lined in silver. "*Une salade,*" she said. "I had Arielle get us lunch before she went to the salon." She sat beside me, placed another container on her lap, sorted out napkins and forks, and passed me mine.

"Thanks." I poked at my salad with my fork. A warm smell of herbs floated up from the rice and veggies and chunks of grilled tofu. I peeked into Camille's container. *Poutine.* Québec-classic style, French fries heaped with cheese and gravy. Heart attack in a bowl I'd heard someone call it. *Poutine* also came in lots of varieties now with much healthier choices.

"The least you could have done is get one with vegetables," I said.

Camille stabbed a fry with her fork and held it up. "*Et ça?!*" she said. "*C'est une poutine végétarienne.* No meat. The whole thing is practically vegetables."

Probably that was debatable. The fry may have started out a potato, but the deep fryer had morphed it mostly into a grease sponge to soak up all the gravy and cheese. A delectable grease sponge that I could be eating, too, if Camille hadn't been all thoughtful and ordered me a salad.

I speared a carrot from my container and released pause on both videos. We ate in silence and watched for a while until I noticed Camille fumbling with her phone beside her. I shot a look at the display as a text came in and hoped it was from Puddles. We still hadn't talked about whatever was going on between them, and my curiosity had me hoping I'd finally find out.

Camille popped up from the couch so fast I didn't get to read the texter's name. Which probably served me right for trying to snoop in the first place. What kind of person snoops on her best friend?

A bored person. That's who. A person stuck watching boring security tapes and eating boring salad while a would-be murderer was on the loose. A murderer trying to snuff out the man who survived a beating and entrusted me with a hippie-doll-guarded flash drive. A man whose sister now counted on me to find said would-be murderer.

I watched Camille toss what was left of her poutine on Laurent's desk, head out of the room, and turn into her own office. I waited a beat then slipped my own food aside and went to Laurent's desk. He had to have a copy of the flash drive some-where, and I wanted to see it. There had to be something impor-tant about it. It just didn't make sense for Johnny to give it to me, otherwise. As much as I may have wanted to be done with the drive, this recent attempt on Johnny's life had me rethinking things.

Laurent's desk consisted of a round, glass-topped table. Not much on it. No laptop, no baskets of junk. Just a stack of papers and a mini clock resembling a hockey puck. A rolling drawer cabinet lived under the desk. A bunch of things were stuffed in there, but no flash drive with stripes. I surveyed the rest of the room—locked file cabinet in the corner, couch along the main wall, built-in shelves surrounding the window that looked out on the lane between this building and the next. The big monitor on one of the shelves streamed the security videos I'd left running.

Various other shelves housed books and more tech gizmos. I crossed over to check out the tech stuff, fingering through a batch of cords, stopping when I found what looked like a white garter contraption with snaps.

"*Bon ben.* I don't think that's your size, *mon petit lapin.*"

I turned to find Laurent watching me, leaning against the doorframe, his arms folded across his chest, his mouth in a grin. He pushed off from the doorframe and walked to me. "But you're welcome to try it on," he said. "Only first I'll have to get you the piece that goes with it."

I stuffed the garter thing back on the shelf and wiped some moistness from my palms. I hated getting caught snooping. Even more, I hated Laurent's ability to sneak up on me like a jungle cat. The man had more control over his body than seemed humanly possible. He claimed it was from early training with a tactical unit. I was beginning to believe it had more to do with genes he'd inherited from the Indigenous ancestry mixed into his bloodline. The same ancestry that gave him the dark hair and even darker eyes. And apparently the ability to tread lightly on the planet. Without making a peep.

I decided there was no point in trying to cover up my snooping. Laurent seemed to enjoy seeing me squirm too much.

"I want to see the flash drive files," I told him. "I know you said they were just shipment logs, but they have to figure into all this somehow."

Laurent slid a backpack from his shoulder and pulled out his laptop. He set the computer on his desk, shrugged out of his jacket, and draped it across the back of the chair he pulled out and waved at me to take. "Have a look."

I sat in the chair and he leaned over me, clicking his track pad until files appeared on the screen. He straightened, and I scooted forward in the chair and took control of the arrow keys to scroll through the files.

Laurent slid a look at the big monitor showing the tapes from the hospital then turned his eyes back on me. "How goes it with the footage from security?" he asked.

"Slow. Typical hospital comings and goings." My foot knocked something as I settled in. The backpack he'd taken on his mysterious errand. "How about you?" I said. "Did you learn anything new? Any more of Johnny's party guests resurfacing besides Duncan?"

"Everyone accounted for, noboby talking."

"I bet," I said, waiting to see if he'd elaborate, turning my attention back to the laptop when he didn't. I clicked open a shipment record and made my way through the other documents to find more of the same. Each file logged a batch of shipments including dates they were ordered, shipped, and received. The logs worked by category, each one covering an area of construction supplies. Most were easy to make out even with my limited French: Bricks, beams, pipes, cement mix. The last one bringing a grimace to my face before I moved on, looking up at Laurent and pointing to some French words at the top of the spreadsheet. "I've seen these before, haven't I? What's it mean?"

He moved to the other side of the table. "*Dépot Deschênes*. The name of the warehouse where Johnny works."

I smiled. Right. Must have been remembering the name from our file on Johnny. "Well, that's it, then. That's the connection between Johnny and the Penguin. They must have crossed paths at the warehouse." I glanced back at the screen. "Only I don't see how these files factor in. They look perfectly normal to me. I don't see anything here worth hurting someone over, do you?"

"*Ça dépend*," Laurent said.

"Depends on what?"

"On many things. The numbers could be wrong, for instance."

"You mean like they could be fudging figures. Maybe claiming more expenses than they have, so they can inflate costs. Or maybe using the accounts to launder dirty money and maybe there are no real supplies. Maybe for appearances they booked space for supply storage at Johnny's warehouse only Johnny noticed the Penguin's storage lockers were full of nothing but air."

I absentmindedly grabbed for a fry from Camille's discarded poutine, popped the fry in my mouth, and went on. "That could explain why they went after Johnny. They wanted to keep things hush hush, but somehow Johnny got hold of the files so then they needed to get the drive back and quiet Johnny." I grabbed for another fry. "Or maybe Johnny was using the flash to try to blackmail the Penguin, and the Penguin didn't take too kindly to someone pecking at his seedy deals."

"That's a lot of maybes."

"But I'm right, aren't I? It could be one of those things."

"Right about what?" The question came from Camille, breezing back into the room, smiling when she caught sight of me bringing a third French fry to my mouth. Or was it a forth? Or fifth?

I went to fetch the napkin I'd abandoned with my salad, and I wiped a gob of gravy from my fingers. If I'd been alone I would have sucked the gravy off, but I thought better of it in front of the Carons. Camille might take it as an admission of my secret love of poutine. And Laurent would probably tease me about it in some evocative way I didn't want to think about.

As I cleaned up, I answered Camille's question by bringing her up-to-speed on what I'd seen in the files from the flash drive and my suppositions about what they may mean.

"Johnny would have to be *un idiot* to blackmail your Penguin," she said. "He'd have to have a death wish."

"Yeah, I think that theory's pretty weak, too." I sat on the couch, pulling my phone from my back pocket so I could slouch back, and

I thought about my conversation with Sister Jane. "His sister said he'd been in trouble before but was straightening himself out now. I don't see him purposely messing with a guy like the Penguin. I think whatever got Johnny involved was more likely accidental."

Camille crossed over to the desk, her eyes darting to the streaming videos and back to me. "She say anything else, Johnny's sister?"

I explained about the parents dying, Johnny's quitting school and striking out on his own. About Johnny's gambling and recent fall off the booze wagon. How Sister Jane worried he wasn't happy about his impending nuptials. And how they had practically no one except each other.

A look passed between Camille and Laurent.

"What?" I said. "You think there's a clue in there somewhere?"

Laurent went to sit in the chair I'd vacated and Camille leaned against the desk, facing me, hands bracing her on either side.

"*Ah non*, Lora. You're getting that look again," she said.

"What look?"

"You know the look. You're getting emotionally involved again."

I crossed my arms and frowned. "I don't know how you get that from what I said, but what if I am? We've been over this before. It's not a crime to care about people."

"*Non, non.* But it doesn't make it easy to do your job. You can't let your feelings mess with your judgment. Whatever his sister said, Johnny is no mister innocent. You're the one who found the shoe clue, no?"

Right. A clue I was starting to really regret. And seriously question.

"I've been thinking about that. Maybe I can't explain how the bottom of Johnny's shoes got muddy, but I find it hard to believe he'd sit through a beating if he could easily get up and walk away."

"The man was knocked unconscious," Camille said. "He wasn't walking anywhere."

Hmm. Fair point. "But that doesn't prove anything." I took a long breath, wishing I'd seen more of the brawl that night from my hunk-a-junk-fake-cake lookout. "Anyway, what does it matter if he was faking or not? That doesn't justify someone trying to kill him. And what if that someone tries again? Johnny's got a pregnant fiancée and a twin sister for goodness sake. They'd be devastated if something happened to him. And Sister Jane did hire us to find out who unplugged Johnny at the hospital. Surely an attempted murder case trumps insurance fraud, right?"

"Technically, Soeur Jane hired *you*," Laurent said, rolling his desk chair sideways out from behind Camille, his eyes catching mine.

Oh boy. I was wondering when we'd get around to that. The man said nothing all afternoon then out this pops.

I explained about the business card dropping out of my pocket at the hospital. The C&C business card with my name on it that Camille and Laurent had had made for me as ID while I was an assistant, I reminded them. "It was an accident," I said. "It's not like I gave it to her. I never exactly said I was an investigator. I stuck to my cover the whole time. It could have happened to anyone."

Laurent held his gaze on mine and I tried not to waver. Or smile. There was still a part of me that was psyched that Sister Jane had mistook me for a full-fledged PI.

"*Vraiment*, Laurent," Camille said, moving over to join me at the couch. "Give the girl a break. Be happy we have two clients paying us for one case."

At this, I smiled a little, on the inside, and made a mental note to get Camille a giant bar of chocolate later.

Laurent stayed quiet but crossed the room and stopped directly in front of me, where he leaned down so close I could feel his breath on my eyelashes.

"No PI of mine uses one of these," he said pulling the clunker phone from my hand. A second later refilling my palm with a brand-new iPhone. "If you're going to start pulling in clients, you have to look professional."

My smile made its way to the outside as I watched him walk out to the hall, saying over his shoulder, "Try not to drown this one."

## 13

---

*M*Y LIVING ROOM looked exactly the same when I got home as when I'd left it that morning. Tina's Babyland'r'Us. My kitchen, on the other hand, had had a complete makeover with every available surface covered in enough takeout bins to rival the all-you-can-eat buffet spread on a cruise ship. Containers, some open some not, some stacked some not, as far as the eye could see. And at the table sat Tina working three plates of chow like she was clearing food from a conveyor belt.

She wore flannel pajamas patterned in mini yellow smiley faces and various food stains. Her hair, tethered into pigtails with mismatched hair bands, had the straw look of horse mane. Her eyes ping-ponged around the table of food as she ate, like she was mentally preparing her next plate-load.

"Tina couldn't decide what she wanted," Adam said from the sunroom doorway, where he appeared, hammer in hand. "So we got a bit of everything. Except sushi. Raw fish isn't good for the babies."

I ventured over to him, the aroma of cabbage rolls melding

with falafel causing my nose to crinkle as I got closer to the buffet spread. "How long has she been going at it?"

He glanced at the clock over the stove. "About fifteen minutes." He set the hammer on an edge of counter and released a pile of nails curled into a fist in his other hand. "Securing the break-in window," he added in response to the quizzical look I gave the pile of nails.

I nodded and peered into the takeout bin nearest me. Brown chunks on sticks over a bed of rice. "You eat, too?" I asked Adam.

"No. I was waiting for you." He circled an arm around my waist and whispered in my ear. "I need to talk to you. Alone."

My eyes wandered over to Tina. With her food fix and Adam talking about her like she wasn't in the room, it felt like we were already alone. But I followed him to the sunroom anyway.

Adam glanced into the kitchen before pulling the door closed behind us and swiping a hand over his hair. "Here's the thing," he said, running his hand through his hair again. "Tina's upset."

I waited and tried to keep my face from showing my lack of surprise. "And?"

He reached for me and planted his hands on my shoulders. "And I hate to ask, hon. But what would you say to throwing Tina a baby shower?"

"A what?" I blinked, surprise springing to my face this time. Full on, shocked, "what you talkin' 'bout Willis?" surprise.

"I know," he said. "It's a lot to ask. But she's got nobody else."

"What do you mean she's got nobody else? What about her mother? Or her mother-in-law? They're going to be grandmas. Grandmas love baby showers. Or her sister-in-law, the one who's going to be the godmother. That's like three good candidates right there."

Adam shook his head. "None of them are doing it. Everyone expects her best friend to do it."

I hit the "find" button in my memory, rooting around for the name of Tina's best friend, and came up empty. Tina always said she had a hard time making women friends because everyone was jealous of her. "Who's that?" I asked.

Adam grinned, his lips tentatively holding position. "You."

"Me?!" I clamped a hand over my mouth to keep from laughing. The only reason Tina tolerated my presence was because I was with Adam. And the fact that our coupledom had lasted longer than a New York minute had Tina thinking her watch was broken. She couldn't wait for me to get out of the picture so she could pencil herself in. No matter that she had a husband and two baby boys coming her way. She needed every male in her life focused on her.

"I know," Adam said. "It surprised me, too. But that's what she told everybody and now everyone's a little miffed you haven't invited them to the shower."

"They're miffed at me? For not inviting them to a shower I'm not throwing and knew nothing about?"

"They think you've left their invites to the last minute. They figure the shower has to be soon because twins come sooner than single babies. So either you're late with the party or late to invite them, and they think it's the second."

"Why didn't Tina ask me herself?"

"You know she has a hard time asking for things. She's too embarrassed."

The remarkable thing was that Adam said that with a straight face. His blind spot when it came to Tina was 360 degrees.

I dipped back and looked through the glass of the sunroom door at Tina still shoveling in food at the kitchen table. More food than I'd ever seen Tina eat at one sitting. She really was upset. If she ate much more those babies would have some serious indigestion. Or be forced out for lack of room.

I sighed. "Fine," I said. "I'll do the shower."

Adam gave me a long kiss on the cheek. "Thanks, hon." He broke away from me and pulled a sheet of folded paper from his shirt pocket. "Here's the guest list and contact info. And don't worry. This won't take all your time. I'll help, too." He reached for the door handle to head back to the kitchen. "But do you think you could tell her yourself? It would seem more real coming from you."

I forced a smile. "Sure." Because this was all about keeping things real. Nothing more real than throwing a sham baby shower for my fake best friend.

And maybe in between tracking down diaper cakes and blue onesies, I'd find the time to track down the real would-be murderer of a fake or not insurance scammer, too.

**FINALLY THE HOUSE** WAS QUIET. Tina tucked away in the hide-a-bed in Adam's office. Again. Adam, me, and the pets, fed and ready for sleep. The evening gone in a haze of baby shower planning with Tina, aka getting instructions, and a slew of texts from Camille. The last one in all caps with five exclamation points, reminding me she was picking me up at one A.M. sharp.

When Adam fell into a pattern of light snoring, I tiptoed out of bed and over to the walk-in closet where I exchanged my nightie for my Batgirl clothes—my answer to Camille's Catwoman haute couture getup for our low-profile, late night prowling. Unlike Camille's sleek catsuit, my Batgirl outfit was less couture and more comfort—black leggings, black turtleneck, black knit tuque, and black sneakers. No bat ears. My kinship with Batgirl as a Gotham city gal ended at bat ears.

In case he woke up and found me gone, I left a note for Adam on the fridge. Then I filled my Batgirl fanny pack with a few essentials and went out to wait for Camille on the porch. As I sat on the top step, a yawn big enough to stash an entire carton of Ben & Jerry's took hold of my mouth, squinting my eyes shut before releasing my jaw, and I bemoaned myself for succumbing to fatigue. Before I'd left the office, Camille and I had come up with this idea to get in a little nocturnal reconnaissance on Johnny's case. I couldn't flake out on that now. Now that this was "unofficially" my case, I needed to step up my game. Batgirl would never yawn on the job. Batgirl was a night person.

A car pulled up and flashed its lights, and I crept down the stairs for a closer look. Sure enough it was Camille, sans Jetta. Instead she drove a ho-hum jalopy. A jalopy that looked vaguely familiar.

I got in the passenger side and Camille hit the gas, my head cleaving to the head rest as she sped away.

"Sheesh," I said, scrambling to get my seat belt clicked into place. "What's the rush?"

"What rush?"

Right. For a second there I forgot I was driving with Grand Prix Camille. Neither late of hour or dark of night would slow her down.

I settled back and gave the car a onceover, trying to place it, nothing tweaking my memory except a faintly familiar scent of sweat and dank fabric. "Do I know this car?" I asked Camille.

"*Oui, oui.* It's the car of the agency."

Oh right. The car Laurent & Camille kept for times when they wanted a forgettable car. One that blended in for trailing people. Or other times neither wanted to use their respective cars on a case. It had been a while since I'd seen the jalopy. The last time there'd been need of an incognito car Laurent had used a sporty rental.

I yawned. "No offence, but I think this car's been in storage too long. It doesn't smell so good."

Camille sniffed the air and buzzed her window down a couple inches. "That's not storage. That's junior league. Laurent's been using the car for his little hockey players."

I glanced to the back seat, half expecting to see a collection of mini hockey men dolls similar to Adam's superhero action figures. "What little hockey players?"

"From his coaching team. Some of the families don't have cars, so Laurent drives the kids to practices and games."

Hmm. Laurent coached hockey for little kids. How did I not know this? The man really was a man of mystery. "I had no idea," I said. "How long has he been doing that?"

"Three years."

"Wow," I said. "That's great."

Camille eyed me, braced the steering wheel with her knees, and reached for a silver thermos in her cup holder. She unscrewed the lid and a waft of coffee streamed out, instantly improving the air quality.

"What would be great," she said, coffee swigged, hands back to driving, "is getting this little mission over with and getting home to bed."

I agreed with her there. But usually I was the one complaining about playing Catwoman and Batgirl. She'd been fine with the plan earlier. Probably her attitude switch had something to do with whatever was going on with her and Puddles. And maybe in a good way. Maybe it was a good sign that she wanted to go home. In which case *I* was good with putting up with her being in a little snit.

She slowed the car to a park, shut off the engine, and smiled, and I got to thinking her coffee had to be some strong stuff to perk her up that quickly. That had to be the shortest snit in history.

"*C'est là,*" she said.

I peered out the windshield to the dimly lit street. We were at our first stop. Chloé's row house, which had two cars parked in the driveway, tucked in snug, nose to end, like a fender bender waiting to happen.

A red Honda Civic sat in lead position. A gold Taurus took the rear. The Civic belonged to Chloé, the Taurus belonged to her work buddy aka Johnny's poker buddy, Thomas Duncan.

Score one for Camille. No wonder she was smiling.

"All right," I said. "I admit it. That's fishy. Maybe you're right. Maybe there is something going on between Chloé and Duncan." I leaned forward to get a better view of the house and felt myself yawn again. The yawn narrowing my eyes so Chloé's house blurred, a tiny streak of light coloring the blur and coming into focus again as my eyes unclenched. The light came from the upper window to the right, thin curtains shading the view to inside.

My tired brain struggled to remember the layout of the house. Was that a bedroom or a bathroom?

"They're not sleeping yet," Camille said. "Someone's walking around."

I turned to see she had binoculars trained on Chloé's lit window. The window my fuzzy brain had finally pegged as a bedroom.

Camille lowered the binoculars and reached for the car door handle. "*Allons-y.*"

I grabbed her arm to keep her from sprinting out of the car, and I squinted into the dark night. "Go? Go where? We can't just march up and ring her doorbell in the middle of the night."

"Of course not. The window's open. We're going to listen from below. Hear what's going on."

I glanced back at the house with its tiny stoop and barren front yard. "We can't. There are no shrubs or trees or anything near the house. There's no place to hide."

She shrugged me off and moved to get out of the car. "That's why we dress in black, no?"

I sighed. I was the kind of person who liked to devise plans, make lists. Control risks, maintain some sense of control. Camille liked to fly by the seat of her pants, and at the moment said seat was hightailing it across Chloé's patchy grass.

I caught up with Camille, hoping the goo squishing below my sneakers was dirt dampened to mud from all the recent rain. I crouched at the base of the house, working to make myself as unnoticeable as possible, and I tried to zero in on any voices from above. Faint tones of Franglais came to my ears, too faint to discern.

"Can you make anything out?" I asked Camille.

Her head did a small shake from where she stood beside me, and her eyes scanned up the brick wall. "We need to get closer."

I followed her scan. No close trees. No drain pipes. Nothing. Thank goodness.

She scraped her hands together, ridding them of loose mortar bits stuck to her palms from bonding herself to the house front. She turned away from me. "*Vite,*" she said. "Get on my back."

"What?"

"My back, my back. If you climb my back you can get up to the window."

I glanced at the window and back at her. Was she nuts? No way was I using her back as a ladder to scale bricks. I was no rock climber let alone a brick climber. Which is what I whispered to Camille.

"*C'est complètement fou!* I don't want you to climb the bricks, just my back so you're closer to hear."

I looked up at the window again. Up high, far, far away. If she expected me to scurry up her spine and stand on her shoulders like the top girl in a cheerleading pyramid, she'd be disappointed. I was no cheerleader back in high school let alone now. And I doubted our combined height in piggy-back mode would get us anywhere near enough to the window. But nothing ventured nothing gained, right? So up I went, feeling like a little kid the time my dad hoisted me on his shoulders once at the Macy Day Parade.

Below me, Camille tottered briefly as I got into position, then she went solid and still as a rock. Not a surprise. The woman had core muscles Pilates instructors probably didn't even know existed.

She also clearly had science skills I lacked. She was right. The added height let me catch snippets of Chloé's words spilling out from the upstairs window. Enough words to guess that the full sentences went something like: "What do you want me to do? I tore the place apart. I can't find the damned thing? I have no idea where Johnny put it."

"Well figure it out," Duncan yelled at her. "That son of a bitch baby daddy of yours fucked everything up. Now you're gonna fix it."

The voices went quiet, the sound of drawers being opened and slammed shut filling their sound void.

"You hear anything?" Camille asked me, her voice barely above a murmur.

"*Oui. Excellente question,* mademoiselle Lora," another voice said from behind Camille. This voice gruff, down a few octaves, and far less friendly.

Camille turned, slowly, and I turned with her, getting a good look at the voice's owner. Brassard. Out of his usual attire, and from my vantage point, out a crop circle of hair from the field of short curls on his head.

Judging by his squared jaw and bulldog shoulders, he was also almost certainly out of patience.

## 1 4

CAMILLE'S HANDS MOVED from where she braced my shins to her hips, her elbows jutting out, arms forming triangle wings.

"Beat it, Brassard," Camille said. "We're working."

Brassard's hands went to his own hips, and he shot a fiery glare at Camille from behind sunglasses, reflective style, shiny and definitely unnecessary in the dead of night. Probably he was wasting the glare. Probably all Camille could see was her own piercing look reflected in the glasses.

The glare wasn't a complete waste, though. From my perch I could see straight through the gap behind Brassard's glasses to his eyes that flared hot enough to burn the devil, and I rebalanced myself to compensate for the loss of Camille's hands anchoring my legs, afraid I might topple over trying to dodge Brassard's sparks.

I held my gaze steady on him, prepared to bob and weave if necessary, wondering if the man ever blinked. Which of course is when he did, briefly, as he got beaned in his crop circle by something from above. Twice.

Instinctively, I scrambled down from Camille's shoulders, three thoughts going through my head—we'd been spotted by Chloé and Duncan, Chloé's ramshackle house was crumbling, or Chicken Little was a bird ahead of his time and the sky really *was* falling.

I was all set to run for cover when an arm grabbed me and flattened me to the wall. Camille. She moved in beside me, placing me monkey-in-the-middle position between her and Brassard. I looked from one to the other of them, each unmoving, breathing slow and steady, almost Zen-like. Both of them looking like they wouldn't break a sweat if we were lined up against the wall in front of a firing squad.

The static of distant bickering voices from above caught my attention, and I looked up to see a small bundle sail out the window and fall at our feet. In the dim glow from the streetlight, the bundle looked white with a strip of purple curling away from it, like the tail of a kite. The white wad sparkled some and recognition hit me. Chloé's wedding favors for the guests. The ones I'd seen all cozy in a basket on her kitchen table. White candies bundled in white mesh tied with purple ribbon, tiny note cards attached citing the bride and groom names and the wedding date.

"*Va-t-en! Va-t-en! Va-t-en!*" Chloé was yelling loud now, another bundle whizzing out the window.

"Stop throwing those things at me," Duncan yelled back.

I felt a tug at my sleeve and Camille pulled me along the wall, leading the three of us in a fast sidestep until we reached the neighboring driveway where we darted over to the neighbor's parked car and ducked down, shielding ourselves from Chloé's front door sightline.

A second later, the door flew open and Duncan stomped out and over to his car. A minute more and his car was peeling up the street. My heart tap danced as I watched him go. Between Chloé's yelling and the car peeling, I figured the whole neighborhood would be up and checking outside to see if everything was all right, and three dark figures crouched by a car might not look so good.

**"THAT WAS CLOSE,"** I said, darting looks up and down the street as I settled myself low in the C&C jalopy and flexed my knees. We'd made it to the car doing the firefighter's low crouch walk, and my knees were feeling a whole new admiration for firefighters. The crouch walk was not easy to keep up for long. Especially with a disgruntled cop breathing down my neck. I couldn't even imagine doing it with fire swirling around me.

Camille started the car and crept it up the street so slowly I looked over at her to see if somehow her Zen mode had slipped into sleep mode. Or if maybe in all the ruckus, I'd missed her being replaced in a body snatcher's kind of thing. If she had been, I couldn't tell. She looked exactly the same. Not even a hair out of place. As opposed to my own hair, which had slipped haphazardly out of my knit cap, long tendrils dangling here and there, one repeatedly dipping into my right eye.

"You okay?" I asked her.

She nodded, her gaze darting to her rearview mirror. "*Reste tranquille*, Brassard," she said. "Your big head's blocking my view."

I turned to look behind me where Brassard sat in the back seat, his fireplug body wiggling like a kid itching with poison ivy. His wiggling stopped when he pulled a set of shoulder pads out from behind his back and a jock strap out from under his butt. Both the shoulder pads and the jock strap were small in size. And both probably belonged to one of Laurent's junior hockey players, but Camille's joke about minimum size requirement when she'd been "tenderizing" Brassard the night of Johnny's bachelor party had me wondering briefly about ownership of the jock strap.

"Pull over at the next corner," Brassard said.

Three car lengths down from the corner, Camille pulled in. There was plenty of space to stop closer to the intersection, but Camille didn't take kindly to people telling her what to do. Brassard was lucky she stopped at all. I wasn't surprised she did, though. She was about as happy about chauffeuring Brassard as she would be about eating mass-market milk chocolate. She'd gladly spit both to the curb the first chance she got.

She kept the engine running and drummed her fingers on the steering wheel. I watched the finger drumming speed up when Brassard made no move to get out of the car.

"Tick tock," Camille said.

Brassard grinned and leaned forward, inserting his head between the front bucket seats. *"Ah, belle Camille.* I was about to say the same to you ladies. You're done here. This is a police case. Your services are no longer required. Pack up your *dossiers* and call it a day."

Camille paused her finger tapping. "In your dreams, Brassard. Our client decides when we're done with the case."

Brassard's eyes skimmed to me. "Don't you mean Lora's client? The client of the investigator with no license?"

I went still like the time in fifth grade when I'd noticed the boy beside me cheating off my test paper and I didn't report it to the teacher. I'd felt just as guilty as if I'd cheated myself. I felt the same way now only this time I deserved some of the guilt. If Brassard decided to make a stink about C&C futzing with regulations, it would be on me.

*Camille smiled. "Agréable de te voir, Brassard. En fait, toujours un plaisir. Now get out of my car."*

Brassard smiled back and tipped his head as he got out and started walking for the corner.

Camille idled the car alongside him and gave him the finger before speeding away.


**I CRAWLED OUT** of bed the next morning, my tongue furry, my eyelids heavy. Given our escapades at Chloé's house, Camille and I had ditched any thoughts we had of further night prowling and called it a day. As I trudged to the bathroom and got a good look at myself in the mirror, I was thinking maybe calling it a day and a half would have been more apt.

En route to drop me off, I'd filled Camille in on what I'd overheard of Duncan and Chloé's conversation and we'd batted around ideas for a while about what it may mean. By the time I got home and fell into bed, I'd conked out like a boxer going down to the mat on his last round. And evidently I'd stayed that way the rest of the night, facedown, mouth open, and now one side of my face looked like an accordion blind encrusted with drool staining it like drips of dried tea. Both my eyes were puffy and dark, and my hair was tangled to the side in a thorny mass. Yuck.

"How two people live with one bathroom is beyond me," a voice said from behind my back. "It's like the third world or something."

I turned from the mirror to find Tina, arms encircling her belly, smiley-face pajama bottoms pooling around her feet. "Could you hurry up? I'm peeing for three here."

I glanced at the floor, hoping she meant that metaphorically, relieved to see she had.

When I looked up again, Tina was staring at me mouth agape, eyes wide.

"Omigod," she said. "What happened to you? You look awful."

I grimaced. Harsh but accurate.

Adam's head popped into view behind Tina. "What's going on?" he said. "Everything okay?"

"Fine," I said, squeezing past Tina and heading for the stairs.

The bathroom door closed and two sets of four paws joined me on the stairs, Adam's two socked feet bringing up the rear. The train broke up when I got to the kitchen and one set of paws went for the back door, the other for the food dish on the floor. Adam paired with Pong at the back door and let her out while I poured kitty kibble into Ping's bowl.

I was bent over the sink, splashing cold water on my face by the time Adam and Pong reappeared.

"What was it this time?" I asked Adam. "Tina forget where she live?"

"Jeffrey's painting the nursery and Tina didn't want to be near the fumes."

I dried my face on a tea towel and sighed. Not a bad reason to stay with us. Probably I could argue that there were plenty of places she could escape the paint fumes in her four-bedroom suburban dream home. But Tina was probably nesting and there'd be no sense arguing with a mom-to-be in nesting mode. Although with all her baby gear still piling up in my living room, I was starting to wonder exactly which nest she was feathering.

Adam popped bread in the toaster, filled the kettle, and looked at me. "Not to change the subject or anything, but you want to tell me where you were last night? I woke up and you weren't in bed."

I dropped food into Pong's bowl, snatched the note I'd left Adam on the fridge, and gave it to him. "Working."

He scanned the note and frowned. "So now it's not enough you work weekends. You're taking on the midnight shift, too?"

I mustered up as much indignity as I could after less than five hours of sleep, and I narrowed my already droopy eyes to mere slits. "What happened to supporting each other's careers and interests?" I said, pointing at the ceiling to remind him what interest of his I was currently supporting. Maybe not happily supporting. But I was, after all, relinquishing my bathroom to his guest while I washed my face in the kitchen sink.

The kettle whistled a time out and we both glared at it.

"Fine," Adam said, breaking the glare and pulling the kettle from the burner. "You're right. Let's just let it go and get on with our day. I'll get Tina fed and out and you can have the house to yourself to clean up or whatever." He gestured at me as he said the last bit, his eyes fixing on the swollen knot of hair jutting out from my the side of my neck like a gnarly goiter.

My hands went to my hips. He had some nerve. Him in his slim jeans and clean white T-shirt and hair that didn't need combing. And his full night of sleep. "Hey. I wouldn't look like this if your friend wasn't hogging our bathroom."

"At least my friend wasn't keeping me out half the night."

"What do you mean by that? I told you. I was working."

"Right. Sitting on some stakeout somewhere chugging java and playing PI with Laurent in a dark car."

"I wasn't "playing" anything. And I wasn't with Laurent. And I wasn't chugging java."

He stared at me and I stared back, our eyes locked like kids in a staring contest. First one to look away loses.

"I smell toast," Tina said, lumbering into the kitchen. She'd changed into a loose dress and leggings, her feet in speckled socks gathered at the ankles. Her hair combed and pinned off her makeup-fresh face. "Breakfast ready?"

Adam and I slowly shifted our stare Tina's way. She sat at the table, letting out a huff as she settled in and moved an empty plate from in front of her to the center of the table alongside a few takeout bins loitering over from the great binge.

Ping took one look at Tina and fled the room, Pong close

behind. And me following suit after nabbing a bagel and a glass of orange juice. Not at all worried about losing the staring contest with Adam. I'd read the same look of surrender in Adam's eyes that he probably saw in mine once we'd both reconnected after Tina's entrance. I felt bad for Adam really. I knew in my heart of hearts that Tina tried his patience at times, too. But I also felt bad for me. I didn't want to lose my turn in the bathroom. While she waited for Adam to make her oatmeal, Tina was socking back tea so fast that I'd be lucky to get five minutes to tame my hair and make myself presentable before she pulled her pregnancy trump card on me again and bounced me out of the bathroom with her baby bump.

I locked myself in the bathroom, took the fastest shower of my life, and was in my bedroom dressed in jeans and sweater and brandishing a blow dryer when Adam slipped into the room.

He moved in front of me and I shut off the dryer.

"Look," he said. "I'm dropping Tina off downtown on my way to the office. Then at lunch you and I are meeting at *Le Pois Chic*. We're going to have a proper meal. Just the two of us. No fighting. No Tina. No work. No talk about alarm systems or break-ins or babies. Just you and me, a bowl of spaghetti, and two straws."

I laughed. "We can't eat spaghetti with straws."

He pulled me into his arms, trapping the blow dryer between us. "Straws. Spoons. Forks. Whatever you want. What'd ya say?"

"I love spaghetti."

"I'll take that as a yes."

And I was taking his lunch offer as an apology for his part in whatever that was we got into downstairs. It was something I learned about men after living with Adam for almost two years. Men rarely apologized with words. With back rubs, movie tickets, even ice cream, yes. But not with words. It's like the words "I'm sorry" stuck in their throats somewhere along with ones like "I need directions." It's not like they never said them, it's just that the extraction seemed to be about as appealing to them as pulling rotten teeth and avoided until all other measures for less painful resolution had been exhausted.

"Lora, you still up there?" Heavy feet moved closer outside the bedroom door and Tina called out again. "Lora?"

I let my forehead drop to Adam's chest. "Yes. I'm here, Tina. But I'm leaving for work."

She thumped her fist on the door and rattled the knob. "Perfect. Then you can take me downtown instead of Adam." The door opened and her body filled the doorway. "We can talk about the shower on the way. There's a lot to plan and you haven't left us much time. We'll need to make the most of every minute we can get together."

I raised my eyes to Adam's, thinking this would be a good time for him to dig deep and pull out an "I'm sorry."

"Oh, and we'll need to get the invitations out pronto," Tina said. "There are a lot of important people on the guest list. They need to book their time."

Important people? My heart skipped a beat. Tina may not have a lot of actual friends, but she did have her heels hooked on the social ladder. What had I gotten myself into? I was going to have to do better than diaper cakes to impress the other social climbers or I'd never hear the end of it. To Tina, social embarrassment was akin to a disfiguring disease, minus the compassion.

I spotted the guest list Adam had given me the night before, the list sitting folded and unread on the dresser. I wiggled free of Adam's arms, ditched the dryer, and grabbed the list. It was long. Crazy long. Tina couldn't possibly actually know that many women. Probably some were being invited as seat fillers. Like at the Oscars. More for effect than affection. I hardly recognized most of the names of the invitees. Just the few family members I knew about and some I guessed at when I saw shared last names. Three quarters of the way down the list, I picked out Camille's name which got a smile out of me. She was going to love that. Then sitting way down near the bottom I spotted another name I recognized, and this one got a furrowed brow out of me. Chloé Malouf, Johnny's fiancée.

I looked up at Tina. "Chloé Malouf?"

Tina nodded. "That's a girl from my birthing class." She moved beside Adam and gave his upper arm a light slap and giggled. "Adam here knows her really well. Adam's on an intimate basis with Chloé and her baby, aren't you mister pillow?"

My eyes travelled to Adam, my eyebrows raising. Mister pillow?

Patchy red splotches sprouted on Adam's cheeks. "It's nothing. Chloé's partner missed class and I helped her out with some of the breathing exercises, that's all."

"All my ass," Tina said. "Shit I said ass. I mean, all my booty." Tina had a swearing habit she was trying to break before the babies came, and she shook her head at herself for her stumble before continuing. "Adam was on the floor spooning Chloé from behind so she could lean on him and do her puffy breathing. He was like one of those giant pillows people prop up on to read in bed, his arms all outstretched rubbing Chloé's stomach. It was hysterical."

Adam looked at me and gave a small shrug. "She was all alone. I felt bad for her. I was just trying to help."

I imagine he was. Just like he was trying to help Tina with her Lamaze breathing when he was undoubtedly on the floor spooning her at the same lesson. But neither surprised me. Adam had a bit of a white knight complex when it came to needy women. What did surprise me was that one of the damsels in distress said knight helped was Chloé. I did a fast calculation and pegged the birthing class as taking place on the day after Johnny's bachelor party. The same day of Chloé and Johnny's would-be wedding. And the same day Johnny was lying flat out on his back in the hospital, comatose, tubes up his nose, his sister the Sister by his bruised side.

If it had been me and my fiancé had just been beaten to an inch of his life and my wedding had been tanked, the last place I'd want to be is a Lamaze class playing in-breath-out-breath with a strange man's hands on my baby belly.

But then I probably wouldn't have been at work two days later or tossing my wedding favors out the window, either.

Which got me wondering just exactly how Chloé felt about Johnny and their cancelled wedding day. And just where she was when someone was pulling Johnny's plug.

$\mathcal{M}$AYBE CAMILLE WAS right. Maybe I did sometimes let my heart cloud my head. All this time I'd been feeling bad for Chloé. Imagining how I'd feel in her place. But I wasn't Chloé and Chloé wasn't me. I needed to learn how to get some distance, keep my perspective open.

"I think we should book the Chalet. That would be big enough, right?"

I slid my eyes over to Tina in the passenger seat beside me in my Mini.

"Excuse me?" I said. With my mind on Chloé, I'd nearly forgotten I was chauffeuring Tina downtown to a hair appointment she had booked at a place on Rue Crescent. Not at all on my way to the C&C office in the Plateau. And if she hadn't spoken up, I may have missed the turnoff towards Crescent street that would take me miles out of my way and make me even later for work than I was already. But on the upside, it would give me an opportunity to practice that open perspective thing.

"The Chalet," she repeated. "At Mount Royal. Wouldn't that be the perfect place for my baby shower?"

Hmm. The Chalet at Mount Royal park. If memory served, that was the lovely old building near the top of the hill. The one with cathedral ceilings and amazing windows and fab art. "I didn't realize you could have parties there," I said.

Tina pulled down the visor and craned her neck forward over her baby belly to get closer to the mirror clipped onto the visor underside. "Jeffrey and I were there once for some political thing he had to go to for his law firm." She paused to smooth her hair. "I figure if they can have a party there, so can I."

"How many people were at the party?"

"I don't know. A few hundred I guess. I think it was a fundraiser and you know those fundraiser types. They always want to tap as many suckers as they can get."

Sounded more like an event to me than a personal party. An event I could imagine taking place there, a baby shower not so much. Lucky for me, my tongue-holding superpower kept me from mentioning that to Tina. Tina might take offense at me even implying her baby shower may be seen by the rental committee as less of an event than a big-scale political fundraiser for bigwigs with big pockets.

"And I think it would be cute to have two of everything," she went on to say. "You know, kind of a double theme since I'm having twins. Two cakes, two main courses, two cocktails, two bands, two ice sculptures."

Two bands? Two ice sculptures? Two cocktails? I'd never been to a baby shower with even one band or one ice sculpture. The baby showers I'd been to had balloons and banners and macaroni salad and baby naming games. And the closest thing to a cocktail served was a fruit cocktail. Most moms-to-be I knew didn't drink. Although the throbbing pain settling into my right eye had me thinking maybe liquoring up the guests at Tina's shower may not be a bad idea.

"Sure. I'll look into it," I told Tina. Not a total fib. I could probably pull off something with a twin theme. Like maybe two Jell-o moulds. They were kinda like sculptures, right?

"Good," she said. "After my hair's done, pick me up and we'll go register for gifts so we can put the registry information in the invitations. God knows I don't want to end up with a bunch of hideous baby clothes and cheap baby monitors."

The throb in my eye went from a thumping to a pounding. I knew just agreeing with her was the way to outer peace at the moment and goodness knows I wasn't getting any inner peace what with the eye throbbing. But I had more pressing things to deal with than keeping Tina happy. Like someone trying to off Johnny. "I'd love to help, but it will have to wait until after I'm done work. I'm booked solid the rest of the day."

Tina's Peach Perfection-lipsticked mouth puffed out in a pout. "It can't wait until tonight? We're late on everything already. We've got too much to do. Can't you take some time off? I'm sure that dreamy boss of yours would understand."

Probably by now my "dreamy" boss had heard from Camille about Brassard's not-so-dreamy threat about my not-so-official first case, and I'd be lucky if tardiness was all I was in trouble for when I got to the office.

We'd reached Tina's hair salon and I slowed the car to a double park, stopping to idle beside a gap between two parked cars so my Mini's passenger door would open into the gap.

"I'll see what I can do. Maybe later in the afternoon. I'll let you know," I told her, figuring the non-committal agreement thing worked with the shower theme and it was worth giving it another shot. If not for outer peace than so I could get in a question of my own before she went off to get her tresses trimmed.

I checked traffic, jumped out of the car, and ran around to the other side to help Tina ease her baby bump out and onto the sidewalk. "I wanted to ask you," I said. "That woman Adam helped at your baby class, do you know her well?"

"Chloé? I know her baby's father is a twin, and I know her baby wasn't, you know, planned." She pouted her lips at me again. "But don't you worry. I was just joking about Adam. Chloé's getting married. The guy's pretty cute, too, even if he is in a wheelchair. Poor guy had an accident. Anyway I don't think he'll be in the chair for long. And Chloé said he's a real catch."

"A catch?"

"Yeah. You know, well connected or something. He didn't look all that special to me, but she should know, right?"

Right. I was getting the impression Chloé knew a lot of things about Johnny and his connections. And if Brassard hadn't got me fired or downgraded back to assistant by the time I got to the office, I planned to find out exactly what Chloé knew. And where Thomas Duncan figured in and why she'd been using him for target practice.

"C'EST VRAIMENT DOMMAGE," Arielle was saying into her receptionist headset when I walked into C&C. She popped her head into the hall, body leaning over her desk, and waved at me, finger going to her lips in the international shush sign.

Across from her desk, Laurent's office door was closed. Arielle waved at me some more, urging me to keep walking right by, her outstretched hand pushing me to the kitchen at the back of the suite.

She'd ended her call and ditched her headset by the time I reached my makeshift work station at the café table.

"No. Not there. Get over by the sink," she told me with a quick glance behind her.

I quick-stepped over to the counter and turned to face her. She had a different look about her than usual. Her nose ring a conservative stud, her hair sleek and flat, fanning forward in a flame-colored fringe from chin to mid torso.

"What's up?" I asked her.

"Tch, tch, tch," she said. "Not so loud. Samuel Brassard is here with Laurent. I was just about to text you to not come. I don't know what's going on. Brassard said something about you and Camille and throwing you out windows."

I smiled. Her "throwing" sounded like "trowing" with her accent, which was good because it distracted me from worrying I was in imminent danger of going out a window. I was almost sure Arielle must've overheard Brassard retelling Laurent about the previous night's events complete with Brassard's beaning by wedding party favors, and Arielle had just misunderstood. Brassard couldn't possibly be seriously thinking of throwing me and Camille out windows. He was a cop. Surely he knew throwing people out windows was frowned upon.

"I appreciate the concern," I said to her, "but I think everything's fine. Brassard just wants us to back off the Johnny case. Camille wasn't so open to the suggestion, so probably he's making the request to Laurent." Hopefully, not along with a request to also have me benched or cut from the C&C team. Permanently.

Arielle brought a hand to her chest and blew hair out of her face. "Ah okay, okay." She pivoted, headed for the hall, and came back a second later texting away on her cell phone, her fingers pausing almost immediately following the sound of a door opening.

I strained my ears and watched the kitchen doorway, hoping to see Camille breeze in, but nobody appeared. I heard a door open again, a brief click clack of footsteps, and then nothing. No feet shuffling, no talking, no window banging. And nobody appeared in the kitchen. The only thing breezing in was silent and invisible, a frosty current rippling through the air like a mist.

Arielle and I tiptoed to the doorway and peered out. Just in front of Laurent's office stood Brassard, toe to toe, boot to boot, with Camille. Brassard had arms crossed at his chest. Camille had arms loose at her sides, hands in fists, coiling and uncoiling with the steady pace of a metronome. She caught my eye, and I resisted the urge to move a step back and take cover. At the best of times Camille's eyes flashed bright with emotion, at the worst of times she turned the flash down to a low glow. At the moment, the flash was all but gone, replaced by a vacant, stony, stare.

Brassard huffed, his arm slipped to the "at-ease" position, and he squeezed himself past Camille and out the front door.

"*C'était quoi ça?*" Arielle said, approaching Camille.

Camille let herself fall back to lean on Arielle's desk, her feet crossing at the ankles. "What was that? That was Brassard being Brassard. *Espèce d'idiot.* He thinks only men can do this work. He needs to get out more and see what women can do."

"*Ben*, the way I hear it, Brassard did see what women can do. Last night. He says he found the two of you playing outside Chloé's house and causing trouble." This coming from Laurent, who seemed to appear magically, leaning, too, on the doorframe of his office, swinging a finger between Camille and me as he said that last bit.

Camille rolled her eyes. "It was not us women getting knocked in the head with candy. If anyone was playing it was him." Then she looked at me and we both slowly started to laugh.

It had been pretty funny. Mister starched and grumpy Brassard getting beaned in the head with wedding swag.

"Maybe when you two stop laughing," Laurent said, "you come into my office, and we talk about how you're going to make nice with Brassard so he doesn't report us for breaking regulations of the *Bureau de la Sécurité privée.*"

"*Mais voyons,*" Camille said, her voice an exaggerated sing-song. "We didn't break any regulations. We stay outside the house of Chloé. We take nothing, we interfere with no one. We did nothing he can report."

"Yeah," I said. "And I wasn't alone. Camille was right there supervising. If you ask me, if anyone was breaking rules it was Brassard. First off, he was casing Chloé's house and second he was stalking us. Plus, he was the one pinging Chloé's candy off his head. Really, we saved his butt. If we hadn't been there to drive him off in our car, he would have been spotted skulking outside Chloé's."

Laurent grimaced. "You don't actually believe that do you? That you saved Brassard?"

"Well," I said. "Maybe saved is a little strong. More like helped. But the rest is true." It was also true that Brassard had us on earlier infractions, but Laurent wasn't asking about those.

The office phone rang, and Arielle sat at her desk and answered the call. A second later, she passed the receiver to me.

"Lora?" the caller said. "It's Sister Jane. What's going on? They've moved Johnny and won't tell me where he is?"

I cupped the phone and repeated her words to the team. Camille looked surprised. Laurent didn't.

"Hang on a sec," I said to Jane and cupped the phone again. "What do you know about it?" I asked Laurent. "Did something else happen to Johnny?"

"*Non,*" he said. "Brassard mentioned the move. It's typical procedure. Keep Johnny more safe."

I went back to Jane and gave her the same spiel.

"More safe?" Sister Jane said, her voice rising to very un-nun-like levels and causing me to ease the phone a little distance from my ear. "He doesn't need to be kept safe from me. Can't you get them to let me see him?"

I had my eyes still on Laurent and saw his head give a slight shake. I knew that shake. That was cop shake. Not easy to break. But I was going to have to try if I wanted to help Sister Jane.

"Let me see what I can do," I told her. I copied her number from the call display into my phone, gave her my direct number, assuring her again I'd be in touch, and I hung up.


**"SO," I SAID.** "It's come to this, has it?"

"*Écoute*, Lora. You have a better idea?"

I leaned forward and scoped the interior of the Tim Horton's doughnut shop where we sat parked outside in my Mini, wedged in at the end of a row of cars big enough to eat my Mini for lunch and still have room to dessert on a Fiat. We had a front row view of Timmy's plate glass window and main entrance, and a good look at the cars spilling out of the drive-through.

"Are you sure Brassard'll be here?"

Camille nodded. "He comes every day. *Onze heures*. Carrot muffin. Dark roast coffee. Two sugars. Three napkins."

"You know a lot about a guy you don't like."

"Keep your friends close and your enemies closer, no?"

At five to eleven a bronze sedan pulled in at the other end of the row, and Brassard got out. He started walking for the Tim Horton's door and stopped just outside to brush streaks of car door dust from the bottom of his overcoat. He was inside a minute later, moving his way to the front of the line.

My fingers loitered over the car-door handle. "You sure I have to do this?" I said.

Camille turned her body to face me, her eyes attempting to soften and not quite succeeding. She hated this as much as I did.

"*C'est juste un jeu.* A game. We all agreed Brassard is using Soeur Jane to get to you. He doesn't really think she is a threat to Johnny. *Alors*, you give Brassard something he wants and Soeur Jane gets to see her brother. That's what you want, no?"

It was exactly what I wanted. I just didn't want to give up anything to get it. And pretending to run into Brassard so I could make nice definitely felt like giving up something. At the very least, a piece of my pride. Probably a few years ago, I would have shrugged it off, but somehow now it felt like a big deal. Particularly since I wasn't sure how far I'd have to go to make nice. Just stroke his ego, Camille had told me. Quid pro quo, she had said. Make him feel like I'm cooperating, give him information he wants to get him to stop using Sister Jane and back off making a formal complaint about me and the agency.

I wasn't sure it would be that easy. Brassard didn't seem like the kind of guy who made anything easy. More to the point, I wasn't even sure I had any information worth a bargain. Probably I didn't know anything he didn't know.

Somehow I'd have to come up with something, though. I didn't want to disappoint Sister Jane, and I needed to clear the agency of whatever trouble I'd caused. Camille and Laurent both assured me they could likely defend any regulations complaint if it came to it, but I knew none of us wanted that. It would be a big, time-consuming hassle and a nasty blemish on C&C. Not to mention a formal complaint could force C&C to suspend Johnny's case and put a serious wrinkle in any of us being able to help Sister Jane find Johnny's would-be killer. And it could all potentially still end in me out of a job.

Reluctantly, I nodded agreement at Camille and watched four more people get in line behind Brassard as he moved on, bag in hand, and made his way over to a sidebar that stocked the expected stir sticks, napkins, sweeteners, and the like.

"Hey, you see that?" I sat forward, spotting something less expected. I let my fingers fall from the door handle. "That guy at the sidebar with Brassard. I swear that's a Penguin goon. Minus the long black coat and Neanderthal stare."

Camille faced front and leaned forward, too. "Binoculars," she said, holding out her hand.

"I don't have any. Who keeps binoculars in their car?"

She glanced my way.

Right. Of course. Camille did. And according to her, anyone in the PI biz should. Make mental note to buy binoculars.

Camille held up her phone and stretched her fingers over the screen. I leaned in to see she had the phone on camera function, zoom mode. Not the power of binocular zoom, but the close-up view sealed it. Brassard's coffee buddy was definitely one of the goons. Goon #2, the one who bulked up the front of his trousers with a gun muzzle.

"That's a goon all right. What's Brassard doing with him?" I said.

"Good question." She clicked a few pictures. The phone went quiet and she panned it back and forth, taking in the shop's exterior, then she slowed and fixed the lens back on Brassard and Goon #2. Taking video this time.

The men had stepped away from the sidebar deeper into the corner, Goon #2 sitting on a stool holding a newspaper, Brassard less than a foot away, standing looking at his phone. Both men's lips moving in alternate rounds, a kind of lip tennis match.

"*Tiens*," Camille said, passing her mobile to me. "Keep the video going." She moved to the door. "What have you got in the trunk? We need to get closer. We need a disguise."

Camille's trunk was like a magician's—filled with everything from clothes to wigs to doodads that seemed to mysteriously materialize as needed. Camille was like the girl scout of PIs.

Prepared for anything. My trunk had nada in it. I'd be lucky if it even had a spare tire.

"I've got a first-aid kit in the glove compartment," I offered.

She groaned. "*C'est tout?* No coats, no glasses, no hats? No clothes from shopping?"

I shook my head, trying not to shake the phone camera along with it. I'd thought about switching to my own phone but didn't want to lose time, and I definitely didn't want to botch Camille's video. "Sorry. I like to keep things organized and neat. I unpack the trunk when I get home from shopping."

She cocked her head towards mine, connecting us just above the ear like we were conjoined twins, both of us sharing the phone view. "They keep talking," she said. "We need to get closer to hear."

Hmm. This was sounding like a repeat of the night before. I hoped she wasn't going to suggest she hoist me on Tim Horton's roof so I could dangle down and listen through the plate glass window.

"Keep watching," she said and darted out of the car.

She slipped away into the sea of cars, and I lost sight of her. I went back to my surveillance of Brassard, curious what she was up to but happy it didn't involve any hoisting of *moi*.

"Uh oh," I said to myself, focus fully back on my quarry. Brassard still had his own cell phone up and had drifted it out in front of him so it faced out the window to the parking lot. Probably he couldn't see me. Probably his phone wasn't on zoom camera mode. But then again he didn't need zoom mode to spot my car.

I ducked down and held tight, muttering some more to myself, searching my brain for training in what to do in situations like this, my brain coming up with nothing. "Okay, okay," I said. "No need to panic. Just wait it out. You can't just leave. If you get up to drive, he'll see you for sure."

There was a tap on my window and I jumped, dropping Camille's phone.

"He sees you now," Brassard said, looming over me through the glass.

I eased myself into my seat and smoothed my hair at the sides, trying for calm and casual, hoping he couldn't hear my thumping heartbeat. Relax, I ordered myself. He couldn't know for sure I'd been watching him. It was a free country. Anybody could go to Tim Horton's.

He wagged a finger at the window, and I hit my ignition to buzz the window down.

"Oh hey," I said.

"Hey yourself," he said. "Let me in."

I hesitated. If I didn't do as he asked, he'd think something was up for sure. But if I let him in my car, who knows what I'd be facing?

My hand went to loiter over the gear shift, tempted to put the car in reverse, back out, and zoom away. My fingers jerked as the passenger door flew open and a gust of air floated over me, relief hitting with the air gust. Camille was back. With any luck, she'd say something tenderizing to Brassard and we'd be out of here.

I turned to greet her and nearly got bulldozed by an arm the size of a log flattening me to my seat, reaching across my chest, winding me. I heard the master lock click and a door swung open in my back seat. Brassard got in behind me and the log arm eased back, its owner settling into the seat beside me. Goon #2. Not Camille at all.

"Drive down the street and pull in the alley," Brassard said.

I looked back to give him my best "who's going to make me" stare and locked eyes with Goon #2, who no doubt had his pants front deflated, because he had his gun enhancer out and proud and pointing straight at me.

# 1 6

*I* DROVE TO the alley as Brassard instructed and cut
the engine, working to keep my knees from knocking
together. Social work training prepared me for many stressful
situations, but being stuck in a car with a scary, starched cop and a
goon with a thing for Penguin thugs and guns was not covered in
Social Work school.

"Put that thing away," Brassard said to Goon #2.

Goon #2 looked down at the gun in his hand. "Sorry. Habit." He
studied the gun, clicked something on it, and shoved it back in his
pants.

Brassard leaned forward and stuck his big head between the
bucket seats. *"Tabarnouche,"* he said. "I told you to get off my case."

I felt beside me for my bag, looking for my new cell phone.
No point in calling Camille since I'd dropped her phone somewhere below me, but I was sure Laurent had himself already
listed and handy in my contacts. If I could maneuver my bag to
get a view of my phone screen, I could make the call without
anyone seeing.

The giant log arm slapped across me again and wrenched my bag away. "Don't make me get the gun out again," Goon #2 said.

Brassard knocked Goon #2 on the shoulder and snapped something French at him and the goon gave me back my bag.

"All right," Brassard said. "Since you're not good at butting out, you may as well be all in. Mademoiselle Weaver *je te présente détective Gilles Grandbois.*"

I hugged my bag to me and looked from Brassard to the goon. Seriously? Goon #2 wasn't just a goon, he was a detective goon? Just exactly what did I stumble on? If it was two crooked cops I was toast. I've seen the movies. Nobody walks away scot free from crooked cops.


**THIS WOULD TEACH** me not to stock my trunk. If I'd had any good disguise fare back there, Camille would never have left me alone in the car and I wouldn't be sitting in a deserted dingy alley with armed cops and nothing to defend myself but my disarming looks and fast talk.

"Look," I said, inching for the door. "I don't need to be all in. Really. I'm good. I just wanted a coconut latte. I mean, who doesn't love a Tim Horton's coconut latte, right?"

"Tim Horton's doesn't do coconut lattes," Goon #2 said.

My brows furrowed. Truth was, I'd never been inside a Tim Horton's. When I wanted a coffee I went to cute neighborhood cafés or Starbucks. But Timmy's was supposed to be really popular in Canada. How could it be popular and not serve coconut lattes?

"Right," I said and switched to a safer food group. "I meant I wanted a doughnut." The place started off as a doughnut shop for cripes sake. Surely *that* was a safe choice.

"*Arrête!* Enough about doughnuts and lattes," Brassard said. "Stop squirming and listen to me. Grandbois here is undercover.

I'm not about to let you go running around poking your inexperienced nose into an operation that's taken months to put in place."

I loosened my grip on my bag. He was looking me directly in the eye, no hedging. Which got me thinking he was telling the truth. Maybe what I'd stumbled on wasn't crooked cops after all. But I'd still stumbled on something and that crack about my nose seemed uncalled for. "Hey, if I'm such a crappy newbie PI, what's that say about you? I spotted the two of you in your little coffee conference, didn't I? If I'm so lousy at my job, you must be even lousier at yours."

Brassard's face flushed red and his hand moved to his jacket. Oh boy. I poked the bear again. What was wrong with me? Another second and *his* gun would probably be out. Or his clicky pen. Probably he could do unspeakable things with that clicky pen.

I risked a look over. He had his hand plunged into his pocket, his phone out, and his finger punching the screen. "Caron," he barked into his mobile, followed by something in French I roughly translated into "we need to talk." Then a bunch more French and he stopped talking, clicked off his phone, and eyed me like he was studying a fresh stain on his new carpet.

I was guessing since Camille didn't have her phone, the Caron Brassard called was Laurent, which I hoped didn't mean I'd gotten the agency into more trouble. The look I was getting didn't fill me with encouragement. I needed to do something to right the situation.

"Look" I said. "I'm not interested in busting up whatever sting you've got going. All I want to do is help Sister Jane find out who tried to kill her brother."

Goon #2 looked away. Brassard's face went blank. Neither said anything.

Hmm. Tough crowd.

"And maybe meanwhile you could let her see Johnny," I added.

"She's his sister for goodness sake and he's in a coma. She ought to be able to see him." I thought about the plan Camille and I had had when we set up our Tim Horton's ambush of Brassard, and I decided to come clean and see where it got me. "Camille thinks you're keeping them apart because of me. If that's true, just tell me what you need me to do so you'll reunite them. I'm nothing if not willing to help. And you really don't have to worry about me outing whatever secret operation you've got going here. I was a social worker. I'm great at protecting confidentiality. You can tell me anything and I won't tell a soul." I did the lock-lips-and-throw-away-key thing.

Brassard studied me like a stain again. "How are you with data entry?" he asked me.

"Excuse me?"

"Data entry. What about Excel? You know Excel?"

I furrowed my brows. "You mean on the computer?"

He checked his watch. "Of course on the computer."

I shrugged. "I know a little about it I guess."

"*Et bien*," he said. "Know a lot about it by tomorrow."

He went for the car door handle and Goon #2 did the same.

"You want me to learn Excel?" I said, completely confused by the request. "And you'll let Sister Jane see Johnny?"

"Right."

They were both out of the car now, and he signaled me to roll down my window again. "Be ready to leave your house by seven-thirty tomorrow morning. I'll have someone pick you up."

"And what? You've got paperwork you want me to key into your computer?"

He grinned. I wasn't sure I'd ever seen Brassard grin before. He had a gap between his two front teeth that instantly took a few years off him. He shook his head. "Not my computer. A job opening just came up at the Port and you're filling it."

Now I was really confused. This was some odd barter deal—taking a data entry gig in exchange for Sister Jane seeing Johnny. Camille had said I'd have to give Brassard something but I never expected this.

Unless...unless this was no barter deal. This was Brassard pushing me into a career change.

"What's the deal here, Detective?" I said. "This job supposed to be permanent?"

"Only if you do it wrong."


"**WHAT DO YOU** mean I can't do it?" I said.

I was back at the office after swinging by Tim Horton's to get Camille. Both of us were sitting on the seat under her bay window, swigging back café grandes she'd made when we came in. Camille didn't have anything at Tim Horton's, but her extended stay there had kindled her coffee itch. Not to mention her need for comfort food. She'd been blocked by a mob of caffeinated teenagers when she spotted my unexpected passengers hijacking my car, and she didn't take kindly to being temporarily ditched. Brassard or no Brassard.

Laurent was standing across from us, his jacket open over a button shirt and fitted jeans. His hair free and thick, his scruff dark and thin, in the early stage of its life cycle.

"*Non,*" he said. "Forget it. Not going to happen."

I slid off the seat and stood a foot away from him. "You don't think I can pull it off, do you? You think I'm going to screw it up."

The "it" being what I learned later was Brassard's idea to have me go to work for Johnny's employer at the warehouse. Incognito. I wasn't entirely clear on the full operation Brassard had going or why, but apparently he needed a mole on the inside and thought

I'd fit the bill. I was hoping his picking me as the mole had more to it than my petite size.

I was also hoping spending time at the Old Port might give me more intel on Chloé. I'd had to put my plans to learn more about her and Thomas Duncan on hold for the morning to focus on Jane's need to see Johnny and the Brassard situation. Now that both were on firmer ground, I was eager to get back to the bigger issue of finding Johnny's would-be killer. Although the odds still tipped in favor of the Penguin and his goons, Chloé and Duncan's recent swag stand-off had me wondering things I probably shouldn't be wondering.

"*C'est trop dangereux*," Laurent said. "It's work for the police."

"Nuh uh," I said. "That's not it. You guys do work for the police all the time. Heck you *were* the police. This is about you thinking I can't handle myself. This is like you putting an alarm in my house. You think I'm just sitting prey."

"*Ben*, wasn't it you who called me to learn how to use the alarm?"

"Well, yeah. I didn't say I didn't appreciate it. I just meant you think I can't do without it. You think I need constant protection from the big bad world. Well, I've got news for you. I've been taking care of myself for a long time and I can take care of whatever it is Brassard wants me to do, too. How hard can it be to be a mole? It's just digging for dirt, right? I can do that."

I had no idea why I was so gung-ho about being Brassard's mole. I didn't even like Brassard. I think it was Camille's café grande talking. She made kick-ass café grande.

"You don't have enough training for something like this."

He had me there. I really didn't have much formal training yet. Mostly I relied on my wits and know-how I'd gleaned as a social worker. I'd only started my PI apprenticeship training recently and had merely a temporaty license that allowed me to train under supervision. Strict supervision. PI training was serious here. No quickie weekend workshop in the back of a strip mall. Regulations were rigid, and I'd been waiting for the Canadian bit of my dual citizenship to kick in before furthering my skills with formal classes. My mother having been Canadian helped earn my claim, but I'd barely had my citizenship a month and the next training session didn't start up for a while. When it did I'd be first in line. After that, I could apply for a permanent license. Until then I was stuck at this lowly status in kind of a nebulous PI land.

"Maybe that's why Brassard thinks I'll be a good mole," I said. "Maybe he thinks I can pass for an office worker more easily because I *don't* have some kind of slick training." Okay, this was a stretch, but it could be true. My years as a social worker did involve some paperwork and office time. Maybe I still gave off that admin vibe.

Camille and Laurent looked at each other then back at me. Not buying it. Arielle walked by the doorway, her head giving a small shake as she glanced my way and walked on.

Oh boy. I was zero for three. I didn't even know Arielle had been listening, but my powers of persuasion were seriously slipping if even *she* didn't buy into my spiel. Buying things was Arielle's favorite hobby.

"Okay," I said. "Look, who cares why Brassard asked me? It's win-win. We get to keep working the case and he doesn't raise a stink about me or the hunk-a-junk-fake-cake incident."

Camille and Laurent looked at each other again. Laurent's face rigid, Camille's less so, a smile forming.

"*Alors,*" she said. "Maybe it could work. *Si* Brassard wants Lora, we give him Lora."

Laurent's face went darker and Camille held up a hand.

"*Écoute-moi,*" she went on to say. "It's Brassard always talking about Lora's supervision. So if he wants Lora on his case, he gets me also. I'll make sure she doesn't get into trouble. *En plus*, once he uses her on *his* case, he can't complain anymore *du tout du tout* about her work with us. She could take a year to do *les courses* and he couldn't complain."

Laurent's eyes travelled over to me.

"But I won't," I assured him. "I promise. It won't take me a year to do my courses. Maybe this will even speed things up. Like getting extra credit for field work. Helping the police has to look good on my record, right?"

He didn't look convinced.

"Look, if this is about safety, don't worry. Camille has been showing me some self-defense moves." Not a lie. She had been showing me. The fact that I couldn't emulate all of them was neither here nor there.

"Camille doesn't do self-defense," Laurent said. "Camille annihilates. Real self-defense means to disable an attacker and run."

"Right," I agreed. "I can do that."

Laurent said nothing but this time I said nothing back, determined to wait him out. If Camille was coming around, that had to weigh in my favor, right?

Arielle appeared back in the doorway, and we all turned our attention to her. Maybe I'd get lucky and she'd weigh in on my side, too.

"*J'm'excuse là*," she said. "There's someone here to see Lora."

Her body got bumped from view and Tina took her place, belly hanging low and wide, hand on her hip, elbow bent.

"There you are," Tina said huffing forward. "Where've you been? I waited an hour at the salon." She hefted her purse onto Camille's desk and dropped herself into Camille's chair. "Have you got a stool? If I don't get my feet up soon, they'll swell to the size of whales."

Tina's usual over-dowsing of perfume mixed with hair products and nail polish from the salon had her smelling like someone who should be standing under a red light somewhere.

Camille was up and across the room, her eyes slits, her trajectory making me think I had about thirty seconds to get Tina out of her chair before Camille found Tina a new place to sit. On the other side of the bay window. Via the direct route, through the glass.

I stepped over to Tina and offered her my arm. "Here. I've got just the place you'll be more comfortable."

She let me ease her up and walk her out to the hall where I steered her towards the kitchen and over to the café table where I deposited her in a chair. I pulled another chair out and hoisted her feet up.

From her place at reception, Arielle caught my eye and smiled. Camille and Laurent were conspicuously out of sight.

"What's that smell?" Tina asked. "Is that coffee? God that smells good." She rubbed her belly. "Maybe I could have just one cup. The doctor said I shouldn't have any, but what does he know? Does he have to cart around two babies all day? No he doesn't. It's exhausting. I could use some coffee. Be a sweetie, Lora, and grab some for me? One cup couldn't really hurt, could it?"

I didn't know a whole lot about coffee during pregnancy except what I'd heard through the grapevine, and I knew it was frowned upon. Especially in high-risk pregnancies, which multiple births often fell into even for the healthiest of moms-to-be. I was not about to add to the delinquency of this mom-to-be by feeding her coffee fix. If normal coffee wasn't good for the babies, I had no idea what damage Camille's coffee might do. What if it messed with their hormones and Tina's kids were born with hair on their chests. Tiny hairy-chest baby boys. Egad. Most men grew enough hair on their chests during their adulthood. I couldn't imagine what would happen if they got a head start in infancy. Or what if the boys were born with caffeine addictions or something. I'd never hear the end of it.

"What about some nice herbal tea instead?" I said to Tina.

"Herbal tea? Yuck." Tina sat back then forward again. "I'll stick with the coffee." She moved to lean back again and let out what sounded like a sharp growl. "Dammit, I mean darn it, Lora. I don't know what you were thinking with this chair. It's awful. It's hard and the back is digging into me." She wobbled side to side, trying to get her legs down from the adjoining chair. "I can't sit here to plan the shower. I'll be too sore to move before we even decide on the orchestra."

Orchestra? Now there was an orchestra?

With the detour my day had taken, I'd nearly forgotten about Tina's baby shower. Or maybe I'd subconsciously blotted it out of my mind. Or maybe consciously.

"How'd it go booking the Chalet? Did you get a good price?" Tina said.

I rooted through the fridge and pulled out a yoghourt I found in the back. I checked the date and plunked the yoghourt in front of Tina along with a spoon, following it up with a glass of water. I figured maybe if I kept Tina's mouth busy, she would stop peppering me with questions. It wasn't the best plan, but since Tina was yanking the top off the yoghourt I might score a few minutes reprieve.

Arielle wandered in and joined me where I'd retreated over by the sink. She made a slow production of rinsing her coffee mug and slipping it into the mini-dishwasher, throwing me sidelong glances. Well not me exactly, more beside me, like she was looking at some invisible person squeezed between us.

"*Alors*," she said. "No ring?"

"Excuse me?" I said.

She pointed at my left hand. "No ring. You're booking an

orchestra and the Chalet. You're getting married, no?"

Yikes. Clearly Arielle's eavesdropping missed a few points.

A sharp noise came from somewhere beyond the kitchen, a drawer slamming shut maybe. "Married?" I said to Arielle. "Nope. Just helping Tina plan a baby shower. Adam and I are perfectly happy living in sin…oh my gosh, Adam!" I grabbed Arielle's wrist and looked at her gold, bangle watch. "It's after one. I'm late for lunch. Adam's gonna kill me." I dashed to Camille's office. "My purse, my purse. Where's my purse?"

Camille looked up from her laptop and backed her chair away from her desk. She pointed at the window seat. *"C'est là."*

I grabbed my bag and stuffed my arm in, rooting around for my phone. "My phone, my phone," I said. "Where's my phone?"

*"Your purse, your phone. Heille-là, qu'est-ce que tu as toi?"*

A guitar strum rang out. My ringtone for Adam. He was calling, probably checking on me. "Shush," I said. "That's it. That's my phone." My eyes travelled the room. The phone couldn't be far. That strum was loud and clear. I pushed aside the cushions in the window seat, looking below each.

*"Allô?"* I heard and turned to see Laurent stroll into Camille's office, my phone at his ear. *"C'est ton Anglophone,"* he said, handing me the phone.

"I guess I don't have to ask why you're late," Adam said when I greeted him.

I shot Laurent a glare and he shot me a grin back.

"Actually," I said to Adam, my feet carrying me out to the kitchen as I spoke. "I'm here with Tina." I held the phone out for Tina to shout a "hello" which she did, gleefully and loud, just like I knew she would. "We got caught up planning her baby shower and lost track of time."

"Let me guess," Adam said. "Laurent's pitching in, too."

I nearly laughed at the idea of Laurent talking onesies and baby rattles with Tina.

"Look," I said. "I can still make it. I can just drop Tina off and—"

"Forget it. By the time you get here I'll be due at a meeting." Adam let out a breath so heavy I could almost feel it in my ear. "Let's try dinner. Same place. Around seven."

I knew I should say yes. A gal had to eat, right? But I had all that computer stuff to learn for my mole gig. If I still had my mole gig, that is. I hesitated before answering.

"Let me guess again," Adam said. "You're working tonight. You and Camille playing Catwoman again?"

Hmm. Adam and I had gone rounds over my late-night excursion to Chloé's, but I didn't remember telling him what I was doing exactly. "Excuse me?"

"I saw your black get-up in the hamper, Lora. The one you wear for your night prowls with Camille. I figure that's where you were last night."

Oh boy. Just who was the detective here? On the bright side, at least Adam wouldn't think I had been lying about being with Laurent. Not that he'd admit being wrong about it. Just like I wasn't going to either confirm or deny his supposition.

Tina waved her hand at me like she was trying to snap her fingers but couldn't make them click. "Let me talk to him," she said. "Let me talk to Adam a minute."

I sighed and passed her the phone.

"Your Anglophone is not happy?"

I turned to Laurent coming up behind me. "Of course he's not happy," I said. "What were you thinking answering my phone?"

He shrugged. "It rang. I answered it. That's what you do with a phone, no?"

I narrowed my eyes and moved to reception out of Tina's earshot. "What were you doing with my phone anyway? The last I saw it, it was in my purse."

"*Ben oui.* That's where I got it. Nice driver's license picture by the way."

I blinked and pinched my lips closed. He had gone through my purse. My sanctuary! *You will not blast your boss, you will not blast your boss,* I reminded myself over and over then felt myself blush. What else had he seen in my purse? Did I leave that junky half-eaten candy bar in there? And what about my phone? What was the last thing I looked at on my browser?

"...you might want to hide it when you're playing mole for Brassard," Laurent was saying when I tuned him back in.

No idea what "it" he was talking about, but the mole bit got my attention. Big time. "What? Did you just say you changed your mind about me being the mole?"

He nodded.

I smiled. "Really?"

"With some rules."

My smile shrank. Uh oh. Rules. As a social worker I knew a thing or two about following regulations, but Laurent's rules weren't posted in some handbook somewhere. His rules were part procedure, part Caron code, and when it came to me, part, I suspected, he threw in for his amusement. I should have known there'd be a catch.

"You mean like the undercover ones?" I asked him. "Because I already learned them on the identity theft case."

"Those and a few more."

"Okay. But I hope it's not a lot. I've gotta be ready by tomorrow, and I still have to learn Excel and whatever other office software Brassard wants me to know. What kinds of rules are we talking?"

He moved in close and dipped his mouth to my ear. "The kind to keep your *petite* mole feet from getting enshrined in cement."

## 17

"*T*HAT'S BLACK," I said. "It's nice, but I was going to go with blue. See, I've got this navy skirt." I smoothed the pencil skirt I was wearing and pointed to a pair of shoes, both by the bed, one shoe resting on its side. "And those navy pumps. I should stick with a blue purse, don't ya think?"

Camille shook her head and held the black purse out to me. "*Non, non.* You take this one. *C'est unique,* special for you."

I looked at the purse again and down at the blouse I was wearing. White with tiny lace-trim cuffs and no collar. It would go okay with the purse, but the purse had a harder edge with its blocky size and no-frills strap. And then there was the black vs. navy issue.

I glanced at my reflection in the mirror on the closet door in my bedroom where Camille was helping me get ready for my date with Brassard's "chauffeur" who was due at any minute. It was early morning and dawning sun beamed in through the window and added a shine to "mirror me," accentuating the blue of the skirt.

"Look inside." Camille passed me the purse and turned to look at her own reflection in the mirror, moving closer to it and swiping a hand under her eye. Probably she thought she was fixing her eyeliner, but Camille's eye makeup was flawless. Like the rest of her. Tall and fit, and at the moment dressed in designer, dark pants and a creamy shirt probably tailor made. Even her short blonde hair was tousled to a chic disarray. And it was barely after seven in the morning.

Of course, she hadn't been up half the night grilling herself on Laurent's mole rules or Arielle's office software tutorial like I had. All of which threatened to spill out of my crack-of-dawn sieve of a brain. I was not a morning person. Which is maybe why the purse Camille handed me made my arm drop a few inches from the added weight. I was no workout queen, but I didn't think I was in that bad shape.

"What's in this thing?" I asked Camille.

She turned back to me and smiled. "Accoutrements for the little undercover mole."

Uh oh. I was nearly afraid to look. The last time Camille outfitted me with undercover accoutrements, they consisted of bustiers and flimsy underwear.

I opened the purse and cautiously peeked inside. Tiny tin of hair spray, key ring, wallet, hairbrush, tampons, blush case, lipstick, toothpaste, travel toothbrush. I looked up at Camille. "Toothbrush? What kind of mole emergency needs a toothbrush? Is that a crack about mole teeth?"

Camille took the bag from me and dumped the contents out on my bed. She held up the toothbrush, compact and folded in on itself for easy travel. She unfolded it and gave it to me. "*Regarde ça.*"

I inspected it closer, turning it this way and that, stopping when a slight tug split the toothbrush in half. Inside the handle end was a hollow bit with metal interior. I cocked my head at Camille. "USB drive?"

She nodded and I went on to examine the rest of the accoutrements. Key ring turned out to be an alarm and flashlight, hair spray spewed something Camille wouldn't let me test, hairbrush handle held various tools, makeup blush was an impression kit, tampon tubes housed matches. I got stumped at the lipstick. "And this?"

Camille shrugged. "Lipstick. It's important to look good."

Right. This harkened back to the undercover tools speech I got about flirting when I was on the identity theft case.

And it wasn't the only holdout from that case. I held the wallet open to Camille, fake driver's license showing, and I frowned.

"I know. It's not the best picture. But it's not bad, no?"

I hadn't even noticed the photo and squinted at it. A headshot of me kitted out in one of Camille's disguise wigs. Long black hair, bangs like a flapper. My eyes a shade too bright, my smile a shade too crooked. "When did you take that?"

She rolled her eyes upward. "I think the night we tried the ice cream floats *avec du champagne*. Remember, to celebrate your citizenship papers coming."

I did remember. That was a good night. Photographic evidence notwithstanding. I tapped the written portion on the license. "Well, the picture quality is not the problem." And it wasn't. The license was fake, but it was a good fake. It was also one I'd seen before, updated photo excluded. It belonged to my alter ego, aka Bunny Bosworth, my previous undercover alias.

"Nuh uh," I said. "I'm not getting stuck playing Bunny again. She had big hair and big makeup and little skirts. Everyone thought she was loosey goosey."

"*Heille!* Watch what you say about my brother's fiancée, eh."

"*Fake* fiancée," I corrected her, referring to mine and Laurent's faux engagement during the identity theft case. "There has to be another undercover name I can use. How about Mary Smith? Nice, nondescript. No one would think Mary Smith is loosey-goosey."

Camille's eyes darted to the alarm clock by the bed. "Mary Smith. Pffft. You are not a Mary Smith. Anyway there was no time to make anybody new." She held the bag up to me again, this time the flap open. "*Et regarde ça.*" She slid her hand along the inner flap edge and her fingers disappeared from view. "In here, you can put anything you want to hide."

"You mean like my real license in case I get pulled over for speeding."

Camille laughed. We both knew I'd never be pulled over for speeding. Going too slow maybe.

We spent the last few minutes I had before Brassard's chauffeur showed up plumping up my makeup closer to Bunny standards and bundling my own hair under the black wig Camille had also brought, the cap off to my mole accoutrements. Thank goodness Adam had had the good sense to clear out early. He would not be happy to hear about Bunny's return or about my new gig as Brassard's mole, which I prudently neglected to mention.

"Wait," I said to Camille as we were heading out. "Doesn't Brassard suspect Johnny and the Penguin are connected? Doesn't he know the Penguin knows me? If whatever connected Johnny and the Penguin came about because of Johnny's job at the warehouse, won't the same thing happen to me? I mean, the wig's not much of a disguise. If the Penguin finds me poking around the same place that got Johnny into trouble, won't he be miffed?"

Camille nodded. "*Probablement* Brassard is counting on it. *C'est probablement ça* that makes *you* his perfect mole."

·  ·  ·

**MOLE? MOLE? I** was no mole. Sitting duck was more like it.

Here I was thinking Brassard wasn't such a bad guy after all. That he was making me his mole because he saw something in me. Some PI potential, some glimmer of competence. But all he really wanted was to throw me into the Penguin's fish net.

"*Mais voyons*, Lora. *Dépêche-toi*. We're late." Camille stood to the side of the open car door, tapping her foot.

I clambered out of the car and onto the street around the bend from *Dépot Deschênes*, the warehouse where Johnny worked. Like the one Chloé worked in a few buildings down, *Mise en Port*, this warehouse was big and wide. Only while Chloé's was more modern, *Dépot Deschênes* seemed to be a holdover from earlier times and was made of brick and mortar, both sullied around the base near the ground from decades of damp. From my spot on the street, I could make out a newer service entrance with the feel of a giant garage door, and a few yards away, a glass side door with sleek, metal surround. People went in through the door. Men dressed in clean shirts and jeans, women dressed in casual office wear and ballet flats or loafers.

I looked down at the stiletto Bunny boots Camille insisted I put on before we left my house. "I need to change. I'll stick out like a high-heeled hack in these, not a seasoned secretary. Moles are supposed to blend in not stand out." I moved to get back in the car and felt Camille tap me on the shoulder.

"Second thoughts?" she said.

Ugh. She knew me so well. Second and third and fourth thoughts. Being a mole for the police seemed exciting, adventurous, a little bad in a good way. Being a sitting duck not so much. Sitting ducks did nothing but, well, sit. And sitting didn't seem like it was going to get me any closer to helping Sister Jane and Johnny. Sitting seemed like just a layover stop on the way to a permanent vacation on the Penguin's ice float. Not exactly the kind of waterway destination conducive to duck health.

Camille followed me back into the car and pulled off her own boots. Doc Martens, black, slim trim along the top. She nodded at me. "*Allons-y*. Take off your boots. We'll switch if it makes you feel better."

Depending on the shoe, Camille and I were about a size apart, me one size down. Taking her boots wouldn't be so bad for me, just a little big. But with the cut of the Bunny boots, Camille would have to cram her foot in to make them fit. Her toes would pinch and her feet would cramp.

"Forget it," I said. "I'm being silly. Nobody will care about my boots. I'm just a bit nervous."

Camille refastened her Doc Martens and smiled. "*T'inquiète pas*. I have total confidence in you."

I took in her words and remembered the other reason I'd agreed to be the mole. To help get Brassard off C&C's back. I owed that much to Camille and Laurent. They had taken little-old-French-challenged me in when no other employer would and were now giving me the chance at a whole new career. I couldn't let a little duck sitting and a case of nerves mess with that. Plus, this was still kinda my own first case. I didn't want to blow that.

I shot Camille my best pseudo-confident smile, and she passed me the soy latte I'd left in the cup holder. The latte had sat there, untouched, since we'd stopped for coffee on the way to the warehouse. I'd been afraid to drink any in the moving car in case I spilled some on my mole clothes. Now I accepted the cup from her and gulped down a mouthful of latte. Confidence fuel. Montreal moxie in a cup.

I hoisted the accoutrement-packed bag on my shoulder, firmed my grip on the coffee cup, and got out of the car again. Ready to be

Brassard's mole or sitting duck or whatever other animal I had to be to get the job done.

**MY CUBICLE WAS** small and smelled of bologna. The walls consisted of four dividers, well three and a half, almost five feet tall, scuffed and stained with mystery splotches in patterns I told myself had nothing to do with the previous occupant's bodily fluids. Given the funky smell, convincing myself was taking some doing.

The guy I was replacing, Giovanni, had apparently quit suddenly to take another job working the bar at a strip club. Which did nothing to allay my fears about the bodily fluids thing.

Giovanni had left the cubicle bare. The L-shaped desk's drawers empty of all but office supplies, and the computer and monitor free of any stickers or otherwise personal touches. The files on the computer were minimal, too. A bunch of folders and no personal emails. Not even any left in the trash file, which was the first place I checked, partly to do mole snooping and partly because it was the only file name I recognized easily since most of the screen icons had been set up in French.

I expanded the Excel file I'd created and cleverly labeled File 1. It had exactly twenty rows of boxes filled in with information I'd pulled from various email confirmations and receipts I'd been told to reconcile by my new supervisor, Huguette. I could see Huguette if I craned my neck out the side of my cubicle. She sat in an actual office, narrow and square, one of many that lined the perimeter wall. Each office had a large window with venetian blinds, a melamine desk, and varied other furniture that differed by office occupant.

When I'd first arrived, ostensibly an experienced clerical assistant sent by an employment agency, I'd been shown to

Huguette's office where I sat across from her in a stiff chair for barely a minute before she'd shown me to my cubicle and got me started reconciling numbers. I'd been in her office long enough to note that she'd positioned her desk to look straight out her open door to the floor of cubicles she supervised. I'd also noted framed photographs on her desk of her and another woman in cozy familial settings. Huguette with piercing blue eyes, short bronzy hair, and the complexion of a pack-a-day smoker in her late thirties. The other woman of similar age with long, straight blonde hair, and the wardrobe of a charge-card-a-day shopping habit.

By the door sat a coat rack with two umbrellas looped on one arm and three jackets covering the remainder spokes, a yoga mat tucked into the rack's base. On the way to my cubicle, Huguette had offered me a stick of gum, and I'd noticed a patch on her arm, making me think the pack-a-day habit was on its way out.

Her accent was thick and her patience long when she'd shown me around and got me started on the computer. She gave me precise and focused direction, like someone who had calmly mothered many small children. If she was thrown at all by my lack of French understanding or vocabulary, she hid it well. And as I ventured surreptitious glances her way while I worked, her gaze from the perch of her desk was more keeper-of-the-herd than prison guard.

A buzzing to my right drew my attention from Huguette to the phone on my desk. A light blinked at the phone's base, it buzzed again, and I picked it up, slowly, minimal fingers touching the receiver sides and holding it just close enough to my ear to hear the caller speak.

"Giovanni?" the voice said followed by a slew of words that sounded part French and part Italian.

"Excuse me," I said when the words cut out. "Giovanni is no longer available. May I help you?"

*"Quoi? C'est qui?"*

*"Sorry, um, désolée. Je ne parle pas beaucoup de Français. Do you speak English?"*

The caller said something more I didn't understand and hung up.

Almost immediately another buzz sounded. This one from the pocket of the blazer I'd snatched on the way out of the house. The buzz was low, the hum of the vibration setting on my cell phone. I peered around at Huguette, still fixed in her chair, tapping away at her computer, and I eased my hand into the jacket pocket and removed my phone.

"What are you doing?" This voice I recognized. Camille.

"Working on spreadsheets," I whispered into the phone.

"You're supposed to be here."

I checked the time on my phone. Ten thirty-five. Oops. She was right. I was late. I was supposed to meet her in the break room at ten-thirty. "Be right there."

I smiled at Huguette as I passed her office on the way out. She smiled back and dropped her eyes to her computer screen, her fingers typing away. For a minute, I imagined her screen filled with spreadsheets of employees' comings and goings. Mine showing how I'd arrived ten minutes late and how I was leaving for break when I should be making up my lost time. And on my first day, too. No gold star emoji for me.

When I got to Camille she was standing by a bank of vending machines, two young women nervously loitering nearby. Somehow, in her plan to "supervise" me, Camille had passed herself off as a surprise inspector, floating through different departments, ensuring all government and legal regulations were being followed. Probably her stint would be very short lived if the powers that be discovered her credentials were as phoney as whatever ID she'd used to gain herself entry.

Of course, the two nervous women wouldn't know that, and I was guessing they had the misfortune to be in a department Camille had surveyed. Probably the women followed every regulation to a T, but one raised eyebrow from Camille had them raking their memories for minor infractions or worried they'd been caught on security camera chatting up one of the hunky guys who worked the docks.

I sidled over to a machine near Camille and spoke quietly, doing my best impression of a ventriloquist. "Maybe we should talk somewhere else," I said.

Camille took a step towards me, and I moved away and closer to the vending machine, tilting my head like I was weighing my choices before making a selection.

She shot me two furrowed brows and nodded towards a door in the back, a big *Sortie* sign lit up in red above. She went to the door and left. Not wanting to join her too fast, I chose a bag of chips from one machine and moved on to get an iced tea from another. I heard the machine gobble my money and then nothing.

A man's arm crossed in front of me and pressed the iced tea button again, the machine chugged, and my can of tea rolled out at the bottom.

I turned to the man and smiled. "Thanks."

"*De rien,*" he said, heavy accent, not French but similar lyrical quality. Spanish maybe. "It sticks sometimes." His English was good, slightly better than his French and his lips widened as he spoke, augmenting their ruby fullness set against his tan complexion. He extended his hand. "Mario."

I let his hand grasp mine, his grip firm, his skin taut and coarse. One of the hunky dock workers maybe.

"Lo...," I started to say then stopped myself and grimaced, remembering my ID resurrecting Bunny and presented myself as her instead. Sheesh. A mole named Bunny. Ugh.

I shook my head to clear the grimace and tipped my lips into a smile for Mario. "I'm new," I said. "Just started today."

Mario nodded, retrieved my tea from the chute, and held the can out to me on his outstretched palm. He leaned in towards me and spoke low. "I warn you, it's not so good."

A chill flitted across the back of my neck. Probably auto response to the cold hitting my skin from the drink I took from him. "Excuse me?"

"The tea," he said and scrunched his nose. "It's no good. Down the street there is a café. Very excellent. At lunch I take you for coffee, tea, whatever you want." His smile had come back, full lips and all. And his eyelids shifted to half-mast.

I replayed his words. More statement than invitation. Hmm. Maybe my body chills were trying to tell me something. Possibly his lack of invitation was more of a lost-in-translation thing, but letch-in-action wasn't completely out of the running. Okay maybe letch wasn't exactly fair. Probably Mario fancied himself more of a Romeo. Probably the half-mast eye thing was an attempt at allure.

Whether letch or Romeo, my instinct was to accept his offer. Part of the whole take-advantage-of-every-opportunity thing I'd learned on my first undercover case. Going to coffee with Mario could give me a chance to pump him for info about Johnny. But I figured I should clear it with Camille first to adhere to the whole "supervisor–trainee" thing. So far, Brassard had given me little direction on my mole role for him, but since the whole mole vs. sitting duck had come up, Camille and I had devised our own mole roles. Part of mine was to use my status as newbie employee to ask my fellow employees questions about my new employer, the work, the people. Anything I could get away with asking stopping just short of "inquiring minds want to know" territory that might sully my motives with smatterings of suspicion.

Camille's face appeared on the outer side of the tiny square window in the exit door she'd taken, the look she was giving me the one that usually went along with her tapping foot.

I asked Mario for his extension number, telling him I needed to check my schedule and would get back to him, and I headed off to meet Camille. On the way, my mobile buzzed. Incoming text. From Tina. Oy. For a fleeting second, I wished Laurent hadn't set up my new phone with my old phone number. Tina wanted her shower date pushed up. She'd found a dress she wanted to wear and was worried it wouldn't fit for long.

I typed back that I was working and would get back to her later, too.

"What took you so long?" Camille said when I reached her.

I pulled my blazer fronts together. The *"Sortie"* sign had led directly outside around the back, where it wasn't spitting spring rain but wasn't real spring temperatures, either. "Sorry," I said. "Vending machine glitch. Then I met this guy. He wants to take me to lunch. I'm thinking I should go and see if he knows anything about Johnny or his run-in with the forklift."

Camille nodded. *"Oui, oui.* I saw you talking. Good call. That's Mario. He's from Brazil. Been in Montréal one year, working here for six months. In the warehouse, same as Johnny."

Right. Of course Camille would have the rundown on him already. Camille probably had background on the guys in tattered coats and grungy beards who I could see hanging out by the pier watching the boats unload. Made me wonder why I should even bother meeting with Mario. Camille probably already knew his shirt size and the last stamp in his passport.

*"Mais alors, qu'est-ce qui s'passe avec les dossiers?"* Camille added, asking me about files—the other part of my mole role. The one where I was supposed to fill my toothbrush drive with files. Files I was supposed to find on the computer I'd inherited from Giovanni. We were looking for a match in schedule to the files on

the doll flash drive. Something that would corroborate dates and details. Maybe show some of the Penguin's goods coming straight into storage. Or better yet, something that might tell us why Johnny thought the doll files were worth hiding in my back pocket and why they may have earned him time in the hospital.

"The computer was clean," I told Camille. "I'm gonna need more time."

"Your supervisor. Try her files."

"Huguette? Huguette is like a sentinel. I've only been watching her for a few hours, but I don't think she leaves her lookout. And if she does, probably she closes out her computer or locks her office. Or both."

I could practically see wheels turning behind Camille's eyes. Like a cartoon character with irises like Ferris wheels. "Not to worry. I'll get her out. So fast she won't bother with *la securité*. *Allez*. I'll give you time to get back to your desk then I'll clear her out of your way."

Before I could move, my phone buzzed again. Another text from Tina. She'd found some new doodad she wanted for the babies and wanted to know if she did a gift registry in two stores if it would ruin her chances of scoring the new must-have, which apparently had a price tag verging on four digits. On sale.

I wrote back telling her I was sure it would be fine. Not that I was sure. The closest I'd come to planning any gift registry was the sham one for my faux wedding to Laurent the first time I'd played Bunny. I knew next to nothing about gift registry etiquette. But I did know a little something about placating Tina, so I was standing by my answer.

I waited a sec to see if she'd text right back. No new words magically appeared. A relief because I was getting antsy having my real phone out and happy to stow it away. I would have been even happier to shut it down, but Laurent made me promise to keep it on vibrate. One of his mole rules. Something about being sure I was reachable in a mole emergency. Sounded practical and professional. At least that's what I was telling myself. It was better than thinking he had other reasons for wanting me tethered to a vibrating phone. Or that he worried I'd dig a mole hole too big for myself and fall in, never to be heard from again.

## 18

*a* **RINGING PHONE** cut out as I reached my cubicle. A millisecond later, Huguette ran out of her office, purse dangling by its strap in her right hand, left hand balled, giant rings squeezed together on two fingers like a mini set of brass knuckles.

Hmm. I was guessing the call was Camille's handiwork. And I was kinda feeling bad for Huguette. And for some guy's snack. She'd run by so fast, she'd knocked into the guy, he'd dropped a white paper bag, and a big sploosh followed when Huguette trampled the bag on her way out.

The man scrambled for the bag and hugged it to his chest, drips of something red and wet soaking the bag and dribbling onto his shirt. Ketchup. No, something with a sweeter scent. Jelly maybe. Like from a doughnut. That was just sad. A jelly-filled doughnut minus the jam. Flattened to a crêpe. And with Huguette's footprint stamped on top. Poor guy. He avoided my eyes as he scurried by, face flushed, upper lip dribbling sweat down to his goatee, short legs moving like scissors. Probably embarrassed by the incident and the giant stain darkening his blue shirt to purple.

More people scampered out from cubicles near me. All trailing after Huguette and Goatee Guy. Wow. When Camille cleared a room, she really cleared a room.

I waited behind, watching and listening until the sound of footsteps faded, doing my best to see over the cubicle dividers to see if anyone had missed the exodus. Nobody I could see. And no heads popped into the hall. No chairs squeaked. No feet padded out to the corridor. Probably it was as good a time as any for me to sneak into Huguette's office.

I snatched some papers from my desk, hugged them to my chest, and zipped off, peering around for onlookers, just in case. I held the papers to me like a shield, at the ready should anyone appear and question my walkabout, prepared to protect myself by shoving the papers at them and fabricating some newbie query about shipment codes or product logs.

At Huguette's desk, her screen sat lit up then started to dim. Egad. Dim was not good. Dim harkened the coming of sleep mode. Huguette's computer was so not going to wake from sleep mode with a kiss. Someone like Huguette probably had a complicated password to wake her computer from slumber. A password to keep snoopers like me from ever entering her hallowed files.

I ditched the papers and jabbed my finger on her spacebar key, holding my breath when the screen went black a second before flaring bright again. Rolling her chair over, I sat and quickly scanned file names. I found two that looked promising and copied them onto my toothbrush drive. Since the drive had plenty more storage, I grabbed some other files, too, ones with French names and info I couldn't place but with corresponding file dates.

The rumble of approaching voices hit my ears while the last file was downloading, and my fingers twitched waiting to eject and disconnect my drive before the voices got closer.

"Bunny?"

I looked up to see Huguette in the doorway.

Her eyes did a quick sweep of her office, darkened, and landed back on me. "You got back fast," she said.

After I disconnected, I'd had just enough time to pick up my shield of papers which I held up to her. "I had a, um, a question." I went to tap the papers for emphasis and realized my hand still held the USB stick aka toothbrush.

A small smile came to Huguette's lips and a hasty explanation jumped to mine.

"Oops," I said. "Sorry about that. I was just washing up after my coffee break." I pointed to my teeth. "When I got back everyone was gone. Did I miss something?"

She ventured forward and scooted behind her desk while I scooted around to the front, like we were playing a game of musical chairs sans song.

"You missed nothing. Some idiot said the big boss was here and called an emergency meeting." She dabbed at the patch on her arm and gave her head a dismissive shake. "What was your question?"

She didn't have to tell me who the idiot was and probably it was better for Huguette's health if I didn't pass along her idiot comment to Camille. I didn't want to see that patch on Huguette's arm upgraded to a cast.

I got some needless clarifications about figures and strode off to my desk. Back in my cubicle, I replied to Mario agreeing to meet him at lunch, and I turned my attention to inputting data. Now and again, I checked on Huguette who didn't seem to budge from her sentinel post. And few of my fellow cubicle dwellers roamed the makeshift halls around me. Possibly they were put off by the bologna scent my predecessor left behind. Or possibly they were dedicated workers. Or napping from boredom.

Whichever it was, I hoped some of my mole digging paid off. I wasn't cut out for spending my days alone crunching numbers in a bologna box. Probably Brassard was joking when he'd said this would be my permanent job if I got my mole gig wrong. But I didn't want to screw up and find out.

## "IT'S GOOD, YES?"

I peered over my bowl of fries to Mario, his head bent over a plate of seafood. Something shiny that slid around on his plate as if it was playing a game of Keep Away with his fork.

"Yes," I said in answer to his question. "It's very good." This was no lie. I had a poutine in front of me, vegetarian gravy, heavy on the cheese. Which was totally healthy because I was sopping up any fat overload with lettuce from my small garden salad on the side.

Mario raised his head and shifted his eyes to half mast like he had in the break room. "You have nice name. Bunny. Soft and cute, like you."

I smiled. Corny line maybe, but I could work with corny. My first go-around as Bunny, I'd learned flirting for fodder was not my best skill. I had no opening moves. So really mister corny was doing me a favor by getting things rolling.

I mirrored his eye stance then slowly opened my eyes wider, keeping my head somewhat bowed, flashing him doe eyes. What I didn't know about flirting, I made up for with oodles of psych courses that had taught me plenty about relating to my fellow man. "Thanks," I said. "I like your name, too. And your accent. It's not from around here, is it?"

He sat back and grinned at me. "Brazil."

By the beaming look on his face I wondered briefly if he was about to pound his chest. Not in an ape-like way. More like Céline Dion when she sang. With passion. I felt simultaneously happy for him that he loved his country so much and sad for him that he was so far from home.

"I hear Brazil is beautiful," I said. "What do you think of Canada so far?"

He set down his fork and reached for my hand. "Canada also is beautiful, especially its lovely ladies."

I didn't bother to correct him about lumping me in with Canadians. He had no way of knowing I hailed from New York. Plus, the point of this banter wasn't to get to know each other. The banter was to loosen him up so he'd talk about Johnny.

I tried to relax my hand below his, quelling my first instinct to pull away. "That's so sweet. And it was sweet of you to help me with the vending machine at work and fill me in on its quirks. I bet there's a lot you could tell me about how things work around there."

"Sure," he said. "Anything you want to know, just ask Mario."

Eek. Another corny line. Something earnest in his delivery, though. Something that was definitely more Romeo than letch. Albeit a corny Romeo.

I leaned forward, my voice low. "To tell you the truth, I'm a little lost. I've got all these shipment details to record, and I don't have a clue how the warehouse works."

He moved his head in so it was mere inches from mine. "You're in luck. That's my department. I know everything." He went back to eating and proceeded to give me a rudimentary rundown of the logistics of the place. Nuts and bolts kind of stuff. Nothing that seemed of much use to me.

"Sounds fascinating." I injected some mock awe with an edge of serious into my voice, hoping to push the chatter into more helpful territory. "And dangerous. I hope you're real careful. Sounds like it would be real easy to get hurt moving all that stuff around and dealing with all that heavy equipment."

"For me, no. Danger is no problem for me."

"I heard some guy had an accident that hurt his back so bad he's in a wheelchair."

Mario shrugged. "Some men can't handle the job. Me I'm very good." He leaned closer again, his head almost over my plate, and reached for my hand, this time raising it and encircling it with his own. "Not to worry. If you visit the warehouse, I take care of you."

Visit the warehouse? Now I was getting somewhere. It would be easier to ask him more specific questions about Johnny at the scene of the crime, so to speak. This PI in training was not trading in her mole role to be a sitting duck in a bologna box. This mole had her own crime to solve and was going to stretch her legs and her digging range.

I shot Mario a big smile. "That would be great. I'd love to see where you work."

The big-lipped smile he shot me back morphed into a round pucker and his eyebrows went up. His chair shook below him and he tottered to the side, his hand whipping away from mine, his arms flailing out like airplane wings.

A throaty male voice came from behind him. *"Je m'excuse."*

I looked up to the owner of the voice, my own brows lowering. I knew who the voice belonged to the second I heard it. Laurent. Barely looking at me now, his attention focused on Mario. Explaining how he'd tripped on a napkin he pointed to on the floor and that he'd accidently bumped Mario's chair.

Right. Accidentally bumped with enough force to nearly send Mario careening to the ground. Not likely.

Probably Laurent found out about my lunch with Mario from Camille. Probably he was tag-teaming her "supervision" of trainee me. How the bump figured in was beyond me. Maybe some form of Caron sign language. Maybe not.

Mario waved Laurent's apology away and assured Laurent his offer of a drink to make up for the bump was unnecessary.

With a smile and a nod, Laurent ventured off from whence he came. Which, judging by my tracking, was a stool at the window counter where a mug and half-empty sandwich plate sat in wait.

Laurent angled his stool so it had a partial view out the window and a partial view of me. His eyes on me made it hard for me to return my focus to Mario. It wasn't easy playing a mole with those eyes making me feel like prey. I couldn't wait until my training was done and I could operate solo.

Mario made a show of pulling out his phone and checking the time. "We better get back. We don't want more trouble from the big boss today."

I pushed back my chair. "More trouble?"

"Like with the meeting this morning. Maybe that one was a false alarm or maybe the time was just wrong. We don't want to take a chance. You were not here before when he made a meeting and made the last three people to arrive to clean the bathrooms."

Ah. Now the earlier mass stampede to the fake meeting was making sense. And why Camille knew calling the meeting would speedily oust Huguette from her office. Images from the movie *Private Benjamin* came into my head of the scenes where Goldie Hawn has to scrub the latrines with her toothbrush.

"Clean the bathrooms?" I said. "Why would he do that? Isn't that for the cleaning staff to do?"

Mario shook his head. "There is no cleaning staff. The big boss doesn't believe in it. He says everyone is equal and has to pitch in. Whoever comes late to the meetings has to do the bathroom wipe-up every evening until the next meeting. The big boss says that's a fair way to assign the chores."

I pushed up from my chair. I'd never heard of such an arrangement. It was hard to argue the community side of it and it definitely didn't sound as bad as Goldie with her toothbrush, but it did seem like an odd way to divvy duties. I could understand nobody wanting to be the rotten egg in that little game. Probably pretty effective incentive to keep meeting attendance timely and on schedule, though. "What happens if the same people are late the next time?" I asked.

Mario shuffled to my side when I stood and he slid my vacated chair back into place. "That never happens. But if it did, it goes to the next closest late person. He's the big boss, he can do anything."

Mario got the check and paid it, dismissing my request to split the costs, which I didn't push. The man's ego had already taken a knock with the chair incident coming on the heels of his accident-proof proclamation. I didn't want to risk anything that may further affront his sense of masculinity.

I let Mario guide me to the door, my eyes flitting to *my* big boss still perched on his stool. His legs outstretched in front of him, his jacket open, his sweater forming to muscles so taut you could bounce a quarter off them. His scruff calling attention to the set of his jaw. A *café au lait* mug in his hand, tipping my way when our eyes met.

His other hand disappeared into his pocket, and a second later my inner pocket buzzed against my side, sending tiny shockwaves to my stomach. I pinched my lips and instructed my face to stay Botox still, determined not to break mole character.

Bzzt, bzzt, it went again. Bzzt, bzzt, big boss calling.

He knew I couldn't answer. Probably he was testing me. Watching to see how I handled myself. He did things like that. Good training he called it. I had a few other names for it. Names that may have on occasion challenged my lip-holding superpower.

I stuffed my hands in my pockets, hoping to block the low buzz of my phone, and followed Mario out onto the street, busy with locals and tourists enjoying one of the first spring days in Vieux

Montréal, winding their way around small pots of flowers outside stores and standing signs beckoning from *restaurants* doorways.

Mario skillfully blended into the crowd. I moved to do the same, maneuvering around a sale rack of dresses some eager beaver merchant had put out. The bzzt of my phone cut out and I sighed in relief, the sigh catching in my throat when I cleared the dress rack to find a new obstacle blocking my path. This one short, dressed in black, and pointing beady black eyes my way. The Penguin. Sans goons. And sans smile.

# 19

"**W**HAT ARE YOU doing in that getup?" he said.

I looked down at the outfit Camille and I had settled on for my mole duty. The white blouse and blue pencil skirt. Blazer covering most of the blouse except the lace cuffs, skirt length hitting well above the Bunny boots, accoutrements bag sagging on my shoulder. "Excuse me?"

He pointed at me with a hand pocketed in his trench coat. The point wide and round and stiff, making me wonder if in the absence of his goonie back-up group he kept his own enhancer, kitted out with a trigger and bullet-sized accessories.

"You think I don't know who you are?" he asked me. More accusation than question.

I stepped away from the rack, out where I could see the café window to see if Laurent was watching. He was. Eyes steady, body poised for action. Down the street I checked for Mario but couldn't see him.

"There you are," someone said from the crowd walking by.

I turned around to find Mario behind me, coming close, then dipping back.

"Go home," Penguin said. "Wash your face. Take off that ridiculous hair. Your mother taught you better than that." And with that he disappeared, floating off in a wave of passersby, leaving me staring after him.

"*BEN, THAT'S IT*. You're out."

"What do you mean I'm out?" I said. "It's working isn't it. Brassard wanted me to ruffle the Penguin's feathers, and it looks like I did. I've never seen the guy without his doowap goons. It has to mean something that he'd make a solo appearance to bawl me out on the street."

Laurent closed the distance between us where we stood by the warehouse back door, the same spot Camille and I had met earlier in the day. This time, Camille was inside doing her inspector 12 thing and it was Laurent who'd beckoned me outside as soon as I'd ditched Mario.

Laurent shot me a head nod to the right, grasped my hand, friendly but firmly, and ushered me behind a deserted freight box. Two men walked by soon after, and I realized the location change had nothing to do with ending my mole career and everything to do with keeping our meeting on the QT.

"Really," I whispered. "I should get to my desk before Huguette thinks I'm not back from lunch."

He stared down at me. "You're not back from lunch."

"This is silly. I've already given Camille one toothbrush stick of files and she gave me a new stick to fill if I find more. And I'm meeting Mario again to dig around the warehouse myself and see what else I can find out about Johnny's accident. I've got to go." I turned to retrace my path to the door, stopping when the hand-lock Laurent had on me pulled me back like a slinky, knocking me into him, focusing my view over his shoulder to the Jacques Cartier bridge spanning the river off the Port.

"Mario?" he said.

I adjusted my feet, shifting my sights from the bridge to Laurent. "Right. Mario. He's going to get me into the warehouse. Then I can see for myself where Johnny had his accident and get more details from an insider. Maybe get a better sense of how bad the accident was. We are still working for the insurance company, too, aren't we? They still want to know if Johnny's faking, right?"

"We all know he's faking."

I held back a sigh. "But knowing and proving are two different things, right? Isn't that what you taught me?"

His stare softened some, and I tried not to smile. I had him. It was darn near impossible to argue with a Caron. I'd learned that much in the time since I'd known him and Camille. But I'd also learned it was just as hard for them to argue back when confronted with their own spiel.

My phone buzzed in my pocket, and my eyes trailed to where Laurent still held my hand. Mostly I felt the phone buzz more than heard it, but I knew with his uncanny hearing the low hum hadn't escaped Laurent. He released my hand, and I fetched the phone and grimaced at the call display.

"Your Anglophone?" Laurent said.

I rolled my eyes to the side. "You should add a little end drum bit to your act. No, it's a text from Tina. She's at the house and can't find anything to eat." Really it was a second text. The first one a short series of bubbles logged at the bzzt time I thought was Laurent and I'd ignored. So not big boss testing me after all.

He raised an eyebrow at me. "Your house?"

I nodded as I texted Tina back telling her about a stash of cookies in the jar on the counter, reminding her that I was working until the end of the day and couldn't help more until then. Stowing the mobile away, I also made a mental note to see about a phone number change when this case was done.

"All right," I said. "We're good, right, so I'm off." I paused to peek out from around our freight-box hideaway. Mostly to make sure the coast was clear. Also to avoid Laurent seeing my face and reading the truth. All the while I'd been working to convince him I wanted to plunge ahead, a teeny part of me was rattled by my run-in with the Penguin. Not because he was a scary dude with nothing but a little cloth standing between me and his pocket gun. That was bad, too. But it was more the topic of his rant and his mention of my mother that irked me. The whole thing felt odd and creepy.

None of which I wanted Laurent to know had thrown me. What I wanted was to end this conversation, get back to work, solve this case, and get the Penguin out of my life.

"*Non*," Laurent said. "Not so fast." He pointed at my neck. "Where is it?"

I shifted my clearance check to look down at myself. "Where's what?"

"Your locket."

My fingers went to my chest, feeling for the outline of my necklace beneath my mole blouse, worry catching in my lungs. I couldn't have lost the locket again, could I?

The familiar bump came to my touch and my knot of worry unclenched, replaced by a tinier knot of annoyance at feeling thrown again.

"It's where it always is," I said, overly nonchalant to cover any thrown vibes I may have given off. I didn't want to lose any ground I may have gained with my earlier win about the knowing vs. proving stuff. "Why?"

"Because this is going back in." He extended his palm towards

197

me, small metal chip resting in the folds of his skin.

I eyed the chip. The tracker he'd kept hidden in my locket on my first undercover case.

"Isn't that overkill?" I said. "I've got the phone. Since you got in to my poker party pics via the Cloud, I'm sure you've got the whole gizmo rigged and probably have location services tracking me already. The mini tracker has got to be above and beyond in the whole supervision thing."

"This isn't about supervision. It's about safety. It's part of the job."

I caught his eye. "So you mean you've got a tracker on you, too?"

He stepped closer and I took a step back. "Do *you* want me to wear a tracker?" he said.

His tone deepened and his eyes held mine as he spoke, and I moved back farther still, this time rounding the corner where the freight box met another box, smaller and smellier.

I stumbled when I recognized *eau de* dumpster, the stumble causing me to pitch sideways, Laurent's arms coming out to right me. Something squished as I set my foot down. An "ew" escaped my mouth and I sprang away, the left heel of the Bunny boots landing down on something too soft to be ground and I jumped again, this time closer to Laurent and braving a look down to where I saw something red spilling out of a white bag.

I put a hand to my heart and laughed at myself. Nothing too gross. Just Goatee Guy's jelly doughnut from the hit and run with Huguette during the great stampede. Probably he'd thrown it out and missed the dumpster.

"Go ahead," I said, looking back up at Laurent. "Make fun of my girly 'ew.' I deserve it."

Laurent stayed quiet, his gaze on the ground, his grip tightening around me.

I looked down at the bag again. There was a lot more red filling leaking out than I remembered. And a wide strip of blue at the top, the blue also smattered with red. And extending far beyond the bag to…no it couldn't be. Was that a chin? With a goatee? And why was it tilting?

## 20

"OKAY, SO MAYBE I fainted a little."

Camille turned from the driver's seat of the work jalopy to the passenger side where I sat.

"A little?" she said. "*Mais voyons*. Nobody faints a little. You melted like a man after sex."

I adjusted my seat from reclined to upright position and wrinkled my nose. "Do you have to put it that way?"

"It is what it is. Body function, that's it. Automatic. It happens to lots of people at the beginning. You're not used to this part of the job yet."

"Did it happen to you?" I said.

She shrugged. "Maybe not me. But lots of cops I know." She thrust a can of apple juice at me. "*Allez*. Drink some more."

I accepted the can and took a sip of juice. I didn't want to be sitting in a car in the parking lot next to the warehouse. I wanted to be at the warehouse learning more about what happened to Goatee Guy. The last I remembered I was looking at his goateed chin lying on the ground next to the dumpster, attached to what I had to assume was the rest of his body.

"Okay. I feel fine now," I said. "Let's go back."

An ambulance pulled out from dockside and onto the street, and Camille's phone pinged with incoming text. The phone ping nearly drowned out by the sound of sirens whirring on up ahead. A good sign, I figured. Sirens meant the ambulance was carrying live cargo. No sirens, no rush, meant corpse.

Camille held up a hand and said, *"Deux secondes,"* protracting wait mode while she checked her text.

I slid my eyes over to her phone screen and immediately ordered my pupils front and center. I had to stop doing that. Curiosity was no excuse to peer at other people's phones. When there was something to tell me, she'd tell me.

I steered my eyes right and watched as a cop car pulled out after the ambulance, half of another cop car still visible sitting around the side of the warehouse. Two men leaned on the car, one in uniform, hand gesturing, head bent. The other sans uniform, arms folded over his chest, head missing a crop circle of hair. Brassard.

A gulp lodged in my throat. Maybe I was wrong about the sirens. If Brassard was on the scene, things couldn't be good. For Goatee Guy or for me. Brassard would not be happy to find his mole missing in the line of duty. Which made two of us because I wasn't so happy being sidelined. Especially in the stinky work jalopy with all the windows closed, the warm sun making an afternoon appearance and stewing the car's locker-room tang into a full-on brew.

And that's not all I was smelling. The red goo on my Bunny heel wasn't helping, either. Plus, it was grossing me out. I was starting to suspect it wasn't all jelly doughnut.

"You got any extra shoes in this heap?" I asked Camille. "And any baggies?"

Camille paused her texting and cast a glimpse my way.

I pointed at my boots. "They got slimed at the dumpster."

She scrunched her nose and hooked a thumb towards the back of the car. "Trunk."

I got out of the car and reached the trunk just as Camille popped it open. A few hockey bags, some slim, some not, sat to the left. To the right, a bunch of totes were filled with various paraphernalia, each tote bearing a boutique name. Camille's stash of emergency snooping supplies no doubt. I rooted through the stash and found a pair of sneakers about my size. No Ziplocks. Just a couple grocery bags tucked into a tote pocket. I set one bag down, pulled off a boot and gingerly lowered it into the bag, balancing myself on one foot, trying to snag the other loose foot with a sneaker. Then I repeated the routine with the other side.

Done, I went to close the trunk and froze when I noticed red on my hands. A dry heave roiled my stomach. Please let that be jelly doughnut.

I pinched my eyes closed, trying to blink away a flashback of Goatee Guy lying in the pool of red, willing the eye pinch to move the image along like the click of an old View-Master moving on to the next slide. I opened my eyes to the world again and got back to closing the trunk, only to stop myself mid-move again. This time when the loud snap of gum hit my ears, evoking another kind of memory. I'd heard the same gum smacking before. From Chloé the day I'd first met her.

Using the trunk as a shield, I ducked down, peered around the side, and spotted Chloé doing much the same thing. Only her gaze was fixed on the cop car in the warehouse lot and she hid, almost fully standing, behind a minivan parked two rows up and one car over.

She tilted sideways, a hand on her burgeoning stomach, leggings visible below her coat, thick-rubber platform Mary Janes on her feet. Odds were she had been at work, heard about the hubbub, and was checking it out. Not a surprise. Quite a few onlookers had gathered and several passersby had slowed to gander at the police presence. None of those folks watched from behind a minivan though. Possibly her desire to hide her curiosity had a simple explanation and was completely innocent, but it looked suspicious to my mole eyes.

Of course, I was one to talk. I was peeking out from my trunk shield.

She pulled back, took out her phone, and held it low, thumbs in motion over the screen. From my angle, I couldn't see her full mouth, but her jaw stayed fixed while her fingers kept moving. Probably texting. She paused and played peek-a-boo with the warehouse lot again, jerking suddenly when a short musical ring tone sang out and she retreated, banging her head on the minivan during her hasty withdrawal.

One hand reached up to rub her head, the other jabbed hard at her mobile screen before snapping the phone to her ear.

I kept low and crept closer, using cars to block my approach, doing firefighters' crouch walk like I had the night of Brassard's swag beaning at Chloé's house. When I got one car away from the minivan, I picked up Chloé's voice, harsh but whispering like a mother reprimanding her child during church service. Only I was guessing the object of Chloé's reprimanding was no kid. At least I hoped not because most of what I overheard belonged in a French dictionary specializing in swear words.

At the end of a particularly colorful outpouring, Chloé turned on her Mary Jane heel, scurried over a cement-block divider, and disappeared from view into a gap between two nearby buildings.

I stood on rubbery legs and waited to see if she'd reappear, inching forward to get a closer look. The alley she'd taken was wide enough for sun to hit ground, giving me a fairly long view, but there was no sign of Chloé.

I scoped the lot, checking to see if she'd maybe come out from another access point. No sign of her. I focused on the alley again. She'd have to be moving pretty fast to clear the end without me seeing. A long shot given her baby belly weighing her down. My guess was either she darted into one of the buildings via a side door or she was playing more hide-away peek-a-boo out of my sight. Whichever way I'd lost her.

"*Voyons*, Lora. What are you doing? I thought you were changing your boots."

I turned to where Camille had come up behind me, and we both simultaneously looked down at the sneakers on my feet. Bright and white in the sun. The kind of shoes that should be running around a tennis court not a parking lot. Probably, part of a get-up that included a short white skirt, collared little top, and ankle socks Camille kept in the work jalopy trunk disguise kit in case she needed to play preppy snoop.

"I did." I explained about spotting Chloé and her game of peek-a-boo while I was making my footwear change. "She was there." I gestured to the minivan Chloé had hid behind. Then my finger retraced the path she'd taken during her vamoose. "And she took off here and went that-a-way."

Camille joined me by the cement block that divided the parking area from the makeshift roadway circling the lot and the "that-a-way" aka alley beyond.

"And you followed her? On your own?" Camille's gaze strayed to the warehouse lot next door where Brassard walked the area in full view. "And with Brassard right there to see you?"

I shook my head. "I spied on her. I didn't follow her when she left the lot." Probably I would have if I'd seen where she went. A fact probably best kept to myself at the moment.

Camille pointed down at the cement block. "Then what's that?"

I followed her pointed finger to a foot-shaped splotch imprinted on top of the divider. A red splotch. I bent, pulled a Kleenex from my pocket, and pressed the tissue to the splotch. Bits of red transferred to the tissue. Still damp.

We both looked at my shoes again, gleaming and white, then back up at each other, realization hitting us at the same time. The red splotch had nothing to do with me or the Bunny boots I was wearing at the dumpster discovery. The red splotch belonged to Chloé.


"SHOULDN'T WE BE looking for Chloé?" I said.

Laurent and Camille sat on either side of me in the back seat of the work jalopy. Neither budged, locking me in place like I was the white layer in a block of Neapolitan ice cream.

"Tell me more about what you saw." This coming from Laurent and not even close to answering my question. Ugh. Camille and I had brought him up to speed on the Chloé Cinderella splotch, and yet he focused on putting me through the usual paces, making me recount every detail like the story was going into a tell-all memoir some day.

The reprieve from spring showers had ended before we got in the car, and fat drops of rain pelted the roof overhead and beat at the windows, clouding the view to outdoors, increasing the claustrophobic effects of my human ice cream blockade. I wiggled my arm free and used it to unlock first one shoulder then the other and ease forward some. "Not much more to tell," I said telling him again what I'd told Camille about Chloé's game of peek-a-boo.

Laurent's gaze on me held when I was done, and for a second I wondered if maybe this time he was putting me through the recounting paces mostly to distract me. I was missing a chunk of time from when I passed out at the dumpster until I found myself horizontal on the front seat of the jalopy. I was guessing he had something to do with my relocation and might have mistaken the momentary wobble in my legs as weakness. Squeamish I may be from time to time but weak I was not.

"Now tell me," I said, placing steady eyes on Laurent, keeping my voice strong. All business lest he be having doubts about me. "Did they catch what happened to Goatee Guy on security?"

Laurent shook his head. "Poor coverage point."

Right. Of course. Just like with Johnny's accident inside the warehouse if I remembered right. Either *Dépot Deschênes* needed better security advice or their weak spots were easy pickings for the camera shy.

I hesitated with my next question. "You know how bad Goatee Guy was hurt? Will he be all right?"

"*Ben*, it's bad but could have been worse. Some bruises, some cuts, a broken arm. The owner of the warehouse is trying to pass it off as an accident."

"An accident? Seriously?"

"*Oui*. They say Marcel, that's your man with the goatee, slipped on some loose garbage and fell."

"But the guy was unconscious."

"They say he knocked his head when he fell."

Right. A broken arm. A possible concussion. All that blood. I found it hard to believe the man's injuries could come from a solo fall. I suspected I wasn't the only skeptical one. "Then what were Brassard and the police doing there? The police being called to an accident on work premises I could see maybe, but not a detective like Brassard."

"Brassard showed up with the police. Nobody would know his job if he didn't tell them."

"And he showed up why?"

"Because I called him."

"Do you think there's a chance it was an accident?"

"*Non.* I saw Marcel's body. The angles of the blood splatters, the force of his injuries, they didn't come from any fall. He was beat up by somebody or more than one somebody."

I worked to keep my face from showing the pangs of sympathy hitting me for Goatee Guy aka Marcel. This was so not his day. First the run-in with Huguette during the stampede and then this roughing up. Hard to imagine Chloé being the one doing the roughing up. But she had left that red footprint splotch behind which likely placed her at the scene. And she did have a violent streak what with the swag beaning of Thomas Duncan and Brassard and all, so I couldn't completely dismiss her possible involvement. Or at least that she knew something. Something that might explain how all this fit together.

Which made me want to get back to my mole duties. I was no doctor. I couldn't swing by the hospital and help Goatee Guy or Johnny. The only way I could help was to figure this mess out. And sitting here wasn't helping any. Something fishy was definitely in the air and it wasn't coming from the river by the Port. First Johnny had his accident then gets a thrashing at his bachelor party, then someone tries to off his machines at the hospital. Then Goatee Guy gets roughed up. I wasn't sure where the Penguin fit in, but there were two common ties possibly related to the rest so far: Chloé and the warehouse.

I really wanted a crack at Chloé, but I was guessing once Brassard heard about her Cinderella foot splotch, any dumpster dirt she'd be divulging would be to him in a tiny room with a two-way mirror. That left me with the warehouse. And if I could just get back in, I may still be able to catch up with Mario and see if I could suss out a clue to the connection. Maybe find out the link to the Penguin.

Which got me wondering. "Did anyone say what department Goatee Guy worked in?"

"Marcel," Laurent corrected me. "*Oui*. Marcel is in logistics. He supervises what comes in and out of the warehouse and when."

Hmm. More connection to the warehouse. "I'm starting to rethink the whole insurance scam thing. Maybe *Assurance Lion* shouldn't be investigating Johnny. Maybe they should be investigating *Dépôt Deschênes*. That's two accidents. And I'm guessing maybe even that dead guy Johnny knew was a work buddy. Maybe he had some kind of 'accident,' too."

Camille and Laurent exchanged one of their sibling looks. "*Quel* dead guy?" Camille said.

"The friend of Johnny's his sister told me about. The one whose death got Johnny drinking again."

Blank looks from both sibs.

"Remember?" I went on. "I told you Sister Jane said Johnny got crushed by his friend's death and fell off the wagon. Poor guy."

Another glance volleyed between Camille and Laurent, and I tried to ignore it. Probably another silent admonishment that I was being too empathetic again.

The phone buzzed in my pocket and I ignored it, too, wondering just how long Camille and Laurent were going to keep us locked up having this tête-à-tête. The longer we sat here talking, the longer we were out of the loop and clues were going stale. Besides, we were in the work jalopy, not the cone of silence under some invisibility cape. We'd moved to park a couple blocks away, and sitting in the back seat brought us some cover, but not much. Anyone passing by might see us together. That wouldn't be good.

"*Voyons*, Lora. Aren't you going to get that?" Camille said, flicking a finger in the direction of my buzzing phone.

I shook my head. "Dollars to doughnuts it's Tina. She can wait."

The recurring bzzt cut out and was replaced by a lone one, likely a text. Tina didn't like going unheard.

Camille tapped her toe on the floor mat, and I sighed, pulled out my phone, and held my display out to her. If she wanted to see Tina's current crisis *du jour* on the tiny screen, she could have at it.

Camille took the phone and turned it back towards me. "*C'est pas Tina. C'est un texto de Soeur* Jane. She got in to see Johnny and she's thanking you for arranging it."

Well that was different. Her I was happy to hear from. I took the phone and double-checked it showed her display name from my contacts and not Tina's, figuring I couldn't be too careful. Then I replied to Jane that I was glad it worked out. At least one good thing was coming from this day and Brassard was holding up his end of our deal.

Jane texted right back asking if I'd made any progress finding Johnny's would-be killer. *I* not *we*, reminding me that this was my very own first case. Unofficially maybe, but still, she'd put her trust in me to help.

I thought of my talks with Sister Jane and how sure she was of Johnny and how he was turning his life around. I'd hoped then that she was right, and I hoped now that I could help her prove it. And I knew in my heart the key to proving it was in that warehouse. With yet another "accident" on its books, the place clearly housed more than crates. Which only made me more eager to get back inside to discover its secrets. And fast. Before any more bodies ended up down for the count.

21

"THIS ISN'T THE way back," I said. "What are you doing?"

Laurent adjusted the gear shift and kept his eyes on the road and his mouth quiet. Minutes before, Camille and Laurent had both made calls. Camille dealing with news her fake inspector role had been cut after Goatee Guy's "accident," and Laurent's call over so quick I didn't catch the drift. Then Camille had slipped out of the work jalopy, leaving only me and Laurent, who I thought was taking me back to the warehouse when the two of us shifted into the front seat and set off. I could have sworn he'd missed the turn street, though, given that we were now taking a tour of Vieux Montréal. A tour that ventured away from the Port.

After a few jigs and jags, we left the tour behind and ended up at a street I vaguely recognized. More so as we turned into a drive-way, and a building with carved medallions looming up top drew closer and closer until we glided into the building's base. We passed through a garage door that closed automatically behind us, and we made our way over to park in a slot by a far wall. I'd been to the building and the slot only once before, but I knew where I was immediately. Laurent's place.

He got out of the car and waited while I did the same then followed him to the stairwell door he unlocked and held open, his arm extended above my head, urging me with his eyes to pass through. That eye message the most communication I'd gotten out of him since Camille had pared down our trio to a duo. I was thinking his lack of chatter and our location change was a message in itself. And not a message I wanted to hear.

As we made our way up the three flights of stairs to his floor I said, "So does this mean you're pulling me from mole duty?"

He veered around me when we got to his landing, opened the door out of the stairwell, and repeated the routine of ushering me through. "Not exactly," he said.

"Then what exactly?"

"*Ben*, consider this a field trip."

I eyed him, unsure what kind of mole duty field trip required a stop at his loft and how this little detour was going to help me on my mission to help Sister Jane. "A field trip to do what?"

"Case review."

I cocked my head to the side. "Didn't we already do that in the car with Camille?"

"*Non.* With Camille we went over new information. This time we talk old information. But not another word until we get inside."


LAURENT CLOSED THE loft door behind us and went to disarm his alarm. "Talk to me about the dead friend," he said.

I cleared the front carpet, something in his tone compelling me to give him a wide berth. Or maybe it was that "case review" comment he'd made that had me on edge. I had the distinct feeling his idea of case review included a lecture about rules and procedures and how I'd broken ranks somehow. Probably about how I'd made some booboo following Chloé solo with Brassard's super cop radar in range.

"I don't know a lot about the dead guy," I said. "Only that Johnny had a friend who died, and he had a hard time getting over it."

The sound of a doorbell went and Laurent shifted the attention he'd set on me to a bank of gizmos beside the alarm panel.

A flutter dusted by my stomach. A visitor. Being in Laurent's lair still had me feeling like I was somehow getting entrée into a heretofore forbidden sanctum. The idea that I'd also get to see who else visited him at his lair revved my curiosity into high alert, momentarily derailing my train of thought.

Laurent turned back from the gizmos. "*Pis?*"

I sat on his *calèche* bench and refocused my mind on our conversation, removing my jacket and shoes as I spoke. "Nothing. That's it. Sister Jane said Johnny had been in a bit of trouble a ways back with gambling and drinking and such, but he'd pulled himself out of it. Until the friend died and he started drinking again. She didn't see how the renewed drinking could get him into any serious trouble, though. Certainly nothing to warrant someone wanting to kill him."

And frankly neither did I so I hadn't given it much weight. The gambling I considered as a factor, which is why I'd theorized with Camille about the Penguin and how Johnny maybe owed him money in gambling debts. But we'd dismissed that theory when the accounting didn't support it.

Some kind of trouble connected to Johnny's dead friend, however, had never entered my mind. Not good. One of the first things Laurent and Camille had drilled into my head was to be suspicious of everything. Since that went against my own personal mantra to see the good in everything, I may on occasion overlook that piece of training. I needed to work on that. Somehow I had to find a way to do both or I could miss vital clues. Or end up on field trips that felt more like remedial summer school.

"Look," I said. "Maybe this would go faster if you could just tell me what I'm missing. What's so important about the dead friend?"

"*Bonne question.*" This coming from a new voice. Laurent's visitor, bustling through the door and shutting it with a barely discernable click. Brassard. His voice and his stance as stiff as the ironed-to-perfection shirt Camille had mocked when we'd seen him at Johnny's post poker/bachelor bash.

Brassard took two quick steps in my direction, glared down at where I still sat on the *calèche* banquette, and added, "Another good question is why didn't you mention you knew about it before?"

**BOY, FOR MEN** who didn't talk all that much, Brassard and Laurent could certainly get testy when they thought someone else was holding out on them. We'd moved our conversation to Laurent's living room where I sat on a couch under a window, Laurent in a chair with its back to the kitchen, and Brassard stood, his feet rooted to the spot like a hundred-year-old tree trunk. I'm not sure who I thought Laurent's visitor would be, but starched and wooden Brassard it was not.

"Look," I said. "I don't know why Sister Jane mentioned it to me. I don't even know who the dead guy was, but maybe if one of you told me why it's so important we could all get on with our jobs."

Both men glowered at each other.

"*C'est fini*, Brassard," Laurent finally said. "No more questions. She's out."

I swiveled my eyes between the two men. Was that "she" meaning me?

"Fine. I don't need her anymore. Take your *petite assistante* back."

*Assistant?* Was Brassard calling me an assistant? What happened to PI in training? What happened to police mole?

Laurent stood and more words zipped back and forth, complicated French bits, zinging out of one man's mouth then the other until I couldn't take it anymore.

"Stop!" I said. When I had their attention, I lowered my voice. Stress management technique 101 for de-escalating tension. Then I moved into my own version of technique 102—distraction, ie: changing the subject. "Look, we've got two guys in the hospital and a pregnant lady running around leaving red goo in her wake. Maybe we could put a pin in the dead guy talk for a minute and get back to that. Did anyone find Chloé yet? Does anyone know more details about what happened to the man at the dumpster?"

Brassard's body shifted my way and the look in his eye changed. Not softening exactly. But more assessing than angry. "What was that about red goo?"

"Hellooo," I said. "At the dumpster. There was red goo on Goatee Guy. The same red goo I saw soaking through the paper bag he'd been carrying earlier in the day. I think it was jelly doughnut, and, you know later some blood. Anyway Chloé left a red shoeprint of the same goo on a cement block in the parking lot nearby. Which means she was probably around the dumpster, too. I thought we all knew that."

The men did some more French bickering. Like they had their own cone of silence à la secret code going on for all I could make out. At one point I figured out why I had such a hard time understanding most of their conversation. Their French didn't sound much like the French I heard in movies. Theirs had home-grown sounds and slangs of deep Québécois. No high-school French class back in New York could have prepared me for their Frenchspeak.

Or for the speed at which it rocketed out of their mouths. Half the time they spoke over each other, too, making it doubly hard to follow.

I wasn't sure if they were doing it deliberately to keep me from understanding or if they'd simply reverted to what came natural. Either way, it left me out. Which I decided could be a good thing.

I eased myself up from the couch and over to the bench in the entryway, picked up my jacket and shoes, and went for the front door.

A hand reached over me from behind and leaned on the upper door, making it hard to open.

Maneuvering around to my side, Laurent said, "What are you doing?"

"Leaving."

"*Non.* We're not done yet."

"We?" I said. "Maybe you two aren't done, but I am. I want to get back to the warehouse. Clearly there's something important about this dead guy and since neither of you are letting me in on it, I need to find out what it is for myself. I may be making a leap, but I'm thinking there's a tie in to Johnny's accident and Goatee Guy's duel at the dumpster. And probably to Johnny's dead friend. Sister Jane never said how Johnny knew the friend, but since you're both fired up about him I'm guessing that man worked at the Port, too, and somehow got himself into his own trouble. Only he wasn't as lucky as Johnny and Goatee Guy. Whatever trouble the friend got into landed him in the morgue."

Most of my thesis I'd worked out while I was sitting outside Laurent and Brassard's French-only "cone of silence." The last bit just came to me, but it sounded about right when I heard myself say it.

"*Tabarnouche.*" This muttered by Brassard, who, when I turned to check the expression on his face that accompanied his lovely

215

vocabulary, I found lowering himself into the chair Laurent had vacated.

Sitting back, Brassard set his elbows on the armrests, bent his forearms towards his heart, and wove his fingers together, crooking one stiff finger in my direction. Not the middle one but close. Like I was being summoned to present my Master's thesis defense to a panel of one. I had no illusions, though. No matter how well I reasoned, I had the distinct impression I would not be rewarded with any Master's degree. Not even for remedial school.


**IT WAS ANOTHER** hour before I got out of Laurent's loft. Past closing time at the warehouse. And, as was made clear to me several times in no uncertain terms, post closing time for my role as a mole.

By the time Laurent dropped me off at home, I was not only minus a new Master's, I'd been stripped of my accoutrement bag, my Bunny ID, and the black wig. There was even a minute before I got out of the car that I thought I'd have to turn in my skirt and blazer.

"It makes no sense," I complained into my mobile as I stomped up my porch steps. "I was right. I was right about all of it and then, boom, they fire me."

"*Voyons*, Lora," Camille said from the other end of the phone connection. "Nobody fired you. I would know if somebody fired you."

"They may as well have." I stuffed my key in the lock on the door. "They haven't even found Chloé. Nobody at the warehouse is squealing. And still Laurent and Brassard cut me from mole duty. *Me*, the one who found Goatee Guy by the dumpster and Chloé's Cinderella splotch. And then they go and practically take me off the case. *My* case. How can they do that?" I wrangled with the lock, my key not clicking right.

"*T'inquiète pas*," she said. "I find out." And the line buzzed to off.

I stuffed my phone away and went at the lock again, two-handed this time. One wrangling the key and one wrangling the doorknob, realizing it wasn't so much the lock giving me a problem, more the knob. It wouldn't turn right. Until it did. And I stumbled inward with a lunging step.

"Lora. Omigod. I'm so glad it's you."

I sidestepped closer to the wall away from my greeter. Tina. Standing one hand at the base of her neck, the other hand holding tight to a braid of sticks with Winnie the Poohs dangling from the ends.

Down the hall, Ping and Pong peered out at me from the edges of the kitchen doorway. Posted on either side, each partly sheltered by their respective doorframe. Smart thinking. Probably they were in no more of a mood for Tina's antics than I was. Or maybe it was the Winnie the Poohs they were dodging. Even Winnie the Pooh could be a little scary when he dangled in multiple doppelganger form from sharp sticks.

Probably the frantic eyes on the lady holding the sticks didn't help any, either. Or the pinched fingertips at her neck, glowing a near red under the lighting from the lamp above.

I dipped back, closed the door, and threw the bolt. I didn't want to overreact to Tina's odd behavior because, well, Tina's breadth when it came to odd behavior was wider than her twin baby belly. But the color on her fingers had me a bit spooked, especially when she brought her hand down and I noticed her neck had the same reddish tone. I'd had enough of seeing red for one day.

"What's up?" I said, my voice as even as I could make it.

"It was awful," Tina said. "A horrible little man was here. Smelly and mean like a mangy dog. He pushed his way in before I could stop him."

I moved past her to the living room. "What man?" I scoped the room, my pulse starting to thud in my ears, my eyes checking to see if the mangy dog man was still around. The boxes in the living room like camouflage, making it hard to pick out my own furniture let alone anything amiss or any uninvited guests.

Ping and Pong had moved as well, from the kitchen to the dining room that attached to the living room. My eyes picked up the movement of their tiny bodies, calming me some. If any strangers were lurking about, Ping and Pong would not be making an appearance. At least not without making it clear that mangy dog men were not welcome.

"I don't see anyone," I said.

Tina huffed over to the one empty seat left on the couch and lowered herself to sit. "He left."

"What'd he look like?"

"Sweaty and smelly. Greasy hair. And his face. I'll never forget his face, wrinkly and really old with beady little eyes."

I was thinking maybe the Penguin until she threw in the really old thing. Now I was lost. "Was he tall?"

"Not for a man. I'm not sure he was much taller than you."

Hmm. That got me rethinking the Penguin. "And how old is old?"

"Oh at least fifty. Maybe sixty."

Oy. Mental head tap. Naturally Tina's version of really old was anyone over forty. Or at least anyone who deigned to let themselves *look* over forty. "What did he want?"

"To see you. But I'm telling you, Lora, he was creepy. Like a stalker or something. And mean. He didn't believe me when I said you weren't home. He forced his way in and ran around checking rooms."

Tina held up the Winnie the Poohs. "I had to grab these to protect myself." She turned to drop the sticks in a box beside her that claimed to house a ready-to-assemble Winnie the Pooh mobile. Cute picture on the box front of the mobile hanging over a laughing baby's crib.

I had to hand it to Tina. The mobile sticks weren't a bad choice of weapon in a pinch. And they seemed to work. Aside from the reddish coloring bits I'd noticed on her skin earlier, she didn't look any the worse for wear.

She reached to her other side, picked up a crinkly bag, and stuck her hand in, pulling out a cheese doodle and ramming it in her mouth.

And now I understood the rusty red fingers. Cheese coloring.

"How long ago did he leave?" I asked her.

"Omigod. It was like only ten minutes ago. He came in, ran around, and left so fast I didn't have time to do anything." She waved her arm in the air and the crinkly bag waved with it. "My phone's around here someplace, but I couldn't find it to call the police or anybody. I was still looking for it when I heard you outside. I thought it was him coming back and I was holding the door so he wouldn't barge in again. A mangy guy like that probably picks locks, right? I didn't want to take any chances."

She had sweat on her forehead and her cheeks were growing similar color to her fingertips. I really wanted to check the house and make sure the Penguin hadn't left any booby traps or unwanted accoutrements of his own, but first I needed to calm the mama-to-be.

"You did fine, Tina. It's all over now and I'm here. You just rest and I'll get you some tea." I strode into the kitchen trying to keep my own anxiety from mounting. The Penguin had been to my house twice now. And this time inside. On the same day I ruffled his feathers and Goatee Guy ended up thrashed and left with the trash. There had to be some kind of connection and it couldn't be good.

Whatever it was still eluded me, and I still had no idea how Chloé factored in, but one thing was clear. As much as Laurent and Brassard wanted to push me off this case, the Penguin definitely wanted to pull me in.

**I PUT THE** kettle on and called something to Tina about how cute the Winnie the Pooh crib mobile was going to be, trying to get her mind back on pleasant things. When she got herself wound up talking about more baby stuff, I quietly made another call to Camille to tell her about the Penguin visit. Probably I should have called Laurent, but truth be told I was still a bit miffed at him for pulling my mole duty. Plus, if he thought I'd needed an alarm in response to the earlier break-in, news of a full-on Penguin invasion may drive Laurent to up security by posting one of his big burly men outside my door. If Adam thought the alarm was a thorny issue, a big burly man keeping watch like a guard at Buckingham Palace would definitely not be seen as a fringe benefit of my job.

"What's going on now?"

I turned from where I leaned on the counter at the far end of the kitchen. When I'd started my call with Camille, Tina's voice still droned dimly from the living room like the background noise of a radio left running. As I stopped to listen now, her voice had been replaced by one much closer and deeper. Adam. Standing near the entrance off the dining room.

"Eh?" he said. "You want to tell me why Tina thinks we need to move?"

I disconnected from Camille and smiled at Adam, peering

beyond him, happy to see Tina hadn't toddled her way out to the kitchen, too.

I didn't want to rile up Adam's worry meter too high, but it wouldn't be right to downplay the Penguin's visit, either. Having people the likes of the Penguin invade our home was serious business, and I needed to take responsibility for it. I hadn't done anything directly to lead the Penguin to our doorstep, but it was my job that had brought the man here. Adam had every right to be concerned.

"Moving may be a tad extreme," I said. "But Tina got spooked. Some guy came and forced his way in. It would scare anyone."

Adam took a few steps towards me, the edge of anger in his face ebbing. "Cripes, Lora. Was anyone hurt? Anything taken?"

I pulled him closer to the far corner and lowered my voice. "Everybody's fine, but I called in to report it. I think it may have something to do with the case I'm working on." I hadn't told Adam about the pizza delivery guy being the Penguin, but I did now. From the need-to-know perspective, it was a little fuzzy when it first happened and was just a suspicion on my part, albeit a likely one. After this second unwanted Penguin visit, though, all the fuzziness around need-to-know had morphed into right-to-know territory.

The kettle whistle blew and both of us turned to the noise. "I'm making tea for Tina," I said, heading for the stove. "You want some?"

"Tina's asleep," Adam said. "She drifted off right after I got in and she told me about how we needed to move. She was barely making sense. She was practically talking in her sleep."

Not a surprise. The pregnancy had her sleeping a lot and probably all that adrenaline revving had zapped her when it finally petered out.

I trailed over to peek in at Tina to see if the kettle whistle had woken her. I found her in the same spot I'd left her, sitting upright, head rested on a throw pillow wedged under her neck, mouth unhinged in an open gap, soft snores puffing out in spurts like a percolator. Her legs were outstretched in front of her, propped up on a box, knees apart like she'd done too many squats over an exercise ball.

"She's still out," I whispered to Adam who had followed me over and followed me again when I trailed back to the kitchen. I made a pot of tea, took a cup, offered some to Adam, and saved the rest in case Tina roused.

Adam accepted his cup without a word, his chin in that jut mode I'd come to know so well. I had no doubt a lot of words were forming beyond that jutted chin. Words I wasn't sure I was ready to hear. "Look," I said. "We'll come back to this I promise, but right now I want to check the house before Tina wakes up. She said the Penguin ran around. It was quick, but I think we need to make sure he didn't do anything fishy while he was here."

Adam swallowed the sip of tea he'd taken and set his mug aside. "Fishy? What'd'y'a think, Lora? You think he left a fish head in the bed? A man like that doesn't put fish heads in your bed. A man like that puts people to bed with the fishes."

Or maybe ditches them near dumpsters. But this didn't seem like the time to mention that possibility to Adam.

## 22

---

*a*DAM WAS RIGHT. We didn't find any fish heads in the bed. Or any other signs the Penguin had left so much as puddles in his lap around our house. Not that that meant the coast was clear for sure. Teeny tiny cameras and eavesdropping bugs could be scattered like sand at the beach these days. I had no idea how to sift those out. I couldn't see what the Penguin would gain by leaving any of that stuff behind, though. Unless he wanted to catch Tina snoring or waddling to and from the bathroom.

She was in "to" mode when I ran into her on my way downstairs. Her eye makeup had softened with her nap, her hair hung lopsided, and the cheese doodle marks on her neck had faded to streaks. Like Barbie Tina had walked off the pages of *In Style* into the real world.

"I'll just be a couple minutes," she said. "Then I want to show you the dress I got for the baby shower. I want all the decorations to match. You can show me what you bought so far to make sure everything coordinates."

In all the hoopla since I'd gotten home, I hadn't even asked Tina what she was doing at our house this time. Truth was, she was around so much these days I hadn't been that surprised to find her here sans Adam. I'd forgotten that her current visit had to do with me and the shower. And it hadn't occurred to me at all that she'd expect me to have shopped for the decorations already. I pasted a smile on my face and nodded, afraid if I told her I'd done no shopping or any other shower planning that she'd have me hanging by the short ends of her Winnie the Pooh sticks.

When she was safely ensconced in the bathroom, I hightailed it back upstairs to my bedroom and closed the door. That guest list had to be around here somewhere. If I could just find it, maybe I could fake my way through party prep chat with Tina by throwing around head count numbers and fudging scheduling complications. I just needed to buy a bit of time. I'd been so busy thinking about mole duties and Penguin run-ins and Cinderella foot splotches and dumpster discoveries that I'd downgraded Tina's shower too low on my priority list. Which was wrong. After all, I had agreed to host it. She may not be my bff, but like it or not she was a friend of Adam's. And if she was important to him, she should be important to me. Plus, he was godfather to her babies. And wasn't the shower really for the babies?

I clicked on the lamp, rifled through some things on the dresser, and found the guest list. The long guest list. Oy. I was never going to pull off Tina's dream shower and impress all her fellow social climbers. She wanted a swanky affair. At a swanky place with swanky people and twin everything. And fast. And now it was all supposed to coordinate with some dress she bought. Double oy.

While I mulled over how to tackle all that, I traded in my defunct mole outfit for some leggings and a comfy billowy blouse, catching a glimpse of myself in the closet mirror. I had a serious case of wig hair. Like hat hair, only the extended dance version.

Somehow wearing Camille's wig all day had turned my usually thick wavy hair into shiny sleek locks, like some before and after transformation in a flat-iron commercial. Not the reflection I was used to seeing of myself. I swooshed my head back and forth, watching the hair swing, something foreign about it yet familiar at the same time.

"Help me with this zipper, will you," Tina said, wandering into my room in a bright yellow striped dress, her gaze fixed on her feet, one hand trying unsuccessfully to reach her back.

"Sure." I zipped her up halfway and the zipper stopped.

Tina tipped her head. "What's the matter? Is it broken? I'm going to kill that saleslady. She swore it worked perfectly when she did it up at the store. Omigod, I bet she lied. I bet she lied just to get the commission. I paid full price, too. And for what? A dress with a friggin' broken zipper. No wonder she rang me up so fast. She just wanted to get rid of me before I found out she was selling me a dud."

"I don't think it's broken," I said. "I, um, think the dress might be a smidge too small."

"That's impossible. It fit perfectly this morning. Try again."

I did. And then again when Tina tried several times to suck in her belly, dancing herself and me across the room in her efforts. The zipper didn't budge.

She turned to face me and my eyes drifted down to the giant bowl of ice cream cradled in the nook of her arm. Possibly the zipper was less the problem than the cheese doodles and ice cream. And the fact that she was growing two human beings who were getting bigger by the day. "Maybe you can take it back and get one that, er, works right."

"This was the only one they had with these slimming stripes. I'd have to get something else. But I won't be getting it there I can tell you. I'm taking this one back for a full refund and taking my money to a store that treats me right."

I clamped my lips together. I had the feeling Tina would never find a store that treated her "right." At least not for long, but I was keeping my mouth shut. Especially since her tight dress was buying me party planning time.

A buzzing came from my bed from where I'd tossed my phone when I shed my mole clothes.

Tina leaned against the window frame and huffed out a sigh. "Do you have to get that? I might need help getting out of this thing."

I glanced at the phone, tilting my head to see if I recognized the caller's name flickering on the display. Looked like Camille.

"Just a sec," I reached for the phone and accepted the call.

"*Réponds- moi seulement par oui ou non,*" I heard when we connected.

"Okay," I said, agreeing to answer whatever Camille was about to say with only a yes or no. Realizing only after I spoke that my "okay" was already breaking the agreement.

"Is the Penguin in the house?" Camille asked.

"No."

"*C'est* Tina with you?"

I scanned the room. Maybe it wasn't the Penguin booby trapping my house with cameras I had to worry about. "Yeees," I said, slowly drawing out the word as my eyes stopped at the window, curtain sheers partly drawn. I stepped closer, keeping a watch on Tina who had rested her backside booty on the end of the bureau while she ladled in the remains of her ice cream. Or more precisely, probably the remains of *my* ice cream stock.

Outside, I caught sight of Camille's Jetta parked in front of my house. And was that the tip of binoculars trained out her passenger window?

"You find trouble in the house?" Camille said.

Since I didn't think me about to confess to Tina that I'd done squat about her party qualified as the kind of trouble Camille was asking about I told her no.

"*Okay*. Then meet me at the car. I give you five minutes to change clothes."

I looked down at my outfit and back out the window. A vision of Camille's vantage point came into my head. Tina, leaning, belly out, shrouded by the sheers like some shadow version of Alfred Hitchcock. Me visible in the open curtain gap, my white blouse picking up the lamp light.

"Um," I said, no yes or no answer going to help me ask her what was wrong with what I was wearing.

"*Voyons*, Lora." Camille said. "Batgirl." The tip of binoculars withdrew from view and the call cut out.

Right. Of course she wanted me to play Batgirl. After all, the Penguin had just made an appearance. Naturally, Camille would want to follow that up with one by Batgirl and Catwoman.

I waited at the window a minute, half expecting to see a torch light appear in the sky flashing a bat with a pink hair ribbon or something. No torch light, but my phone lit up again. This time with a call from Brassard.

I hovered my finger between the accept and decline buttons. Probably by now he'd heard about the Penguin doing laps at my house and Brassard wasn't happy. And it was a good bet he'd be even less happy to hear that his grounded mole was about to take flight as a bat.


**I SLID IN** the seat beside Camille and pulled the Jetta door closed before my batwing got clipped as Camille whipped away from the curb.

"You're wrinkled," she said as she sped up the street.

I rubbed at my thighs, smoothing the crinkles in my black leggings. "I had to pull the pants out of the hamper. I haven't had time to wash them since the stakeout at Chloé's house the other night. Speaking of, has anyone found Chloé yet?"

Camille shook her head. "*Et* Thomas Duncan *non plus*. Neither is at their houses or their works. Didn't Brassard tell you?"

"I, um, haven't talked to him since I left Laurent's."

She slowed for a stop sign and glanced my way before coasting through. "He didn't call you?"

Hmm. Just how good were Camille's binoculars?

"He did but I couldn't pick up," I told her. "I was with Tina." Technically true. It would have been hard to talk to Brassard about confidential bits with Tina listening in. At least that's what I'd told myself when I'd hit the decline button on his call.

Camille shot me her "that's a load of bull cocky" look.

"Fine. You got me," I said. "I didn't want to pick up and listen to him rant. I figure he'd find some way to blame me for the Penguin showing up at my house, and I didn't want to hear it." Which was also why I'd ignored the couple of pings I'd gotten from him since. Ditto one from Laurent.

She smiled. "It's better than that. Brassard wants you locked away."

A sudden heat rushed my body. "Locked away where?" I shifted my eyes to the door lock then out the window to concentrate on my surroundings, trying to peg Camille's route. "Is that what this is about? You're not taking me to the PDQ, are you?"

"*Non, non. Absolument pas. Brassard est un con. Un con typiquement masculin.*"

I scrunched my nose. She'd lost me with more French than I could follow. I sort of understood the words but not the context. "What?"

"Brassard wants you locked up safe somewhere until the case is over. He thinks you figured out too much and the Penguin knows it."

The heat rushing my body rerouted to my head. "But it's my job to figure things out. And it was Brassard's idea for me to go to the warehouse and ruffle the Penguin's feathers. I'm not even sure how I did. All I did was grab computer files and go to lunch with Mario and trip over Goatee Guy's body. It's not like I put the guy there." I fell quiet, a sinking feeling of doubt coming over me. One that had been creeping around most of the afternoon. A niggling feeling of guilt that maybe somehow my feather ruffling *had* played some part in what happened to Goatee Guy. Logic kept telling me otherwise, but even the slightest possibility that something I did could have got someone hurt was unthinkable. And only made me more itchy to solve this mess once and for all.

"Anyway," I went on, "What does Brassard care? He already took me off his case. He called me an assistant. Told Laurent to take me back. Like I was some piece of equipment out on loan that they were shuttling back and forth."

Camille pulled the car in front of a driveway, cut the engine, and pivoted my way. "Pass me your phone."

I grabbed my cell from my Batgirl fanny pack slung across my torso beauty queen sash style, punched in my password, and handed the phone to Camille, watching as she tapped away at the screen and handed it back.

"Brassard is a pain in the neck," she said. "He's a macho chauvinist who thinks all women belong behind desks. *Mais aussi*, he's a good cop. *Probablement* he thinks he made a bad call putting you in the warehouse. Locking you up is how he fix his mistake."

If I had hackles on my back, I'm sure they would have bristled. "I'm not buying it. This was no mistake. Brassard wanted me there. Maybe not so much to be a mole, but he was using me for something. My guess is whatever that something was took a turn he didn't expect."

Camille fidgeted in her purse as I spoke, and when I was done she tossed me a square of dark chocolate that I gratefully accepted. Whoever said honey is the nectar of the Gods never had chocolate. Liquid, solid, melted into a warm cookie, embedded into ice cream, or otherwise. If I learned anything since I started working with the Carons, it's that chocolate is the ultimate nectar of the Gods.

She took two squares for herself and popped them into her mouth. Chocolate was also Camille's cure-all for any situation. Like a heat sensitive missile, chocolate had the power to target her needs, zero in, and modulate accordingly. Sometimes it soothed her. Other times it acted like rocket fuel. Probably it would be another minute or so before I knew which this dose was going to do for her.

For me, my dose was bringing me focus. "Look," I said. "As far as I'm concerned Brassard can talk all he wants, but he's not locking me anywhere. I held up my end of the deal and I expect him to hold up his and leave me and C&C alone. I'm done being his mole or sitting duck or whatever. What I care about is Sister Jane and helping her protect her brother from being unplugged permanently. Maybe Johnny did commit insurance fraud, but if he did I'm thinking he had his reasons. Obviously, something funky is going down at his warehouse. And I don't think it ends there. Laurent and Brassard got very interested when I mentioned Johnny's dead friend. What I don't know is why. And neither of them was willing to tell me. That's when they got into a big fight and fired me."

Camille rolled her eyes. "*Encore ça…* Nobody fired you. I talked to Laurent about it. He's not happy with Brassard. It's got nothing to do with you."

"What about this talk about locking me up?"

"That's just crazy Brassard. Mister macho. It's just talk. *Dis-moi* did the friend die three months ago?"

"I don't know," I said. "Maybe. If Sister Jane said a time, I don't remember."

Camille pulled out her own phone and worked it, zipping from scroll mode to click mode and back again. "I think I found your man. *Le gars* fell through the ice of *Fleuve Saint-Laurent.*"

"Excuse me?"

"After you told us in the car about the dead friend I looked into it. It was in the papers. Three months ago. A man who worked at *le Port* fell through some ice on the river and drowned." She held her phone up so I could see.

Oh my. The news was surprising, but Camille's uncovering it was not. When it came to finding Internet info, Camille's fingers didn't just walk, they sprinted.

"That's awful. Did the article say where he worked?" I asked. "If it was an accident?"

She skimmed her phone screen. "*Mise en Port.* The same place as Chloé and Thomas Duncan. *Et oui c'était un accident.* At least according to this."

Okay that placed him in Johnny's Port posse sphere, but it didn't mean the guy was the friend Jane told me about. "It could be the guy," I said. I texted the dead man's name to Sister Jane to confirm it was the right man. She answered back that Claude Morin, the name of the man in the paper, was indeed Johnny's deceased friend.

If Jane had any curiosity about my question or found it odd, she didn't say. Probably some nun code not to ask too many questions. Or maybe a sign she had faith that whatever I asked of her was for the good of Johnny and the case.

I sent off another note asking what Jane knew about Claude. To that she was less helpful, not knowing any more details other than that the two men met through work.

"Okay," I said to Camille and stowed my phone away. "So we have the right dead guy, but we still don't know why the mention of him got Brassard and Laurent so riled up. Maybe you should ask them. Just because they wouldn't tell me doesn't mean they won't tell you."

Camille had her nose in her phone and said nothing. A minute went by and I figured she'd zoned out, so I made my suggestion again.

"We don't need Brassard and Laurent," she said, swiveling her mobile my way again. "*Regarde ça*. It's from the files you took from Huguette."

I focused on the list filling the screen. "And?"

"*Et bien*, it has a folder logging problems with some shipments being screened before coming into the country."

I squinted, trying to see better, and skimmed my finger over the phone display to toggle through the lines of info. "What kind of problems?"

"Times the x-ray machines were not working."

"X-ray machines?"

"*Les autorités du Port* uses some x-ray type machines to scan into packages, shipping containers, and so on. It's more fast than having inspectors search each piece. If the machines see something that might be a problem then someone goes in and checks it."

"You mean for drugs and stuff?"

"*Oui, oui*. Anything that could be smuggled in."

"All right," I said, not quite getting the significance. "And that connects to the dead man how?"

"It was his job to work the machines."

Hmm. Interesting but still not clear how that factored him into the case. "So let's say Claude did work the x-ray machines and was maybe even on duty when the x-ray machines were down. How is that important? What happens then? Do they open and inspect everything by hand?"

Camille shrugged which I took to mean ideally that should happen, but in reality maybe yes maybe no. "*Le Port de Montréal* is one of the biggest in North America," she said. "Very busy. Not just for Canada. You want something in Chicago, it's faster to go through here than New York. *Le Port* here has to process a lot quick and manual checks aren't quick. *En plus*, the people, the sniffer dogs, they don't have as many anymore. Cutbacks."

Camille showed me another page she'd pulled up on her phone. "*Puis regarde ça.* A file from your hippie doll flash drive."

I browsed the file she had up and spotted what was likely the link that had Camille thinking we were onto something. "Looks like the Penguin's shipments went into storage at Johnny's warehouse on the same dates the x-ray machines were down," I said. "And all before Claude's drowning." I looked back at Camille. "Maybe that does tie things together somehow. Maybe Claude knew something about the Penguin's goods. Maybe when the x-rays weren't working, Claude inspected things and found something wrong. Something the Penguin wanted kept quiet."

"*Peut-être*," Camille said. "Or maybe Claude knew already there was something not good in the Penguin's boxes."

"You mean like ahead of time? Like maybe Claude only pretended the x-ray machines were broken so he could pass the packages through himself? Like he was on the take or something?"

Camille nodded. "Bingo, as you would say."

I nearly smiled despite the gloomy circumstances, glad to have picked up on the connection so quickly and that Camille was picking up on my lingo as much as I was picking up hers. The Bingo may be a bit premature, though. Felt to me like we may be starting to fill in more squares on our Bingo card and make some links, but we still didn't have enough to make a solid row. It also didn't explain why Brassard and Laurent were worked up about Claude. It may take a whole other Bingo card to see how that lined up.

"So let's get this straight," I said, going into a list—my go-to for helping my brain keep track of things. "We've got four people who all work at the Port and who know each other: Johnny, Chloé, and Johnny's two friends—the dead one Claude and Thomas Duncan, the man Chloé argued with at her house. Then we've got the Penguin and his goons who may have something fishy going on at the docks that Johnny and his entourage know about or are maybe even involved in. Plus, we have Goatee Guy, also maybe involved somehow."

"*Évidemment* he's involved," Camille said. "A man doesn't get beat up for nothing."

"Right. But we've got no proof. All we have so far is a bunch of suppositions. We need more. For starters, maybe a work log to see for sure if Claude even had his shift when the x-rays were down," I said. "Or more information about the Penguin's shipments." I checked the record from the flash files of what went into storage to see what had been declared, making my best efforts to understand the French wording. "Says here it's some kind of metal stuff for construction I think. But I'm betting there's more to it than that. And if Johnny knew what that more was, maybe that's why someone tried to kill him." I sat back and sighed. "This is so frustrating. If only my mole career wasn't over or you weren't tanked as a fake inspector. If only we had a way to find out what was in the Penguin's boxes."

Camille snapped on her black Catwoman gloves, reached for a bag in the back seat, and said, "*Oui*. If only."

## 23

CAMILLE DROPPED THE bag onto my lap. From inside, I pulled out a slim, mid-length red coat and another wig similar to the one I'd worn earlier in the day. Same color, same bangs, shorter length in the back.

A car beeped behind us, an arm waving frantically out the driver's window. In the rearview mirror, I could make out the driver's lips moving. From his facial expression I was guessing the words had something to do with Camille moving her Jetta caboose the heck out of his driveway.

Camille got the car going and sent the guy a smile that looked like it had him rethinking exactly where he'd like to see her caboose resettle itself.

I set the coat in my lap and finger combed the wig. Camille made a right at the corner and a left at the next one, her route sure and deliberate. And starting to look familiar. It was quickly gaining a familiar feeling, too. An unmistakable bumpy rocking that settled into my own caboose. Like a massage. A seat massage.

The kind that comes from rolling over cobblestone streets like the ones she'd brought us to now in Vieux Montréal.

Camille slipped the car into a lane between two brick buildings with large windows and small entryways headed by vine-covered black iron gates. The kind that promised something enchanting beyond.

"*T'as faim?*" she asked. She cut the engine and turned her attention to me, waiting for my reply to her question asking if I was hungry.

A fast check-in with my stomach told me I was. It had been nearly dinner time when I'd gotten home to Tina and her Winnie the Pooh sticks. Between dealing with her, Adam, and the Penguin invasion aftermath and then answering Camille's call for Batgirl, nary a breadcrumb had crossed my lips. The fact that we were barely a cobblestone's throw from a whole loaf of French buttery baguette was not lost on me. But neither was the wig and coat sitting in my lap that were sending me a "Guess Who's Going to Dinner?" vibe. Leaving the car for buttery baguette could mean stepping into some ill-fated episode of Batgirl meets Molegirl. With me playing both roles.

I held the wig up to Camille. "Just who are you asking?"

She smiled, and I think I caught a glint of glee in her eye. Impossible. Camille didn't glint.

"*Dépêche-toi,*" she said. "You'll be late."

Hurry? Uh oh. "Late for what?"

"Your date."

Now that time I saw it for sure. Not quite a glint, but something shimmered behind Camille's baby browns.

Probably something flashed in my not-so-baby blues, too. Clandestine reconnaissance I expected maybe when we'd donned our prowling duds, a mystery date I did not.

"Okay, spill," I said. "You did not just happen to pull me out into the night to send me on a blind bat date."

"Who said anything about blind? Your date is with Mario."

I felt my eyes widen. "Mario asked me on a date through you and you accepted?"

"*Non, non.* Of course not. *You* asked Mario on a date and *he* accepted."

I may miss a few things now and then but that I would remember. "Nuh, uh. I so did not."

*She nodded. "Regarde ton cellulaire."*

I found my phone and checked the history. Sure enough there was a text exchange between me and Mario. Not long ago. About the same time Camille asked me to hand her my phone and like a dummy I had. No questions asked.

"Wait," I said, checking the messages again. "That's not my phone number Mario's texting. How did it get on my phone?" I didn't bother asking how Mario's number got there. Camille had a habit of collecting numbers and other details on a case that she pulled from nowhere like a magician materializing scarves from his sleeve.

"*C'est sûr*, Lora. I'm not going to use your real number with some stranger on a case. *C'est un numero de téléphone jetable.*"

I gave the phone a once over. It was mine all right. At least the new one Laurent had given me. Complete with my usual contacts and a bazillion texts from Tina. "This isn't a throwaway phone," I said.

"I didn't say *téléphone jetable*," Camille said. "I said *un numero de téléphone jetable*. *Un numero de téléphone jetable* is easy to get now and good for some of our work. It's a burner number and only temporary. Laurent put the app on your phone just in case."

Hmm. I doubted the "just in case" Laurent had in mind was Camille making me a bat date with Mario. But overall I could see the use of a burner app, especially if it meant having access to various incognito number lines on one phone.

"What exactly am I supposed to do on this date?" I said.

Camille leaned towards me, a hair net materializing, and she swept my hair up into the net. She took the wig from me and slid that on me, too, adjusting as she went, pulling the fake hair into a short ponytail spun into a knot and pinned. "*Mais alors*. See what more he knows."

I glanced at her as she pulled a small cosmetic bag from her purse and began upgrading my makeup to Bunny standards. I considered relieving her of the blush brush dusting my face and doing the job myself. Or pointing out that she was pretty much resurrecting my mole self when I'd been de-moled by her partner and brother, aka Laurent, and super cop Brassard. But with Camille it was best to pick my battles, and I was sensing a more critical one may be imminent. One foreshadowed by the way she avoided my attempts to catch her eye, her evasions taking some doing since she was leaning right into my face.

"And?" I said.

"And what?" she said.

"No. That's my question. Something tells me this is not just about gathering intel. What exactly is it you think a date with Mario is going to get us?"

She sat back, studying her handiwork, still avoiding eye contact. "His pass card."

I burbled out an incredulous laugh touched with a hint of panic. "You mean his employee pass card for the warehouse? How am I supposed to get that? I'm no pickpocket. I can't just ask him for it. And there's a good chance he won't even have it with him. What am I supposed to do then? Ask him to run home and get it?"

"You'll find a way."

Right. "What's the point anyway? The warehouse is closed. And

it has security. No pass card is going to get us past all the security."
And if it did, it wouldn't get us past all the cameras which I'm sure
would be up and working just fine this time. "And if you're
thinking it's going to get us into the Penguin's private storage box,
think again. There are locks on those, too." She, of course, would
know that as well as me, but it seemed like a good time to
remind her.

"*T'inquiète pas*. Leave all that to me."

Don't worry she says. Leave all that to her she says. She wants
me to hoodwink Mario out of his pass card so Batgirl and
Catwoman can wade into a warehouse in the dark of night and
plunder the Penguin's secret booty. Yeah, that plan had "don't
worry" written all over it.

**NO BOOTHS. STONE** walls, slate floors, beamed ceiling, dim
lighting, the scent of simmering herbs. But no booths in the land
beyond the enchanting iron gates of the *Jardin de Pilaf* restaurant.

I let out a sigh. I was hoping for booths. And crowded together
tables. Like popular restaurants back in New York where diners
were packed together so tight they ate elbow-to-elbow with
strangers. As best as I could figure, sitting near enough to bump
elbows with Mario was my only hope of getting his pass card away
from him without him knowing.

"*Bonjour.*" A young man in white shirt and dark pants had come
up beside me where I stood mere steps away from the maître-D
desk.

I turned to his smile and returned it along with a *bonjour* of
my own.

"May I take your coat?" he said.

My smile dimmed just a little and I shook my head, thanking
him for his offer but declining. Below the coat were Batgirl

clothes. Wrinkly Batgirl clothes. Appropriate for prowling or cave dwelling or maybe even a gym or an old Beatnik club, but not for enchanting upscale restaurants. Coming from Camille, the coat was haute couture and at the moment the only thing cloaking me with a modicum of class. The coat and a pair of heeled booties pulled from Camille's trunk that I'd swapped for my Batgirl shoes, which screamed comfort not class.

And apparently class was very much in vogue at *Jardin de Pilaf*. Not stuffy, nose-in-the-air class. The kind of class that came from knowing it's fun to dress up and kick back with a glass of wine and a fine meal now and then.

Across the room of tables sans booths, I spotted Mario, seated, in profile, fiddling with a tiny silver jar of flowers. I watched as he propped the tallest flower in the middle of the mini bouquet, centered the jar on the pristine white tablecloth, and sat back, his attention shifting to one of the paned, double windows set deep into the stone walls that could easily belong to some ancient villa in Europe.

I headed over to Mario's table, the young coat-check guy in tow and pulling out my chair for me in a move so swift and seamless it had me thinking dance was the man's real profession.

He retreated with the same soft-shoe shuffle, leaving me alone with Mario who had classed himself up with a blue suit, a slathering of hair product, and a shot of cologne. Not bad given the short notice he'd had to prepare for our fast fix-up.

Beaming at me, Mario said, "You look beautiful tonight."

His eyes trailed from my face to my body, and I watched him work to hold his beam in place. Probably the red coat. It was nice and all, but it wasn't the kind of outfit that would have most guys jumping to beautiful.

He reached for my hand and his smile turned sly. "I see you

have kept your coat. *Muy excitante.* Leave the surprise underneath for later, yes?"

Yipes. That wasn't just some corny line. That line didn't say date. That line said booty call. And so did the look Mario landed on my mouth. A look that said he was imagining a lot more than what I was wearing beneath the red coat.

I did my best to put the brakes on the flush heating its way up my cheeks. It never occurred to me that Mario would mistake Camille's text to set her Penguin booty plunder plan in motion for a bootay booty call with mole Bunny, aka *moi.* Especially when Camille had made our date for dinner at a place like the *Jardin de Pilaf.* The *Jardin de Pilaf* had too much class to be a booty call pre-show venue, didn't it?

Of course, the faux-date text had been for a last minute *rendez-vous.* Probably that didn't look good.

I slid my hand away from Mario's and grabbed for the menu sitting by my place setting. "So, what looks good? I've never been here before. You have any suggestions?"

Mario grinned at me. "Many. But none from the menu."

Ugh. If my appetite hadn't already dulled from his earlier remarks, that one would have sunk it for sure. There was cute corny and then there was tacky corny.

I had a hard time working up a smile for him but smile I did. I had to keep him on the hook, didn't I? The tricky part was keeping him on a hook that I could use to bait him to get what I wanted without letting him think he'd get what he wanted.

A waitress approached, took our order, and sauntered off.

I snatched a bread roll from the basket she left on the table and set my eyes on Mario. "I'm sorry we didn't get to connect in your warehouse this afternoon," I said. "I was really looking forward to seeing you work. I have to say when I heard someone had another accident, I worried something happened to you." Step one in my hook-him plan. Express interest and concern.

He sat back and grinned some more. "You were worried about Mario, eh? No need. Mario is right here for you."

I hid the "oy" making its way to my lips behind a smile. "I *was* worried. I'm still a little shaken about the accident and then all those police guys crawling around." I let a shudder skim my shoulders. Step two in my plan. Appear vulnerable. "I just keep thinking about the man who was hurt. Marcel I think someone said. I heard he had to go to the hospital." I lowered my voice. "I also heard what happened to him may not have been an accident." Step three. Steer the conversation to the latest accident and set the groundwork to pump Mario for info.

Mario's dimple tightened for a fraction of a second. "Marcel is having accidents always. He loses keys, he drops boxes on his feet, he forgets his computer passwords. He's a walking disaster, but he'll be fine. He always is."

Hmm. Those weren't really the same kinds of accidents. Then again, Marcel aka Goatee Guy had fumbled and dropped his doughnut bag when Huguette had passed him. Maybe he was accident prone. Or maybe a nervous Nellie type. But that didn't mean the dumpster dive he took was because he was a klutz. Laurent said Goatee Guy had been beat up and I believed him. Laurent wasn't wrong about stuff like that. Laurent was rarely wrong about anything.

I reached for a dish of butter shaped into mini seashells, buying time to form my next question. Also, giving in to the smell of warm bread resurrecting my appetite.

Mario caught my arm before my fingers closed in on the butter dish. I trailed my gaze up my arm to his face, a blur of movement over his shoulder catching my attention, like a cat spotting a strand of dangling yarn. Through the window, the blur moved again then slowed and came into focus. Camille. Making a whirring motion at me with her arm, revving her hand in circles like she was cranking a pasta maker. Her sign language loud and clear. She wanted me to hurry things along.

I felt the pull of Mario's grasp on my arm as he drew my hand to his mouth and kissed my palm. His message just as clear as Camille's and just as suggestive about wanting to rev up the evening's activities. Only his idea of the end goal likely had me relieving him of more than his pass card.

A prickling started in my toes and slowly rose up my legs. Revulsion maybe. Or panic.

Maybe Brassard was right. Maybe I wasn't cut out to be a mole. I wasn't even feeling a lot of confidence in my Batgirl abilities at the moment. I'd played Mario and he'd played right along by upping his overtures, only now I had no idea what to do next. I was all flapping wings and no bite. Some bat I was.

Camille gave me one final hand gesture then disappeared from sight, leaving me to suck up my insecurity and flap on.

"What do you say we get our food to go and move it to my apartment?" Mario said. "I live very close. Five minutes to walk."

Slowly I eased my arm away from Mario, the prickling in my limbs growing into a full-blown itch. I checked my hand for welts, sure I was developing hives. It was one thing to draw him out with banter in a public restaurant. It was another thing to move the banter to somewhere private. I went quiet, needing a moment to process how to respond.

Mario got up and came over to me, pulling my chair out. Reflexively I stood, the itching in my legs feeling like mosquitoes had found their way under my Batgirl pants and couldn't find their way out.

We got the food and paid the bill, and while Mario retrieved his jacket from coat-check, my processing went from thinking I needed to figure out a way to decline Mario's offer to thinking I should see it as a lucky break. Look for the bright side. Like probably Mario would be less guarded talking at his place. And I'd definitely have access to his pass card. Both good things. Maybe this turn of events wasn't so bad. Maybe it was the path to getting what I needed that Camille was so sure I'd find. The "take advantage of opportunity" undercover rule Laurent said I needed to be ready to recognize at all times.

I felt Mario's arm settle on my shoulders and his hand grip the soft flesh near my bicep, squeezing me closer to him as we headed for the door. Somewhere in the back of my brain, I could hear Laurent drilling some other PI rule into me about keeping people more than arm's length from my body. Something about safety and access.

While I considered the best way to extricate myself from Mario and put a little distance between us, more of Laurent's words popped into my head. Ones about me not having enough training yet to pull off undercover work on a case like this. I scratched at a renewed itch on my leg and tried to push the words away, hoping with all my might that that was one of the few things Laurent had wrong.


*WAIT*, **I SILENTLY** told the spreading itch on my legs. There's no need to panic. I can handle this. I made home visits to clients all the time when I was a social worker. Going to Mario's apartment was no different. The problem wasn't that I couldn't be a good mole or play Batgirl. The problem was forgetting that underneath the Batgirl outfit and mole wig, I was still me. I may not have a lot of PI training, but I did have social work training. And I'd honed my skills in New York—not exactly easy street.

Okay, so it wasn't like I worked the grit and grime of TV shows like NYPD Blue or a CSI or something, but I did manage my share of sketchy situations and dodgy people. I was not without survival skills. I may not know how to crush a man's windpipe like Camille, but I did know how to crush a man where it counted if the circumstances called for it. And I also knew how to turn a potentially negative scenario to my advantage.

When we exited the gates of *Jardin de Pilaf*, Mario steered us right. Clouds lingered high in the sky, streets were dry, and the air chill, making me grateful for the borrow of Camille's red coat. As we strode along, rather than distance myself from Mario, I burrowed closer to him and wrapped my arm around his waist.

"Brrr," I said. "It sure got cold, didn't it?" I let my body shudder again, this time not in a suggestion of vulnerability but more of a shivery chill.

Mario nodded. His muscular build and Latin temperament probably kept his internal heat gauge on a permanent slow burn, but hailing from South America likely the Montreal damp and cold could get to him, too.

I took advantage of his agreement nod by snuggling closer and dipping my hand in the pocket of his jacket. The jacket was decent quality, the all-weather type I imagined had a zip-out lining for reinforcement. The kind of coat a guy gets when he appreciates good clothes but needs to stretch his pesos by buying things like jackets that work just as well in the fall as the spring and go from a daytime to nighttime with nothing more than an accessory upgrade.

My social work had prepped me for noticing things just like multi-purpose coats, and I was banking my assessment skills were still sharp enough, too, for my educated guess to be right that Mario had worn the same coat to work earlier and may have absent mindedly stashed his pass card in one of the pockets. Hopefully the one my fingers were currently probing. Otherwise,

Mario and I could be in for another misunderstanding between us.

He turned a smile my way and slowed his stride to stop at a corner intersection. I paced my probing with his slowdown, and my fingertips grazed something sharp cushioned in something soft that had the feel of a glove. Gingerly I felt around some more. The something sharp was thin, rectangular, and smooth with a hard bump-out at one end. Promising enough for me to palm it, scoot my arm back to me, and slip the something under my red coattail in a move I hoped went unnoticed. Sliding slightly aside, out of the way of foot traffic, I bent and feigned adjusting the heel of my shoe, using the ruse to steal a peek at my pickpocket pickings. Bingo.

I tucked the card in my waistband and stood to face Mario, bundle of takeout crooked in his arm, perfect toothy grin in place. Now that I'd figured out how to get what I wanted from him, I needed to figure out how to let him know he wasn't getting what he wanted from me and ditch him.

## 2 4

"**WELL THIS IS** a big disappointment," I said.

Camille crouched beside me and killed the flashlight. "Shush."

I tilted my head so one ear faced higher, as though that would improve my hearing. "What?" I whispered. "I don't hear anything."

She tapped a hand to my leg and I went quiet and listened some more. My knees started to lock and my instep pinched from perching myself on the balls of my feet too long. That's what I got for faking a queasy stomach to ditch Mario and following Camille into the dark depths of *Dépôt Deschênes* which, true to her word, she'd gotten us into but was having a much harder time getting us out of.

My stomach growled and Camille shushed me again. Hey, was it my fault I had to scurry out on my bat date before I got to eat?

I pressed an arm to my stomach to muffle the new growl I could feel coming, and I repositioned myself closer to the nearest palette, piled high with pipes, in an attempt to hide from whatever threat Camille had detected. I had no idea what the threat could be but was not going to let my traitorous stomach be the thing that gave us away to whatever it was. I was already feeling like the evening's episode of Catwoman and Batgirl Go a'Plundering was a bust. All I needed now was for us to get busted.

It had taken some of Camille's best cat burglar skills, and I was guessing some purring in the right ears, to gain us entry to *Dépôt Deschênes* and inside the Penguin's booty box, where we'd found nothing but palettes filled with steel tubes on one half of the storage locker and a whole lot of nothing on the other. We'd found some white powder resting in the nothing. Drugs, we'd thought. Until Camille had tasted it and found her tongue tainted with cement mix instead. Major letdown. As were the steel tubes, although they were making for a handy hiding place.

"*Mais voyons*, Lora," Camille said. "It's you."

I slid a look her way. "I'm sorry. It's my stomach. I'm hungry."

"Not that. The whirring sound. It's coming from your back."

Whirring sound? I didn't hear a whirring sound. Except then I did. In tempo with an itch at my back, like the imaginary mosquitoes in my Batgirl pants earlier had migrated. I felt behind me to find in reality my fanny pack had done the migrating. And the whirring was my phone, tucked into the pack, buzzing on vibrate.

"Is that what we're hiding from?" I whispered to Camille.

She rolled her eyes at me and stood up. I rose, too, slipped my pack front and center, and freed my phone to find its screen filled with missed calls and several texts. A few of each were from Tina and Brassard, but the majority came from Laurent. His earliest texts blasting me for turning off Location Services tracking. His later messages laced with concern and requests for me to reply.

My brows furrowed. I hadn't turned off any services on my phone, let alone tracking ones. I wasn't even sure I knew how to turn them off.

I glanced at Camille. "Did you do anything to my phone besides make the bat date with Mario? Like maybe turn off the tracking service?"

"*Bien entendu.* You're with me. Nobody needs to know where you are."

Translation: Nobody needs to know where *we* were. Not when we were in a warehouse we shouldn't be in doing plundering we shouldn't be doing.

"Right," I said and texted Laurent back that I was fine and would talk to him in the morning.

Immediately his message bubble popped up and filled with dots. Seconds later the dots faded out and the bubble disappeared.

I tucked my phone away, slipping it to the side of my Batgirl pack, checking the other side for bat nibbles. Usually I stocked the pack with protein bars, but I'd left the house fast and forgotten so the Batpack pantry was bare.

I sighed and my shoulders sagged. My mind went to Mario with all that baguette and butter. If I'd gone with him at least I'd be full up on bread by now. And possibly more info about Johnny's accident and the shady goings-on in the warehouse. Instead, all I had to show for the night was an empty stomach and a futile frisking of a half-empty storage unit.

Camille shook her head at me and passed me a chunk of chocolate. Where she had it hidden a moment before I had no idea. Her Catwoman suit showed no pockets I could see and she wouldn't be caught dead in a fanny pack, even a cute one like mine slung over her shoulder.

I ate the hunk of chocolate and shook a kink out of my leg and a sticky blob off the bottom of my shoe as I scanned the Penguin's tubes-of-steel booty. If I stood back, it was like looking at a wall of shiny circles. And if I squinted a little the circles looked like a wall of doughnuts. Glistening with glaze. Maple. Or maybe honey.

Oh geez. I had to get my mind of off food.

"What do you suppose the Penguin needs with all these pipes?" I asked Camille. "They don't look like plumbing pipes. Those are usually thinner and copper."

She came to my side and waved her hand at the palette of tubes. "Who cares? We're too late." She swept her wave over to the bare side of the locker like a magician flaunting his trick. "The good stuff is already gone."

"Or maybe there was no good stuff," I said. "Maybe we're wrong about the Penguin. Maybe he is just shipping and storing construction supplies. Maybe he's got nothing to do with whatever's going on here."

Camille knelt by a strip of the white powder lacing the floor. "*Non, non.* He's doing something. Brassard wouldn't be running undercover plans and making you a mole for nothing." Her eyes methodically scanned the high corners of the storeroom. "*En plus,* someone's got more cameras in this locker. Not every locker has this many cameras. Either someone wants extra *sécurité* or someone's watching."

I looked over at the gizmo Camille had placed on the floor near a wall when we'd come in. I knew it did something to scramble or disable something. I thought it messed with possible alarm triggers, but maybe it futzed with camera feeds, too.

I walked the length of the leftover palettes, peering between. "Well, whatever Brassard's after isn't here. Anyway if it had been, wouldn't he have just seized it or something? I mean he's a cop. Isn't that what they do? Make busts? Search and seizures? Stuff like that."

"Search and seizures?" Camille said.

"Yeah, something like that. I heard it on TV."

She arched a brow at me and sighed. At my TV comment or the concept, I wasn't sure.

"*Non, non,*" she said. "Brassard is after something bigger. I can feel it."

I caught a look of something in Camille's eyes. Close to the same glint I'd seen earlier when she told me about my bat date with Mario.

"Is that why we're here?" I asked her. "Is this about Brassard? Or more specifically you and Brassard and this crazy feud or whatever you two have going."

"*C'est quoi ça* 'feud'?" Camille said, asking what feud meant. Which was ridiculous. She knew exactly what feud meant. Pretending she didn't know an English word was just a diversion tactic she used when she wanted to avoid something. I knew that. And she knew I knew.

But if this plundering bit had something to do with Brassard, it explained a lot. Seemed to me, this bit did more than stretch the rules in the PI handbook. It had to be closer to snapping them. Camille was big on rule stretching, but this was as close to rule snapping as I'd seen her go. Something big had to be motivating her. I was a fellow rule stretcher but not a rule snapper. I only went along with the plundering plan because I trusted Camille. And because that's what best friends do. Ethel never abandoned Lucy or Lucy Ethel in *I Love Lucy* no matter how hair-brained or risky the messes they got into. They always trusted each other and had each other's backs. And if my bff wanted to keep her motivation for this scheme to herself for the time being, I'd just have to stand by that as well. Partly because it was the supportive thing to do. But mostly because I knew eventually she'd snap on that, too, and tell me.

"Okay," I said. "Have it your way. But I say we go now. We've done all we can here and I'm hungry." Past hungry really. Bordering on delirious hungry it seemed. One of the pipe doughnuts higher up was starting to look cream filled, more like a cannoli than a doughnut.

Camille swiveled to face the wall of tubes. "What are you staring at?"

"Nothing. My imagination's playing tricks on me. I thought I saw something filling that pipe." I gestured loosely towards the cannoli of my hunger vision.

She squinted and moved forward. "*Mais alors*. There *is* something in there." She hooked her thumb towards her back and bent her knees. "*Allez. Monte.*"

Oh boy. Not this again. The piggy back thing to hoist me closer to the cannoli, just like she'd hoisted me closer to the window at Chloé's.

"This isn't going to become a thing, is it?" I said, scrambling up her back. "Because truth be told I'm not all that fond of heights."

She raised up and slid over to where I'd seen the cannoli mirage. "Can you tell what it is?"

I reached for the closest pipe to still myself from a wobble. "Scooch a little to the left." I felt a shift below. "Okay, stop. Got it." I placed my fingers in the pipe center and pulled out something white and stiff yet soft to the touch. Not cream filling. Something papery.

Camille lowered down, and I returned my feet to the ground and unraveled the paper. A buttery soft canvas with a painting of a woman reading under a tree.

I glanced from the painting to the pipe where I'd found it then to Camille. "What's a painting doing with a bunch of construction supplies?" I said.

Camille smiled and took some pics of the painting with her phone. "*On verra.*" She rerolled the canvas, extended her arm up as far as it would go, and pitched the painting into a steel tube. "Whatever it is, Brassard will be the last to know."

. . .

"IT'S SIX IN the morning. Who would come knocking at six in the morning?"

I rolled onto my back and nestled my head into my pillow. "Hmm?"

Adam flopped his arm across me onto my side of the bed. "Someone's at the door," he said. "It's early. Just ignore them and they'll go away."

I murmured a sleepy "okay" and shifted again, this time to burrow my backside into the warmth of Adam's body.

Bang, bang, bang, bang, bang. Bark bark bark.

I eased open one eye. Fabulous. Now the dog was blaring out a duet with our early, and apparently persistent, visitor.

"I don't think ignoring them is working," I said. "I'm surprised Tina is sleeping through it."

"Tina isn't here. She went home last night." Adam turned onto his back and covered his eyes with his hand. "You would know that if you hadn't gotten home at the crack of dawn."

Bang bang bang. Bark bark bark.

"It wasn't the *crack* of dawn." Had felt like it, though. On the way home from *Dépôt Deschênes* Camille and I had grabbed some takeout fettuccini and ate it camped down the street from my house, keeping watch to make sure Brassard wasn't going to pop out of somewhere and make good on his idea to lock me up.

Since he'd been instrumental in my demotion from mole duty, Brassard was making quick time reinstating himself as a pain in my caboose. And given that Camille had mentioned him several times during our plundering, I was guessing he wasn't figuring too far from her mind, either.

Not that either of us talked about him. We had more important things to do like eat and spitball hypotheses about how the painting got in the Penguin's pipe—smuggling stolen art being our top guess.

When we'd felt sure Brassard wasn't lurking and got tired of spitballing, I'd dashed home and tiptoed off to bed, safe as a mole in a hole. Only now said mole, on duty or not, had an eager beaver pounding on the mole door.

Adam flipped open his covers, and I caught his arm when he had one leg out and headed for the floor.

"What are you doing?" I said.

"What do you think I'm doing? I'm getting the door."

I had a vision of Brassard tossing me into an *actual* hole. "Wait," I said, rising to a sit. "We don't want to be hasty. I mean, whoever it is isn't being very nice, banging like that. We don't want to reward that kind of behavior, do we?"

Adam groaned and his eyes shut too long to be a blink. "Is there something you want to tell me?" He opened his eyes and directed them at me. "Am I going to go downstairs and find your Penguin friend on our doorstep expecting to barrel his way in again?"

Penguin friend. Egads. I hadn't thought about that. What if the Penguin went to the warehouse to check on his painting pipe and found the painting in the wrong hole? Camille had just flung it into a random empty tube. What if he knew Camille and I had messed with his painting and he was coming to mess with us?

"Of course it's not the Penguin," I said to Adam, hoping wishing would make it true. It was bad enough I had to worry about Brassard. I didn't need to come nose to beak with the Penguin this early in the morning. "And he's no friend of mine." I eased out of bed and tread stealth-like to the window and peered out from an edge of curtain.

No goons leaning on a car, no fish heads in the street, no cop cars, no bronze sedan with a Tim Horton's cup on the hood.

The tightness from holding my breath released and I let the

curtain drop. It had been at least two minutes since the last round of banging from downstairs. Maybe whoever it was had left.

Bark bark bark.

Or maybe not. I flicked the curtain again, something across the street catching my attention. Something familiar. A car. A dark Beamer to be exact.

A sharp inhale filled my lungs and I backed away from the window. Uh oh. It was worse than Brassard or the Penguin. My early visitor was no doubt the owner of the Beamer. An owner I knew all too well. Laurent. And Laurent banging doors at six in the morning could not be good.

$\mathcal{T}$HE TIGHTNESS THAT had left my chest shifted to my stomach as I grabbed my robe and padded out to the stairs. Laurent was usually at the gym at six A.M. Not paying house calls.

When I unlocked the door and let him in, he took two steps towards me, his eyes burning into mine, his hands about to clasp my shoulders, then his gaze rose above my head and he retracted his arms and stilled.

"*Salut*, Adam," Laurent said. "Would you mind giving Lora and me time to talk shop."

I turned my head so I could see Adam who had come downstairs after me, taking time to jump into jeans and throw on a T-shirt. His hair, recently trimmed, rested on his head, tidy and neat. No sign he'd just been propelled out of bed. His stubble, the only tell he'd yet to start his day, added an angular accent to his cheeks. Something dim passed through his eyes as he weighed Laurent's request, which had come out less question and more directive.

"Actually," Adam said. "Since your agency has opened up a

branch "shop" in my home with break-ins and alarms and fishy characters taking themselves on unguided tours around my house, I'd be more than happy to talk shop, too. As in, closing this one."

I looked back to Laurent, his body remaining still, his own hair untamed, his scruff longer than usual, and the crinkles at the outer corners of his eyes nearly showing as lines. Only the barely perceptible lowering of one eyebrow his tell that he had any feeling at all about Adam's reply. And the tell was only a giveaway to someone practiced in Caron sign language.

I shot Adam a pleading look. "Just give us a sec, okay?"

Adam returned my look with a "don't push it" one. "Fine. You've got five minutes. Then you and I are having a talk of our own." He walked down the hall and into the kitchen where I heard the back door open and Pong scamper out.

I tightened the belt in my robe, stuffed my hands in the robe pockets, and faced Laurent. "So what's up?"

Laurent cut the distance between us, forcing us both through the vestibule doorway and shutting the door behind him. "*Ben*, get yourself together. We're leaving."

My hands went to my hips. "Leaving? Nuh uh. You heard what Adam said. When you and I are done with whatever this is about, he and I have stuff to talk about it. And last time I checked, this was our house and we got to make the rules." I gestured to the living room, leading the way as I invited Laurent in. I turned to check his progress and found him unmoved. Except for the edge of his eyebrow which had gone from its earlier lowering to a lift at the edge. Sign language for amused.

Which I found completely un-amusing. Especially when I followed Laurent's glimpse around the living room full of Tina's baby bounty and had to concede that in its current state the place didn't look like it belonged to Adam and me. I stood my ground, though, because my point was still legit and because in a strange way I felt encouraged by Laurent's moment of amusement.

Nothing would amuse him if he was here to tell me something truly awful like that Johnny or Goatee Guy had tipped from hurt to dead. Or that somehow the Penguin found out Mario's pass card had been used after hours, discovered there'd been a game of musical painting, and was holding Mario accountable somewhere. I had tossed and turned all night worrying about that last possibility, even though Camille assured me she was managing things so no one traced Mario's card use to him or us.

As if she sensed my anxiety meter starting to edge up and wanted to offer an assist, Ping scurried her little feline body out from behind a box and curled herself around my legs. I picked her up and held her to me, fortified to have a tiny ally, and I looked at Laurent expectantly. He looked back at me saying nothing, a new expression in his eyes I couldn't quite read. Something that made them darker somehow and made my pulse quicken.

"Okay, now you're scaring me a little," I said.

His eyes seemed to darken more. "Good. Then we're even."

"Even? What do you mean even?"

"Forget it. Go. I'll wait while you get ready."

I rolled my eyes at him. "I told you, I can't just leave. Adam will be mad."

"*Ben,* Adam could be a lot more than mad if you *don't* leave."

"Now you're scaring me a lot," I said, but I set the cat down and started to move past him to go upstairs and get dressed. It wasn't like Laurent to exaggerate or imply things he didn't mean. Camille maybe, but not Laurent. Instantly, all my earlier fears spun in my head again.

By the time I was washed up, dressed, and back downstairs, both men were in the kitchen, sipping steaming cups of tea and watching Ping and Pong munch kibble.

Adam put his mug aside and fixed Laurent with a head nod when I entered the room. A minute later, another visitor was banging on the front door, and Adam was kissing me goodbye, ushering me into the sunroom off the kitchen, and out the back door, Laurent steps behind me.

"This is all very cloak and dagger, but will somebody tell me what's going on?" I said.

"We're getting you the hell out of here," Adam said.

We? Since when were Adam and Laurent a we?

"Scratch the cloak and dagger," I said. "This is starting to feel all caveman. I'm perfectly capable of getting myself out of the house, thank you. And since when did *you* want me to leave?"

The front door banged again. "Since now," Adam said. "We'll talk later."

I hesitated, confused, intrigued, and annoyed at the same time. Confused about exactly what was going on, intrigued that Adam and Laurent appeared to be on the same side in something, and annoyed that they were keeping that something from me and ordering me about.

I reminded myself that offering the benefit of the doubt was always the best policy and decided to trust they had good reasons. With a last glance at Adam, I strode out the back door, Laurent on my heels, and I crossed my patio to the driveway gate.

Laurent gripped my arm from behind and redirected me to the back fence.

I glared at him. "I've had very little sleep and no breakfast. Are you sure you want to do that?" Just because I was sticking to the benefit of the doubt trust thing didn't mean I had to be cheery about it.

He released me and I walked to the fence, found a gap between some bushes, and hoisted myself up and over, landing on my backside in my neighbor's petunia bed. All readied for spring early with fresh soil and judging by the smell, fresh fertilizer. Yuck. Damp dirt seeped into my jeans, and I scrambled up and brushed as much of it off me as I could, knowing full well it was too late, my entire lower half feeling like it had just been treated to a mud bath. Which it had since it was too early in the season for petunias to sprout.

I swiped more dirt off the jacket I'd thrown on over my sweater. "Just so you know," I said to Laurent. "I'll be billing the cost of new jeans as a work expense."

He grinned at me, his own clothes pristine clean, having cleared the fence with space to spare and landed on his feet. "*Ah oui*. Worth every penny."

"LET ME GET THIS STRAIGHT," I said. "You showed up at my house before sunrise because I didn't answer my phone?"

Laurent set down his *demi-tasse* of coffee, shoved aside his empty plate, and leaned across the bistro table. "I tell you you jeopardized Brassard's operation to bring down a major crime figure, an operation that's taken much time and money to put in place, and you hear only the part about your phone?"

No. I heard it all. I just didn't want to focus on the crime boss bit. I had no idea how to reply and "Camille made me do it" didn't seem like the most mature response. On the other hand, it was kinda accurate. It was also kinda true that this was as much Laurent's fault as anyone else's. If it wasn't for his secret cop code, we wouldn't be sitting in a café several blocks from my house, tucked into a secluded corner, cramped around a teeny table with barely room for one person let alone two, and talking about the plundering expedition Camille and I had done the night before.

"You know," I said, "none of this would have happened if you and Brassard had been straight with me. Camille and I wouldn't have had to sneak into the Penguin's box at *Dépôt Deschênes* if you had just told me why you and Brassard got in such a snit about the dead friend of Johnny's."

Laurent sat back, keeping his eyes locked on mine, his cop face expression in place. I couldn't tell if I'd made a good point, if he thought I was nuts, or if he was thinking of following up his veggie omelet with a croissant.

"I don't think Brassard sees it that way," he finally said.

"I figured. I'm guessing that was him at the door when we left the house via the back exit and hoofed away by the scenic route instead of taking your car. I bet now Brassard wants to lock me up *and* throw away the key."

"*Ben*, something like that."

"And you came by to whisk me away so he wouldn't find me."

Laurent's legs brushed against mine as he shifted in his chair. "Something like that."

"Well thanks," I said. "But isn't this all just a little silly. And why am I catching all the flak? What about Camille? How come he's not all mad at her?"

"He is, but she's not the one he told to hang up her mole clothes and butt out."

Laurent went quiet again after that and I had the feeling there was more to it. Like maybe Brassard was also afraid of Camille, but some guy code prevented Laurent from adding that bit. Cop code and guy code could be a tough combo to crack.

My shoulder bag buzzed beside me from where I'd dangled it off a chair spindle. I reached in and pulled out my phone as it vibrated again. A new text appeared from Adam saying the coast was clear.

I showed the text to Laurent. "Looks like you can get your car now."

"We," he said, taking my mobile, holding it side-by-side with his own and glancing between the two, then passing mine back. "*We* can get my car."

I shook my head and pointed to the underside of my chair. "Aren't you forgetting something? I need to go home and change. And Brassard's gone. He won't be back anytime soon. He's got better stuff to do than play some grandstand game with me. Anyway, I bet he's just a sore loser because Camille and I found a lead that he didn't."

Laurent's face went impassive. Neither confirm nor deny mode.

I took a sip of the cocoa I'd ordered to quash the early morning spring chill and the dampness of my impromptu mud bath. "Either way," I said, "whether Brassard likes it or not, you've got to admit finding that painting is a good lead. It could explain a lot. It could be the reason someone's trying to kill Johnny. I mean if there's a smuggling ring or something going on and Johnny knew about it, that could make the ring leader pretty unhappy, right?"

"That's a big if."

"Maybe. But it fits with Johnny having that flash drive with details about what was supposed to be stored in that unit and only that unit. And since the Penguin and his goons have been after the drive since we got it and the Penguin's the owner of said unit contents, it's more than just a good hunch."

On that Laurent smiled. We had a wee history debating the merits of my hunches versus educated guesses of more seasoned professionals, aka him and Camille. Although already I knew Camille agreed with me about this particular hunch, so really it had the seasoned professional stamp of approval, too.

"What about the mademoiselle Chloé and monsieur Thomas Duncan? You have hunches about them?"

I had the feeling Laurent was partly teasing me now, but I did actually have theories about Chloé and Duncan. "I think the flash drive is what Chloé tore her flat apart looking for and what Duncan was upset she didn't find. My guess is that Johnny's posse of Port friends knew he had it. I'd like to think Chloé has been trying to get it back to protect Johnny."

Laurent raised a brow at me. "Like to think?"

I shifted my mud-soaked derrière. "Well, she's his fiancée so she might be trying to protect him. But something's niggling at me. Something Tina of all people said. She met Chloé at a birthing class and told me Chloé said Johnny was a catch. And there was a definite financial aspect to his 'catchness' implied. Like maybe he was due to come into some significant money soon."

Laurent sat back. "You didn't mention that before."

"It didn't really click before. It was obvious from their financial background checks and lifestyle that neither Johnny or Chloé were exactly living the high life. But what Tina said sure made it sound like Chloé was expecting to be high stepping soon. And maybe the flash drive factors into attaining said high life."

"Like someone's willing to pay for its return."

"Right. Or maybe more than one somebody would pay a lot to get their hands on it."

"Only one problem with that theory," Laurent said. "The police already know what's on the drive. If it's housing a secret, the secret's out."

"True. But Chloé and Duncan may not know that. Have you met Brassard? You know as well as I do that he's not big on sharing. I bet the man never even shared a popsicle when he was a kid." I stopped to swig more cocoa. "Also, who said the information was worthless just because the police know about it? Maybe there's something else on there that's important to somebody. Or maybe some rival smuggler wants it because they think it will give them some kind of clout or psychological advantage."

"*Et voilà*. That's my little social worker talking. Always bringing everything down to emotions."

"Everything always *does* come down to emotions. Even the big crime motivators you've drilled into my head all stem from feelings—jealousy, greed, love."

Laurent smiled. "*Oui*, love is a particularly good one."

"It would be here if Chloé's motivation was love for Johnny and wanting to protect him. That's what I'm hoping. What I can't figure out is what she'd be doing hanging around Goatee Guy at the dumpster. I've been wondering if maybe he was in on it, too, and they had some kind of posse meeting that went wrong. Or maybe she got there late and missed seeing some confrontation or something." I let a breath in and out, trying to cleanse another niggling thought lurking in my mind. "I don't suppose anyone's found Chloé yet, have they?"

Slight head shake from Laurent, doing nothing to help ease my niggling thought.

A woman slipped by our table, and I stayed quiet, waiting for her to clear earshot. Her eyes barely strayed to Laurent as she passed and I silently congratulated her on her subtlety. Even Laurent's early-morning look didn't seem to keep him from attracting more feminine attention than a Bloomingdales' sale.

A fact he either didn't notice or ignored because his gaze stayed steady on me until she was gone. "*Ah, mon petit lapin*. I recognize that look."

"What look?"

"*Ton coeur tendre* look. You have concern for Chloé."

"Maybe. She is kind of missing. I mean Brassard's got a whole police force on alert. How hard can it be to find one pregnant woman? Maybe she did have something to do with Goatee Guy's dumpster dive, but what if she didn't? What if she saw something and she's running scared or something happened to her, too? Or what if she was involved in Goatee Guy's "accident" and when he got out of the hospital he went looking for payback?"

Laurent's dark eyes got darker and he plucked a leftover pear from my fruit plate. "*Bon ben.* If he did, his collection didn't go well."

"How do you know?"

"Because the only thing your Goatee Guy, Marcel, collected last night is water. While you were getting your text from your Anglophone, I got a text that Marcel's broken arm and the rest of him turned up this morning. Wet, cold, *pis* very stiff and very much alone. Unless you count the fish in the *Fleuve.*"

---

## 26

EAD. GOATEE GUY was dead?

This was all I could think about when I got home, stripped out of my mud and fertilizer splattered clothes, and got in a hot shower. That and that Chloé was still MIA. As was Thomas Duncan. But it was Chloé who weighed on me. What if something did happen to her? What if she was floating out there somewhere in the *Fleuve*, aka river, too, and she just hadn't surfaced yet? Probably I'd been the last to see her when she'd skulked out of the parking lot leaving only her Cinderella splotch behind. PI rules or not, I was kicking myself for not following that splotch. Especially when the owner of said splotch had a baby on board. Whatever Chloé did or didn't do, the baby had nothing to do with any of it. The baby was an innocent bystander.

A quick check in with Sister Jane told me Chloé hadn't made a visit to see Johnny at the hospital since the day before when she'd barely made an appearance that morning. Johnny still had security with only two visitors allowed—his sister and his fiancée. Sister Jane took full advantage of her visitor status and spent most of her days by his side. Possibly because she never got the cameras posted in Johnny's room she requested and may not have had complete faith in the police protection. Even nuns probably had some crises of faith now and then. Or possibly she was afraid the powers that be would keep moving Johnny around and forget to tell her.

Chloé, on the other hand, claimed hospital germs weren't good for the baby so she kept her stays to a minimum. Yet from the reports I'd been getting, she had stopped by each day until now. As a big fan of organization and order, I didn't like the break in pattern.

Just as I finished getting redressed, my doorbell went and my phone text binged within seconds of each other. The signal I'd worked out with Camille to let me know the doorbell ring belonged to her. Laurent had gone to prowl the docks where Goatee Guy washed up while the water trail was still damp. If I'd had my druthers I would have gone, too, but my "druthers" needed a cleaning first so the plan was he'd go on ahead and Camille would come meet me and we'd follow together. That was until a new plan occurred to me. One I thought best to run by Camille instead of Laurent. It had been hard enough to get him to agree with the first plan that left me with nothing but the fancy new alarm system to keep me safe from Brassard or the Penguin should they stop by before Camille arrived with her windpipe-crushing maneuvers.

I clipped my hair into a ponytail, trekked downstairs, cut the alarm, and opened the door to Camille who rushed in with Arielle trailing after her.

"Woah," Arielle said, eyes wide. She'd shed her shoes alongside Camille's, stepped into my hall, and fixed her eyes on my living room. "*C'est super ça.*" She made her way into the room, fingering some of Tina's baby wares, then tipped her hand sideways and gave it a good shake as though ridding it of excess water after a swim. "*Oh lala. Toute une séance de shopping.*"

By *séance de shopping* aka a good shopping session, it was tough to tell if Arielle meant expensive or expansive. Probably both applied so probably it didn't matter. Either way I knew immediately that I'd made the right call asking Camille to bring Arielle along. She was no slouch in the shopping department herself and had more connections than a box of Lincoln Logs. Perfect for making my plan work.

"*Mais alors,*" Camille said, hands on hips. "We're here. What's all this you said on the phone about a plan?"

I pulled Tina's guest list from my back pocket and I turned to Arielle. "How fast can you throw together a baby shower?"


**TURNS OUT THE** answer to my question was lightning fast.

By three that afternoon, e-invites had gone out and twenty-five guests had already RSVPd to attend a "Twindig" in Tina's honor later this evening at *Ciseaux*, a combo hair salon and spa owned by Camille's cousin, Albert. Evidently, inviting a bunch of women to freebie spa treatments guaranteed results. Even at the last minute. Especially when almost half the women were preggers and a massage and mani-pedis were involved. And when the other half had heard rumors that the spa's new masseur, Raoul, worked wonders with his hands.

And all it took was one little fib on my part: that Tina's doctors had ordered her on immediate bed rest in the hospital as of tonight, so we had to expedite the shower. No need to give too many gory details, either, since everyone knew twin pregnancies could be tricky. Nobody questioned the fib. And nobody asked Tina to confirm it because the shower was billed as a surprise.

Okay so maybe that was two fibs, but that one didn't really count because it would be a surprise when Tina got there.

Arielle's phone pinged, and I looked up from my dining room table where I was bagging beauty supplies Albert had sent over as party favors. I cinched the cellophane bag I'd just filled while Camille secured my cinch with blue ribbon.

"Is that her?" I asked Arielle.

Arielle pumped an arm in the air and smiled. "*Oui. Elle va venir.*"

I smiled, too, because the "her" in question was Chloé, and she was coming to the shower. Lucky for me, even Cinderella footprint leavers in quasi-hiding wanted free mani-pedis. But more importantly her response meant she was alive and kicking on dry land and not sipping river water with the fishes. Very good news. But also, truth be told, I was gleeful my plan to flush her out had worked. So far, nobody else had had any luck finding her. Not the police, not Laurent, not Brassard. Nobody. And aside from worrying about her, my instincts kept telling me she was the key to this whole case. The filling holding the cake together. Or at least the domino tile with the transitioning dots.

Her e-invite had been sent out separate from the others and my name as the "bff" shower-thrower omitted. Sneaky maybe some may say, but I preferred to think of it as strategy. Especially since it seems to have worked.

Camille finished off her ribbon tying with a bow, backed away from the table, and high-fived me. "Take that, Brassard. *Et ne dis pas que les femmes ne sont pas aussi bonnes que les hommes pour faire le boulot.*"

I tilted my head, quizzical. I didn't quite follow the French.

"Score one for girl power," she said, clarifying.

I laughed and nodded, knowing there was a dig at Brassard somewhere in her original statement, too, but focusing on the girl bit. "You don't get much more girly than baby showers and spa days," I said. "Estrogen. The secret ingredient in the girl's guide to PI tools." I paused. "Although to be fair, we couldn't have pulled this off without Albert and his willingness to host a gaggle of women shower-goers after hours." Or without Tina for that matter and her guest list complete with email addresses people actually checked.

Camille shrugged. "*Oui*, but Albert is no Brassard. Albert thinks women are beautiful and *capables*. Not Brassard. Brassard wants women only in the kitchen."

I smiled some more. Now I understood her ongoing digs at Brassard and her willingness to push the rules. She didn't just want to solve the case. She wanted to do it before Brassard so she could tell him to eat dust.

Which reminded me of the painting we'd found in the Penguin's storage area and Camille's reluctance to share our find with Brassard. From my conversation with Laurent, it was pretty clear her wish had not been granted. How Brassard found out was less clear, but I had the feeling that in Camille's mind our finding Chloé first was somehow righting that wrong. Or at least tipping the power back in her direction. A good thing since it improved her mood and made it easier for me to broach the painting subject.

"Speaking of Brassard," I said, "you find out if the painting we found has anything do to with the undercover sting he cooked up? Did you trace the painting? Was it stolen like we thought?"

She nodded. "*Oui et oui.*"

"So aside from his crooked construction games, the Penguin's also an art smuggler?"

Camille crossed to the buffet side table in my dining room where she'd placed her mobile. The phone had chimed once and went again. She checked the display, pocketed the phone, and turned back to me. "It looks that way."

"I never really got the point," I said. "I mean if everyone knows

THE MÉNAGE À TROIS

a piece of art is stolen, what's the thief get out of it? He can't just sell it at a Christie's auction or something. I know in movies there's always these 'private' collectors who'll buy stolen stuff for the sheer thrill of owning it, but is that really something that happens in real life? Seems to me someone who gets off on owning something they think is hot stuff is the exact kind of person who gets off on showing off that hot stuff, not keeping it locked away."

"Who says they don't show it?" Arielle added in. "I saw a movie once where this *gars* made a very valuable collection of stolen rare things—things owned before by celebrities and old weapons and all kinds of junk. When he wanted to impress with the collection, he brought some poor *con* home to see it. Then the gars kills the *cons* after and adds them to his collection."

"Eww," I said. "That sounds like an awful movie. Nobody would really do that."

Camille and Arielle rolled their eyes at each other.

"Hey," I said. "I saw that. Anyway I seriously doubt that's what's going on here. But I do think somehow Johnny and his Port mates either found out about the Penguin's secret stash or played some part in processing it."

"*Moi aussi,*" Camille said and picked up a whack of beauty product party bouquets. "And in about an hour Chloé's going to tell us which."

I grabbed an armful of "bouquets" and carted my bundle to the front of the house where Camille had set her bundle down and was easing open the door.

"What makes you so sure Chloé'll tell us anything?" I said. "So far she's given us nada." Which wasn't such a bad thing in my book, since I'd added her lack of sharing to the pro side of my mental list of signs that she was protecting Johnny—either because she knew he was in on the smuggling and was keeping him off police radar or because she wanted to keep him safe from further attacks by the Penguin.

Camille signaled the all clear and stepped onto the porch. "*Voyons*, Chloé will talk when I tell her you saw her with your beat-up mister Goatee at the dumpster and when I show her the picture on my phone of her red footprint when she was running from the scene."

We'd made it down to the sidewalk and over to Camille's car with our armloads. Camille popped the trunk and shifted her armload to raise the lid.

I moved forward to unload my beauty bundle. "We don't know Chloé was running from the scene," I said. "And I never actually saw her hurt Goatee Guy." Let alone send him to a watery death in the river mere hours later.

Camille tossed her bouquets into the car alongside mine and slammed the trunk closed. "That part we won't tell." She pulled sunglasses from her pocket and put them on as she strode towards the front of the car. "*Pis alors*, just because you didn't see it doesn't mean she didn't do it."

## 27

IKES. COULD I have just invited a murderer to Tina's baby shower? I was so busy congratulating myself on finding a way to reach Chloé and draw her out that I'd spent little time factoring in the idea she could be dangerous. Very little time. As in zero.

In less than twenty minutes, *Ciseaux* would be crawling with a bunch of shower-goers expecting spa treatments and tot talk. Not some would-be black widow type who may have spun a few webs of deceit and was taking out time to get the kinks worked out of her spidey legs before tightening threads around her next victim.

This could be bad. Very very bad. What was I getting everyone into?

I felt my breath catch in my chest and reminded myself to exhale. *Wait,* I told myself, taking a few deep breaths. This was crazy. I was letting my brain run on overdrive. I needed to focus. Chloé could be completely innocent in all this. I couldn't let an offhand remark from Camille get me this rattled. I wanted to flush Chloé out of hiding to find out the truth and protect her if need be. I needed to hold on to the thought that she was helping Johnny. Where was my positivity? Where was my open mind?

From my position in the back room, I peeked out at the crowd of women who'd started to arrive. Just a few early stragglers so far. All milling around Raoul, the masseur who was getting double pay to stay late and work his magic on the ladies. Raoul had the look of a Mediterranean Tarzan, if Tarzan had a voice like butter and was clothed in dark pants and a light shirt open at the collar and rolled at the sleeves to expose muscular forearms with dark hair that could double as a shag carpet.

Standing over by the entrance was Camille's cousin Albert, owner of *Ciseaux*, on meet and greet duty. Far from having enough hair to make a shag carpet, Albert was so manscaped and pumiced to smooth perfection that if he stood stock still he could be mistaken for a mannequin. A mannequin with tidy brown hair wearing tight pants and a tighter shirt, silky and tailored right down to the wide cuffs. His height average, his build slight. Adding even more to the mannequin effect. If the mannequin had once had aspirations of *Cirque du Soleil* stardom dashed after a nasty fall off his bike as a teen that landed him a broken knee that never set right and a stint in beauty school.

"Oof." I pinched my eye closed and eased back at the feel of something wet hitting my cheek. A blue blob. A blue bubble blob to be exact. The third one to get me since I'd arrived.

I wiped the wet mess off my face and refocused to see Albert leave his post at the door and scoot over to the corner where he'd set up a bubble machine to add festive ambiance for the occasion to the glass and marble and bamboo décor of *Ciseaux*.

Albert crouched, fiddled with a lever to the side of the machine, and the bubbles slowed from hyperactive mode to mellow. If I had to guess, I'd say the mellow would last about five minutes before the machine revved itself again to spew bubbles faster than a group of kids mainlining sugar. That was about as long as it'd been since the last time Albert had adjusted the speed to low only to have it gear up to high on its own. Probably Albert didn't get lessons on working bubble machines at beauty school.

He stood, nearly bumping his head on a navy blue banner proclaiming *"Félicitations!"* in bright silver letters. Congratulations. Just one of many banners draped around the room, some with more specific baby messages, most in French. All decorations Albert had added here and there, above manicure stations, over glass counters filled with cosmetics. None of them outdoing the three main *pièces–de-résistance* of the night.

Filling a salon chair banked against a strip of white wood wall stood the first *pièce*—the largest cake I'd ever seen. Made entirely of diapers fashioned into precut slices of white cake and decorated so realistically it was hard to tell if it was food made to look like diapers or diapers made to look like food. Only the smell gave it away when I'd checked it out earlier and got close enough to take it in. But I couldn't resist touching it just to be sure.

The second and third showpieces sat hidden from view, sectioned away with the shampoo stations, awaiting their reveal when more guests arrived. Two fountains on stands. Each three tiers. Each flowing blue liquid à la Niagara Falls.

When I'd arrived, Albert had me taste a sip from each. Which I did, expecting that since the blue concoction looked like blue Kool-Aid that it would taste like blue Kool-Aid. It didn't. It tasted delicate, like a tisane. An herbal tea with a hint of a kick.

Albert had smiled as he watched me try to place the kick. "Vodka," he'd said and pointed at the other fountain. "And for the mommies-to-be, no vodka."

Truthfully, I'd been touched at how much trouble Albert had gone to for the impromptu baby shower. And amazed at how quickly he'd pulled so much together. Especially on a work day. He must have put every available staff member on prep duty for the afternoon. Probably even pulled in favors from friends and family. As grateful as I felt, I wasn't surprised. If rallying together was an Olympic sport, the Caron clan would win gold every time.

"*Elle est déjà là?*" Camille said, coming up to peer out beside me, asking if she was here. The "she" in question I figured to be Chloé. Although to be fair, since technically Tina was the guest of honor she was also a possibility.

"Chloé or Tina?" I said.

An unmistakable scent hit my nose as Camille popped a chocolate and made a sound that resembled a Frenchified tsk. Okay. So not Tina then. Not that it mattered to my answer really since neither had arrived.

"No, not yet."

Camille sauntered over to one of the Niagara fountains, pulled a plastic champagne cup from a stack, filled it to the brim with blue brew, and drank it down like a chocolate chaser.

"You know that's got vodka, right?" I said.

She set the cup down and traced fingers down her throat. "I do now."

My phone bleeped from my thigh where I'd tucked it into the band of my stocking. Arielle had insisted I dress for the evening before we'd left my house. I'd hemmed and hawed, but she'd pointed out that as the hostess of Tina's shower I would be expected to look the part. The part, according to my two in-house fashion gurus, meant a dress and stockings and shoes befitting the ensemble and not from my Birkenstock collection. Only after I'd gussied up did I realize the outfit left me no pockets. And since I had learned the hard way that my phone was an essential PI tool best kept on my person than in my purse, it was either tuck the phone into my stocking or try to hide my fanny pack under the dress my gurus had pulled for me from my closet—a vintage sequined number of my mom's from the '60s that left little room for breathing let alone covert fanny packs. So tuck option it was. Lucky for me, I'd discovered on my first undercover case that lingerie, too, had many handy uses in the PI toolkit.

The phone bleeped again as I slipped it out. Sister Jane checking in for news. I kept the call brief, sticking a finger in my free ear to drown out some of the pre-party chatter from the main room while I exchanged updates with Jane. Mine as encouraging as I could make it and hers letting me know Johnny's status was unchanged.

I clicked off and my phone pinged almost immediately with incoming text.

Camille turned from the fountain where she was refilling her glass, and she arched an inquisitive eyebrow my way. "More Jane?"

I shook my head. "No. Adam," I said, "letting me know Tina is five minutes away."

I'd enlisted Adam to get Tina to the shower and he'd obliged with little complaint. In fact he'd seemed pleased and maybe a tad surprised I'd come through with the baby shower. Which sparked a momentary bristle of offense somewhere inside of me that was replaced quickly by guilt when I reminded myself that Arielle and Albert had done most of the party work, and that I hadn't told Adam that I'd turned Tina's shower into work work and was using it to lure Chloé out of hiding. I preferred to think of that last bit as simply efficiency on my part by achieving two things in one go. Or "healing two hearts with one hug" as my mom always said as a metaphor whenever she got two things accomplished at once.

Which in this case was kinda accurate, too. After all, Tina was getting the chic shower shindig her little heart desired. And fingers crossed real hard, Chloé would show up and tell us she was no murderer and her heart was in the right place trying to protect Johnny, and we'd get to help her, too.

"Shushhh," a woman said from the main room, her own tone nowhere near shush range. "Hide everyone. Tina's coming."

Scurry sounds followed, and Camille and I went to our peek-out posts.

Days had gotten longer and it was still light out. With *Ciseaux's* plate-glass windows, the interior was far from dark. Attempts to hide in the wake of Tina's approach futile. A few guests ducked behind chairs, some behind the reception area. A queue formed behind Raoul. Free-floating blue bubbles bounced in the air, hitting ground here and there or bursting in mid-flight, leaving sticky mist on the polished concrete floor.

The number of guests seemed to have quadrupled since I'd last checked, and the Raoul line had the look of bunny hop dancers minus the music. The last hopper smacking gum so loud the hopper before her shooting her the finger-to-lips quiet thing.

I smiled and focused in on the gum-smacker. My ears would have recognized that gum-smacker even if my eyes didn't see the baby bump stretching out her purple tube dress. Chloé. In full-on purple glory. My plan had worked. She was out of hiding and in my sights.


**NOW THE TRICKY** BIT. Timing my entrance.

As the hostess, etiquette would have had me mingling with the guests already only etiquette didn't take Chloé into account. More specifically, the need not to have her spot me too soon and recon-sider her attendance. Chloé had gotten a baby shower invite to celebrate Tina, her fellow birth-class cohort. Chloé wasn't expecting to see the two women who showed up unannounced at her workplace asking about Johnny and his bachelor party that went from betting to beating and then some. Odds were good that if she saw either me or Camille too soon, she may spook and run.

Once Tina arrived, the plan was for Albert to lock *Ciseaux* from the inside, barring the way for Chloé to make a quick exit. Camille and I needed to time our appearance to maximize visibility for Tina's entrance but minimize chances of being conspicuous to Chloé.

Out the window, Adam's head came into view, bobbing as he walked up to *Ciseaux*, his tall height making it easy to track his progress. Beside him, a blondish high pony-tail whooshed in and out of sight. Tina I supposed. Her head lower and blocked by the strip of lettering etched onto *Ciseaux's* storefront glass.

"What could you possibly have to get *here?*" I heard Tina huff out as Adam led her inside, careful to keep his body between her and the roomful of party-goers.

When Tina was fully in, baby belly and all, Camille and I slipped into the crowd just as Adam stepped aside and everyone yelled surprise.

Tina's body trembled like a fleeting earthquake aftershock. "What the fuuunk."

A few people laughed, someone fixed Tina with a camera on video mode, and a tall, older woman rushed forward, grasping Tina in a loose hug.

The woman looked vaguely familiar. Tina's mother-in-law judging by the family resemblance to Jeffrey, Tina's husband. It had been a few years since Tina and Jeffrey's wedding, but I'd met the mother-in-law then along with some of the other familiar faces in the room. I didn't have the best memory for names. Faces I remembered, and a lot of these I'd seen at the wedding or one of Tina's hobnobbing soirées over the past couple years.

Most of the unfamiliar faces around me I pegged as moms-to-be from Tina's birthing class. If their baby bellies didn't give them away, their smiles thrown Adam's way clued me in. Chloé's mouth stretching into the biggest smile of all as she trudged over to him.

Camille slid a sidelong glance my way.

"What?" I said.

She held her hands up like the start of patty-cake. "*Rien.* You didn't tell me Chloé and Adam were *chums*."

My eyes did an involuntary eye-roll. "They're not *friends*," I said accentuating the friend thing to distinguish it from the other meaning when Camille said "chum" as in people dating. "They met at Tina's pre-natal class."

A few more of the expectant mums moseyed over to Adam, slipping back some when Chloé flashed them slitty eyes.

Hmm. Maybe Camille was right. Maybe Chloé wasn't as innocent as I'd hoped. The slitty eyes didn't convince me she posed imminent physical danger, but they sure got me questioning her loyalty to Johnny. The man was out of commission less than a week and here she was trying to lay claim on a replacement. The replacement being my boyfriend no less.

I took a step forward and Camille pulled me back. "*Attends.*"

Reluctantly, I paused to wait like she asked, tracking her gaze over to Albert over by the door who turned our way and flashed a thumbs up.

"Okay *voilà*," she said. "The door's locked. Go ahead."

I moved forward, got another blue bubble in my face, and paused to clear the goo as it slid towards my chin.

"Lora!" Tina said, stepping into my path and shaking a finger at me. "I should be so mad at you. You didn't tell me a thing." She slid a hand down her body like she was brushing crumbs away. "You should have warned me. Look at me, I'm a mess. I didn't even get to wear a new dress. I look like a porker in this thing." She gestured again to her clothes, black leggings topped with a smock filled with dizzying multi-colored lines. "And look at my hair! It's in this filthy pony tail." She stopped herself with a giggle. "But how can I possibly stay mad when you've done all this. I can't believe you even got twin cakes like I wanted."

I craned my neck to see where she was looking and sure enough, another cake had joined the diaper one, identical in look but this one most certainly edible. Both now holding court on twin tables.

I caught Albert's eye and he looked back at me, hands going to clap position covering his mouth, his shoulders squishing in and up in glee.

I mouthed a thank you. Knee injury or not, the man deserved to be part of *Cirque du Soleil* as a mind reader slash miracle worker. Twin cakes, twin fountains, and now that I noticed, many of the signs and decorations had doubles strategically placed to create a mirroring effect. Even the goodie tables that mysteriously appeared had double sets of treats set on pedestals like an English tea, each top level showcasing doll-sized boys made of chocolate, one topped in a blue hat, the other in yellow.

"I'm so glad you're pleased," I told Tina.

She shuffled closer to me and lowered her voice. "Pleased? Omigod. You've got to be kidding me. You even got Evelyn Perrault to come. Nobody gets Evelyn Perrault. She declines everything."

I checked the room for a woman who looked like she made a pastime of declining invitations, scanning for Chloé at the same time, not locating either.

"Um. Sure," I said absently to Tina as I continued to pan the room for Chloé, checking for Adam as the sun she would invariably be orbiting around but not spotting him. "Anything for you and the babies, Tina."

Instantly Tina fell on me in a hug, smothering me with Chanel N° 5 and something that smelled suspiciously like coffee breath. There was a surprisingly homey feel about it all that caught me off guard. Tina and homey were not two words I ever thought I'd put together, and as she pulled away I could swear there were tears in her eyes. Not Tina's usual drama queen ones, big sappy ones that made her bottom lip quiver. Mommy hormones. That had to be it.

I liberated myself from Tina and steered her in the direction of the gift table, relieved when I saw her eyes latch on to the pile of bags and boxes in bright shiny colors and she ventured forth.

With still no sign of Chloé, I went on a venture of my own, checking the various beauty stations including the wash area behind the partial wall where the fountains had originally been stashed. No sign of Chloé. Or Adam. Camille I did find, cup of blue infusion in one hand, mobile phone in the other, sitting in a chair bordering a shampoo sink.

"I lost her," I said to Camille.

"Mmmm."

"Chloé," I said. "I lost her. Tina intercepted me before I could get over to her. Did you see where she went?"

Camille looked up from her phone to me. "*T'inquiète pas.*" She waved her thumb towards the archway to a hall beside the back-room where we'd spent part of our time in hide mode earlier. "She's in back with Raoul."

"Raoul? Last I saw, she was chatting up Adam."

"Adam left. *Probablement* a salon baby shower with a bunch of women was too girly for him. After, I put Chloé for her *dix minutes* with Raoul. It wasn't easy. It was the turn of the woman with the fingernails like icicles. I got Albert to bump her so we could get Chloé alone in a room. Raoul is holding her there until we arrive. I was waiting for you. Your plan, your case, no?"

I smiled. It *was* my plan and it was working and this was good. Way better than confronting Chloé in a crowd. Now we'd get her all to ourselves. And she'd be all relaxed from Raoul's detaining techniques. If the rumors I'd heard were true, ten minutes with

Raoul was more potent than a Valium.

We went down the hall and stopped in front of the first of six doorways, two on one side, three on the other, and one at the end. The two on the right had old-timey figures of a man and a woman painted on the doors—unisex bathrooms I guessed. The three doors to the left were numbered in the same old-timey fashion with curlicue script *à la 1, 2,* and *3.* Numbers *1* and *3* were open and darkened, shadowy interiors showing each outfitted with spa table, bank of cabinets, small sink, towel stacked shelves. No Chloé or Raoul. Door number *2* was closed, soft light filtering out through the slender space at the bottom.

I slipped over to it and stopped.

"*Et alors?*" Camille whispered beside me and fanned hands between me and the door. "*Dépêche-toi. Entre, entre.*"

I went to knock, changed direction, and went for the doorknob, then back to knock position again, tapping softly with my knuckles. Nothing, so I tapped again louder. Still nothing so I tried the knob. It didn't budge.

"It's locked," I told Camille.

She tried for herself. Same results. "I'll get the key from Albert," she said.

I glanced back at the door. "Has Chloé been in there ten minutes? Maybe we should wait the ten minutes."

Camille shook her head, one brow slightly cocked, and rushed off to fetch the key, leaving me with guard duty.

I eyed door number *2,* easing closer, listening for movement on the other side. Careful not to listen too hard in case there were details I didn't want to hear. I knew Albert wouldn't encourage any intimate line-crossing at his salon, but sometimes the personal nature of massage could sound intimate. Not that it mattered at the moment since I heard nothing. I put my ear to the door and tried again, concentrating harder, growing concerned. Maybe something was wrong. Maybe it wasn't a good idea to leave Chloé alone with Raoul.

A thud. I could just make out the sound of a faint thud.

I knocked again. Still no answer. Just another thud. Thuds couldn't be good. Where was Camille with that key?

I slipped to the end of the hall and peered around the corner to see if she was coming, and I nearly bumped into a redhead, hair a mass of frizzy curls as wide as the belly she was supporting as she puffed past me to the washroom. She fumbled with the door, and I moved in to help her.

"Sorry," she said, waving her hand in my face. "It's these pudgy fingers. They're so swollen they can't grasp the knob right."

"No problem." I held the door until she made it inside.

"Thanks." She sucked in air and twinkled her fingers, the tips gleaming pink with fresh polish. "I hate to ask, but you think you could help with the zipper on my skirt, too?"

Her face was flushed, her eyes aglow, and she shifted on her feet. Probably one too many blue drinks swishing in mommy bladder.

I darted a look at door number *2*, dipped into the washroom, started the redhead's zipper for her, and dipped out in time to see a flash of purple as the door at the end of the hall edged closed. A door with a big red *Sortie* sign above it.

Oy. Chloé! Spiriting off again under my watch!

I dashed out after her, the door clinking shut behind me, the purple flash moving to the end of the narrow passageway ahead. Trash cans and recycle bins lined the alley, fowling the air as I rushed after her. Solar sconces barely lit my way as my heels struck ground with sharp clicks, and tiny drops of rain pecked my head.

Chloé was amazingly fast for a pregnant lady and her lead on me solid, so I risked calling her name, hoping to slow her enough to catch up and coax her back inside.

Her head turned my way, and another figure appeared in front of her, cutting off her path. The figure reached out, grabbed her by the arm, and snatched her away, her shrill scream piercing the air then fizzling as she disappeared from view.

## 28

*I* FISHED UNDER the hem of my dress and yanked my mobile from its hideaway in my stocking. Running after Chloé, I punched in my code, pausing when I reached the spot I'd last seen her where the *Ciseaux* alley ended in a T with a laneway of uneven, cracked asphalt. The laneway was bordered by ridges of grass patches between various gates and openings, each leading to neighboring businesses. Lighting was spotty making it hard to see. I looked right then left, like I was crossing a street, while I placed a call to Camille and told her I lost Chloé. Again. And how.

Camille told me to sit tight until she got to me and clicked off just as a floodlight blinked on three gates down the lane. From the same direction, a man swore like a seasoned sailor, his words vocal breadcrumbs to my ears.

Crumbs I could lose if I sat tight, so I trailed the man's cursing, moving in long strides as quietly as I could until I reached the gate. Beyond was a small patio, unkept, with a shed tucked in the corner. By the shed, Chloé and her abductor stood huddled together, his hand still gripping her arm.

I focused in on the adductor. Male, medium height, slightly hefty build. The back of his head like a basketball with teacup handles for ears. No, not teacup handles. Coasters! Like Thomas Duncan, Johnny's friend from the poker party with the fidgety hind quarters.

Last time I'd seen them together Chloé was pelting the man with wedding favors. Either this time the tables had turned or he was holding her arm down in case she was packing more candy souvenirs.

I crept closer, cleaving myself to bushes just inside the gate.

"You think you can play me?" Duncan was saying to Chloé. "You think you can keep the money for yourself? You got another thing coming, Sunshine."

"What are you talking about? I told you. I can't find it. And Johnny didn't put the bank numbers anywhere else."

"Yeah, you told me. I don't believe you anymore." He flapped papers at her. "Don't think I don't know about your little trip. I got the boarding pass you printed out." He snickered. "Don't you know you can just flash your phone at the terminal now? You bitches are all the same. You don't know nothing about technology."

She snatched at the papers with her free hand. "You were in my house? What were you doing in my house?"

"Looking for what's mine. You and I both know that money belongs to me." He stuffed the papers in his pocket out of Chloé's reach. "It was Claude and me that set this thing up. It was Claude and me that rigged the machines and hid the paintings. And Marcel who made sure nobody found out. Johnny didn't do a thing. Johnny didn't have the balls to do anything but shuffle boxes. And he couldn't even do that without fucking up his back."

Chloé's chin thrust out to a sharp point. "Then why did Claude give Johnny the bank deets and not you? You're the dumbass. Without Johnny you've got nothing."

Duncan twisted her wrist and she cried out.

"I don't need Johnny," he said. "I've got you and you're gonna give me the numbers and the passwords or you'll be spending your reunion with Johnny in the hospital bed next to his." He poked her belly with his free hand. "And your baby, too."

I sucked in air and moved out from the bushes. No way was he going to hurt Chloé or the baby on my watch. The heel of my shoe tangled in the scraps of moist grass at my feet, and I jerked it free and stumbled onto the patio.

Duncan's head snapped around. "You there. Get away from here before I call the police."

Ha. I was no poker player like him, but even I knew that was a big fat bluff.

"*You* get away," I said. What was I? Five years old? Where did I get that comeback?

I walked closer to them. My heart did a little bop in my chest, and I used the beat to pace my steps.

"You!" he said as I neared. "You're one of them dumb bitches snooping around after Johnny got his head thumped." His eyes narrowed and he slid a look to Chloé. "You letting her mix into our business?"

Chloé shook her head. "I don't even know her." She rotated her arm in his grasp, but he held firm.

"Let her go," I said. "Or I'm calling the police." I held my phone up to him to prove I meant what I said. Truth be told, this was also kinda a bluff because I was calling the police either way. I already had, really, since I'd called Camille and knew she'd be along any second.

He lashed out with his free hand and bashed the phone from my palm, cracking my fingers so hard I heard a snap.

"You ain't calling nobody," he said. He kicked at my mobile where it landed to his side, and the phone skidded away to the rear of the shed. "I'm not telling you again. Get the fuck out of here."

Another snap rang out. This one behind me. I thought I caught the faint scent of chocolate in the air, and I smiled. Camille.

I cast a look to be sure and felt a searing tug at my hair that whipped me from where I stood and landed me so close to Duncan's coaster ears I could make out the bushy hairs sprouting out.

Duncan's burly arm surrounded my waist and slapped me to his body, my back to his front, his fistful of my hair holding me in place.

Finally free, Chloé backed away. Beyond her I saw Camille, standing maybe ten feet from us, hands out in front of her in a back-off type gesture I was sure was meant to calm Duncan who only yanked harder at my hair.

A high-pitched shriek rang out that I thought must have come from me until I spotted another person beside Camille. This one so still I nearly missed him. His hands flanked his face and the shriek went again and perfectly sculpted eyebrows curved up. Albert.

Another scream flew from his mouth, and my eyes pinched shut and my hands went to flank my own face to shield my ears, my fingers meeting something hot and gooey. Something sliding down from the top of my head, gliding along my cheek, and dropping in drips.

I wiped away one of the drips and brought it into view. Blood. Lots of it. Streaming down from my scalp. Wisps of hair falling along with it.

. . .

**BALD, BALD, BALD**. The Duncan creep is pulling out my hair. I'm going to be bald.

*Lora, get a grip. That's the least of your worries.*

I looked down and sure enough, the voice in my head was right. I was staring into the shiny glint of a knife blade, tucked in between Duncan's fingers pressing into my stomach.

On the bright side, Chloé and her baby were a safe distance off, being waved even farther away by Camille whose eyes darted about nearly seamlessly like a tiger assessing danger status in the jungle.

*Disable and run. Disable and run.*

This time Laurent's words flew into my head. His mantra of self-defense. Not crush a man's windpipe like Camille. Just disable your opponent enough to make a getaway.

I wanted to pry Duncan's arm from me or gouge him in the ankle with my heel. But he had a knife. What if it slipped and sliced into me.

I could tell by Camille's expression she had similar misgivings. Breaking someone's hold was one thing. Breaking that hold when that someone had a sharp weapon already grazing your flesh was another.

Ditto Camille overpowering Duncan. I had no doubt she could rush him and take him out. But could she do it without me getting a permanent memento in my belly? Neither of us wanted to find out the answer to that the hard way.

I needed another disabling approach. One more my speed. One less about physique and more about psyche. And I needed it fast. The blood stream from my scalp had stopped. And I hadn't seen any more hair slip away. With any hope, the wound was small and settling, but I wasn't sure how long the settling would hold.

"Johnny gave the numbers to me," I said.

I felt Duncan stiffen. "Don't fuck with me," he said. "You don't know what you're talking about."

"I do," I told him. "At the poker game the other night at the club. I was there and Johnny gave me the bank numbers to keep safe."

Even in the dim light I could see Chloé's lips tighten and her arms cross over her chest. Duncan may not be pressing the buy button on my story, but Chloé was putting it in her checkout cart.

Duncan squeezed me and tugged my hair. "The only bitch at the party was a stripper. You ain't no stripper."

Camille took a step forward, pausing when I flashed her my hand like a stop sign.

I recounted a couple events from the evening that only someone with a firsthand account could know. "I was in the cake," I added. "I saw everything. And I saw Johnny after everyone left."

Duncan's grip slackened some. I had his attention.

"Then where is it?" he said.

Hmm. It. He must mean the flash drive. The bank numbers must be somewhere on the drive. In code maybe. Clearly he didn't know the police had the flash now.

"It's inside. In my purse." I knew by the pile of poker money Duncan had racked up at the bachelor party that he was no slouch at the game. I, on the other hand was a novice and I was bluffing big time. Lucky for me, we were both facing the same direction and he couldn't see my face.

Duncan went still and quiet. Weighing his next move maybe.

"You," he finally said, gesturing loosely with the point of the knife towards Albert. "Go get her purse." He tipped the knife a little to Albert's side towards Chloé. "And you go with him. Make sure he doesn't call the police or this one gets it." He jabbed the knife at me, the tip point pricking through the delicate fabric of my mother's dress to my skin. "And don't get no ideas about running off with anything yourself or I'll hunt you down after I'm done with her. And you'll both be going for a swim."

Yikes. Going for a swim. Just like Johnny's friend, Claude, and Goatee Guy. Did that mean Duncan was responsible for their trips up the *Fleuve* without a paddle? And if so and they were his partners, maybe even friends, and he did that to them, there was slim chance he'd have a problem sending me on the same ride.

Okay maybe my disabling approach wasn't working out quite how I'd hoped. But at least it got Albert and Chloé in the clear. And I had no doubt Albert would be calling for backup. My confidence in Chloé was a tad shakier, though. I knew she wouldn't score anything in my purse besides an old candy bar, but I could see her taking off anyway. For all I knew that trip she had scheduled had an imminent flight time. Maybe she'd stopped by Tina's Twindig on the way to the airport to get a mani-pedi to look good for her trip.

I tried to telepathically pass my thoughts to Camille like she and Laurent did their sibling silent communication thing, but when I looked her way it was Albert who caught my attention. The expression on his face reminded me of ones I'd seen on preschoolers I'd worked with back in New York. An expression of focused preoccupation, usually when they were about to hurl.

Truth be told I could relate. It wasn't every day I was threatened with stabbings and drownings. Or really ever. If I hadn't been so worried about Chloé and her baby and protecting them, probably I'd have hurled already when I saw the blood and hair falling from my head.

Albert's face changed again and a second later I was seeing it up close and personal when he catapulted himself into me, leaping up and swinging his body from a branch overhead, catching both me and Duncan by surprise with an aerial attack and separating us instantly. I staggered forward, glancing back as Albert swiftly lunged himself from the branch again, barreling his two feet into Duncan's chest with enough momentum to knock Duncan to the ground, his knife skittering down after him.

Camille had the knife scooped up and Duncan in a hold by the time I got to my feet, a hand to my heart to still its pounding against my ribcage. Albert lowered himself slowly from the branch, his legs fully extended, his arms and torso rigid with control. He went to stand by Duncan and muttered something to him in French that got Camille to smile.

I turned to check to see if it got a smile out of Chloé, too. She wasn't where I'd last seen her, and my heart kicked up its battering drumbeat again as I scanned to make sure she hadn't been hurt in the ruckus or fainted from the stress. But I didn't see her anywhere.

*H*IGH-PITCHED SQUEALS. I could hear them loud
and clear the closer I got to *Ciseaux*. The back door off
the alley had been locked when I'd retraced my steps in search of
Chloé, so I hightailed it to the front street entrance where I heard
high-pitched squeals as I approached. Through the window, the
interior looked like a fish tank with air bubbles floating against
streaks of blue streamers and bright colored figures swooshing
about.

I had to knock to be let in and got swooped up in the stream
like a doll caught up in a river current.

"*Lâche-moi*," a woman shouted.

"You let go," an older woman yelled back.

I recognized the first voice and followed it. Chloé. Talking
from somewhere to my left. Projectile bubbles in the air made it
hard to see clearly, but soon three women came into fuzzy view.
Two having a tug-of-war over something stretched between them.
And another tugging at one of the warrior-women, attempting to
pull her backwards.

"Omigod, Lora. Help, will you. This woman is trying to steal your purse."

The speaker was Tina, who I could barely make out as one of the warrior women. The other Chloé. And to Chloé's backside, the older woman. Tina's mother-in-law.

I zig-zagged my way across the room to the bubble machine gone wild in the corner and pulled its plug. When I turned around, the women were still going at it and the party guests were scattered watching, some from manicure stations, some splayed out in styling chairs, others standing. Some quiet, wearing deer-in-headlights faces, and some giggling. It wasn't hard to tell which blue fountain the latter group had been frequenting.

Beyond the warriors was another deer-in-headlights face. Albert. Next to him, Raoul, who seemed to have survived just fine whatever had caused the thudding in his massage room earlier with Chloé.

Camille caught my eye as she strode in with Duncan, escorted by a newcomer wearing a look more of awe than deer-in-headlights, like he was getting a behind-the-scenes peek at the making of his favorite movie. The newbie cop who'd bought Camille's three-women-in-a-cake story. Officer Tessier.

Two more newcomers stood to the side, their faces not betraying emotion. Brassard, standing arms crossed over his battery chest. And Laurent, leaning against the partial wall.

By the time I wrangled the warriors, all the fight had gone out of the women and Tina's breathing came out in puffs keeping her words to a minimum as she handed me my purse, her eyes glowing with triumph. Or maybe exhaustion.

I slipped the bag over my shoulder, thanked her, and whisked her into a reclining chair, insisting she stay there and rest for a while. Once I got her mother-in-law settled beside her, I headed over to Albert.

"I'm so sorry about the mess, Albert." I went on tiptoes and kissed his cheek. "And thank you. You're a lifesaver." I smiled at him. "You've got some very impressive moves. *Cirque du Soleil* doesn't know what they're missing."

He waved his hand in the air, the same dismissive gesture I'd seen Camille do a thousand times, then he pulled me into a hug. "*T'inquiète pas* about the salon. It looks like this at least once a month. And the thing outside was nothing. Teamwork. Nobody saves anybody. Every performer learns about that. It's all about timing and teamwork."

I agreed. Every woman learned that, too. Timing, teamwork, and cooperation. Not one person saving the day, but everyone doing their part. Still, without his part I may not be standing here thanking him.

"Well you've got impeccable timing, too," I said.

He shrugged. "I couldn't just leave. It was then or never. I worry you get hurt, but to surprise him was the best shot."

I gave Albert another cheek kiss, and he grabbed my hand. "Come. Let me clean up your hair."

My hair? Right. I'd almost forgotten that the pain in my head was more than just a bad headache.

I felt a light tug on my other hand. Laurent, his touch loose and gentle. "*Merci*, Albert," he said. "Maybe first we let a doctor worry about her head then we worry about her hair, *hein?*"

I eased myself free of both their hands. "Thanks. But I think it can wait until we're done here. There's still a lot we don't know. I think Duncan may have killed that guy last night and the other one three months ago, but I don't know if he acted on his own or for the Penguin or something. And I know Johnny wasn't part of the art smuggling or anything, but I don't know how Chloé figures in. I do know she wasn't trying to steal my purse, she just wanted the hippie doll flash drive."

"Flash drive? What flash drive?" Chloé said from the chair Brassard had moved her into for questioning. "And what doll? If you mean that old thing Johnny carried since his accident for good luck, you can have it. Some good luck she bring him." She rolled her eyes. "You said you had Johnny's phone in your purse. I'm not a thief. I wasn't going to take your purse or any drive. I just wanted back the phone."

The latecomers to the party exchanged looks.

"Didn't you get Johnny's phone from the hospital when you took his wallet?" I said to her.

She pulled at the purple spandex holding in her baby bump and sighed. "There was no phone at the hospital because you had it already, no?" She went quiet and turned her attention to her fingernails. Varying lengths, some chipped. It was too bad for her she'd spent Tina's Twindig out back. She really could've used a mani-pedi.

And I was starting to think I could've used a cheat sheet on this case. All this time I'd been laboring under the assumption that everyone was after the hippie doll flash drive I'd found in my pocket. But all along what they really wanted was Johnny's phone. Which I didn't have. After running through a mental list of possibilities, though, I had a good idea who did.

I turned to Laurent, "I think I will see that doctor now. But I need to make a stop first."


**ACTUALLY I MADE** TWO STOPS. First, by the shed down the lane to retrieve my phone left behind from when Duncan had knocked it from me. Then on to Johnny's room at the hospital before getting my head checked at the ER.

By the time Laurent got us past the guard outside Johnny's room, I'd already confirmed my suspicion. All it took was a text to

Sister Jane. Technically the text went to Johnny, since it was his phone where I was reaching her. She didn't have a phone of her own and had appropriated his during her stay. It had taken her only a few tries to get past his password before she hit on it—the date of their parents' deaths. When she used the phone to connect with me, I'd naturally assumed it was hers and already had her name associated with the number in my contacts.

I wasn't surprised Chloé didn't think to ask Sister Jane about Johnny's phone, though. I'd seen firsthand Jane's reaction to phone use in the hospital. Chances were slim Chloé would have ever seen Jane with the phone. Especially since Chloé hadn't been visiting Johnny much. Or maybe she assumed nuns didn't use cell phones. Seemed there was a lot about Johnny's family Chloé didn't know.

Lucky for us Sister Jane knew more, and she identified Johnny's pattern of using family dates for passwords. When we asked for her help, it hadn't taken many more tries for her to figure out the passwords for the files with the bank account info everyone wanted.

The bank details had come by emails from Johnny's friend Claude before he died. Turned out the accounts held money Duncan, Claude, and Goatee Guy aka Marcel decided to skim from the art smuggling scam and keep for themselves. Claude did the bookkeeping for the squirreled-away funds, and he oversaw the bank accounts. He'd asked Johnny to hold onto the specifics for safekeeping—as backup and as insurance in case any of the partners got greedy and tried to cut another one out. A prediction that proved true since Duncan did just that when Claude wanted to end the scam, and Duncan didn't agree and decided to end their partnership permanently instead. But not before Claude put his own partnership provision into place by changing the account passwords and sending everything by email to Johnny.

Johnny saved the info in protected files for added security and stored them on his phone.

The same phone Laurent collected from Sister Jane and turned over to Brassard. The phone file discovery was a good break in the case. Brassard hoped the bank info would establish an undeniable tie-in with the Penguin.

Brassard had been working the smuggling angle for months. He knew it involved disabling screening at the Port via *Mise en Port* where Thomas Duncan, Claude, and Chloé worked. He also knew it involved warehouse storage at *Dépôt Deschênes* where Johnny and Goatee Guy aka Marcel worked. But Brassard didn't want to just bust the little guys. He wanted the big fish—the Penguin. And he wanted to get him with hard evidence the Penguin's lofty lawyers couldn't dispute. Anything showing money changing hands like the bank trail Johnny's phone could unlock would be good proof.

Not that I heard any of that from Brassard. Laurent had filled me in while we waited for my turn in the ER that left me with a clean booboo held together with special tape that acted like stitches in cases like mine where the skin damage was small. Big relief. From the oodles of blood it had leaked, I was afraid I'd have a crater in my head, but apparently even small head injuries can produce lots of blood. The hair damage, on the other hand, felt not-so-small. Hair had been pulled out in a clump, hard enough to cause the skin tear. The hairless patch I was assured was barely noticeable. Probably like those zits everyone tells you they can't see, but are about as subtle as shiny red beacons.

"There's something I don't get," I said to Laurent as he drove me home. "If Johnny wasn't part of the art scam and his friend only gave him the bank info on the hush hush, how did anyone know Johnny had anything? I mean, it's not like the dead friend could've let it slip. How come three months later, it all of the sudden became an issue?"

Laurent had been on the phone getting updates while I was being treated, and I felt like the girl who missed the finale episode of a gripping TV show that everyone else saw.

"For that, he can thank his lovely fiancée," Laurent said. "After Claude died, Chloé got it in her head that Johnny could take the scam money and they'd go off to live on an island somewhere after the baby was born. She told anyone who would listen that soon they'd be rich. It was only a matter of time before the wrong people heard and wanted back what's theirs."

Hmm. Got me thinking Chloé probably wasn't the brightest, but it fit with what Tina had said about Chloé finding a "catch" of a fiancé.

"But Johnny wasn't even one of the scammers," I said. "Duncan was very clear about that. It wasn't even Johnny's money. And if Johnny didn't want to be in on the scam, there's no way he'd be the kind of person to steal money like that."

Laurent's gaze slid to me. "Maybe not. But Chloé might. It was her fighting your pregnant, whiny friend for your purse."

That was true. And she did seem to be in some kind of cahoots with Duncan. Maybe with Johnny out of the way, they'd made some kind of deal. When Camille and I had first seen them together, they had been pretty friendly. Maybe Duncan was right and Chloé had decided somewhere along the line to double-cross him and keep all the money for herself only she couldn't find Johnny's phone to get access to the bank accounts.

Which got me thinking another unpleasant thought. "Maybe Johnny's accident at the warehouse wasn't such an accident, either. Maybe someone tried to get him out of the way, and another drowned dock worker so soon after Claude's death was too risky, so they tried to rig a different type of work accident. And maybe when it wasn't fatal, Johnny decided to keep himself off the premises for a while by exaggerating his injuries. Maybe that's why he had the little doll with the flash drive, too. Not so much for good luck like Chloé said, but as insurance. Probably he got it, too, from Claude and held onto it thinking it had something he could bargain with if he found himself facing another faux accident."

Laurent's eyes slid my way again. "Maybe."

"And if so, his plan seemed to work. At least until the poker party tousle and the unplugging at the hospital." I let the back of my head sink into the headrest, my booboo throbbing suddenly bringing a heaviness with it. "I guess we'll find out for sure when Johnny wakes up." I let my eyes close. I imagined Sister Jane by Johnny's bedside, holding his hand as he went through questioning from Brassard and his clicky pen. Probably I'd be thinking about Brassard and his clicky pen for a while.

"Hey." My eyelids flew open and I sat up straighter. "If Brassard already knew about the art smuggling scam, why did he send me in to *Dépot Deschênes* as a mole?"

"He likes you."

"He likes me?! The man doesn't like me. He makes fun of me. He calls me an assistant. He makes threats about reporting me as an unlicensed PI!"

"Right. That's what Brassard does when he likes people. *Pis* the information you got as a mole was useful to him. And it was you who got him the flash drive. He knows you were helpful."

"Right. So helpful he fired me and wanted to hide me away? What was that about?"

Laurent pulled the car to a stop at the curb in front of my house. He turned to me and reached to glide his fingers along my temple just below my bandage. "*Ben,* when this heals, you'll have *une toute petite et sexy* scar to go with your tattoo."

I held his eyes. "You know nothing about my tattoo," I said. "And you're avoiding my question."

He withdrew his hand, moved it to the breast pocket of his jacket, and pulled out an envelope. "Brassard gave me this tonight. *Je te jure*, if I'd seen it earlier you would not have been a mole."

Laurent passed me the envelope and I took out a photograph. Old and square, thin white band along the edges. Two teenagers sitting on a picnic table, trees behind them, both smiling. The girl holding something small in her hand. Some kind of camp logo sign above the boy's head, a *feu interdit* message on another sign to the right.

I leaned in for a closer look at the faces and my heart stopped. It felt like a full minute before it started up again.

"That's my mother," I finally said of the girl in the picture. "Why did Brassard have a picture of my mother?"

Laurent reached to hold my hand. "He didn't. He had a picture of the boy with her."

I flipped on the overhead light with my pinkie, checked the photo again, and shrugged. "Don't know him," I said.

"You might. If he had on a long coat and slicked his hair back."

I looked again. "Are you telling me this is my mother with the Penguin?"

Laurent nodded and released my fingers to point at the little object in my mom's hand. "And that's the doll from your pocket." His gaze stayed steady on me. "When Brassard found the picture, that's when he wanted to hide you away."

# 30

"**I**T'S ALL OVER," Camille said.

I shuffled my phone away from my sheets so I could hear her better. "What time is it?"

"Early. *Mais alors*, it's done. Duncan is in custody officially. He admits to the art scam with Claude and Marcel and to sending them up the *Fleuve* with no water wings. Even to pulling Johnny's plugs at *l'hôpital*. He denies knowing anything about the Penguin. He says it was all a scam of their own."

"Really? What about the painting we found in the Penguin's storage locker? In his construction tubes? How does Duncan explain that?"

"Handy hiding place, that's it."

"That's crazy. He'd be stupid to hide paintings in the Penguin's stuff."

"*Oui*. But also maybe more stupid to point fingers at the Penguin. *Probablement* Duncan would rather face criminal charges and live out his life in jail than face the Penguin and join his friends in the *Fleuve*."

My head bandage brushed my pillow, bringing back memories of the night before, my sore knuckles flashing me reminders, too. Yes, of course. Goatee Guy/Marcel ended up taking the same swim with the fishes as Claude. Probably as Duncan got closer to getting the cash, he bought into the less-is-more theory. As in, the less people to share with the more for him. Conveniently, it also left no main partners to contradict Duncan's story. "What about the bank info? Won't that show the Penguin's involved?"

"*Peut-être*. They're working on it. But that's not the same as Duncan ratting him out."

"And Chloé?" I asked.

"Chloé went home after they finished with the questions. She didn't break any laws. Like Johnny she knew about the scam, but I don't think they'll charge her for that." She paused. "*T'es correcte?*"

Was I okay she wanted to know? Was I okay with the bombshell Laurent dropped that my mother knew some big-time criminal when she was a kid. Was I okay knowing that criminal may have recognized me and been toying with me all week?

I leaned over, afraid my early morning call would wake Adam, but his side of the bed was empty.

"I will be," I said to Camille. "When I can tell Sister Jane that Johnny is safe. And when he wakes up and we can clear him of the insurance fraud business with *Assurance Lion* once and for all."

Camille went quiet. When Camille went quiet things were never good.

Finally she broke her silence with a long sigh. "*Okay-là*. Laurent told me your theories about that, but even if Johnny exaggerated injuries for good reasons, *c'est quand même* fraud. Don't forget his dirty shoes."

Again with the shoes! I wish I'd never spotted Johnny's muddy shoe treads. "What shoes?" I said. "I don't remember any shoes. I

remember Johnny staying in his wheelchair all through his bachelor party."

"Fraud is fraud, Lora."

"Potato potato," I said, infusing the second word with my best
British accent.

**I WENT DOWN** to the kitchen to get a cup of breakfast tea and
found Adam at the table reading from his laptop.

"Humming," he said. "Someone's in a good mood."

"Was I humming?"

"Uh, huh. The old *Walking on Sunshine* song. I'm guessing you
haven't looked outside or you'd be humming *Raindrops are Falling
on my Head*."

I glanced out the back windows, over the café curtains to the
yard. Adam was right. More spring rain.

"I guess I am kinda in a good mood," I told him. And I was.
Despite everything, I had just completed my own first unofficial
case working for Sister Jane, and I counted it as a success. She
wanted me to find out who pulled her brother's plug and I did. Her
brother was safe, and before we'd ended our call Camille had said
the doctors were so pleased with Johnny's progress, they'd be
bringing him out of the coma early. I was thinking, too, that his
body had probably detoxed while he was out, and he'd have a good
chance of staying on the wagon once he was filled in on Duncan's
shenanigans and had some closure concerning his friend Claude.

How Johnny might take the news about Chloé was still TBD,
but I'd seen couples work through worse. Especially when there
was a baby on the way.

"How about you?" I asked Adam. "How's your mood?"

I'd gotten home late but Adam had been even later, and I'd
conked out the minute my booboo hit the pillow.

"I'm good," he said. "Now that I'm going to be a godfather I've decided to learn how to let things go. Be more a 'go-with-the-flow' guy. I've been practicing the deep breathing I learned at pre-natal class and it really helps. For instance, I'm not even going to ask about that big piece of masking tape on your head."

I resisted the urge to touch the tape mending my scalp. "It's nothing really. Just a small cut. But if you want to know—"

Adam held up a hand. "Nope. Don't need details. Am I thrilled your job is dangerous now and then? No. But am I going to try to back off and deal with it? Yes. I can't promise I'll be good at it, but that's part of compromise, right? And this case is done, right?"

"Right and right."

The kettle sang, and I felt Adam's hands slip around my waist. "Besides, I wouldn't want to mess with a woman in a good mood." He kissed the exposed skin near my shoulder where the T-shirt of his that I'd worn to bed didn't cover. "I'd rather make her feel even better."

I turned from the counter to face him. "Why, sir. Are you suggesting something improper in the kitchen?"

He took my hand and led me into the dining room. "It's quite proper I can assure you," he said. He let me go and did an abra-cadabra move towards the adjoining living room.

My eyes went from him to the room. "They're gone. No more boxes! The coffee table is set right. The couch, the floor, the chairs —they're all clear." I went to the front window and eased it open. "Light's coming in again. And air." I moved to the middle of the room and did a spin. "It feels huge. Was it always this big?"

Adam laughed.

I stopped mid-spin on my second round. "Wait. It's not all in the basement, is it?"

"Nope. Tina and Jeffrey cleared everything out after the shower last night. They hauled everything home. All the presents. All the stuff they had here. Everything. I thought for sure all the noise would wake you up, but you slept right through it."

After the shower. Uh, oh. I'd turned Tina's shower into a crime scene. She must be mad. Or maybe afraid for her safety. She didn't want anything to do with us. She was gathering up her kit and caboodle and heading for the 'burbs. Adam had asked me to do one thing for his friend and I'd blown it. Well maybe not one thing, but one party thing. And I'd botched it. Maybe ruined their friendship forever.

"I'm sorry," I said. "Is she very angry?"

Adam's head tilted, his brows bunching. "Who?"

"Tina."

He laughed again. "Tina? Tina's ecstatic. Tina's the queen of her own social media empire. Thanks to you, her baby shower is all anyone's talking about. And some business bigwig, Evelyn some-body, wants to bottle some drink she got at the party and market it as the next must-have for baby showers. The last I read, Tina had a link on her Facebook page to three mockups for glass bottles filled with pink, blue, and green stuff that looks like fruity tea. Labels to come."

I smiled. Relieved. Too funny. If Adam knew what was holding that tea together, he'd smile, too. Tina's Twindig Toddies. Only really they were Albert's concoction, so she'd have to cut him in on the deal if it ever went beyond Facebook fantasy stage.

"I'm glad she's happy," I said. And I really was.

"Someone posted a video of her saving your purse. She's very happy. She's a superhero for the day. Which reminds me." He strolled to the fireplace mantle. "Look what showed up on the doorstep this morning." He picked up three tiny plastic men and displayed them on his palm.

"Your superhero dolls!" I said.

"Figurines," Adam corrected me. "I went to take the dog for a walk around the block and when I got back they were sitting on the doormat."

Some of my brightness dimmed. "Just like that? No note? No bag? No box?"

"Nope. Just wrapped in a napkin from the pizza place down the street."

Uh oh. "Can I see it?"

Adam went to the hall and got it from the entryway table. The napkin was just like Adam said. Just a plain ordinary napkin. Nothing scrawled on it but the name of the pizza place printed at the top.

I was sure it was from the Penguin. Maybe the police didn't have enough to arrest him yet. Maybe they thought they did, but his lofty lawyers got him off already.

At the thought of him out there somewhere, I expected my skin to crawl. The hair at the back of my neck to stand on end. My throat to get tight. But I felt none of that.

Probably because despite some odd behavior, the guy never hurt me. And because instead of the short man with the flappy coat and the greasy hair and the Neanderthal goons, the image that flitted into my mind was the young boy in the picture with my mother. The boy who probably had no idea he'd grow up to have backup goons. Nobody starts out with a rap sheet.

I told Adam I'd meet him back in the kitchen in a few minutes and headed upstairs to the little office I'd made for myself in the front room. The room that held the sum total of my life in New York. My bookshelves, my sofa, my desk, my mementos. My life.

I went to the closet, pulled out the bin of family photos, and rooted through it for the small, mini-album with the blue-eyed cat on the cover. One of my mom's childhood keepsakes. I flipped through the pages, stopping when I hit on a picture of her sitting on the same picnic table as the one in the picture Laurent had showed me. I knew I'd recognized something about it. In this photo, only my mother sat on the table, the same doll in her hand to her side. Tiny and barely recognizable, but it was the same. My mother smiled shyly at whoever was taking the picture. Her body in cut-off jean shorts and a flowery sleeveless blouse showing tanned limbs, ring of love beads around her neck. Her hair, a mass of near-ringlet waves, sun-streaked strands that otherwise matched my own tone.

My mother before I knew her. My mother who grew up in the country I was just getting to know and who, once upon a time, went to a summer camp not far from where I sat.

I felt for the locket around my neck. Her locket, now mine.

When I'd packed up my life to join Adam and live in his mother's house, I knew a part of me did it because I wanted to get a taste for my own mother's roots. But it never occurred to me when I started working at C&C that I may have been drawn to my new job for similar reasons. Not just because I wanted to help people solve the problems and mysteries in their lives, but because I may want to solve some mysteries in my own life. Like who my mom was before I knew her and what parts of her had found their way into me.

The doorbell went and Adam called up that it was someone to see me. I pulled on a pair of leggings under Adam's T-shirt and got downstairs, surprised to see Adam laughing with Laurent. Both men stood by the living room fireplace and stopped their conversation when I neared.

"I was just showing Laurent that video of the fight over your purse," Adam said, laptop crooked in his arm. "Want to see it?"

I shook my head. Having caught the live show, I didn't need to see the video. "Maybe later."

Adam's computer dinged with email and he excused himself to respond, wandering off to the kitchen.

"Does it hurt?" Laurent asked me, his face turning more serious as he tipped a finger at my booboo.

"Some. Not too bad."

He nodded, taking in my answer. I saw his eyes travel to the kitchen doorway through the dining room, and he moved out of view over by the couch. "*Tiens*," he said, handing me a bag.

I took it and looked inside. The tiny hippie doll that had covered the flash drive. The doll my mother had held in the old photos.

"I don't get it," I said. "Are you giving this to me?"

He nodded again.

"Is there something you want me to do with it?"

"Just keep it."

"I still don't get it. Isn't this part of evidence or something? Doesn't Brassard want it?"

"*Ben*, I told him it got misplaced."

I blinked. Laurent didn't misplace things. And he certainly didn't withhold evidence.

"It did?"

"*Oui*." He shrugged a shoulder. "*Des fois* it happens."

Now I nodded. "That's true. Things do go missing sometimes."

He headed for the front door. "*Alors, c'est tout. Je m'en vais.* Take a long weekend to rest. We'll see you next week."

I walked out to the door with him and watched him go to his car, droplets of rain dotting his path. Even now that I'd seen his home, the man was still a mystery to me. I sighed. Just what I needed. Another mystery to shake up my life.

⚜

# ACKNOWLEDGMENTS

While writing is often done alone, bringing a book to life is not.

I'm a lucky gal to have much support from my family, friends, and early readers. I thank them all.

This book especially, though, owes a lot to French proofreader/editor *extraordinaire* Maud L. *Grand, grand merci.*

And to my readers, who have so patiently waited for this book. Your enthusiasm for the Lora Weaver series is much appreciated. As is your kindness in leaving comments and reviews and sharing in Lora's journey. I so hope you enjoy this next step on the road in Lora's new life:)

# CHECK OUT THE AUDIOBOOKS!

**Hear the Lora Weaver Series In Audio!**

The wonderful Vanessa Labrie brings Lora to life beautifully in the audiobooks. Plus, Vanessa knows first-hand about life in Montréal and adds fabulous authenticity to the French characters.

Hear clips at:

Amazon * iTunes * Audible

# ABOUT THE AUTHOR

Katy Leen grew up on baguette and chocolate milk in a house full of pets and books. She writes the Lora Weaver mysteries and is currently working on the next book in the series.

Join Katy's *Nouvelles* newsletter where she shares more meanderings and insider info about the books:)

Pop by katyleen.com to check out the Q&A and her blog or Follow Katy at:

# ALSO BY KATY LEEN

The Lora Weaver series is still growing! Pop over to my website for news about the latest books.

The series is available in print, ebook, and audiobook.

I hope you join me for more of Lora's adventures:)

Happy reading!

**Series in Order**

The Demi-Tasse Début (prequel novella)

The First Faux Pas

The Nearly Nixed Noël (holiday novella)

The Pas de Deux

The Lost Love Liaison (Valentine novella)

The Ménage à Trois

The Easter Egg Ennui (Easter novella)

**Bundle Books**

The Lora Weaver Bundle

The Lora Weaver Holiday Boxed Set

Made in the USA
Las Vegas, NV
04 June 2022

49774083R10177